THAT OLD WITCH!

THE COFFEE COVEN'S COZY CAPERS: BOOK 1

M.Z. ANDREWS

That Old Witch!
The Coffee Coven's Cozy Capers: Book #1

by
M.Z. Andrews

Copyright © 2017 by M.Z. Andrews

ISBN-13: 978-1977880291
ISBN-10: 1977880290

Cover Character Illustration by Crissha's Art
Edited by Clio Editing Services

CONTENTS

1

*B*aritone waves of thunder grumbled overhead as storm clouds poured across the sky like molten lava, chasing away the midnight-blue sky and filling in the empty spaces with blurry waves of charcoal and graphite etchings, choking out Polaris and the Big Dipper. The delicate tinkling of a wind chime hanging from a porch ceiling floated in on the air, lending a sweet melodic sound to counter the deep tenor of the rumblings.

As the storm front moved in, a sudden, fierce gust of wind whipped at the newly budded tree branches and sent a spray of gravel dust up into the air, exfoliating the front of the three-story Victorian and the back end of the old jalopy parked in the dirt driveway. The air seemed to split apart as the sky belched a sudden streak of incandescent light, electrifying the air. Seconds later, rain pattered against the parlor's bow windows and settled the swirls of dust in the air, coating the dusty old road with a layer of much-needed spring precipitation.

In the backyard, the storm skirting around the perimeter of her rose garden didn't faze Katherine Lynde. In fact, the old woman smiled a crooked smile as she stood barefoot in her ankle-length blue cotton night-gown next to the stone fountain and held her hands out, high above her head. The pale, wrinkled skin on her outstretched arms sagged from just below her elbows to her armpits, her short elastic sleeves doing little to carry the burden of the excess baggage. Hanging wild and free around her shoulders, Katherine's long salt-and-pepper hair danced around her shoulders in the wind and battered at her face.

With her eyes closed, she chanted silently. Only her lips moved, murmuring the words from the open book on the iron garden table in front of her. Words she'd memo-rized from years and years of use. Still, she brought the book. It was a time-honored tradition. And old witches such as herself were nothing if not creatures of habit.

The black cauldron at the epicenter of the garden had just begun to bubble. A thick green substance swirled inside, permeating the air with the sweet scent of spring and the colorful aroma of freshly picked roses. Arched white trellises covered in pink and purple clematis and lavender-shaded wisteria anchored themselves centrally at each of the four cardinal directions. A white picket fence connected each of the four arbors and enclosed the garden, isolating the intricate beauty from the simplicity of the rest of the backyard. The storm the old witch had called didn't dare enter her garden without her consent. Instead, it soaked her Kentucky bluegrass and drenched the lilacs just outside the fence. Rain on her precious rose garden would be the grand finale.

With her nose still pointed towards the clouds, Kat opened her eyes and ever so slowly dropped her chin. In turn, she slowly lowered her arms like a graceful ballerina with her fingers knitted together and her palms cupped heavenward.

Only she could hear the low buzz of the chant she continued to recite. Each recitation made the cauldron bubble with more fervor. Each verse lifted the substance higher in the oversized black pot. Each solemn word dared the liquid to overflow. Finally, she sucked in her breath and, with a great flourish, threw her arms into the air. The cauldron spewed the green liquid out sky-high in a tremendous neon gush. Kat watched proudly as the glow of her miracle rose potion met with the clouds. The combination of her magical fertilizer and the spring rain would surely bring her another bumper crop of the most deliciously fragrant Lady of Shalott roses, and with it the coveted Aspen Falls Master Gardener award.

Kat clapped her hands together. Folding them into her chest, she let out an excited squeal. Springtime was her favorite, and tending her garden her pride and joy. When the thunder boomed overhead once again, she shut her spell book, tucked the heavy brown leather-bound tome under her arm, and headed for the house. She had only a few minutes to get out of the garden before the magic fertilizer mixed with the rain coming down. Soon, like her precious flowers, she'd be coated with a fragrant layer of green slime.

On arthritic bare feet, Kat ambled towards the arched trellis on the west side of the garden. No sooner had she stepped foot onto the cobblestone paver pathway that would lead her back to her house than the rain pelting her yard soaked her hair and her nightgown. The skin on her arms and legs pebbled, but Kat was suddenly aware that it wasn't from the coolness of the rain. She felt the distinct presence of someone behind her. Her upper torso turned slightly, just enough to catch the shadowed outline of a dark-cloaked figure behind her.

A streak of lightning burst overhead, and she caught the reflection of the shovel as it swung back. Kat's heart surged and her breath caught in her throat. She felt the spell book tumble to the ground as she raised her arms to defend herself, but the shovel was too fast. The blunt force to the back of her head was enough to make Katherine Lynde's world go black.

a bell chimed above a heavy wooden door, and two elderly women dressed in black ambled into Habernackle's Bed, Breakfast, and Beyond, a home-style restaurant in the heart of downtown Aspen Falls, Pennsylvania. The familiar scent of bacon grease and the pungent aroma of coffee welcomed the women.

Phyllis Habernackle glanced out across the restaurant. A smattering of people dotted the booths and tables in the dining room, but no one sat on the barstools across from them at the long counter.

"Should we sit at the bar today, Char?" asked Phyllis, clutching a brass urn in her gnarled hands. Though her last name was on the sign out front, it was her daughter and her grandson who owned the cozy little establishment.

Charlotte Bailey shook her head, her black veil rustling over the top of her short white curls. "No. I'd prefer our usual table."

"Fine by me."

Char led Phyllis to a round table in the middle of the room, just a few tables away from a tableful of men enjoying their midmorning cup of coffee.

The men were absorbed in a political debate of one type or another, and only one of the men acknowledged the women's entrance. He was a distinguished gentleman with a perfectly groomed flattop of white hair, wearing a crisp blue gingham button-down shirt with a starched collar.

"Good morning, ladies," he said with a polite nod.

"Not really," grumbled Phyllis. Her chair made a scratching sound as she pulled it backwards across the hardwood floor.

Sitting at the table with one impeccably creased trouser leg crossed over his knee, the man leaned his head backwards and lifted a single white eyebrow. "Let me guess. You're coming from a funeral?"

Phyllis eyed Char. Like herself, her friend wore a black veil, a black dress that nearly covered her ankles, and sensible black shoes. "No, Sergeant, we're coming from a birthday party," replied Phyllis as she set the urn she carried on the table and took a seat in front of it. She nodded towards the urn. "This was our parting gift."

With his arms folded neatly in his lap, he merely blinked, unfazed by her sarcasm. "I'm sorry, you're right. That was an observation posed as a stupid question. It must be a hard day for you both. Is the deceased from Aspen Falls?"

Char nodded as she pulled the black pillbox hat with

attached veil off her head and set it on the table. She ran a hand over the top of her hair to settle the strays. Her blue eyes were rimmed with red as she pulled a wadded lipstick-stained tissue from the pocket of her skirt and blotted at her pinkened cheeks. "Katherine Lynde. She lived on the west edge of town."

The sergeant's silvery-blue eyes widened as he motioned towards a man with a camera bag in front of him just across the table. "Benny just mentioned the other day that Katherine had passed away."

Phyllis glanced over at the small pointy-nosed man who barely managed to take his eyes off the front page of the *Aspen Falls Observer* in front of him while cutting his cherry Danish with a fork. "I wrote her obituary for the paper," he said offhandedly.

Although Benny Hamilton was quite a few years younger than many of the retired gentlemen at the table, he was the only man to experience the unfortunate irony of saving a bundle on shampoo bills. Though he claimed to be only in his forties, the majority of his scalp was barer than a plucked chicken's butt, yet he allowed two tawny tufts of hair to take up residence behind his ears. Phyllis wondered why men of his follicly challenged state didn't just shave it all off completely. What was the sense in keeping the tufts? *Are there women out there who find such a thing attractive?* she wondered.

"It's a shame how it all happened," said the sergeant with a bit of a sigh.

"How it happened?" Phyllis leaned forward in her seat and lifted her veil back over her head to expose narrowed emerald-green eyes of suspicion. "It was accidental, you know."

He nodded and sat forward in his seat as well, turning his torso so he was able to see her better. "Well, how they found her anyway. I can't imagine being that paperboy and finding her after all that time. I'm sure it wasn't a pretty sight."

Char frowned as a hand went to her stomach. "Sergeant Bradshaw, we were just about to have a bite to eat, do you mind?"

"Oh, I'm so sorry. That was incredibly rude of me. You're right. One shouldn't talk about such things, especially in the presence of ladies. How did you two know Katherine?"

"We went to school with her years ago," said Phyllis.

"Oh, are you all Aspen Falls High alums?"

"Actually," began Char slowly, "we all went to the Paranormal Institute for Witches together. Katherine was my roommate. Phyllis lived down the hall from us."

That seemed to be a conversation killer. All the men at the table looked up and stared at them then. Char and Phyllis were used to it. Being a witch in Aspen Falls wasn't that big of a deal, really. At least a third of the small town's population had supernatural powers of one type or another, thanks in large part to the Institute's presence in the community. But there were still people who either got a kick out of seeing a real live witch in their midst or were annoyed that witches were so prevalent in the community. The other portion, and the majority of the Aspen Falls residents, simply went about their lives, not caring if someone had magical powers or not.

Sergeant Bradshaw cleared his throat and looked up as a woman in a green apron split open a pair of swinging doors behind the bar. "Of course, what was I thinking? I believe I did know that you attended the Institute, it simply slipped my mind. Gentlemen, Phyllis is the Habernackle matriarch. She's Linda's mother."

Phyllis glanced up at the woman coming their way. Not one for dillydallying, she gave the men a tight smile, the kind that didn't so much as crinkle the deeply etched crow's-feet near her eyes. "If you'll excuse us, gentlemen, our waitress is here. Have a nice day."

Sergeant Bradshaw tipped his head in a gentlemanly nod. "You have a good day as well. My sincere condolences."

"Thank you," said Char before taking a seat across the table from Phyllis and turning her back to the men.

The waitress stopped at the table and looked down at the two women. Her red hair, peppered with strands of white, was rolled up and fastened behind her head in a long brown hair clip. "Good morning, Char. Good morning, Mom," she said, giving both of the women a friendly smile.

"Hello, Linda," said Char.

"Good morning, sweetheart," said Phyllis, waving away the menu offered to her. "We're starved. Char and I will both have coffee and your special."

Char frowned. "What's the special today?"

"Two eggs, toast, and a side of bacon or sausage," said Linda, pulling a pencil from her hair.

Char shook her head. "I better not. I'm trying to watch my cholesterol." She looked at the woman across the table from her. "You should be watching yours too, Phil. We aren't spring chickens anymore. Look at poor Kat. It just goes to show, you can't always count on tomorrow being on the other side of your pillow."

Phyllis frowned. "Kat slipped on a paver and hit her head on a rock. She didn't die from eating eggs and bacon." She looked up at her daughter. "I'll have the special and a double order of bacon, please. Bring Char a glass of ice water and a spoon."

Char narrowed her eyes at her friend. "You're so funny, you old witch." She looked up at Linda. "I'll have a bowl of oatmeal and a side of whole wheat toast, please."

Linda nodded as she jotted the order down on her notepad.

"And make sure to give me my senior discount, please," added Char as she readjusted her bottom on the cushioned vinyl seat.

Phyllis rolled her eyes. "Yes, Linda, do make sure to give my friend her ten-percent discount. What will that be today? Twenty-five cents?" she mused.

Char swatted at her friend across the table. "Oh, you just hush. I'm on a fixed income. Every little penny adds up."

After writing the order down, Linda looked up at the women. "How was the funeral?"

Char sighed. "How funerals always are. Depressing."

"It's not fun watching all your old friends die," agreed Phyllis.

"Were there many people there?"

Phyllis snorted out her nose. "I can count on one hand how many people were there, and I'd still have two fingers left over."

Linda's eyebrows lifted. "Kat didn't have any friends or family?"

Char shook her head sadly. "The woman never married. I tried to visit her once or twice a month, but she never seemed to mind being all alone. She had her garden, her garden club, and her books to keep her busy."

"Didn't anyone from her garden club show up?" asked Linda, leaning one hand on the back of Phyllis's chair.

"Not a single one of them," said Char. Her voice took on a chastising lilt as she crossed her arms over her ample bosoms.

Linda lifted an eyebrow. "Well, then, who was the other person there?"

"Her paperboy, if you can believe it," scoffed Phyllis.

"I don't think you can call a forty-five-year-old man a paperboy anymore," said Char, shaking her head. Then she lowered her voice. "Especially one that just married a twenty-four-year-old stewardess."

Phyllis's eyes swung towards the ceiling. "What do you call him, then? A paperman?"

"That doesn't sound right either, does it?" Char scratched at her chin.

Linda's head volleyed back and forth between the two women. "The paperman was at Kat's funeral?"

"Yeah, paperman definitely doesn't sound right," murmured Phyllis after she heard it roll off her daughter's lips.

Char ignored Phyllis's musings. "He was the one that found her. I suppose he felt obliged to show up for the funeral."

"Puh," puffed Phyllis. "I certainly wouldn't feel obliged to show up at the funeral of someone I found dead and bloated in their backyard."

"Do you mind?" barked Char, holding her stomach. "I'd like to eat."

"I'm just sayin'." Phyllis rolled her eyes and looked away. "So how do you know he's shacked up with a twenty-four-year-old?" she barked. Her heavy voice seemed to fill the empty spaces around them.

Char's eyes immediately scanned the room as she sucked in a reproachful breath. "Do you have to yell?" she hissed. "I was told that in confidence. And they're not shacked up anymore. They actually tied the knot."

"Well, excuse me," quipped Phyllis, waggling her head. "Who told you he married the girl?"

Char leaned forward. "Well, Amy Bartley lives next door to him. Her mother is in my bridge club, and she said that Amy told her that Ruben moved the girl in about a year ago, and three months ago, they flew off to Vegas and made it official. That girl is young enough to be his daughter."

"I wonder what he sees in her?" asked Phyllis.

Char let a puff of air out her nose. "I'll tell you what he sees in her. Her triple Hs, that's what he sees in her."

Phyllis covered her face with one hand and lowered her head. "Oh Lordy, here we go."

Char waved a hand in protest. "No. I won't go there. Today is Kat's day. I won't even get started on that. Of course, I think it's silly what some men will do when they hit middle age, but that's neither here nor there. I'm just a fuddy-duddy old grandma, what do I know?"

Phyllis rocked back on her seat and threw her hands in the air as if to scream *Hallelujah!* "Don't even get me started on grandkids," she bellowed.

Linda looked around uncomfortably. "Where's Vic?" she asked Char in an attempt at changing the subject.

"Oh, I left him at home. He didn't think it would be proper etiquette to bring him to the funeral."

Linda nodded her head knowingly. "Yes, I suppose that makes sense. Though if it was just the three of you, I don't think it would have mattered."

Char shrugged. "How were we to know that no one else would show up?"

Phyllis looked over her shoulder towards the kitchen. "Linda, where are my grandchildren?"

"Well, Mercy and the girls are all in class right now."

"And how about my grandson? Where's Reign?" she asked, craning her neck towards the kitchen.

"Reign went out for a jog. He's trying to get in shape. He's started dating, you know," said Linda in a hushed voice.

"That's what I heard," said Phyllis. "Don't let him pick someone I wouldn't approve of."

Linda rolled her eyes. "You're going to stay out of my son's love life, Mother. You've caused enough damage to the poor boy to last forever. You leave him alone, got it?"

Phyllis threw both hands into the air. "See what I'm saying? Grandma doesn't know best if you ask them. Got it, got it. Jeez."

Eyeing her mother seriously, Linda walked backwards towards the bar. "I'll go get your order started and have your coffee out in a jiffy."

"Thank you, Linda, dear," said Char with a polite smile. She looked at her friend. "Well, I don't know about you, but that was one of the strangest funerals I've ever been to."

Phyllis unrolled the napkin full of silverware on the table and placed it across her lap. "How so?"

"That new priest. He was so rude."

"Oh, him. Yeah, I didn't appreciate all that pagan mumbo jumbo. Father Bernie is so much more relatable to the residents of Aspen Falls."

Char sighed. "Yes. I cannot wait until he comes back."

"Where's Father Bernie at anyway?"

"He's on a retreat until the middle of May. Father Donovan's just a loaner from Bakersdale. He's been here for about three weeks, and none of the parishoners likes him."

"Well, he certainly doesn't understand that Aspen

Falls is different than other parishes, does he? You've got to cater to a wider range of people here."

"Exactly. And to perform services for a witch, you'd think he'd have been a little more open-minded. I just thought the whole service was laced with his own agenda. Kat was probably rolling over in her urn."

The two women looked down at the gold-colored container on the table. "Hard to believe that's all that's left of her," whispered Phyllis. "What are we going to do with her ashes?"

Char shrugged. "I don't know. I'm not ready to think about them yet. We'll figure something out. I'm still thinking about how much I'm going to miss her. We had some really good times together." She blotted the tears that formed in the corners of her eyes.

"I'm really going to miss her, too," said Phyllis wistfully. Then a slow smile played around the corners of her mouth. "Do you remember during the first semester of school at the Institute, when we snuck into Beverly Schmidt's room while she was sleeping and stole all her bras so she'd have to go to class without one?"

Char giggled. "Of course I remember! That was all Kat's idea. She thought that was so funny." Char pointed her finger at Phyllis. "I also remember that it backfired on her. That evening at the mixer between us and the Paranormal Institute for Wizards, Kat was slow-dancing with Charlie Daniels, but when he saw Beverly come in without her bra, and she was *perkier* than every other girl at the dance, he dropped Kat like a hot potato."

Phyllis' elephant-sized laugh filled the dining room.

"Oh man," she said through her laughter, tears filling her eyes. "That was hilarious. The joke was on her, huh?"

Char nodded. "And then there was that time that Gwyn Prescott, Loni Hodges, Kat, Auggie Stone, you, and I came downtown at midnight Halloween night and put all the police cars on top of the buildings around Aspen Falls."

Phyllis's eyes nearly disappeared into her cheeks as she guffawed. One hand covered her stomach, and the other covered her eyes. "That was hilarious! That one made the papers if I remember correctly. They had to bring in a team of second-year witches from the Institute just to get the cars off the tops of the buildings! Everyone at school talked about it for weeks!"

"That one was Loni's idea!" said Char, chuckling.

"Oh golly," said Phyllis as her laughter began to subside. "I haven't thought about Loni Hodges or Gwyn Prescott for years!"

Char harrumphed. "Loni lives in Aspen Falls, you know."

"You don't say!" said Phyllis. "Well, then, why wasn't she at the funeral?"

"I'll tell you why. She's gone batshit crazy from what I've heard. She rarely leaves her house. I know she keeps up with Kat, but after that little *incident* after graduation, I haven't heard from or spoken to her or Gwyn. Nor do I want to."

"I haven't spoken to them either. After the mess between Auggie Stone and me, I sort of fled Aspen Falls and never looked back. Being back in town after all these years has been quite the trip down memory lane, that's for sure."

Char leaned forward and covered her friend's hand with hers. "I'm so sorry about everything Auggie put you through. I had no idea."

Phyllis patted her hand. "Thank you, dear. I'm sorry for what she put you through as well."

Char nodded. "It wasn't all her fault."

"I know," agreed Phyllis, "but it might as well have been."

"Well, at least I have him still. You poor thing. You went through so much more. If only I'd known…"

Phyllis frowned. "I managed. I just can't believe she didn't get locked up over that whole mess with Vic."

"I'm a little surprised too, but you know those Stones. They always manage to get their way."

"Yes, I suppose they do," agreed Phyllis. "Well, I'm just so glad that I've got you, Char. And I'm even more thankful that I don't ever have to think about any of those girls again!"

3

"*This* is the good room?"

Gwyndolin Prescott sighed. "Yes, Mother. This is the good room." She set the two suitcases she carried down on the threadbare carpet, unwound the hanging bag from around her neck, and dropped herself onto the faded pink floral armchair beneath the window.

Hazel Prescott's droopy eyes widened. "If this is a good room, I'd hate to see the bad rooms!"

Gwyn ignored her mother's complaints. She was too tired from being on the road for the last seventy-two hours. It had been the longest three days of her life, driving her mother from Scottsdale, Arizona, to Aspen Falls, Pennsylvania. But they'd made it. *Finally.* All she wanted to do now was sleep before she had to report for duty in the morning.

Hazel tapped her cane against the floor. "They call

this carpet? I've seen thicker rugs on Dean Martin's head."

Gwyn sighed. "Mom, it's a retirement village, not a Hilton."

Hazel nearly spat out her dentures as she pointed her cane at the window. "You call this a village? A building built around a tree does not make a village."

With mighty effort, Gwyn pushed herself off her chair and looked out the picture window to the courtyard. A mammoth scarlet oak tree stood proudly centered above the cobblestone patio. Black cast-iron benches surrounded the tree with matching end tables at each of the four corners. A pair of senior citizens sat quietly reading beneath the shade tree.

"Mom, the courtyard is lovely. Do you remember promising not to complain if I took you out of Scottsdale Manor?"

Hazel frowned at her daughter. "I promised not to complain if you took me somewhere better. This isn't better."

"It's better, Mom. And it's part of my salary package. Free room and board for both of us. It doesn't get much better than that." She strode over to the suitcases, hefted them up again, and carried them to the hallway off the small kitchenette. "Come on. I'll let you pick the good bedroom."

Hazel followed behind her daughter, twirling one finger in the air. "Oh, the good bedroom. Yippee."

Gwyn had to suck up all the patience she had left not to bark at her mother. It was her mother's fault that she'd been forced out of her job at Scottsdale Manor. She hadn't told her that, of course, but the retirement community had asked her to find a new home for her mother. They thought she required more care than they could give. And they weren't referring to her medical care. Hazel was a handful.

Not only did she have a tendency to wander off and get herself into *predicaments*, as the Manor liked to call them, but she was also an accomplished poker player and used her *special gift* on more than one occasion to swindle money out of unsuspecting residents. When the families discovered Hazel was taking money from their parents and complained to the management, a strict no-gambling rule was implemented at the Manor, which made Hazel want to find a new place to live. Of course, Gwyn couldn't just up and quit her job and move—where would they go? Eventually, the Manor had asked her to find Hazel a new place to live. At that point, she realized she had no other choice than to quit.

That was when the job search began. Not many companies wanted to hire someone of Gwyn's advanced age. She'd probably sent out fifty resumes before she'd discovered that the retirement village in the small town where her old alma mater was located was hiring an activities director. And one of the criteria was experience dealing with the paranormal. *Hot damn!* Gwyn had filled out the online application that very day, and within a week she'd had a phone interview with the board of directors. She almost couldn't believe it when they'd called the very next day to offer her the position.

Packing up had been a breeze. Gwyn and Hazel didn't own much. They'd been gypsy wanderers the last twenty years or so. With Gwyn being a single mother, once her daughters had become adults, moved away, and started their own families, there was really no reason to be tied down to the house in which she'd raised them. And by that time, Hazel was aging rapidly and needed someone to keep an eye on her around the clock. So, Gwyn did what she thought was best and sold the house and all her furniture and unnecessary possessions and gone to live with her mother. When the money from the sale of her house had begun to dwindle, she'd realized it was time to get a job. But she wasn't sure how she'd make a job work with Hazel's needs, and that's when she'd gotten started working for assisted living centers, nursing homes, and retirement villages. As long as the place would let her mother come and they could live together, Gwyn happily took the job.

But the older Hazel got, the more problems she seemed to cause. Of course, it had taken a year or two at each location before management got snippy enough to pull the plug on Hazel's residency, but it was always inevitable. This time was no different. Gwyn had seen the writing on the wall for a while, but she'd grown to like Arizona's climate and the friends she'd made at the Manor, so it had been a disappointment to have to leave their comfy little apartment just as she'd gotten comfortable.

Now she looked around wistfully. The beige walls with cheaply framed pictures of snow-capped mountains and wildlife bored her. The kitchenette was small and filled with miniature appliances and cheap cupboards whose doors didn't seem to fit right. The living room had only enough space to fit a small boxy sofa, the faded armchair, and a twenty-seven-inch flat-screen television on a pressed-wood rolling stand. Both bedrooms had extra-wide doorways to accommodate wheelchairs and medical equipment, but the rooms themselves were tight. There was just enough room for the bed, nightstand, dresser, and a closet. Gwyn didn't want to complain, though; at least the room had come furnished.

"Which one's the good room?" Hazel snapped from behind her, pulling Gwyn out of her little reverie.

From the doorway, Gwyn looked back at the other room. Her eyes were vacant from exhaustion and weary resignation, so she couldn't readily tell the difference between the two rooms, though someone had told her on the phone that one of the bedrooms was bigger. Standing in the doorway, she thought both rooms both looked equally small.

Hazel's head swiveled from left to right. "They look the same to me."

Gwyn pointed to the room behind her. "That one has two windows," she said, trying to muster up a glimmer of excitement.

Leaning her weight on her cane, Hazel lifted her other arm and jazz-handed the air. "Well, wooey!"

"Mother!" The chastisement in her voice was distinct. She was too tired to try to hide it.

Hazel shrugged. "Fine. I'll take it."

Gwyn lugged her mother's suitcases to the room across the hall and put her bags on the bed. "Why don't you start unpacking, Mom? I'm going to run out to the car and carry in another load."

"What?" asked Hazel, cupping her ear.

"I'm going out to the car to get another load," Gwyn hollered into her mother's good ear.

The fleshy pouches of extra skin beneath Hazel's sunken eyes lifted as she made a face. "They don't have any bellboys for that?"

"No, they don't have any bellboys. I'll just be a minute. Can you be good for just a minute?"

"What do you mean, *can I be good*? I'm always good," shouted Hazel. Her hearing wasn't as good as it had once been, and her voice had gotten louder the worse her hearing had become.

"Just don't wander off. Stay in the room. Okay?"

Hazel didn't acknowledge her daughter's words.

Gwyn walked around her mother to look her in the face. "Don't wander off, please. Stay in the room, okay?"

Hazel lowered her chin and frowned. "I don't need a babysitter, Gwynnie."

"I know you don't, Mom," she sighed. She knew her mother didn't like being treated like a child. She hated having to treat her like one, too. Gwyn mustered up a smile and a spoonful of fake enthusiasm. "I just want to explore the place together. Okay?"

Hazel thought about it for a second. "Fine. We'll explore together. Hurry up, though. I'm hungry."

"We'll look for the dining hall when I get back."

Gwyn stood with her hand on her hip in the doorway of her mother's new room, watching her mother's slow movements. It didn't matter where they were or what they were doing, they were together, and she was thankful for that. Quietly she pondered whether it was safe to leave her mother unattended for the few minutes it would take her to go to the car.

Hazel's hand paused as she unzipped the suitcase on the bed. She looked up at Gwyn. "Well, don't just stand there. Hurry up, then."

Gwyn sighed. "Yes, Mother."

———

*A*t the intersection of the corridors, Gwyn looked down the hallway in all four directions. She couldn't believe how quiet the hallways were. *Is it always this quiet here on a Sunday afternoon?* she wondered. Scottsdale Manor always bustled with activity on Sunday afternoons, with families coming and going. Music poured out of the dining room, enticing families to join the scheduled events and proving to them that their loved ones were in good hands.

But this place was a ghost town. Even as Gwyn and Hazel approached the dining room, the only sound she could hear was her mother's cane tapping the floor and her feet shuffling as they walked. As the new activities director, Gwyn made a promise to herself right then and there that she'd fix that. It would be her first order of business to implement a family fun day every Sunday.

"Where is everyone?" Hazel asked from her stooped walking position.

"We must have missed family hour," suggested Gwyn. She didn't want to call attention to the fact that she guessed they didn't *have* a family hour here. That would only give her mother one more gripe.

"You sure this is a retirement home and not a funeral home?" snapped Hazel.

Gwyn looked down at her mother. Hazel Prescott had shrunk over the years. Gwyn remembered a time when she and her mother had been the same height, and then Gwyn had surpassed her by an entire inch and stopped growing. Now, she looked down and could see the top of her mother's short grey hair. Granted, it was due in large part to her mother's stooped posture, but even when she tried to stand taller, Hazel still stood several inches shorter than her daughter now.

Gwyn ignored her mother's dig. She was always worse when she was hungry. "Let's get you some food, Mom."

They turned into the dining room. It was a bright, pleasant enough space that smelled of disinfectant and tomato sauce. A wall of windows and sliding patio doors lined one side of the room, facing the courtyard. A piano sat against one wall, beneath another set of generic mountain and wildlife paintings. The far wall had a big-screen TV on it with a handful of sofas and chairs arranged around it. The rest of the room had nearly a dozen square wooden tables, each with four wooden chairs and padded navy seat cushions and seat backs. *Not bad.* When the first thing out of her mother's mouth wasn't a crack on the dining room, Gwyn knew her mother agreed that it was nice.

"They better be serving lunch," said Hazel, instead of commenting on the decor.

"Why don't you go sit down, Mom? I'll go check the kitchen."

"I want French fries," Hazel called out after Gwyn had walked away.

"I know, Mom. You always have French fries. I'll see what they have. Save me a seat."

Hazel laughed. "I don't know, Gwynnie. That's asking a lot. How will I ever find a spot for both of us with all of these people?"

Gwyn sighed and walked around the partial wall that separated the dining room from a serving area. There was a buffet line, but only a few partial tins of lasagna and some green Jell-O remained. Gwyn could hear the clanging of pots and pans in the kitchen, so someone had to be nearby. "Hello?" she called out.

The clanging stopped, and a short round woman walked out of the kitchen. She wore a white apron, a hairnet, and yellow rubber gloves. "Lunch service ends at two," she said in an orotund voice.

Gwyn looked down at her watch. "You don't serve food past two? Darn it. It's two fifteen. We just got here. I've been driving all day, and my mother is starving."

"From eleven to two, we have a full-service dining room. After two you serve yourself. We put the leftovers on the serving line," she said and pointed at the small bits of food left over in front of her.

Gwyn grimaced. There weren't any French fries. "I don't suppose you have any French fries back there?"

The woman shook her head. "Those are always the first to go."

Gwyn sighed. Then she held her hand up over the glass sneeze guard. "I'm Gwyndolin Prescott. I'm the new activities director."

The woman looked put out to have to remove her glove, but she did and shook Gwyn's hand. "Georgia Lange. Folks around here call me Miss Georgia."

Gwyn smiled at the first coworker she'd met, besides the facilities director, who had met her briefly to give her the key to their new room. "It's nice to meet you, Miss Georgia. You can just call me Gwyn."

Georgia gave her a half-smile. "You start tomorrow?"

Gwyn nodded. "Yes. Is it always this quiet on Sundays?"

"Around here it is. Most folks go to chapel on Sunday mornings and then read in their rooms in the afternoon. It might pick up a little at suppertime."

Gwyn smiled with relief. She was glad it wouldn't be dead all day. She'd likely climb out of her skin if she had to stare at the beige walls and listen to her mother complain for the rest of the day. "I don't suppose I could convince you to put some fries on for me? It's the only thing my mother likes to eat, and she's so hungry she's darn near biting my head off right now."

Miss Georgia considered the request for a moment.

Gwyn made a cross in front of her heart. "I promise we'll be on time to every meal from this day forward. We just rolled into town. We've been driving for three days straight."

Her matted strawberry-blond hair, smudged makeup, and the deep purple circles beneath Gwyn's eyes told the story of their last few days on the road. Miss Georgia's face softened slightly. "Alright. I'll put on some fries for your mother. Do you want some too?"

Gwyn shook her head. "No, thank you. I'll make do with this lasagna."

Miss Georgia pointed to a self-service counter behind her. "There's a microwave back there if you'd like to heat it up. It's probably cold by now."

"Thank you, Miss Georgia, I really appreciate it."

"I'll bring 'em out when they're done," she said before disappearing back into the kitchen.

Gwyn served up two plates of food and ran both of them through the microwave before returning to her mother.

"Took you long enough," Hazel barked, looking down at the plate of food her daughter put in front of her. She sucked in her breath. "Where are my French fries?"

"They have to make you some fresh ones. They'll bring them out." Gwyn took the seat across from her mother.

Hazel poked at her lasagna. "Is this homemade or store-bought?"

Without skipping a beat, Gwyn replied, "Homemade."

Hazel eyed her daughter suspiciously. "How do you know?"

Gwyn didn't know, but what she did know was that her mother would refuse to eat it if it were store-bought. "I asked," Gwyn lied.

"Gwynnie, don't lie to your mother."

"I'm not lying, Mom." Gwyn crossed her fingers under the table. She didn't have the energy to deal with her mother's idiosyncrasies right now. She really needed a nap. "Just try the lasagna. It looks good." Gwyn forked off a small bite and popped it in her mouth. "Mmm, it is good. Try it."

Hazel's hand shook as she cut a small piece off with her fork. She lifted it to her nose and took a whiff. "It smells store-bought."

Gwyn palmed her forehead. "Oh, for the love of Pete. Take a bite, Mom."

Hazel set her fork down and buried her hands in her lap. She turned her head stubbornly, giving her daughter her side profile. "I'll wait for my French fries."

Gwyn didn't have the energy to argue. She'd force-feed her mother at the evening meal if she had to. Maybe by then, they'd both have a nap in, and she'd have gotten her second wind. "Fine. You'll be starved by supper."

Gwyn chewed the tasteless, rubbery lasagna in silence, lost in her thoughts, while Hazel sat across from her, stubbornly refusing to eat until finally Miss Georgia came out with a basket of French fries and set it on the table. "I think these are for you?" she asked, looking down at Hazel sweetly.

"Well, they aren't for the dog!" snapped Hazel.

Miss Georgia's eyes widened.

"Mother!" snapped Gwyn. "That was rude. Miss Georgia went to special trouble to make you those."

Hazel wagged a wrinkled, stubby finger in the air in front of her. "Don't make it sound like she whipped me up some big culinary delight, Gwynnie. The woman put some fries from a bag into a basket and lowered them into some grease. McDonald's hires children to do that."

Gwyn felt the heat rush to her face as she looked up at Miss Georgia in horror. "I'm so sorry, Miss Georgia. My mother hasn't eaten yet, and I think her blood sugar's low. She's really not that rude in general." Gwyn kept her fingers crossed under the table.

Miss Georgia's face softened. "It's alright, I understand." She turned around to walk away.

Hazel held a hand out to touch Miss Georgia's arm before she could leave. "Is the lasagna homemade or store-bought?"

"I get it frozen from the company," she said.

Hazel nodded her head knowingly and let the woman walk away. When she was gone, Hazel leaned forward and smiled knowingly at her daughter. "I told you not to lie to your mother. Have you forgotten I can read minds?" She tapped a finger to her temple.

Gwyn sighed as she leaned her elbow on the table and let her chin fall into her palm. "No, I haven't forgotten, Mother." It was going to be a *long night.*

4

Char Bailey flipped off *Kathie Lee and Hoda*, set the remote control on the two-tiered midcentury end table that was so old it was now considered retro, and stood up. "Time to get crackin'," she said to the small tan-and-white Chihuahua in a ball on the sofa.

The Chihuahua's batlike ears perked up excitedly as his body uncurled. His sticklike feet poked out first. Elongating his body, he stretched one leg and then the other. When he finally stood, he put his two front paws out in front of him, lowered his chin to the cushion, stuck his butt up in the air, and arched his back in a downward dog yoga pose. When he was properly stretched out, he sat back down on his bottom and looked at Char with interest. His bulbous black eyes shone in the light as he tilted his head to the side. "What's on the agenda today, my little love muffin?" he asked quite clearly in a bouncy voice.

"I thought I'd go get the mail, and then we'll go for

our walk. Then maybe this afternoon we can make some muffins to take to Sarah Henderson's little boy. You know, poor little Patrick broke his leg playing soccer last weekend, and he's stuck with a cast and crutches right now. I thought if we brought him some of his favorite muffins, we could sneak in a little bone-healing potion. Plus if he gets to see you, it might cheer him up a little."

Victor Bailey's eyes widened. "Brilliant idea, sweetheart. Count me in! I'll go through my recipes and see what I can find!"

Char scratched beneath her husband's chin and laid a chaste kiss on his forehead. "Perfect! I also told Phyllis I'd meet her for lunch and coffee this afternoon. I hope you don't mind me leaving you alone for an hour or two?"

Vic jumped off the sofa and looked up at his wife. "I don't mind at all. Maybe you could drop me off at the bakery, and I'll see how Sweets is getting on."

"Brilliant idea. That's why I married you, you're full of brilliant ideas," said Char. She walked to the door, pulled a hot pink visor from the hook next to the front door, and slid it on over her puffy white curls. Then she lifted a miniature tie-dyed visor from the next hook. "Do you want your visor too?"

Vic looked at her suspiciously. "Just the visor?"

Char held up two hands defensively. She hadn't been allowed to dress up her Chihuahua since her late husband's spirit had accidentally inhabited her dog, Regis, thanks to a group of young, inexperienced witches, one of whom was Phyllis's granddaughter, Mercy. "I swear, just the visor. No tutus, no hunting vests, no kilts—

although you've got to admit that Scottish kilt is so adorable. Are you sure you don't want to wear the kilt?"

Vic palmed his forehead with a paw. "Sugarplum, I'm absolutely sure I don't want to wear a kilt, it's just a fancy name for a skirt."

"But it comes with a matching beret!"

"I don't want to wear a beret either. I'll wear a visor to keep the sun out of my eyes, but that is it. It's not a fashion statement. It's just practicality."

Char waved a hand towards him dismissively. "Fine. Suit yourself. I'm going to go get the mail, and then we'll go." She dropped the visor next to him on the floor and headed for the door.

The screen door on her small bungalow had no sooner slammed behind her than she noticed a familiar car pull up to the curb. The door popped open, and Phyllis nearly flew out the driver's side. *What in the world?* she wondered as she looked at her watch. "Well, it's barely eleven! I thought we were meeting at noon."

With her white hair in a wild bun atop her head, Phyllis ignored Char's questions and instead padded towards the woman. "Did you get your mail yet?"

"I was just walking down to the box to get it, why?" asked Char, noting Phyllis's wild hair, bathrobe, and house slippers. "Golly! Where's the fire? You couldn't even bother to put on pants before leaving the house this morning?"

Phyllis waved a letter in the air. "Check your mail!"

"I'm working on it, for cryin' out loud."

Phyllis grunted. "Oh, just stay there, I'll check it for

35

you." She popped open the box and pulled out a handful of items.

"Do you mind? That's private information," grumbled Char from her front step.

Phyllis rifled through the letters while walking up the sidewalk. "Oh, you got one too!" She held up a letter with an embossed seal in the corner.

"Well, what is it?" Char asked, snatching the letter out of Phyllis's hands.

Phyllis took a deep breath, but Char held up her hand to stop her. "No, don't tell me. I'd rather read it for myself."

Phyllis blew out the breath she'd just sucked in. "Well, then, hurry up already."

"Come on in," said Char, opening the front door.

Phyllis followed Char inside and sat down on the couch. "Good morning, Vic," said Phyllis.

"Good morning, Phyllis. I thought you two were meeting for lunch later?" he asked, peering up at Phyllis beneath the brim of the little visor he'd managed to get on his head.

"I had to stop over and see if Char got the letter from the lawyer too."

Vic's beady black eyes widened. "Lawyer?" He looked at Char. "What's a lawyer want with the two of you, Pumpkin?"

Char's eyes scanned the official-looking letter. *The Estate of Katherine Lynde. You have been named in her will. Meet at my office this Wednesday at 9:00 a.m.* Char's eyes swiveled up to look at Phyllis. "Kat put us in her will?"

Phyllis nodded excitedly. "It looks like it. I wonder what she left us."

Char shrugged. "Does it matter? Our friend is dead."

Phyllis lowered her head sorrowfully. "Yes, I know that. But who doesn't like being named in a will? It's like finding buried treasure."

Char sat down in her chair. "I suppose it is. It just makes me sad that we had to lose a friend to find that buried treasure."

"We're all sad about losing Kat, but if she left us something, you know she'd want us to be happy about it."

Char nodded. "You're right. Should I pick you up on Wednesday morning?"

Phyllis stood up too. "I'll be waiting with bells on!"

---

*T*he offices of Jerry T. Marlow were located in a stately brick building two blocks east of the Aspen Falls Police Department. The grass was a lush shade of green, and on Wednesday morning at 8:55 a.m., a groundskeeper had already set up shop on the lawn when Phyllis Habernackle and Char Bailey pulled up to the curb.

Phyllis looked out the passenger window towards the law office. "What do you think she left us?"

Char shut off the ignition and threw the keys into her purse. "I have no idea. But we're about to find out."

The women emerged from the car and together made their way to the frosted glass doors painted with the words

Jerry T. Marlow, Attorney at Law. As she touched the handle of one of the doors, a sudden feeling of unease rolled across Phyllis's body. She rubbed her bare arms as her skin began to pebble. Something didn't feel right. "I suddenly have a bad feeling about this."

Char wrapped her own hand over Phyllis's and peeled back the door. "Too late now," she said, holding the door open for her friend. "We're here."

As they walked into the law office, Phyllis's feeling of unease didn't automatically dissipate. She'd had the feeling so many times in her life that it didn't immediately cause her to turn tail and run. It was one of her many *gifts*; she could sense when bad things were about to happen. Sometimes her abilities came in little bursts of anxiety and amounted to little more than getting bad news like an overly inflated bill from the plumber or finding out her favorite television show hadn't been picked up for a new season. Other times her abilities came in the form of full-fledged body-numbing panic attacks, and she discovered a loved one had passed away or that there had been a terrible accident involving someone she knew.

The receptionist looked up at the two women with a polite smile. "Hello. May I help you?"

"We have an appointment to see Mr. Marlow at nine," said Char.

"Yes, Mr. Marlow will be right with you. Please have a seat." The young woman tipped her puffy blond hair towards the small lobby.

Char took a seat on one of the red padded armchairs

and plucked a magazine off the end table. Her sunny yellow polyester pants rode up on her calves, revealing the long white socks sticking out of her white New Balance sneakers.

Phyllis took the seat next to her. She glanced over at Char, casually flipping through the magazine. She leaned towards her, resting her face in the palm of her hand with her elbow on the armrest. She wished the feeling in the pit of her stomach would go away. There was no way she could read about Martha Stewart's tips for lining her cupboard shelves with rolls of cork instead of adhesive shelf liners. With a heavy sigh, she shifted her weight to her opposite cheek, leaning her elbow on the armrest on the other side. Seconds later, she fidgeted again and rocked her weight back onto her left hip until finally, Char had to lay a hand on her thigh.

"For heaven's sake, Phil, sit still. You're getting me all flustered. You need to relax," Char chastised.

Phyllis tucked her hands under her bottom in an attempt to keep still. "I can't. Now that we're here, I'm getting this really strong sense that something *bad* is going to happen."

Char let out a sigh and flipped the page in her *Martha Stewart Living* magazine. "You're just being paranoid. What bad thing could possibly happen in a *lawyer's* office?"

"Good morning, ladies," boomed a deep voice across the room a second later.

The women looked up to see a man in his late fifties

in a dark suit and tie standing next to the secretary's desk. He wore a bad salt-and-pepper toupee on his head, and his shoulders were dusted with dandruff flakes. The broad smile he wore on his face curved up high on both sides of his cheeks like a drawn-on clown's smile. "I'm Jerry Marlow. Come on back."

Phyllis's unease continued as she and Char stood up and followed Mr. Marlow down the blue-speckled hallway into his office. Four chairs sat empty around his desk. He gestured towards them. "Have a seat, ladies. We'll get started in a minute. We're just waiting for everyone else to arrive."

Char and Phyllis exchanged glances. *Who else would Kat have named in her will?* Phyllis wondered. *Maybe she left something to the paperman. Maybe that's why he showed up at the funeral.*

"So, how did you two ladies know Ms. Lynde?" he asked, attempting small talk with them while they waited.

"We went to school with her," said Phyllis. She brushed a hand in front of her face, signifying that the length of time she'd known the woman was so far in the past, it belonged in a history book somewhere. "Years and years ago."

"I was her roommate," added Char. "I kept in contact with Kat over the years, checking in on her once or twice a month. We were really sad to hear that she'd passed."

Mr. Marlow's smile faded, relaxing the overexaggerated curves of skin beneath his eyes, and he nodded sadly.

"Katherine was a sweet woman. I always enjoyed our visits."

There was a knock at the door, and then the receptionist's blond-headed bird's nest poked inside the room. "Mr. Marlow, Ms. Prescott is here for the will reading."

His hand lifted off his desk as he gestured her in with two fingers in the air. "Send her in, please."

Phyllis's eyes widened as she turned to stare at Char. *Gwyndolin Prescott? It couldn't possibly be! Gwyndolin Prescott doesn't even live in Aspen Falls!*

An older woman's voice carried in from the hallway. "You're going to keep an eye on her, right?"

The receptionist's voice trailed in. "Yes, your mother will be just fine in the lobby."

"She tends to wander…," said the voice with hesitation.

"I won't let her leave my sight."

"Not even to use the restroom? Because if there's a window…"

"Okay, umm, yes, all right," the younger woman stammered uncomfortably.

A woman with shoulder-length strawberry-blond hair wavered in the doorway with her back to the room. "Maybe I could just bring her into Mr. Marlow's office with me?"

"I'm sorry—as I said, only those named in the will can be present for the reading. Don't worry, I'll keep a very close eye on her," promised the receptionist.

"Okay, yes. Thank you so much for watching her."

The older woman's fingers knitted together nervously as she turned to face the room.

The woman's eyes barely had time to scan the faces in the room before Phyllis stood up and bellowed, "*Oh, hell no!*"

The woman's hand shook as it went to her mouth. She looked like she'd seen a ghost. "Phyllis Habernackle?" she breathed.

Phyllis wagged a finger in the air at the lawyer. "Oh no, we aren't doing this with *her*."

Gwyn's eyes swung in shock down to the other woman seated in the chair. "Char?!"

Char's head lolled back on her neck, and her eyes swung up towards the ceiling. "I can't believe this is happening right now," she murmured.

"Did Kat put you two in her will too?" asked Gwyn, slowly lowering her hand.

"No, we're here filing a sexual harassment suit against Harvey Weinstein," snapped Phyllis. "Of course she named us in her will! *We* were her friends!"

Gwyn's spine stiffened. "I was her friend, too."

"A hundred years ago, maybe. Where ya been since then?"

"Raising a family, taking care of my mother. But I always kept in touch with Kat."

Char's arms crossed across her chest as she harrumphed. "Funny. You never kept in touch with us!"

Gwyn's eyes narrowed. "Of course not, not after what you did!"

"After what I did?" An indignant look passed across Char's face as she sat poised on the edge of her chair, ready to jump to her feet at any second.

"What you *both* did," Gwyn said, pointing her finger between both Phyllis and Char.

"Ladies," said Mr. Marlow, putting his palms flat on his desk and pushing himself to his feet.

"*What we did?!*" demanded Phyllis, feeling the jittery spike of adrenaline shoot through her limbs. "*I* certainly didn't do anything!"

"Neither did I!" hollered Char.

It was Gwyn's turn to cross her arms across her chest. "Oh, I beg to differ. Kat told me exactly what you two did."

Mr. Marlow cleared his throat. "Ladies…"

"Well, Kat told *us* exactly what *you and Loni* did!" cried Char without so much as a glance in Mr. Marlow's direction.

"Loni and I didn't do anything!" huffed Gwyn.

Mr. Marlow looked down at his watch. "Speaking of Ms. Hodges, have any of you heard from her? It's time we got this meeting going." He glanced around the room, unsure of which woman to direct his question to.

It was Char's turn to stand up then. "*Loni's* coming too?"

Phyllis palmed her forehead and sat down on her chair. "Oh, for heaven's sake. This is turning into a three-ring circus!"

Gwyn's head shook nervously. "I haven't heard from

Loni in a while. I just got to town a few days ago. I'm trying to get us settled into our new place, and I haven't had time to visit her yet."

Char's neck practically snapped as she turned to regard Gwyn. "Are you telling us you've *moved* back to Aspen Falls?!"

Gwyn's jaw tightened as she frowned at her. "Not that it's any of your business, but, yes, my mother and I just moved here on Sunday."

"I can't believe this," murmured Char, shaking her head.

Phyllis clucked her tongue. "I told you I was getting a bad feeling," she reminded Char. "This! This is why! The devil herself just moved in next door."

Char poked a stubby finger into the top of Mr. Marlow's desk. "Can we just get on with this?"

Mr. Marlow cleared his throat and straightened his tie. "Not without Ms. Hodges." He reached a hand for the phone. "Perhaps I could give her a call."

Char sighed. "That old loon doesn't answer the phone if she doesn't recognize the number."

Gwyn plopped down in the last of the four chairs, putting a space between her and Phyllis. "Char's right. Loni is a bit on the *paranoid* side."

"Do you think she'll show up? We could give her another five or ten minutes if we need to. My next appointment isn't until ten thirty."

Gwyn used her fingertips to knead the sides of her temples as if she were suffering from a headache. "I kind of doubt it. From what I understand, Loni hasn't left her house in a while."

"What's a while?"

Gwyn's head bobbed from side to side. "Oh, the last twenty or thirty years or so," she said.

Mr. Marlow smiled. "Surely you're joking."

Char lifted a brow and pursed her lips. "No, that woman's a recluse. I wouldn't be surprised if it were more like *forty* years."

"Well, I'm sorry, but the will specifically states that you *four women* must be in each other's presence when the will is read, and it must be read in *my* office."

"Surely if one of the women is flat-out looney bin nuts, exceptions can be made," suggested Phyllis.

He shook his head. "Ms. Lynde was very clear. The four of you must be here together when the will is read. No exceptions, unless of course one of you preceded her in death."

Phyllis eyed Gwyn with contempt. "I'm sure arrangements can be made."

"*Phyllis Habernackle!* That is a *horrible* thing to say!" breathed Gwyn as a hand fluttered to the base of her throat.

"Oh, don't go getting your granny panties in a knot, *Gwyndolin Prescott*," spat Phyllis. "Why don't you skedaddle on outta here and get your precious little Yolanda Hodges over here, post haste. I have things to do."

Gwyn wrung her hands uncomfortably. "I—I have to

go back to work. I just started a new job. I can't go over there right now."

"You still have a *job*?" clucked Char.

"Aren't you a little *old* to be starting a new job?" asked Phyllis.

Gwyn looked offended. "There's nothing wrong with starting a new job at my age."

Phyllis wrinkled her nose.

Gwyn's light blue eyes swung up to meet Mr. Marlow's. "I can go visit Loni this evening. We can meet again tomorrow over my lunch break?"

He slipped on his reading glasses, flipped a page on his desk planner, and picked up a pencil. "Noon?"

She gave him a curt nod.

He looked at Char and Phyllis over the top of his glasses. "Noon work for you two?"

Phyllis groaned as she looked at Char. Char gave her an almost imperceptible nod. "Fine," she grumped. "Noon is fine."

5

*I*t was nearly dark by the time Gwyn packed her mother up into her old silver Buick and left the retirement village. The Aspen Falls streetlamps had just begun to flicker on, and a cool spring breeze rode in through her open window, bringing with it the sweet smell of freshly cut grass. Gwyn leaned her head back against the headrest and inhaled the familiar scents deeply before slowly letting the air out of her lungs.

It was the first time she'd sat down all day. She'd spent the day on her feet, teaching Village residents to macramé plant holders and dream catchers, and all she really wanted to do now was curl up in the bathtub with a good book and a glass of wine. She wished she had the energy to muster up a little more excitement about meeting up with her old friend, Yolanda Hodges, but she was too exhausted. She would have liked to have done this little excursion in a week or two, when she'd gotten back into a routine and had a Saturday afternoon to spend with her old friend.

Hazel peered out her window as they cruised down a side street. "You sure you know where you're going?"

Gwyn glanced up at the street signs. It had been years since the last time she'd been to Aspen Falls. She'd practically been a child back then. In fact, only being in her late teens, she had been the youngest of all of her friends. Not that she'd let that stop her from having just as much fun as the rest of the girls, though. Seeing the familiar land-marks as she drove through town made her smile. The waterfall in the center of town that they'd gone splashing in at midnight on more than one occasion. The kitschy little downtown shops with their colorful awnings and lit window displays hadn't changed a bit—though the merchandise in the windows had progressed with the times. She cast a sideways glance towards the road that would take her up the hill to the Paranormal Institute for Witches, her alma mater. One day soon, she'd make it a point to pack up her mother and go visit it for old time's sake. Maybe she'd even find a picture of a younger version of herself on a wall somewhere.

Then her mind drifted to the Hodgeses' house. Loni had lived there her entire life, except the two years she left to go to the Institute. She'd begged her parents to let her live on campus so she could have the *real college experience*. They'd allowed it, and she and Gwyn had been room-mates for both years of witch school. Since Gwyn's family had lived so far away, Gwyn had spent many a holiday and extended weekend at Loni's house, so she knew the place well.

With one elbow of her periwinkle-blue cardigan poking out the open window, Gwyn leaned her head against her fingertips while steering with her right hand. "Yes, Mother. I know where I'm going. Loni was my roommate, remember?"

"Of course I remember that she was your roommate. I might be old and hard of hearing, but I'm not forgetful," snapped Hazel.

Gwyn sighed. She really needed that glass of wine. *Or three.* She looked out the window and watched the familiar scenery pass her. She remembered that big, tall sandstone building on the corner. She and the girls had put a car on top of that building one Halloween night. She smiled to herself as she passed a familiar dilapidated gas station. *My goodness, they haven't done a thing to that place since I left Aspen Falls!*

"Did you call her and tell her we were coming?" asked Hazel.

"I tried. Loni didn't answer."

Hazel clucked her tongue at her daughter and then turned her head to look back out the window. "Folks don't like people stopping in unannounced," she chastised.

"I don't have a choice, Mom. She didn't answer the phone, and I know she doesn't leave the house."

Hazel shrugged. "Don't be shocked if she's runnin' around the house naked as a jaybird, is all I'm saying."

Gwyn smiled an amused smile at her mother.

"Nothing would shock me when it comes to Loni Hodges. She's a little bit *different*." Gwyn gripped the steering wheel a little bit tighter as she turned down Hemlock Road. *Different* was an understatement where Loni was concerned. Gwyn didn't want to be offensive and call her old friend eccentric, but facts were facts, and Loni was eccentric. Gwyn pushed the thoughts aside. Maybe things had changed with Loni, and she'd be normal as the day was long now.

Gwyn slowed down in front of the last house on Hemlock Road. Loni's was the very last oversized lot at the end of the dead-end road. A large newly planted cornfield sat just beyond the dead end sign. A narrow dirt-packed alley wound its way behind her house.

Hazel peered out her window. A solitary streetlamp lit up the otherwise darkened corner, casting an eerie glow across the overgrown weeded lawn. "This is where she lives?" There was skepticism and a hint of fear in Hazel's voice.

Gwyn rolled up her window and shut off the car's engine. "Yep."

Hazel's eyes widened as she sucked in her breath and hunkered down into her seat. "I'm not going in there."

"Don't be ridiculous. Yes, you are, Mom."

Hazel crossed her arms across her chest and jutted her chin out defiantly. "No. I'll stay out in the car."

"I'm not leaving you out in the car. You'll wander off."

"No, I won't."

"Yes, you will."

Hazel held on to the seat belt that crossed her chest. "I'm not going anywhere."

"Don't make me carry you in, Mother."

Hazel's eyes narrowed as she glowered at her daughter. "You wouldn't!"

Without a word, Gwyn shoved her door open, slung her purse over her shoulder, got out of the car, and walked around to her mother's side. She opened the passenger-side door and unbuckled the old woman's seat belt. "I've done it before. I'll do it again." Her tone was authoritative and tight as a plucked guitar string.

"You'll throw your back out!" Hazel challenged.

"I've done that before too."

Hazel looked past her daughter at the unkempt, rickety old three-story house. "Ghosts live in houses like that."

"You're a witch, Mother. Ghosts don't scare you."

"Houses like that do."

"I'm carrying you in," said Gwyn. She ducked her head down low towards her mother's lap, preparing to throw her over her shoulders in a fireman's carry.

Hazel swatted at the back of Gwyn's head. "Oh, for crying out loud, I have two feet. I'll walk!" When Gwyn pulled her head back, Hazel grabbed hold of the cane that rested in the web of her skirt and touched the concrete curb with the tip of it. Then she smacked her daughter's legs, just below the knees. "Move, Gwynnie. How am I supposed to get out with you standing over me?"

"I was going to help you get out."

Hazel stuck her free arm out to her daughter. "Well, then, pull, why don't you?"

Gwyn pulled, and soon the two women were standing on the sidewalk in front of Loni's house. A cool gust of air whipped between the trees, making a rustling sound, and an owl hooted ominously in the distance.

Hazel rubbed her goosefleshed arm. "This place gives me the willies."

Gwyn didn't want to admit that it gave her the willies too, but she knew she didn't have to admit it. Her mother was likely reading her mind as they stood there.

She led her mother to the wooden porch. The paint on the balusters, which had at one point been a pristine white, was now flaking off, and in some spots they were bare right down to the wood grain. The entire porch leaned towards the street and slightly to the left. If a big windstorm came, it could likely take the porch with it in one big gust. Old newspapers and soggy, misshapen cardboard boxes littered one end of the porch, and the other end was mounded with split firewood. Next to the front door sat a faded wicker chair with a floral pad covered in clumps of cat hair. Three bowls filled with cat food were placed in various empty spots around the garbage. An old dog leash was tied to one of the tall columns, but no dog lay on the other end. The screen door hung from its last hinge, and the screen was torn and frayed in three spots. Gwyn remembered when Loni's folks had still been alive. Her father had kept the place in tip-top shape, so it saddened her to see what the years of no maintenance had done to the once remarkable home.

"No lights on," remarked Hazel. "No one's home. Let's go." She turned on the stairs to go back to the car.

Gwyn caught her arm and scowled at her mother. She'd had it. She pointed at the leash. "Don't make me chain you to the porch."

Hazel squinted her eyes and sneered at her daughter. "You wouldn't."

Gwyn lifted one pale eyebrow. "Try me."

Hazel let out a *puh* sound but didn't move.

Gwyn helped her mother across the porch to the front door. Keeping one hand firmly on Hazel's back, she knocked with the other hand. She waited a few seconds and didn't hear anything, so she knocked again. No answer. Gwyn started to get worried. *What if something happened to Loni?* She pointed to the wicker chair. "Sit, Mother."

Hazel's eyes widened. "Oh, I'm not sitting on that!"

"Don't move, then!" ordered Gwyn. She let go of Hazel's arm and stepped carefully over the old boxes and newspapers, keeping an eye out on the dimly lit porch for animals hidden amongst the rubbish. She got closer to the picture window and cupped her hands to peer into the glass. A curtain hung on the other side of the glass, ruining her view of the interior. *Darn it*, she thought. Just as she started to walk away, she thought that she caught a glimpse of a tiny bit of the curtain swaying. *Did that just move?* She peered in the window again, and this time, she heard something inside the house. She knocked on the glass. "Loni! Is that you?"

Gwyn stepped back over the garbage and went to the door and knocked again. "I saw something move," she said to her mother.

Hazel stood in front of the chair with both hands resting on the knob of her cane. "It was probably a ghost. I told you this place was haunted!"

"It had to have been Loni." She pounded on the door again. "Loni! Open up. It's Gwyn Prescott!"

Gwyn was sure she could hear someone shuffling about inside of the house then.

"She's probably got to get dressed after running around naked and all."

"Who runs around naked in their house?" asked Gwyn, staring at her mother.

Hazel made a face. "I'd run around naked if you'd let me."

Gwyn rubbed her temples with the tips of her fingers. "Ugh, you just gave me a mental picture I didn't want to have, Mom."

"As if you'd look so great naked?"

"Just stop, Mom."

Hazel shrugged and pinched her lips tightly to her teeth.

"Loni! I need to speak to you. It's important!" Gwyn hollered into the door.

Suddenly, the handle of the interior door turned, and the door creaked open just a crack. Gwyn couldn't see anyone through the screen's dirt-caked mesh.

"Who is it?" asked a froggy voice.

"It's Gwyn!"

"Gwyn who?"

"Your old roommate, Gwyn Prescott."

"I don't know a Gwyn Prescott."

"Stop playing, Loni. Of course, you do." Gwyn silently wondered if her old friend was suffering from sudden-onset dementia or Alzheimer's.

"How do I know you're telling the truth?"

Gwyn was at a loss. *Because I wouldn't lie*, she thought. She looked at her mother. "Because I brought my mother with me."

The person on the other side of the door paused. "How do I know that's your mother?"

Gwyn poked the short woman in front of her. "Tell her you're my mother," she hissed.

"I've never seen this woman before in my life," said Hazel.

"Mother!" admonished Gwyn.

"The woman picked me up off the street and forced me to come with her," Hazel added. She turned toward the street and tried to hobble away. "Call the police!"

Gwyn sidestepped and stood in her mother's way. "Stop it, Mom."

"See! She's got me against my will. Call the police. Call the FBI. Call your senator!"

"You're not the FBI?" the woman asked from the other side of the door.

"Of course we're not the FBI," said Gwyn. "It's Gwyn and Hazel Prescott, Loni. We just moved to town."

"Why are you coming so late at night?" asked the voice.

"Because I just got off work."

"Where do you work?"

"The Aspen Falls Retirement Village."

"More like the Aspen Falls Funeral Home," snarked Hazel. "That place is worse than death."

The door opened a little wider. "Did anyone follow you here?"

Gwyn looked behind her. "I don't think so. Why would they?"

"You can never be too sure," said the low, gravelly voice.

"Can we come in and talk inside?" asked Gwyn.

"You got any ID?"

Are you kidding me? Gwyn wondered. She sighed, but dug into her purse, pulling out her wallet. She flipped it open and flashed it at the dark crack.

A hand reached out, shoved the screen door open, and snatched up the wallet, pulling it inside with her.

"Hey! Loni!"

"You got any ID on the loudmouth?"

"Trust me. She's my mother. I wouldn't be hauling this woman around unless I was related to her by blood."

Hazel bent slightly to the left and stared up at her daughter, giving her the stink eye.

The voice on the other side was quiet for a moment. Finally, the door swung open all the way. Only darkness could be seen inside. "Come in. Hurry up."

Gwyn pulled the screen door open all the way and shoved her mother forward. "Let me do the talking," she whispered.

"Quit pushing. This body hasn't hurried up in forty years, it's certainly not gonna start now," said Hazel as she crossed the threshold slowly tapping at the dark ground in front of her with her cane.

Gwyn followed her mother inside, and the minute the door cleared her bottom, it slammed shut behind her back. Gwyn and Hazel stood in complete darkness.

"Did you forget to pay your electric bill?" asked Hazel.

"I don't put the light on in this room after dark," said the gravelly voice. "Follow me."

Gwyn stepped around her mother so she could go first, but Hazel held her arm tightly. "Don't make me go in there, Gwynnie," she pled. "I don't wanna die!"

"Mother, please!" begged Gwyn, tugging her mother along behind her.

Hazel sighed. "So this is how I go. Chopped up into little pieces by a psycho axe murderer. I'm leaving your sister my estate."

"You don't have an estate, Mother," whispered Gwyn. "And I don't have a sister."

"Maybe not, but if I *had* another daughter, *she* wouldn't make me go anywhere scary. She'd be the *good* daughter."

Gwyn frowned in the darkness. Her heart jittered in her chest. She wasn't exactly excited about blindly trusting her old friend Loni either. After all, Loni seemed to have gone off the deep end some time ago. Were they walking into a trap?

Gwyn grasped hold of her mother's arm, and

together they did their best to follow the sound of Loni's footsteps across the hardwood floor. The further they walked, the tighter Gwyn and Hazel grasped each other's arms.

"Where are we going, Loni?" asked Gwyn with her pulse pounding in her ears.

Suddenly, the sound of the footsteps in front of them stopped. They heard a noise, and then the light flipped on.

Gwyn's eyes narrowed as the light caught her off guard and temporarily blinded her. She looked up.

"Ahh!" screamed Hazel.

6

"*L*oni!" breathed Gwyn. "Is that you?"

Hazel's frail body pressed tightly against Gwyn's back. She peered one eye around her daughter.

The woman standing before them stood about five feet nothing tall. She wore a wide-brimmed pink velvet hat with pink and orange flowers on the brim. She had on round black-rimmed Coke bottle glasses and wore a pink boa around her neck. Her shift dress was green-and-yellow paisley and looked like something she'd kept from the sixties. And to support the whole outfit, she had on a pair of purple galoshes.

With grotesquely enlarged eyes, the woman peered through her thick lenses at Gwyn. "You wearing a wire?" she asked in a coarse voice.

"A wire? Why would I be wearing a wire, Loni?"

Loni nodded her head towards Hazel. "How about that one? Is she wearing a wire?"

Gwyn peeked around her back to look down at her mother, who was holding on to the tail of Gwyn's sweater tightly. "No. Mother's not wearing a wire."

"Then you won't mind if I frisk you?" asked Loni.

Gwyn's eyes widened. What had she gotten herself into? "Frisk us?! You can't be serious! Can't you just take my word?"

Loni shook her head. "I need to be sure."

Gwyn felt the woman's hands on her sides and down her back. With her arms straight down in front of her, she squeezed her breasts together between her biceps to protect them. When Loni came at her chest, Gwyn swiveled her shoulders. "That's quite enough, thank you," snapped Gwyn. Gwyn hadn't been felt up in years, and she wasn't about to let cuckoo Yolanda Hodges be the first to have that honor.

Apparently satisfied that Gwyn wasn't wearing a wire, Loni moved on to Hazel.

"Touch me, and I'll cane you," said Hazel, holding out the business end of her wooden cane. With the cane slung over her shoulder, Loni and Hazel squared off, staring each other down.

Finally, Loni relented. "Fine. I'll need to check your bag," she said, pointing at Gwyn's purse.

"My purse? Why?"

"Standard procedure," said Loni without taking her eyes off of Hazel and her cane.

"It's really not necessary, Loni. I don't have anything important in there…"

Despite Gwyn's protests, Loni pulled the bag off her

shoulder and dumped the contents onto the floor. Tubes of lipsticks, a box of Tic Tacs, a comb, wadded-up tissues, the car keys, and several handfuls of crumpled receipts tumbled out.

"Loni!" breathed Gwyn as she looked down at the mess on the floor. Gwyn squatted down and began reassembling her items. "What is going on?"

Loni picked up a tube of lipstick, pulled off the cap and twisted it to reveal its contents. "Is this really lipstick?"

"Of course it's really lipstick! What else would it be?"

Loni rubbed the bright red lipstick across her mouth, smudging it out of the naturally formed lines of her lips and into the wrinkled creases that outlined them. "So it is," she said before handing Gwyn the tube. "What's this?"

Gwyn looked at the small box Loni had just picked up. "Tic Tacs?" she asked, bewildered. This was the strangest encounter she'd ever had in her life.

Squatted down next to Gwyn, Loni sniffed the container. "What are Tic Tacs?"

"Breath mints," said Gwyn curiously. "Haven't you ever had a Tic Tac?"

Loni put the box in the pocket of her dress. "I'll just hang onto these until the contents can be verified."

Gwyn couldn't believe it. Her friend had truly gone off the deep end. *What happened to make Loni so suspicious?* she wondered. *She certainly wasn't like this in college.* Gwyn shoved the rest of her belongings back into her purse and stood up.

"May I please have my wallet back?" she asked indignantly as she shoved the purse high up on her shoulder.

Loni blinked without changing expressions. Then, slowly, she looked down at the wallet in her hand and began to study Gwyn's identification, giving Gwyn a chance to look around the room.

They stood in the kitchen. The inside was much like the outside. Stuffed with junk, covered in cat food, and badly in need of cleaning and repairs. The whole house reeked of cat urine and cigar smoke, and Gwyn had a difficult time taking in a deep breath as the odor was so pungent.

"This says you live in Arizona. What are you doing in Pennsylvania?" Loni's question sounded more like an accusation.

"Mom and I just moved here." Gwyn scanned Loni's clothing choice. "That's an interesting outfit you're wearing."

Loni handed Gwyn her wallet back. "Why did you move here?"

"I got a job at the Aspen Falls Retirement Village," said Gwyn as she tucked her wallet back into her purse.

"So it's really you?" asked Loni.

Gwyn sighed. She wasn't sure what else she needed to do to prove to Loni that she was indeed her old college roommate. "Yes, Loni. It's really me."

"What was our headmistress's name in college?"

"Sorceress Halliwell," said Gwyn. "And we all loved her."

Loni blinked again behind her round glasses. Her

oversized eyes like those of a slender loris. "Anyone could have found that out."

Gwyn palmed her forehead. They were getting nowhere at a snail's pace. She was getting frustrated. "We pulled a prank on Halloween night. Put all the police cars on top of the downtown buildings."

That made Loni smile, and for the first time, she revealed her caffeine-stained teeth to the girls. "He-he," she cackled in a slow chuckle. "I had almost forgotten about that. That was funny." Just as she'd been quick to smile about the incident, she was quick to allow her smile to fade, and the suspicious looks returned. "But it also made the papers. Anyone could have figured out that was us. What else you got?"

Forced to replay old memories in her mind, Gwyn thought about it for a long moment. Her eyes scanned the familiar walls and the wooden stairs just off the kitchen. She could see a young Loni sprinting down those stairs in her mind. Loni had been wild and crazy and full of life. They'd been the best of friends back then. The thought made Gwyn want to try harder to bring the old Loni back. "I stayed here in this house with you many, many times. I met your mom and dad and your brother and sister. Your room was on the third floor. We snuck out once by crawling out your window and down the tree in the backyard. Your skirt got caught in the branches and tore off a huge chunk of the rear of your dress."

Loni made a funny noise, almost a snort, and then said, "That tree came down in a storm about twenty years ago."

Gwyn smiled at her. "See? How would anyone else know that?"

With her arms hanging limply by her side, Loni finally broke character and slowly reached out to touch Gwyn's face. "Is that really you, Gwynnie?"

Gwyn sighed. Finally, she'd gotten through to her! "Yes, Loni. It's really me." Gwyn stood awkwardly as Loni felt her face with the tips of her fingers. Then suddenly, Loni's arms were around her, and she was pulling her in for a tight hug.

"I've missed you, Gwynnie!"

With Loni's head pressed between Gwyn's breasts, her pink felt hat tipped off of her head and smashed Gwyn in the face. She leaned her head back on her neck and patted Loni's back. "I've missed you too, Lon."

Just as suddenly as she'd embraced Gwyn, she let go of her and rushed back towards the front door and into darkness. Loni wove through stacks of possessions and pulled back the curtain at her front window. Carefully she peered outside. "You're sure no one followed you?"

Gwyn knitted her eyebrows together. "Pretty sure. Who are you scared of, Loni?"

Loni held a hand to her lips and hissed at Gwyn, "Shhh!" She stared at the window.

Gwyn looked down at her mother. Hazel swirled a finger in circles up by her temple. Then she made a psychotic face and pretended to stab Gwyn repeatedly with her cane. Gwyn rolled her eyes and shook her head at her mother as if to say, *No, Loni's not going to kill us.*

Finally, Loni returned to the kitchen, causing Hazel to

retreat back behind her daughter again. "I think we're safe," said Loni, sounding a little more normal than she had thus far.

"I'm glad to hear that." Gwyn stepped aside to reveal her mother, but Hazel stayed glued to her back and moved when she did. Gwyn had to twist around to peel the old woman off her. "Loni, this is my mother, Hazel," she grunted while working to detach Hazel's grip from her sweater. "Do you remember her?"

"No," said Loni, sniffing in Hazel's direction. "I never met your mother."

"Yes, you did. It was on move-in day of our freshman year."

Loni shrugged and looked at Hazel. "So you're Hazel."

"And you're a loon," said Hazel matter-of-factly.

"Mother!" gasped Gwyn. "I'm so sorry, Loni. My mother has a tendency to blurt things out."

"I just call things as I see them. Nothing wrong with that," said Hazel with a shrug. "Besides, she called me a loudmouth."

Loni nodded. "I can appreciate that. Too many people pretend to be something they're not. I prefer blunt people. It's nice to meet you, Hazel. Come on in, girls." She led the duo further into the kitchen between two tall rows of stacked magazines to a kitchen table covered with mail, papers, books, and a calico cat bathing herself. The chairs around the table were all covered with random things. Baskets of buttons, bins of thread, a box of candles. "Let me clear off a spot for us to sit down." She waved her hand towards the cat in a shooing motion. "Get down, Callie."

The cat squawked at her as it jumped down off the table.

"Well, I'm sorry," she snapped back at her as she sauntered away. "I didn't know we were going to have guests either!"

Gwyn stepped uncomfortably around the tight space while her friend emptied three chairs. "Is that your only cat?" Gwyn asked politely.

The woman looked up at Gwyn with a broad smile. "Yes."

By the cat stench in the house, Gwyn was shocked to hear that this was the only cat contributing to the odor, but it was the only one she'd seen.

Loni looked back at the cat. "Oh. Do you mean is that my *only* cat?"

Gwyn nodded. She wasn't sure how else her question could have been interpreted.

Loni shook her head. "Callie is my only *calico* cat. Her brother died a year ago Saturday, and as you can tell by her attitude, she still isn't over it. Now technically she does have a third cousin that's part calico. But I really don't count that because her mother was Siamese."

Gwyn lifted her brows and pursed her lips. "So you have other cats?"

Loni moved a basket of candles to the floor and motioned for Hazel to sit. "I have twenty-seven other cats."

Gwyn's jaw fell open. "You have *twenty-eight* cats total?"

Loni's head bobbled on her neck. "Oh, give or take a few strays."

Hazel eyed the chair Loni had just cleared off for her. "You some kind of crazy cat lady or something?"

"Mom!"

Loni laughed. "It's alright, Gwyn. She's probably got me pegged accurately."

Gwyn's face fell. "Oh. I—I'm sorry…"

"Sorry? For what? I love cats. They're my family." Loni looked at Hazel. "I talk to animals, you know."

Hazel's baggy eyes widened. "Oh. I didn't know. I read minds."

"I think I remember Gwyn telling me that." Loni nodded. "Please, have a seat. Can I get you something to eat or drink?"

Gwyn's stomach rumbled, but one look at the cat food covering the dishes in the sink and on the counter told Gwyn she could wait to grab a bite when they got back to The Village. "Oh no, we're positively stuffed," she lied instead.

Hazel looked up at her sharply, as if to say, *Liar.*

Gwyn kicked her mother's leg under the table. "Loni, that's quite the interesting outfit you're wearing."

Loni looked down at herself. "Oh, yes," she said, unwinding the boa and letting it drop on the floor. She took the hat off too and put it on the counter, on top of a bra and a pair of nylon stockings, then slid her bare feet out of the rain boots. "That was just a disguise."

"A disguise?" Gwyn looked down at the small gold watch she wore. "It's late, Loni. Why would you be wearing a disguise in your own home?"

Loni ignored the question and glanced down at Hazel. "Hazel, would you like some coffee?"

A black-and-white cat approached and began lapping milk from a coffee mug on the floor. His face was white, but he had a black Hitler-like mustache below his nose and a swirl of white and black like a yin and yang symbol on the left side of his rump. Hazel eyed him suspiciously. "Have cats licked out of all of your mugs?"

"Mmm, not these," said Loni, pulling two mugs from the cupboard.

Gwyn looked at her mother. If Hazel had caffeine now, Gwyn would never get her wine, bath, and book ritual in before bed. "Mom will pass. It's too late in the evening for her to have caffeine. It makes her jittery and then she won't sleep."

Hazel frowned and crossed arms across her sagging breasts. "You're really becoming no fun. Didn't I raise you better than that?"

Gwyn ignored her mother. "You were saying what the disguise was for?"

Loni poured a mug of coffee and put it in the microwave to warm it up. She shrugged simply. "I thought maybe you were someone else."

Gwyn lifted an eyebrow. "Oh, who did you think we were?"

Loni shrugged nonchalantly and pulled her coffee out when the timer beeped. "I don't know. The FBI, maybe."

"The FBI? Why would the FBI be knocking on your door so late at night?"

Loni sat down with a big sigh. "Oh, you know, that's how they getcha. By coming at night."

"It is?" asked Gwyn. She wondered why the FBI would even be coming in the first place but thought maybe it would be rude of her to ask.

Loni nodded as she kicked her birdlike legs out in front of her. "So, tell me everything!"

"Everything?"

"Yeah, you know. Everything that's happened since we last saw each other."

7

"*W*ell, gosh, Loni. That's a lot of stuff. It's been decades since the last time we've seen each other. We've talked on the phone over the years, though. Don't you remember any of our conversations?"

Loni lifted one thick black markered-on eyebrow. "Eh. Some." She tapped a finger against her skull. "The memory comes and goes. You live with your mom, right?"

That made Hazel chuckle. "He-he. Yeah. You hear that, Gwynnie? *You* live with *me*." The old woman thumbed her chest.

Gwyn rolled her eyes. "My mother lives with *me*, yes."

Loni leaned forward. "Do you still have *the touch*?" she asked with a wicked smile.

"*The touch*?"

Loni wiggled her fingers at the books on the table in front of her. "Yeah, you know, *the touch*."

Gwyn smiled the kind of smile where she refused to

part her lips and show her teeth. It was simply a polite gesture. "Oh. That. Yes, sometimes. It comes and goes as I've gotten older. But for the most part, yes."

Loni smiled and rubbed her hands together. "Do something for me?"

Gwyn slumped in her seat now. She was exhausted and didn't feel like spinning any magic. "Like what?"

"Anything!"

Gwyn hated being put on the spot with her "talent," but she equally hated letting people down.

"Okay," she said reluctantly and flexed her fingers out in front of her. She pulled her hands back, so they were just in front of her shoulders and wiggled her fingers towards the book on the table.

The book bounced an inch off the table and sprung open wide, the pages spilling apart. Leaves sprung forth from the pages, and the spine magically evolved into a terra-cotta pot. The hard cover disintegrated into soil and fell neatly into the pot. The leaves continued to grow as a thick stem shot out of the soil and lifted the foliage. When the little magic show was complete, a beautifully potted maple sapling sat on the table in front of them.

Loni's eyes widened as she clapped her hands. "Oh, you've still got it! Just like old times! You haven't changed a bit, either. You look great! Love the hair," she said.

Gwyn fingered her hair with a light smile as Hazel rolled her eyes and leaned back in her seat. "It's from a bottle," said Hazel mockingly.

Gwyn's face glowed red as she sighed. This was why she didn't have any friends. "Mom," she begged quietly.

Loni chuckled. "It's alright, Gwynnie. I still like it, and you still look great. You've aged well."

Gwyn lifted her cheeks again. She wished she could say the same about Loni, but the woman's sagging face, overgrown nose complete with wart, and coffee-stained teeth told Gwyn that that would be a lie. Instead, she decided to change the subject.

"Thank you, Loni. It's really great to see you, too. So, what's going on with you?"

"Not much," said Loni. Swiveling in her seat, Loni pointed a finger at the counter behind her. A pile of loose papers shifted magically, and a small box emerged from the rubbish. She curled the finger towards herself, and the box floated across the short distance and landed gently in her hand. She put the box on the table, pulled a cigar out of it, and placed it between her bright red lips. "Mind if I smoke?" she asked, snapping her fingers and igniting the air in front of them.

Gwyn frowned as she shifted in her seat. "Oh, uh—it might not be good for Mother," she said in a hushed whisper. "Asthma."

Loni looked at Hazel, who shrugged before looking away. She shook out her fingers, extinguishing the flame, and put the cigar back in the box. "Alright," she sighed.

"Sorry."

Loni waved a hand. "No problem. I'll have one later." The women stared at each other for an uncomfortably long moment until finally, Loni's eyebrows furrowed. She pointed at Gwyn. "Hey, do you mind taking that sweater off?"

Gwyn looked down at the cardigan she'd thrown over her white cotton top. The evening had been cool when they'd left, and she'd put it on before they'd even gotten to the car. "My sweater? Why?"

"It's blue," said Loni as if that were a complete explanation.

Gwyn slowly shrugged off her sweater. "What does that mean?"

Loni made a face as if Gwyn were crazy. "Blue? You know, that's a color."

Hazel looked up at her daughter and lifted a brow.

"Yes, Loni. I know that blue is a color. I don't understand why you want me to take my sweater off."

"Oh. The color blue bothers me," she said simply.

"It does?" Gwyn shoved the sweater behind the small of her back in her seat. "Why?"

Loni leaned forward in her seat. "I can't talk about it either," she whispered, covering her mouth with a hand. "It makes me want to urp."

"Urp?" asked Hazel.

"Yeah, you know." Loni made a vomiting gesture with her other hand while keeping the first hand on her mouth. "Urp."

Hazel's eyes widened as she scooted her chair closer to Gwyn. "Please don't. I have a very bad gag reflex. If I so much as see it, we're all changing clothes."

Gwyn scooted herself backwards in her seat. "Loni, are you feeling alright? You're acting a little..." She trailed off, trying to think of the most politically correct way of saying what she was thinking.

"Nuts," Hazel filled in.

Gwyn wanted to chastise her mother, but she'd said what Gwyn couldn't. Gwyn looked at Loni uneasily. Would she take offense?

"Oh. Now that the sweater's off, I'm feeling fine," she said happily, rocking back in her chair. "I'm very glad you came to visit me. I haven't left the house in a while, and you're the first real guest I've had in a few weeks."

"How do you get food if you don't go anywhere?" asked Hazel.

"The grocery store delivers," explained Loni.

"What about your cat food?" asked Hazel as she watched three cats dash by.

Loni laughed. "Delivery. Check this out." She stood up and walked to her pantry. She opened the door and pulled on the string in the middle of the small closet. The room lit up, and from their chairs, Hazel and Gwyn could see that the pantry was completely full of bagged cat food. There were at least sixty bags of cat food stacked inside!

"Holy tarnation!" bellowed Hazel. "Whaddaya need with that much cat food?"

Gwyn looked appalled. "Loni! You don't—*eat it*, do you?"

Loni laughed. "Of course not!" She shrugged as a devious smile spread across her face. "The delivery boy is nice to look at."

Despite feeling completely out of her element in Loni's house, Gwyn couldn't help but laugh. It reduced the uncomfortable tension in the room a little bit. Gwyn wondered how she'd broach the topic she'd come to discuss. She wasn't even entirely sure that Loni knew that Kat had passed away. They were all silent for a few seconds before Gwyn finally said quietly, "Loni, do you read the paper?"

Loni looked around. "I get the paper. Can't say I read it all that much. Doesn't really make much difference to me what folks are doing around town."

"Yes, but it keeps you updated on important world events."

"World events, shmurld events," she croaked, waving a hand dismissively.

Gwyn caught her mother nodding in agreement.

"It also keeps you caught up on those who've passed away."

Loni laughed. "Well, I've got Kat for that. She always calls me when someone important kicks the bucket. You remember Kat Lynde from school, right?"

Gwyn winced. *She doesn't know. This is going to be difficult.* "Yes, I do. When's the last time you heard from Kat?"

Loni scratched the wiry pair of whiskers poking out of the bottom of her chin. "Oh. I don't know. It's probably been a week or two. Maybe three. I don't keep track of time much. I suppose she'll be stopping by any day now."

"Do you ever check your mail?" asked Gwyn, eyeing the pile of unopened mail on her table.

"Sometimes I ask Derrick to grab it on his way up the walk with the cat food," she said. "I never get anything good, so it doesn't really matter."

"Do you *open* your mail?"

"Sometimes, why?" asked Loni, sitting forward. She was getting suspicious now.

Gwyn fidgeted with her watch. *How am I going to tell her this?* Gwyn wondered. *She has no idea, and I hate to be the bearer of bad news.*

"Kat's dead," said Hazel plainly from her seat.

"Mom!"

"You didn't want to tell her, so I told her." Hazel shrugged, her hands folded in her lap politely. "You're welcome."

Gwyn looked at Loni uncomfortably. The woman stared at her out of her thick Harry Potter–looking glasses. "I'm sorry, Loni."

"Sorry for what?" she asked blankly.

Gwyn furrowed her eyebrows at her. "Did you hear what Mom just said?"

"Yeah, but surely the woman was joking. It's not a very funny joke, I might add," she said, chastising the little old lady between them.

Hazel merely lifted her eyebrows but sucked her lips between her dentures.

"It wasn't a joke, Lon. Kat passed away. Her funeral was last week. We couldn't get here from Arizona in time for it."

Loni's face froze. "There's no way she's dead. I just saw her a few weeks ago."

Gwyn nodded. "Yeah, it happens fast like that sometimes. I heard she slipped and fell and hit her head on a rock in her garden. The paperboy found her."

Loni shook her head. "What? How would I not know?"

"You haven't seen a paper?"

"No," she croaked. Then she stood up. "You're wrong. I'll call her and prove it to you." Loni walked over to the black rotary phone hanging on her wall. She lifted the spiral-corded receiver and dialed Kat's number. The phone rang and rang and rang.

"She's not going to answer," whispered Gwyn sadly. "She's gone, Loni. I'm so sorry."

Loni slammed down the receiver. "Prove it!"

Gwyn stood up and did what she'd wanted to do since she sat down at the table. She began to sort through Loni's mail. She pulled out letter after letter, sorting the junk mail from the letters that were obviously bills until she came to a professionally embossed envelope. "Here it is."

"What is it?"

Gwyn swallowed hard and handed it to her old friend. "Just read it."

Loni took the envelope, tore off a strip along the narrow side and dumped out the paper inside. Her hands shook as she unfolded the letter and read the words on the page. "Estate of Katherine Lynde? Oh my God," she breathed, lowering the paper. "Kat's really gone?"

Gwyn nodded. She stood up and put her arms around Loni's shoulders, hugging her old friend to her tightly. "I'm so sorry to have to be the one to tell you."

"But I didn't even get to say goodbye," said Loni as tears stained her cheeks.

"I know. Neither did I. I'm so sorry."

Loni let go of Gwyn and paced around the kitchen anxiously. "I can't believe this is happening."

"I can't either," admitted Gwyn. It had definitely been a shock to her when she'd heard the news as well.

As Loni passed by them, Hazel handed her a scrunched-up paper towel that had been on the kitchen table. Loni blotted her eyes beneath her glasses. "What's the letter about?" asked Loni when she'd finally gotten control of herself.

"Kat named us in her will," Gwyn explained. "She named Phyllis Habernackle and Char Adams too."

"Kat told me that Char's a Bailey now. She just married Vic Bailey. He owns a bakery here in town," said Loni through her sniffles.

Gwyn nodded. "The will reading was earlier today. Both Char and Phyllis were there."

"The nerve of those witches to show up at *our friend's will reading!*" exclaimed Loni.

Gwyn nodded. "They were very unfriendly with me."

Loni's face flushed. "How dare they! They don't have the right to be unfriendly to you! It's *us* who should be unfriendly to *them* after what they did!"

Hazel looked up at the two women. "What did they do?"

"I'll tell you exactly what they did!" cried Loni.

8

*G*wyn sat on her hands. She'd never told her mother about what Char and Phyllis had done to them. What would have been the point of that? At one time, Gwyn had thought she and the five girls she had befriended as a college student at the Paranormal Institute would be friends for life. But after everything that had gone down after she'd left Aspen Falls, she'd tried to forget about those girls, despite the wonderful friendship they'd once shared.

Loni looked at Hazel wearily. "Do you remember who lived with whom?"

Hazel shook her head. "I don't remember what I had for breakfast this morning," she snapped.

Gwyn rolled her eyes. "What was it you were saying to me earlier about not being forgetful, Mother?"

"You expect me to remember who roomed with who in *your dorm* over a million and a half years ago? Hell,

Gwynnie," cursed Hazel, "I didn't even know who the roommates were then, why would I know now?"

Loni chuckled. "It's okay, Hazel. I'll fill you in. Of course, Gwyn and I were roommates. And then it was Char Adams and Kat Lynde together, and Phyllis Habernackle and Auggie Stone. Can you remember that?"

Hazel tick-tocked her finger in the air and murmured to herself as if she were writing it down or making a mental note. Finally, she nodded. "Got it."

"Well, here's what went down. For starters, on graduation night, Phyllis and Auggie had a falling out. A *major* falling out, which caused all of us to turn against Auggie. But that's another story, for another time and place. So Auggie wasn't there when Sorceress Halliwell, our headmistress, pulled the other five of us into her office the day we were moving out of the Institute."

"We all loved Sorceress Halliwell," remarked Gwyn. "She was such an amazing mentor. We all learned so much about magic during those two years."

Loni nodded. "She was terrific. I miss her a lot."

Hazel waved a hand to prod the two women along. "Get on with it. It's past my bedtime."

"Right," said Loni with a little smile. "So it was Gwyn, me, Char, Kat, and Phyllis in Sorceress Halliwell's office the morning after graduation. She told us what amazingly talented witches we'd become and how we were all moving on to bigger and better things. She also told us how she admired the friendship we shared and how a witch's coven was one of the most powerful things a witch could ever possess and that we should cherish it always."

Loni's words brought a sudden unexpected ache to Gwyn's heart. She had to swallow hard to move the lump she felt forming in the back of her throat. Tears welled up in her eyes.

"We were all such good friends," she whispered. "It makes me sad that we aren't friends anymore." She pulled a crumpled tissue from her purse and blotted at her eyes.

Loni swatted at Gwyn's hand. "Well, don't cry about it! Get mad about it! Like me. It makes me angry!" she cried, her eyes opening wider. Her finger trembled as she pointed it in the air. "What those girls did to ruin our friendship. I'll never forgive them!"

"Well, for heaven's sake, what did they do?" demanded Hazel.

Loni sucked in a deep breath. "So Sorceress Halliwell gave us a spell book as a graduation gift. It was a very powerful spell book. We were instructed to share it by passing it around to one another throughout the years. It was supposed to keep us all close and bring us together over the years."

"It was such a thoughtful gift," said Gwyn with a sniffle, trying to avoid letting Loni see her dotting at her eyes again. It saddened her that Sorceress Halliwell's parting gift hadn't worked as it had been meant to.

"But *those witches* stole the book from us! I haven't seen the book once since the day I moved out of the dorms! It was supposed to bring us all closer together. Instead, it drove a wedge between us," spat Loni. "I'll never forgive them for ruining our friendship by stealing the book!"

"How do you know they stole the book?" asked Hazel curiously.

"Kat told us! She told us she asked both Phyllis and Char about getting the book and they told her that they were keeping it and there wasn't a darn thing she could do about it!"

Hazel tipped her head to the side and lifted her shoulders. "Eh. Easy come, easy go."

Gwyn frowned. "I still can't believe Char and Phyllis would turn on us like that."

"Believe it!" croaked Loni. "Once those girls turned on us, I stopped trusting people. I mean, if you can't trust your friends, who can you trust?"

"Oh, Loni," breathed Gwyn. "Is that why you've holed yourself up in this house for all these years?"

Loni's eyes shifted away from Gwyn's. "Part of the reason. But there are others," she said mysteriously.

"I'm so sorry if that's even *part of the reason*. You can trust *me*," Gwyn promised.

Loni eyed Gwyn carefully. "You know, Gwynnie, I think I can. You and Kat were the only two friends that kept in touch with me over the years. And I thank you for that. Because I never left the house, I had to rely on Kat to push Char to return the book, but Kat continued to tell me she refused her, time after time."

Gwyn shook her head. "It just isn't right! Sorceress Halliwell gave that book to all of us."

Loni's nostrils flared. She slammed a hand on the table and stood up defiantly. "We should get it back!"

An idea began to form in Gwyn's head. "I know a way, Loni. If you're serious about getting it back..." Gwyn's head tipped towards Loni.

Loni slapped her hand on the table again. "Of course I'm serious. That book is rightfully ours just as much as it is theirs!"

"They're both going to be at Kat's will reading tomorrow. We'll confront them about it there. There will be a lawyer there. Maybe he can help us get it back!"

Loni's smile disappeared almost instantaneously. Her head trembled as she slowly sat back down on her chair. "N-no, I can't do that."

"What do you mean you can't?"

Loni pushed her glasses back further up her nose. "I don't leave the house."

"Well, why not?"

Loni shifted about uncomfortably. "Well, for starters, I don't have a driver's license."

Gwyn smiled. "Neither does Mom. It's okay. I'll pick you up."

Loni reached across the table and patted Gwyn's hand. "Thank you. It's a sweet offer, Gwynnie, but I can't."

"But, Loni, Kat left us all something in her will. Aren't you curious what it is?"

Loni sighed and slumped back in her chair. "I'd rather have my friend back."

"I would too," whispered Gwyn. "But we can't get her

back. But maybe you could have a memento that would remind you of Kat. Wouldn't you like something of hers so that you could remember her always?"

Loni looked up sharply. Gwyn could tell that interested her. By the looks of her house, Loni was a hoarder. She liked stuff—nothing in particular, just *stuff*.

"Couldn't the lawyer just mail me whatever it is that Kat left me?" asked Loni.

Gwyn shook her head. "No. Kat specifically put in her will that the four of us—you, me, Char, and Phyllis—must be present, and we must go *to his* office."

Loni sighed. "Just like Kat to try and get me to leave the house. She tried for years, you know."

"I'll pick you up tomorrow at eleven forty-five sharp."

"I can't, Gwynnie. I'm scared."

"What are you scared of?" asked Hazel.

Loni waved a hand. "That's neither here nor there."

"It *is* here or there," scoffed Hazel. "You won't leave the house because you're scared. The only way I can get out of that funeral home they call a retirement village is to get a windfall from this Kat woman. So come hell or high water, you're going to that will reading! Even if my Gwynnie has to throw you over her shoulder and drag you there kicking and screaming!" Hazel pointed a crooked finger at Loni. "And she'll do it, you know. It's not just a scare tactic."

"You think Kat left us a windfall?" asked Loni.

Hazel shrugged. "Something's better than nothing, isn't it?"

Loni glanced up at Gwyn. "You'll pick me up?"

Gwyn nodded. "A quarter to twelve."

Loni's hands trembled as she leaned back in her seat. "Alright. We'll give it a go."

---

*I*t was exactly eleven forty-four when Gwyn Prescott turned her car onto Hemlock Road the next day. This time, the sun was shining brightly, and it was a perfect seventy-five degrees.

"Loni's house looks so much better during the daytime," Gwyn said to her mother as they pulled up to the curb of Yolanda Hodges's house.

"I'd sure hope so. I'm not sure it could look any worse," grumped Hazel from the passenger seat.

Gwyn honked the horn to alert Loni that they were waiting. "I think the darkness just gave it a sinister appearance. It still looks unkempt, but at least it doesn't look sinister."

"Puh," puffed Hazel. "Still looks sinister to me."

Gwyn looked down at her watch and then at the house. "I wonder what's keeping Loni."

"The whack job probably changed her mind."

Gwyn shot her mother a look of frustration. "You're not allowed to speak when she gets in the car. You're rude to her."

"She makes it easy," said Hazel with a snort. "She's a slow-moving target."

"I mean it, Mother. If you say one single cross thing, no French fries for a week."

Hazel reared her head back and cast a horrified glance at her daughter. "You can't do that! That's elder abuse!"

"No, it's not. And I have power of attorney over you. That means I also have power of French fries over you. Read it. It's in the fine print," quipped Gwyn.

Hazel sulked and looked out the window.

Gwyn honked again. "Hurry up, Yolanda, we're going to be late for the meeting with the lawyer."

"Well, maybe you should just go in there and get her," suggested Hazel in a mocking voice.

Gwyn sighed. She really hated to leave her mother alone in the car, but it would take her twice as long to unpack her mother from the car, walk up to the house to get Loni, and then pack everyone back up again. It was like trying to leave the house as a new mother with the diaper bags and the strollers and the babies. It just about wasn't worth the effort. She pointed her finger at her mother. "No leaving this car. Got it?"

Hazel shot her tongue out at her daughter and widened her eyes.

"I hate having to be the mother, too," said Gwyn quietly. She got out of the car and rushed up the cracked and weedy sidewalk and onto the ramshackle porch, glancing back at her mother the whole while.

Hazel waggled her fingers under her chin at her daughter tauntingly.

Gwyn sighed and faced the house, knocking on the door. "Loni, it's Gwyn. We have to go!" she hollered. "We're going to be late."

Gwyn heard a noise at the picture window and saw the curtain rustle. She stepped over the mess on the porch and peered in the window. Loni's over-made-up face appeared, startling Gwyn.

"Go to the back," Loni hissed through the glass.

"What?" asked Gwyn, cupping her hands to the window and squinting inside. "We have to go, Loni."

"I need to talk to you. Go around to the back," she hissed. "Through the gate on the side. I unlocked it."

Gwyn sighed. She didn't have time for this nonsense. She only had an hour lunch break, and she didn't want to be late getting back to work. But she felt like she didn't have a choice but to follow Loni's directions, crazy as they were.

She stepped back over the cat food and the wet newspapers, down the steps, and around the porch to the side of the house, where a wooden fence ran around the backyard. Gwyn looked back at the car. Her mother was still sitting quietly in her seat. Gwyn opened the gate and rushed into the backyard. In the backyard, broken-down lawn mowers, old appliances, and washbasins covered the weedy yard. In one corner sat a teal-colored golf cart with a plastic roof, partially covered by an old tarp. Gwyn went to the back door and knocked. "Loni, let's go!" she hollered.

The door opened, and a weathered hand reached out and pulled Gwyn inside.

"Loni, it's time to…" Gwyn sucked in her breath when she caught sight of Loni. "What in the world are you wearing?"

Loni wore the bottom half of a bird costume. Like Big Bird on *Sesame Street*, but in place of the bird's head, she wore a Charlie Chaplin mask.

"Shh," she hissed through the mask. "We don't have much time."

"Loni, this is highly unprofessional. You can't go into a lawyer's office looking like—like—*this*!"

"You want me to go, or not?" demanded Loni impatiently.

"Well, yes, b-but don't you own any *normal clothes*?"

"Of course I do. I'm in disguise."

"Where in the world did you get a bird costume?" asked Gwyn. She didn't know what to say. The woman looked like a lunatic.

"Kat gave it to me years ago. She found it at a rummage sale, but it didn't have the head. Now enough about that—listen. Here's the plan. My property is surrounded by a privacy fence. I'm going to go out this door. You drive around the alley. There's a gate back there. Park by the gate and wait for me. Make sure you aren't followed. You weren't followed here, were you?"

Gwyn cast a wary glance over her shoulder. "I—I didn't see anyone."

"Good. Go around to the alley. Don't honk or anything. Don't make any noise. Just pull up to the gate in back and park. I'll come out through there."

"No one's out front, Lon. I swear."

"Just do it. Now go," she said before shoving Gwyn out the back door of her house.

Gwyn sighed. She was starting to think Loni Hodges

had become a total nutjob since the last time she'd seen her. She walked back around to the gate, pulling it shut behind her before walking towards the car. She'd gone no further than five paces when she realized the front passenger seat was empty!

"Mom!" she breathed. Immediately her eyes began scanning the sidewalks looking for a little old lady with a cane. "Mom!" Gwyn hollered.

All the sidewalks were empty. *Dammit, how could she get so far so fast?* Gwyn's mouth went dry. Her heart plunged into her stomach, and suddenly she couldn't breathe.

Unsure of what to do next, she rushed to her car and started the engine. She pulled the car ahead and peered down the alley, hoping to see her mother walking along the dusty alley, but saw nothing. With no other options, she followed Loni's directions. "Four eyes are better than two," she whispered to herself and drove around the corner to the gate. She only had to sit for a second before the gate popped open and Loni literally flew out, wearing her ridiculous bird getup. She launched herself into the backseat.

"Go, go, go!" she hollered, ducking low below the windows.

Gwyn frowned. "I can't go. My mother took off," she said.

"What do you mean, *took off?*"

"On foot. She got out of the car while I was in the back of your house, and she disappeared."

Loni poked her head up an inch past the bottom of

the back window. "She's a feeble old woman with a cane. How far could she have gotten?"

Gwyn pulled the car through the alley. "She's sneaky. She probably hid somewhere. I'll circle back around the block."

"No! You can't go around the block. They might be waiting for me there. They'll see us!"

"Who?"

"The FBI!"

"The FBI was not out in front of your house. I was just there."

"Yes, they are. They hide. They're sneaky little bastards. You have to go straight to the lawyer's office and then bring me straight back."

"Loni! I can't leave my mother!"

"She got out of the car. It's her own fault."

"Well, yes, but——"

"Do you want to go to that will reading or not?" demanded Loni.

The back of Gwyn's throat tightened. She didn't know what to say or what to do. It could take her hours to find her mother if she'd found a good hiding spot. Gwyn rubbed her face with the palms of her hands. "Ugh," she groaned. "What am I supposed to do?"

"Go to the lawyer's office! You can find your mother later."

Gwyn sighed. "What if something happens to her?"

"In Aspen Falls? What's going to happen to her in Aspen Falls? How long can it take to read a will? Five minutes? You'll be back in a jiffy. And she's a grown woman. She can take care of herself for five minutes."

Gwyn peered in her rearview mirror and scanned the alleyway. "Oh, fine," she said. She drove slowly, eyeing the backyards of every house she passed as she drove to the other side of the alley. *I hope you'll be okay, Mom. I'll be right back for you, I promise!*

9

*C*har and Phyllis waited quietly inside the offices of Jerry T. Marlow. Char drummed her fingers on her arm, wondering what was taking Gwyn and Loni so darn long. She'd promised Vic they'd go to the park later and have a little fun.

Mr. Marlow looked at his watch. "Maybe Ms. Prescott was unable to convince Ms. Hodges to make an appearance today."

"It wouldn't surprise me," said Char.

Phyllis leaned her head back. "This is getting ridiculous. Can't we just do this without Loni?"

He shook his head. "I'm sorry. I—"

He was cut off by his office door being flung open by a giant yellow bird wearing a Charlie Chaplin mask. "Let's get this show on the road," said a croaky, hollow voice from inside the mask.

Mr. Marlow stood up. "Excuse me, what's going on?! We're in the middle of a meeting."

Gwyn Prescott followed the odd-looking bird inside the room and shut the door behind them. "Mr. Marlow, this is Loni Hodges," she said. Her face was visibly heated as she grinned uncomfortably.

"Why are you wearing that costume, Ms. Hodges?" he asked with a horror-stricken voice.

Char and Phyllis stared at their old friend with shock as well.

"Take that ridiculous outfit off, Loni!" cried Char. "You're making a mockery of the memory of my friend!"

Gwyn wrung her hands nervously. "She was uncomfortable leaving the house and felt she needed a disguise," she said.

"A mockery of *your friend*? Kat was *our* friend, you backstabber!" hollered Loni in a muffled voice from behind the mask.

Phyllis stood up. "*You're* the backstabbers. We didn't do anything wrong!"

"Ha!" hollered Loni, pulling her mask off. "Say that to my face, witch!"

Phyllis got closer to Loni and looked down at her. She poked a finger into her feathery chest. "*You're. The. Backstabber!*"

"You wanna piece of me?" asked Loni, digging her hands into Phyllis's chest and shoving.

Phyllis sucked in her breath. "How dare you!" she spat, shoving Loni back.

"Ladies, I'm really going to have to ask you to sit down," said Mr. Marlow uncomfortably.

"How dare I? How dare I?" screamed Loni over him. "This whole thing is your fault."

Wringing her hands nervously, Gwyn touched Loni's wing. "Loni, we don't have time for this," whispered Gwyn. "I need to go find Mother."

"I'd really like to know how this is *our* fault!" said Char, backing up Phyllis.

"Ladies!" Mr. Marlow finally boomed over the shouting women. "I can't have this shouting in my office! I have another appointment in fifteen minutes. We need to get on with the will reading."

Loni and Phyllis stared each other down.

Gwyn tugged on Loni's wing. "Loni, please," she begged. "I need to get back to find Mother."

Loni looked at Gwyn and then took a step back behind the chair. "Fine," she grumped, crossing her wings across her chest. "Get on with it."

"Thank you, Loni," said Gwyn, taking her seat on one of the four chairs.

"Oh, yes, yes…" said Marlow as he took a seat behind his desk. Flustered, he seemed more than a little surprised that both women had given up quite so easily. He flipped through some papers while Phyllis and Char took their seats as well.

He cleared his throat and adjusted the reading glasses atop his nose. "This is the last will and testament of Katherine Anne Lynde," he began formally. "Being of sound mind and body and in the presence of witnesses, I hereby bequeath my estate as follows: to my oldest and dearest friends and my only living family, my very own witch's coven, Gwyndolin Prescott, Yolanda Hodges, Charlotte Adams-Bailey, and Phyllis Habernackle, I bequeath my entire estate, including my home located at 1715 Blue Spruce Lane, my 1949 Ford F1 truck, and all of the contents of my home with the stipulation that you *must not* sell the home, but instead use the house as a way to reconnect lost friendships and mend broken fences. Please know that despite everything, I loved you all." Mr. Marlow removed his glasses and looked at the women. "Janice at the front desk has the keys to the property and copies of the will for each of you. Do you have any questions?"

The four women sat stunned and speechless. Kat had left them *everything*. Char's mind raced. She already owned a home. Loni owned a home. Phyllis had just rented an apartment over a building downtown, and Gwyn had just moved to town as well—surely she had a place to live. What were they supposed to do with a house if they weren't allowed to sell it? What in the world had Kat been thinking?

"What are we supposed to do with her house if we aren't allowed to sell it?" asked Loni. "I already have a house, and I'm certainly not moving in with *them!*" she spat.

"Don't flatter yourself, Loni. We wouldn't move in with you if George Clooney were asking and offered to share his bed!" Phyllis shot back.

Gwyn shook her head at the lawyer. "No, you don't understand. My mother lives with me. I can't leave the retirement home," she whispered to Mr. Marlow. "She needs round-the-clock care."

Char nodded and added her two cents. "I'm a newly-wed. My husband and I aren't about to go living with a bunch of old witches during our first year of marriage!"

By now all the women were staring at Mr. Marlow for answers. He held up his hands defensively. "I'm sorry, ladies. Ms. Lynde didn't specify what you were to *do* with the property. Only what you *weren't* allowed to do, and that is to sell it. I imagine renting it out would be acceptable if you don't want to reside on the premises. Or perhaps one or two of you could buy out the others' shares."

Phyllis frowned. "I don't have that kind of money."

"Neither do I," agreed Gwyn.

"Well, Loni and I already own our homes, so I don't think we'd want to buy anyone out," said Char.

Mr. Marlow lifted his shoulders and hands. "I think it's something you'll need to discuss. Together. That was the point Ms. Lynde wanted to get across. She wants your friendship restored to its original luster."

"Kat always was the make-peace-not-war one of the group," sighed Phyllis.

"Now, ladies. If you'll excuse me. I have to prepare for my next appointment. If you have any questions, please take one of my cards on your way out and feel free to give me a call or send me an email."

The women were still stupefied as Mr. Marlow ushered them out of his office and closed the door behind them. Dazed, Char stopped in the lobby to get the key to the house and her copy of the will.

"So what do we do now?" asked Gwyn. "I'm kind of in a hurry and don't have much time to talk about things right now."

Phyllis threw her hands up in the air. "I have no idea. This is ridiculous."

"We'll have to meet at the house to figure it out. What time do you get off work, Gwyn?" asked Char.

"I'm not meeting *anywhere*!" bellowed Loni, tugging her mask back on her face.

"Take off that ridiculous mask, Loni," said Char. She was embarrassed even to be associated with Yolanda Hodges. "I can't even look at you!"

Gwyn ignored Char's comment. "I could be there around five thirty today."

Char blew out a breath of frustration. "Oh, fine. We'll meet at Kat's at five thirty. Does that work for you, Phil?"

Phyllis nodded.

Loni crossed her bright yellow wings across her chest. "Well, I won't be there."

Char pushed her way out the front doors of Jerry T. Marlow's office. "Suit yourself, you looney bird. We'll decide what to do with the house and all of Kat's things without you, then."

"hat a bunch of hooey," ranted Loni from the backseat as Gwyn drove. "I can't believe Kat expects us to forgive those women for what they did!"

Gwyn clutched the steering wheel tighter as she drove. Her head pivoted on her neck, slowly scanning the neighborhood for any signs of her mother. "It would help me immensely if you'd sit up and help me look for Mom," she said, her jaw tightening.

"I can't. Someone might see me," chided Loni in a hushed whisper.

"So what? You're wearing a disguise. No one will know it's you. Isn't that the point of the disguise?" After all of that at the lawyer's office, Gwyn was exhausted and short-tempered. Not only had Loni and Phyllis's little showdown worn her out, but the thought of having to deal with Kat's entire estate made her want to curl up and take a nap. And *now*, she had to deal with trying to find her mother before something bad happened to her or she got herself arrested. Not to mention the fact that she was due back at work in under fifteen minutes.

Loni sighed and sat up as requested, but slumped down in her seat.

"Thank you," said Gwyn in a clipped tone.

"I mean, what are we supposed to do with her house if we aren't allowed to sell it?" asked Loni, continuing her rant while taking an ineffectual glance out the window.

Gwyn shrugged. "I guess we rent it out or something. We'll figure it out tonight."

"Well, all I know is I'm not going," she said, crossing her arms pointedly.

"Suit yourself, but I bet there will be a lot of interesting treasures we'll all get to pick through," said Gwyn, lifting an eyebrow as she peered into the rearview mirror at Loni.

Loni groaned. "You all can't just *take* things, though. Everything in there is one-fourth mine!"

"If you don't show up, then they'll be able to take anything they want!" sang Gwyn. She was quickly learning how to push Loni's buttons.

And indeed, she'd seemed to set Loni's butt on fire. "Oh, hell no!" she bellowed from behind the mask. "They stole that spell book from us. They aren't going to steal all of Kat's prized possessions from us too!"

"Well, then, you better go with me tonight. We can confront the thieves about that spell book while we're there."

Loni nodded as she mulled over Gwyn's words. "You might be right. I suppose if we ever want to see that book again, we need to sort it out now."

Gwyn smiled at her. "So you'll come with me?"

"Yes. I suppose I'll have to," she whined.

"Okay, good. I'm glad we've got that settled. We're almost to your house, and I haven't seen hide nor hair of Mom," said Gwyn.

She had no idea where to even begin looking. Hazel didn't know her way around Aspen Falls. Where would she even have gone? At least in Scottsdale, Gwyn knew which local haunts to search first when Hazel went missing. She usually started with the pool halls and the casinos. And if Hazel wasn't there, it usually meant she was hungry, and Gwyn would try all of Hazel's favorite French fry joints. McDonald's was her favorite. But there were no casinos or pool halls in Aspen Falls, and there certainly wasn't a McDonald's. Today, she'd be searching blind.

Gwyn's hands shook as she turned down Hemlock Road. What would she do if she couldn't find her mother? She could be in trouble somewhere. Or worse, hurt or even dead in a ditch! She shouldn't have left to go to the will reading. She should have rescheduled and figured out how to get Loni convinced to go on a different day. But then Char and Phyllis would have thrown a fit. Maybe Loni would have changed her mind about going altogether. Gwyn's mind replayed all the possibilities of what could have happened, trying to rationalize her idiotic decision not to look for her mother the minute she'd discovered her missing.

"Why are you going to the front of the house? You have to take me to the alley!" cried Loni, slinking down in the backseat so that her head was no longer visible from the windows. "I can't go to the front, they'll see me."

"I'm looking for Mom!" said Gwyn. "And you're being ridiculous. There is no one monitoring your house."

"You *think* there's no one monitoring my house,"

hissed Loni from the floor of the backseat. "That doesn't mean there isn't."

As they pulled up to Loni's house, Gwyn had to squint, but she thought she saw someone sitting on the old wicker chair on Loni's front porch. She pulled up to the curb and rolled down her window. "Mom!" she breathed, throwing the car into park. Gwyn launched herself out the door and rushed to the porch. "Mom! There you are! Where have you been, are you okay?"

"Hell, Gwynnie. I've been waiting here for nearly an hour," Hazel exaggerated. "What kind of daughter are you? You just up and leave an old woman alone the first chance you get? In this ghost house?"

Tears of relief filled Gwyn's eyes. "Oh, Mom! You ran off. I didn't know where to look for you!"

"Ran off? I didn't run off. I went inside to use the bathroom. I'm old, you know. My bladder's the size of a walnut. Wait until you get to be my age. Hopefully, *your daughter* won't up and leave you the second you go to use the john."

Gwyn practically collapsed on top of her mother. Fear had gripped her since she'd left Loni's house nearly thirty-five minutes ago. "I was so worried about you."

"Obviously. I could tell by the way you just took off," snapped Hazel, using her cane to pull herself to a standing position. "I'm starving. It's past lunchtime, and if we're not back by two, I won't get my French fries. Let's go." Hazel pushed past Gwyn and shuffled across the porch to the steps. "Come on, Gwynnie. I can't be late for lunch. That Miss Georgia's a real stickler for minding the clock."

With her heart still throbbing in her chest, Gwyn followed her mother down the stairs and helped her into the car. She walked back around to the driver's side, slipped into her seat, and turned on the ignition. Once she'd put her seat belt on, Loni's head popped up between the two seats.

"Finally! Now take me around to the back."

"Ahhh!" screamed Hazel, shoving the butt of her cane into the Charlie Chaplin mask in the backseat.

Loni's hand went to her head in the place that Hazel had just caned her. "Oww!" she cried. "What are you doing, Hazel?! It's me. It's me!"

"It's Loni, Mom," said Gwyn, putting a hand on Hazel's shoulder.

"Oh for pity's sake!" Hazel's hand went to her heart. "What the hell are you trying to do? Gimme a heart attack?"

Loni rubbed her forehead but stayed low. "Shh, they'll see you talking to me!"

Hazel looked out her window. "Who will?"

"The FBI."

"FBI? Are you plumb nuts or only partially nuts?" asked Hazel.

"Mom! French fries!" said Gwyn.

Hazel sucked her lips between her teeth as her eyes widened.

"Can you *please* just take me around to the gate in the

back of the house and drop me off?" asked Loni, still rubbing her head.

Gwyn sighed. Hazel and Loni in the same car were just about too much for one day and one person's sanity. "Gladly."

10

*C*har and Phyllis were the first to pull into Kat Lynde's driveway that evening. Kat's beat-up old green Ford pickup was parked off to the side of the stunning three-story Victorian house.

Phyllis approached the truck on her way up to the porch and kicked one of the tires with the toe of her black leather orthopedic walking shoe. "Does this thing even run?"

"I guess I never asked Kat if it ran. I assumed it didn't." Char peeked in the window. "It's still in pretty good shape. Maybe it does."

"It's a nice-looking piece of steel," said Phyllis. "Maybe we should take it for a test drive." She attempted to open the driver's-side door just as an old silver Buick came rambling into the driveway behind Char's car.

"Oh, look who's here," said Char, clucking her tongue. "The thieves themselves."

Loni Hodges jumped out of the backseat of the car before Gwyn had even pulled the car to a complete stop. Loni had lost the chicken costume, but had donned a grey rabbit fur vest over a silver satin blouse, leather chaps over a pair of hot pink leggings, purple rain boots, and a black veil that covered her face. She'd topped off the whole ridiculous ensemble with a cowboy hat with a big yellow feather sticking out of the band. She held up a hand.

"You just hold it right there, Phyllis Habernackle! Don't you go touching anything that's one-fourth mine until we get a few things straight."

"I'm sorry, did you lose your horse, cowgirl?" asked Phyllis with a chortle. "I think it's time someone put you out to pasture."

Char didn't even attempt to cover up her giggle.

Loni bunched up her face as she came storming towards Phyllis. "I mean it, Habernackle. That truck is mine!"

Phyllis looked at Char incredulously. "Is she trying to steal Kat's things *already*?"

Gwyn got out of the car. "Girls," she huffed. "This is embarrassing. We're already fighting out in the driveway? You can't wait until we get into the house, at the very least? What will the neighbors think?" She stalked around to the other side of the car to help Hazel out next.

"I don't give a damn what the neighbors think," hissed Phyllis. "I'm going to get a few things off my chest today."

Char ran a hand across the back of her neck as she

peered at the house next door. She'd lived in Aspen Falls longer than most of these women, and she wasn't particularly keen on her business being the topic of conversation at all of the social gatherings for the week. "Gwyn's right. We should take this inside. We all have a lot to say to each other, and it's none of the neighbors' business as to what that is." She looked at the little old lady hobbling towards her. "Who's this?"

"This is my mother, Hazel Prescott. Mom, this is Char and Phyllis," she said, pointing at the two women in the order she'd introduced them. "I take care of my mother. I can't leave her alone, or she gets herself into trouble."

"I just have a little fun is all," snapped Hazel. "My daughter doesn't know how to have fun anymore."

"Mom, I know how to have fun. And you don't just have fun. You get police escorts home is what you get. I don't consider that fun at all."

Char shrugged as she smiled at Hazel. "It's nice to meet you, Hazel."

"I'd say likewise, but that would be a lie, and I've always taught my daughter it's not right to lie," she said without pausing as she walked past Char. Then, lifting one finger into the air, she added, "And I *always* know when she's lying."

Char looked up at Gwyn. "Spitfire, isn't she?"

Gwyn blushed. "You could say that. Just don't encourage her. She doesn't need any encouraging."

"Alright, girls. Let's go inside, then. We'll air our grievances in there," said Char, leading the troops up the wooden porch steps past Hazel. About two dozen folded-up newspapers sat in a pile in front of the door. Char shoved them out of the way with the toe of her white sneaker and then pulled back the screen door and stuck the key the receptionist had given her into the lock. "There's a light on inside the house."

"But she died outside," Gwyn pointed out.

"I know that, smarty pants," snapped Char. "I was just making conversation."

Loni grimaced. "No need for sweet-talking us now. Hurry up and get that door opened. I got a lot to say."

"Slow your roll, Loni Hodges," groaned Phyllis.

"Don't tell me what to do, *Phyllis Habernackle*."

Gwyn sighed. "Will you ladies *please* act civilized? You're giving me a headache."

Char pushed the door open. A pungent smell wafted out the front door, making Char gag almost immediately. "Oh my word!" she bellowed, pulling the collar of her sweatshirt up over her nose. "What is that smell?"

Hazel pushed Char aside. "I don't smell anything," she snapped. "I need to use the little girl's room."

"Down the hall to the right," said Char. "Come on, girls. We need to figure out what that smell is before we do anything else."

Phyllis entered next. "Smells like rotten food to me."

Gwyn entered and immediately pulled her shirt up over her nose too. "Yeah, that's got to be her garbage or something."

Kat's house was of a similar age and style to Loni's,

but Kat's was immaculately kept. Everything was in its place and neat and tidy, so it was a shock that it smelled so badly. The women walked through the house to the kitchen, where they found the light that had been left on. A cup of coffee sat on the counter along with a small jar of sugar next to it.

Gwyn sucked in a puff of air. "Oh, she was having coffee," she said sadly.

"One minute you're here and the next you're gone. What a shame," agreed Char sadly.

Loni took her cowboy hat and veil off and walked towards Char. "How dare you be sad? You weren't a friend to Kat during her life, so you don't get to pretend you're sad that she's dead."

Char furrowed her thinly penciled-in eyebrows at Loni. "Kat was my friend, too. I visited her a few times a month since college!"

"Liar. You did not. Kat would've told me that!" said Loni.

"Maybe she didn't tell you everything. Ever think of that?" asked Char.

"Girls, can we please address this smell before World War III breaks out?" asked Gwyn. "I can hardly breathe. It smells like Kat died in *here*, not out there." She tipped her head towards the glass sliding doors off the eat-in kitchen.

Phyllis pointed at the garbage can while the other women opened cupboards and drawers searching for the smell. "Garbage is empty. It's not coming from here."

Gwyn walked over to the sink. "Oh no," she said,

holding her nose and gagging at the same time. "Kat must have been starting supper before she died."

Char looked over her shoulder. A small glass bowl was in the sink with an uncooked chicken breast and a thigh in it. Kat must have taken the chicken out to thaw, then gone outside and slipped and fallen. *Poor woman!* "Yup, three-week old raw chicken will make that smell. Someone find a bag so we can wrap this up."

The women looked through the cabinets until they found a box of trash can liners. Gwyn put the chicken in a bag and then double-wrapped it in plastic.

Char held out a hand to Gwyn to take the wrapped chicken from her. "I'll just put that outside," she said, opening the sliding glass doors leading to Kat's famed rose garden. She set the bag behind the house. "Remind me to take that to the curb and put it in her garbage bins before we leave, so an animal doesn't get into it."

Gwyn nodded and sprayed the air with a bottle of air freshener she'd found underneath the sink. "Maybe you should just leave that door open to let some fresh air in."

"Yes," said Char. "Good idea."

Phyllis looked at Loni contemptuously. "Now what were we arguing about?"

"I don't remember, but I have something I need to get off my chest," said Loni, pointing her bony finger towards Phyllis.

Phyllis snarled at her. "Well, it certainly isn't your breasts, because *those* are on your stomach!"

Loni scowled at Phyllis. "You're an evil witch, Phyllis Habernackle."

"Takes one to know one," Phyllis retorted, rolling her eyes.

"Get on with it," snapped Char. "We don't have all night. What could *you* possibly have to gripe about?"

Loni snarled at them. "Ha! You've got to be kidding! You mean *other* than the fact that you and *that woman* stole our book?"

Char's eyes widened, as did Phyllis's.

"Stole your book? What book?" asked Phyllis.

"You know what book, don't play dumb with me," barked Loni.

"Are you talking about the spell book that Sorceress Halliwell gave us for graduation?" asked Char.

"Damn right I'm talking about that spell book!" hollered Loni in a huff. "What other book would have torn us apart all those years ago?"

"You're talking about the book that *you stole?*" clarified Char.

"That *we* stole?" asked Loni, pointing at herself curiously.

"Yes, that *you* stole!"

"We didn't steal the spell book," said Gwyn from the other side of the room.

"Of course you did. Don't try and deny it," said Phyllis, pointing at both her and Loni. "I'm surprised Kat was even speaking to the two of you thieves."

"*You* were the ones that stole the book," said Gwyn calmly.

Char made a face. "Who told you that we stole the book?"

"Kat told me!" said Loni.

"Kat? Kat told me that *you two* took the book and refused to give it back," said Char.

Gwyn shook her head. "I would never do something like that!"

Phyllis laughed. "Oh, you can quit the goody-two-shoes act, Gwyndolin Prescott. We all know you have an ornery streak in you a mile wide and a football field deep."

Gwyn's back stiffened. "Well, so do you two!" she snapped back.

"That's why we made such good friends in the first place!" said Char. "And to think it was all ruined because the two of you were so selfish."

Loni lowered her eyebrows. "Katherine Lynde told me that you and Phyllis took that book. Gwyn and I did not take the book."

Phyllis frowned at her. "I don't believe you," she said bluntly. "Kat wouldn't have lied to us for all those years."

"I don't think she would have lied to us either," said Gwyn loudly. "That's why I don't believe *you*!"

Just then they heard the shuffling of feet coming down a hallway, followed by a steady thud as Hazel's cane tapped along the floor. She stopped to pause in front of Gwyn and pointed her finger up at her. "Believe them. They're telling the truth," she said to her daughter. "They don't have the book."

Gwyn sucked in her breath. "Mom, y—you read their minds?"

"No, it was written on the bathroom wall," she snapped.

Gwyn looked down at her mother, horrified.

"Of course I read their minds!"

"Your mother reads minds?" asked Phyllis skeptically.

Gwyn nodded. "It's one of her favorite *gifts*. Makes her a lot of money at poker."

Char walked towards the little old lady. "And we're just supposed to believe that your daughter and Loni don't have the book either?"

Hazel nodded. "My daughter doesn't have the book. If she did, I'd tell you. It's no skin off my wrinkled old butt."

"What about Loni?" asked Char.

Hazel glanced at Loni.

Loni stared back at her. Her pop-bottle eye wear reflected the kitchen light off the glass, giving her a vacant expression.

Hazel shook her head. "I'm not going in that fun house. I may never get back out!"

Gwyn sighed. "Please, Mother."

Hazel looked at Loni again and after a beat replied, "She doesn't have the book."

"So you're just expecting us to believe your mother?" Char asked Gwyn with a raised lip.

Hazel looked at Loni again. "Look at her. You have to be sane to lie. Does that look like the face of a sane woman?"

Everyone stared at Loni. Finally, Char narrowed her eyes at Hazel. "Prove yourself. What am I thinking?"

Hazel squinted her eyes and ground one of her fingers into the side of her temple and pretended to be in deep thought. "You wish I was your mother." Hazel threw her hands into the air. "Too bad, so sad." She smiled a dentured smile at the women.

Char frowned. "Try again."

"You were thinking if *they* don't have the book and *we* don't have the book, then who has the book?" said Hazel flippantly.

"That was obvious," said Char.

"Not my fault you don't have an original thought in that puffy white head of yours."

"You really don't have the book?" Phyllis asked Gwyn, staring at her closely.

"We *really* don't have the book." Gwyn's words came out genuine.

Char suddenly wondered what had truly happened to the book that had torn them all apart all those years ago. The realization that their lifelong feud had all been based on a lie was shocking.

Loni hopped up on a stool in the kitchen. "What exactly did Kat tell you two?"

Char leaned against the doorjamb to the dining room. "A million years ago, I mentioned to her that it was my turn to borrow the book. I asked her if she knew who had it because I thought she'd had it first," she began. She took a deep breath and continued, "She said that she'd given the book to you, Loni. I thought, fine; I'll wait awhile and let Loni have her turn, and I'll ask for it then. So I waited six months, and I happened to stop over to Kat's house to visit her, and she said she'd asked Loni for the book back so she could give it to me, but Loni had sent it to Gwyn."

Gwyn furrowed her eyebrows. "Loni never sent me the book!"

"That's because I never had the book!" shouted Loni.

"So Kat just lied about it?" asked Char.

"That old witch!" breathed Phyllis. "What did she tell you girls?"

"Basically the same thing," said Loni. "I'd asked her to run over to Char's place one time and see if I could use it, and she came back and said that Char had sent the book to you and that the two of you were just going to keep it for yourselves."

Phyllis shook her head. "I never got the book either. Not even once!"

"This is shocking to me that Kat's lied to us all those years," said Gwyn. "So did she keep the book for herself?"

"She had to have. She wouldn't have given it away," said Char. "It's too valuable."

A lightbulb went on in Phyllis's head. "That's why she gave us the house and all its contents. I bet the spell book is in this house."

"And she didn't want us to sell it until we found the book!" said Gwyn as a slow smile spread across her face.

The pieces of the puzzle were all starting to come together in Char's mind. "I bet forcing us all to be in the same place at the same time was also part of her plan to reunite us and allow the truth to come out!"

"To think! We missed out on being friends for decades just because of Kat's lie!" sighed Gwyn. "How terribly sad is that? I've missed you girls so much."

"Oh, I've missed you all too," said Char, holding her hands out wide. "Bring it in, girls." Gwyn was the first to go in for the hug, and then Char waved Phyllis in. "Come on, Phil."

Phyllis, who wasn't much for displays of affection, grudgingly joined the hug. Gwyn looked back at Loni, who had remained seated on the stool. "You too, Lon."

"I don't do hugs," she barked gruffly.

"Well, I do," said Gwyn. She reached out and pulled Loni off the stool and into the hug.

"It's been way too long, girls," said Char, leaning her head on theirs. "I'm so glad we're back together now!"

From behind them, Hazel crossed her arms across her chest and harrumphed.

Char cast a glance over her shoulder. "With Kat gone, we're missing our fifth member of the group. Whatever will we do?" she said loudly.

Hazel lifted her eyes to the ceiling and pretended she hadn't heard that question.

Phyllis nodded. "We definitely need a fifth if we're going to be any kind of good witch's coven. Doesn't anyone know a witch that might want to be part of a *fun* witch's coven?"

The women could see Hazel look at them out of the sides of her eyes.

"Oh!" said Loni. "I know of someone. But she tells it like it is. We'd have to be willing to accept her for who she is."

"I'm willing," said Char. "How about you, Gwyn?"

A big, brilliant smile covered Gwyn's face. "I'm more than willing!"

"Hazel? We're looking for a fifth member of our witch's coven. Would you be willing to join us?" asked Loni.

"Eh?" hollered Hazel, cupping her ear.

"You want to be the fifth member of our witch's coven?" shouted Loni.

Hazel thought about it for a second. "What's in it for me?" she asked.

"You get to have all the fun you want when we're around," said Loni.

Hazel's eyes widened with interest as she glanced up at her daughter. "All the fun I want?"

"Within reason, of course," began Gwyn tentatively. She glanced around at the faces of her friends as they groaned.

"Come on, Gwyn, lighten up on her when she's with us," sighed Phyllis.

"I just don't want her to be rude to you…"

Char smiled. "We're tough old witches. We can handle it."

Gwyn looked down at her mother. "You're sure? What if she runs off?"

"Then we'll hunt her down together," said Phyllis.

Hazel eyed her daughter with one raised eyebrow. "What do you say, Gwynnie?"

All four women looked up at Gwyn expectantly. Finally, she sighed. "Fine, all the fun you want," she relented.

The oldest woman in the room smiled from ear to ear as she brought it in for a hug. "Deal!"

11

*G*wyn's eyelashes batted as she stared down at the fingers she'd knitted together in front of her. "So now that we're friends again, what do we do?" she asked the group. She couldn't help but think that there should be more. After all these years, their coven was finally reunited, and it felt a little flat. Like something was missing.

Kat's missing, said a tiny voice inside her head. She grimaced. Even though she hadn't seen Kat in years, just knowing that her dear friend was only a phone call away had meant a lot to her. Gwyn knew having Kat only a phone call away had meant a lot to Loni too. It was still hard for Gwyn to wrap her mind around the fact that Kat had been the one to steal their book all those years ago and had been the cause of a destroyed friendship with the rest of the girls. While there was shock and surprise, Gwyn was finding it difficult to be mad at Kat. Could a person really be mad at a dead woman? Did she *want* to hold that grudge for the rest of her days?

She glanced over at her mother and pictured the broad smile she'd flashed only moments ago. How sweet it had been for the girls to include her mother in their coven. Gwyn swallowed hard as she thought about loosening the reins on her mother. Was it so wrong of Gwyn to want to protect her mother? It was just that she was always so quick to get into trouble. What if something horrible ever happened to her? What would she do without her? She shoved her thoughts aside as Phyllis responded to her question.

"What do we do? About our friendship?"

"No, about this house!" said Gwyn. "Kat left us this house for a reason."

"She left us the house because she wanted us to be friends again. Her plan worked," said Char dusting her hands off in front of her. "Case closed."

"No, I get what Gwyn's talking about," said Phyllis. "She feels like there's more to Kat leaving us the house than just reuniting us. Am I right?"

Gwyn leaned inward. "Absolutely. There has to be more. We couldn't have gone through all those years for nothing, could we?"

"She had the book. She wanted us to find it," said Loni knowingly. "She wants to give it back to us."

Char lifted her brows and let out a heavy sigh. "You might be right. And we want to find it. So do we just start looking?"

Gwyn's eyes swept the room, scanning the centuries-old house—the overabundance of furniture, the excess trinkets, and the multitude of hiding spaces. "I think that's exactly what we do. That book has got to be in this house somewhere. We just need to look."

"This is a *huge house*," said Phyllis. "It could take us weeks to go through it all!"

"Not if we split up," suggested Gwyn. She felt her ability to organize kicking in. It would be just another project, and Gwyn excelled at projects.

Char nodded. "Gwyn's right. We split up the house and we'll find it faster."

The nods of agreement around the room emboldened Gwyn. Her eyes lit up as she started passing out marching orders. "Phyllis, you take the basement. Mom and I will take the first floor because stairs are hard on her knees."

"I'll take the third floor," volunteered Char with a little wave of her hand. "I'm probably in the best shape here. I walk every day, some days twice a day. Stairs don't bother me a bit."

"So I guess I'm taking the second floor, then?" asked Loni. "Who wants to take the turrets?"

"Tourette's?" cracked Hazel with a hand to her ear. "Who's got Tourette's?"

"Not Tourette's, Mom, turrets," Gwyn shouted.

Hazel's eyes opened wider. "Oh." She formed a circle with her mouth. "I thought maybe we had a screamer in the group," she said with an open-mouthed cackle.

"I'll climb up there when I'm done with the third floor," said Char.

"If I get done with the basement, I'll come up and help you," offered Phyllis.

"Alright. If anyone finds anything, holler!" said Gwyn, smiling ear to ear. Nothing made her happier than having a plan when it came to starting a project.

Phyllis, Char, and Loni all went their separate ways while Gwyn and Hazel stayed behind.

"Well. Where do we start?" asked Gwyn, looking around.

"I'm going to start in the living room. On the recliner," said Hazel as she hobbled away.

Gwyn sighed and followed her mother to the living room, where a recliner sat invitingly in a corner with a burgundy chenille blanket slung over the cushioned back rest. What she wouldn't give to be taking a nap in that cozy chair right about now. "I guess I'll be checking the main floor by myself, then, huh?" she asked as her mother settled herself into the chair.

Hazel pulled the wooden handle, extended her feet, and closed her eyes. "Wake me in an hour, Gwynnie."

"So much for the fifth member of the coven," murmured Gwyn as she shut the living room light off and turned on a dim lamp in the opposite corner of the room. "I guess I'll be checking the living room last."

***

*H*ours later, the sunshine that had poured in through the windows earlier was long gone. In its place, oversized pieces of furniture cast long shadows on the carpet and across the hardwood floor in the foyer. Phyllis had no sooner come up from the basement than Loni came down from the second floor. Both of them wore long faces and immediately fell onto the sofa in the living room.

Seated at the base of a floor-to-ceiling bookshelf in the living room, Gwyn rubbed her lower back. Her spine ached from leaning over the pile of books in front of her for so long. She wished she'd thought to throw some ibuprofen in her purse before they'd left the retirement village.

"Did either of you find anything?" she asked as she moved book after book to a new pile, verifying each wasn't the book they were looking for.

Hazel sat behind her, paging through an old issue of *People* magazine. "Did you know that George Clooney has finally become a father?" she asked the group. "He's fifty-six years old! Imagine a woman having a baby at fifty-six. People would say she was being selfish and call her a geriatric mother. But not men," she chided. "A man has a baby at fifty-six, and they throw him a party!"

"I see you're working hard," said Loni.

"Eh?" asked Hazel, squinting one eye shut and looking at Loni curiously.

Loni waved a hand in front of her face. "Never mind," she sighed. She looked at Gwyn and Phyllis. "I didn't find anything, and I looked *everywhere*."

Phyllis nodded. "Me too. I went through every box, every nook and cranny. Nothing. The book wasn't down there."

They all looked at Gwyn.

"I've gone through all her cupboards, her drawers, and her closets. Anywhere a book could fit, I checked. I just have this bookshelf to finish going through. I didn't readily see it, but I'm still checking all the books to make sure that she didn't put a false cover on it or something."

"Good idea," said Phyllis with a nod. "Maybe I'll go upstairs and see if Char could use a hand."

"Loni, you want to help me finish looking through these books?" asked Gwyn.

"Sure," she said just as Char came trudging down the stairs.

"Well, I'm bushed," she groaned, falling onto the sofa in the living room next to Phyllis.

"I take it you didn't find anything?" asked Loni.

Char shook her head. "Not a single inkling of that book."

"You checked the turrets?"

"Yes! I checked there first. That's where Kat did her spells. She's got a casting circle up there, and all her candles and potion ingredients. Really and truly, if that book were to be anywhere in this house, it should have been up there. She even had a book stand, but it was empty. I thought I was going to go up there, find the book, and come right back down."

"That's so strange that it wasn't up there, then," said Gwyn, a frown flitting across her face. "I just have to finish checking this bookshelf. Otherwise, we've all checked everywhere else."

Char shook her head. "You're not going to find it on

the bookshelf," she said. "Kat wouldn't want it out in plain sight like this. What if I came over and saw it?"

"I'm checking the books to make sure the insides are what the outsides say they are," explained Gwyn. "I'm almost done. If we all go through them together, we'll get done a lot faster."

Char sighed but sat up in her seat. "Pass me a stack."

"Me too," groaned Phyllis.

Loni passed out two stacks of books, and then everyone looked at Hazel.

"What?!" she asked, staring all of the women down. "I can't help right now. Some woman named Katy Perry is ranking her celebrity lovers from best to worst. I've got to see which one's the best one." She looked down at her magazine. "Just for future reference."

Gwyn palmed her forehead. "Oh, Mother," she sighed.

"Inquiring minds want to know," said Char with a laugh.

---

*T*hirty minutes later, the women lounged around the living room in various positions, rubbing their sore body parts.

"I think it's time to call it a night, ladies," said Phyllis, massaging the balls of her feet.

Char stood up and arched her back, stretching an arm out over her head. "I agree. I don't think we're going to find the book tonight."

Gwyn's head rolled back on her shoulders. "I don't know that we're ever going to find it. I don't think it's in the house, girls. We've looked everywhere."

"We'll sleep on it. Maybe we'll think of another place Kat might have hidden the book," said Loni.

Phyllis stood up and put the last stack of books back on the bookshelf. "Lon's right. Maybe we should meet back up tomorrow night."

Gwyn sighed. "I can't tomorrow night. I'm taking a group of my Village residents on a night walk to the Falls Festival. I think it will be neat seeing the Falls all lit up at night. I think my group will enjoy it."

"Oh, I was planning to go to that with Vic. Mind if we tag along?" asked Char.

Gwyn smiled broadly. Having company might be kind of fun. *And* if Char and Vic went, they could help her keep an eye on her mother. "Sure! That would be great! You're all welcome to come!"

"Well, I can't," huffed Loni. "You're lucky I even left the house to come over here."

"You need to get out more," chided Char. "It's not healthy to keep yourself locked away in your house like that, day after day and week after week. You're breathing in the same old dirty air day in and day out. You should come with us."

Loni lowered her brows as she peered at Char. "My air's not dirty."

Char smiled at her. "I didn't mean your air was dirty. I just meant you need to get some *fresh* air. It's not healthy to stay cooped up all day."

Loni crossed her arms across her chest in a pout.

"How about you, Phil?" asked Gwyn. "I'd love to have you!"

Phyllis nodded. "Alright, I suppose I could make an appearance. It might be fun."

Gwyn threw both hands in the air. "Yay! Oh, girls, this will be fun getting to hang out again. I've missed you all so much over the years!"

"Gwynnie," Char began, "Phil and I meet for coffee at her daughter's restaurant every morning. You're sure welcome to join us. You and Hazel, that is."

"You too, Lon," added Phyllis.

"Oh, yes, of course. I wasn't trying to exclude you, Lon," said Char. "I just figured if you wouldn't leave the house for a night walk, you probably wouldn't want to come have coffee with us in public in the light of day."

Loni sat quietly in her spot. Gwyn could see the wheels quietly turning in her mind.

Gwyn smiled at the girls. "Mom and I would love to join you for coffee. What's the name of the restaurant?"

"Habernackle's Bed, Breakfast, and Beyond downtown," said Phyllis. "It's a B&B, but they also have a nice little restaurant."

"What time do you meet in the mornings?" asked Gwyn.

"It varies on occasion, but generally we like to be there by eight," said Char. "We get a little chat session in and then get on with our day. I like to go walking before it gets too hot in the afternoon."

Gwyn nodded. "Eight it is! I like to have projects at

The Village started by nine, so that will work perfectly." She looked outside. "Well, girls, it's getting late. We should probably go. Char, don't forget to take that chicken to the curb."

"Yes!" she said, holding a finger up as if she'd just remembered as well. Char locked the front door. "Why don't we just all go out the back? That way we won't forget to take that with us." She shut the lights off in the living room as Gwyn pulled Hazel up from her recliner. Slowly, the five women filtered out of the house through the sliding door in the kitchen.

Char locked the door behind them and stuck the key in the pocket of her pink polyester pants. Gwyn stooped over to pick up the chicken they'd bagged. She could still make out a faint scent, even through the plastic.

"Ooh, this is horrible," said Gwyn, holding the bag out by two fingers at a distance. "Where are her garbage cans?"

"Around the corner. We'll put them in there and drag the can down to the curb, so that the garbage men will take them. Tomorrow is trash day on this side of town, I believe."

The moon was bright, but it was a windy evening. As a breeze whipped through the backyard, it moved the trees overhead, causing moonlit shadows to dance across the rose garden in Kat's backyard. Gwyn stopped short of walking around the house. "What is that?" she asked with surprise.

"Kat's flower garden?" asked Char. When Gwyn

nodded, she continued, "My goodness, that woman had quite the green thumb."

"She used to talk about her flowers when we visited on the phone, but I had no idea her garden was quite so elaborate!" breathed Gwyn with a broad smile.

"Would you ladies like to take a quick tour?" asked Char.

Loni's eyes darted uncomfortably around the back-yard. She'd put her veil and cowboy hat back on inside the house, and the backyard was fenced in, but on a bit of an incline, and it looked down at her house, which was only a block away. "We can't stay out here long. I don't want anyone to see me!"

"Oh, hush, Loni Hodges. You're being ridiculous! No one cares that you're over here, and if they did, they certainly can't see you!" hissed Phyllis.

"Especially in that ridiculous ensemble," added Char.

"Fine," grumbled Loni.

Gwyn looked out over the garden. She couldn't believe what she was seeing! Four arbors with vining flowers growing all over them stood central at the four sides of the garden. A picturesque white fence ran around the perimeter, and an amazing assortment of carefully cultivated rose bushes covered every square inch inside of the fence. "It's so lovely!"

"Isn't it?" asked Char, entering the rose garden beneath the arbor nearest the house.

The rest of the girls followed and everyone oohed and aahed over the beautiful plants. The vegetation was already lush and green. The fresh, floral scent was intoxicating and made Gwyn smile from ear to ear. A few of the early bloomers had already begun to show signs of blooming, but many plants were still working on their buds.

Gwyn stopped in the center of the garden, where a big black cauldron had collected a hazy green load of rainwater. "This is going to be a mosquito magnet," she said.

Phyllis stopped walking and looked down at the cauldron. "What's Kat got a cauldron in her garden for?" she asked.

Char held a hand to the side of her face. "If you ask me, I think Kat liked to tip the scales in her favor."

Gwyn looked at Char curiously. "What does that mean?"

Char gave a little shrug. "Kat was very *particular* about her flowers. She entered them in the gardening contest every year, and every year she won. I suppose the fact that she's a witch might have had a little to do with her success. If you know what I mean?"

Gwyn sucked in her breath. "You mean she used her powers to enhance the flowers? She cheated?!"

Char laughed. "If you call that cheating?"

"I *do* call that cheating!" breathed Gwyn.

"Oh, relax, Gwynnie. Everyone can't be as perfect as you," sighed her mother from behind her.

Gwyn's mouth snapped shut. She hated when her mother told her she was perfect. She wasn't perfect. Far from it.

"There have to be *some* perks to being a witch," said

Char. "Don't you think? It can't all be 'burn her at the stake.'"

Phyllis rubbed her chin. "You don't suppose she was *cheating* the day when she slipped and fell out here, do you?" she pondered. "Maybe it was the spell that killed her?"

"Maybe," said Char with a shrug. They were all quiet for a few long moments, considering what the possible fate of Kat had actually been. Suddenly, Char sucked in a breath. "Omigosh, girls! I just thought of something!"

12

"*D*o tell," said Loni excitedly.

"Does anyone know exactly what day it was that Kat passed away?" asked Char, scanning the faces of her friends caught in the moonlit shadows of Kat's rose garden.

Phyllis shook her head. "All I heard was that she was found dead by the paperb—*paperman*. He and the cops said she'd been there for quite a while, by the looks of it. At least two weeks."

"Right, but we don't have an exact date, do we?" asked Char.

"No, not that we know of," said Gwyn. "Why?"

Char smiled and gave her a tip of the head. "Bear with me for a few minutes, and I'll explain why I want to know." She took a breath. "Okay. So it was the paperman that found her. If I'm to understand what he told the police, he noticed that something was wrong because Kat's papers were piling up in front of the door, which he

135

found odd. Kat usually picked her paper up off the porch every day. So that means…"

Gwyn cut in excitedly. "That the oldest paper on her porch was either from the day that she died or the day after!"

Char's hands lurched out with gusto. "Exactly what I was thinking!"

"Let's go check it out," said Phyllis, leading the charge to the front of the house.

Loni sighed and left the flower garden to sit on a swinging love seat between the house and the garden. "I'll just stay right here. Someone might see me out in front."

Hazel nodded. "I'm with crazy pants here. All this running around is too much for me. I'll keep her company back here," she said, hitching a thumb over her shoulder.

"Alright, let's go, girls," said Char. Then she looked over her shoulder at Loni and Hazel. "We'll be right back. You two sit tight."

"Sit tight? I can't sit any tighter than I am right now," cracked Hazel. "Heck, I'm so tight, I can barely touch my knees. They shouldn't call it getting old—they should call it getting tight."

Gwyn pointed at Loni. "Please don't let her out of your sight."

Loni saluted Gwyn. "Aye-aye, Cap'n."

Char, Phyllis, and Gwyn rushed around to the front of the house. On their way, Gwyn tossed the rotten chicken into the garbage, and she and Phyllis pulled the garbage can around through the gate and to the curb.

Then they met Char up on the porch. She was already holding her awakened cell phone over the newspapers at the front door, trying to read the dates in the dim glow.

Gwyn and Phyllis sat on the front steps next to her. Each of them pulled out their phones too, lit them up, and began organizing the newspapers. "I've got papers from the fourteenth and fifteenth," said Gwyn.

"I've got the twentieth, the twenty-first, and the twenty-second," Phyllis called out.

"I've got all the ones from this week," said Char, bundling them up and scooting them off to the side.

Phyllis made a face. "Why are they still delivering papers to a dead woman?"

The thought hadn't occurred to Char. She plunged out her bottom lip and widened her eyes. "Maybe her bill's paid through a certain date," she suggested. "Maybe they have to."

Gwyn ignored that topic of interest and announced, "I found papers from the tenth, eleventh, and twelfth. Girls, I don't see anything prior to April tenth, do you?"

Phyllis shook her head. "Nope. I don't have anything before the nineteenth."

Char shook her head too. "Me either."

Their eyes widened in unison. "That means that on the tenth, Kat didn't get her newspaper. When are papers delivered around here?" asked Gwyn.

"We get ours first thing in the morning. Usually before the sun's even up," said Char.

"Alright, then. Well, if the newspaper gets delivered in

the mornings, then we know Kat had to have died the night of the ninth," rationalized Gwyn.

Phyllis frowned at her. "She could have died on the tenth."

Gwyn shook her head. Her face was serious, with furrowed eyebrows and a mouth set firmly in a line. "Not likely. Kat had taken that chicken out to thaw for supper. I don't know about you ladies, but I don't usually take my meat out to thaw until about lunchtime. Chicken doesn't need to be sitting out all day. She probably took it out that afternoon and had gotten her paper that morning. I think she was alive the morning of the ninth and dead before the next paper showed up on the tenth."

Char clapped her hands with fervor. "Oh, Gwynnie, you're so smart."

Phyllis groaned. "Well, any of us could have put that together."

Char swatted at Phyllis's shoulder. "Is it past your bedtime? You seem grumpier than usual."

Phyllis rolled her eyes and leaned back against a baluster on Kat's porch. "Yes, as a matter of fact, it *is* past my bedtime. What's the point of all of this? I'd like to go home and get my beauty sleep."

Char let out a puff of air. "Hold your damn horses, woman. I'm getting to it." She took a deep breath, lowered her torso, and began her theory. "Here's what hit me when we were out in Kat's garden. In early April, this huge peculiar storm rolled through town late one night. Everyone in Aspen Falls speculated about it. In fact, it was so strong that it even made the papers that next morning."

Phyllis wagged a finger at Char while nodding. "I remember that storm. Damn near blew the chair off of my patio. I had to go out in the rain to get it before it blew over the railing. Got soaked to the skin in that storm!"

"Yes! I remember you telling me that," said Char. Then she looked at Gwyn. "Every year around the same time, we get a storm that is eerily similar. The forecasters are never able to predict it. It's never on any radar. It's like it just pops up out of nowhere. The only thing consistent about it is that it always happens sometime in the early spring."

"You think the storm had something to do with Kat's death?" asked Gwyn.

Char lifted a single brow and tilted her head to the side. "What if *Kat* was the one that's brewed those storms up all these years?"

Gwyn sucked in her breath. "You mean it was part of a spell?"

"Do you think that's why the cauldron was in her garden?" asked Phyllis.

"Could be. Maybe she was doing a spell, and somehow, it killed her," suggested Char. "Now, here's what I'm thinking. We look at the papers from the tenth or the eleventh. If either one of those talks about that storm, then we know that was probably Kat messing around with the spell book."

Gwyn smiled excitedly as she clasped her hands to her

chest in front of her. "Eee," she squealed. "Char, you're a genius. I could kiss you!"

Char made a silly face and then held out her palm to distance Gwyn. "I know you're probably sexually frustrated because you're without a husband and all, but we should clarify things right now. I'm not interested. I'm a married woman, in case you didn't know!"

Gwyn giggled.

"Would you two quit flirting and give me those papers!" chided Phyllis. "I'm dying to know if Char's theory is right!"

Char took the two oldest copies of the *Aspen Falls Observer* and opened them both up. "Only one way to find out!"

She flipped open the paper from April eleventh to the weather highlights and saw nothing related. Then she opened the paper from the tenth. Char's eyes widened as she jammed a stubby finger at the headlines on the front page of the paper. "Aha!" she yelled. "*Forty-Fifth Annual Freak Storm Hits Aspen Falls, Meteorologists Fail to Predict Once Again,*" she read out loud. "A freak storm unleashed chaos on Aspen Falls in the late evening hours of April ninth, causing trees on the east end of town to fall on power lines. Power outages lasting over three hours were reported in parts of Aspen Falls."

Gwyn's blue eyes widened. "You were right, Char! It had to have been Kat!"

"It had to have been," echoed Phyllis.

"Well, now we know when she died, and we also know

that she was likely doing a spell in her garden when she died," said Char. "You'd think after forty-five years of doing the exact same spell, she'd have known to be more careful."

"Poor Kat," whispered Gwyn. It broke her heart that her old friend had died in such a careless accident.

"But now we know she probably had the spell book with her outside when she died," suggested Phyllis.

Char nodded. "This is very true. But it's not out there. That paperman was the one to have found her. Maybe he found the book and decided to keep it."

"We may never know," said Gwyn quietly.

Phyllis's head reared back. "My heinie we'll never know!" She stood up. "If he stole the book, we're going to get it back!"

Char nodded. "I agree with Phil. That's *our* book. It kept us apart for decades. I'm not about to let it go. Kat *wanted* us to have it."

Gwyn wrung her hands nervously. "Well, how do we get it back?"

Char rubbed her chin. "I don't know. I need some time to think. Let's meet for coffee in the morning and work out a plan!"

Phyllis rubbed her hands together devilishly. "Whoever stole that book better watch out. The Coffee Coven is on the case!"

13

*T*he next morning, Habernackle's was a hopping place. As usual, Sergeant Bradshaw and his friends took up residence in the big booth in the corner. He sat on a chair at the end of the booth as he had the day before. A group of tourists with young children sat noisily reading menus in another booth against the outer windowed wall, likely in town for the Falls Festival that evening. Several other tables were filled with couples having breakfast and chatting pleasantly. And to the left of the front door, a big group of some type had spread out across three tables and a booth. A man with brown curly hair stood in front of them, delivering a lecture of some sort while the group stared up at him, listening with interest.

Phyllis and Char entered the restaurant, saw their usual spot open, and made a beeline for the round table near the men having coffee in the booth.

"Good morning, ladies," said Sergeant Bradshaw as

the women walked past him. "A little breezy, but otherwise a beautiful day out there, isn't it?"

"It's always a good day when I wake up alive," said
Char with a grin.

The bell above the door alerted Char and Phyllis that
Habernackle's door had opened again. They looked back
to see Hazel amble in, leaning heavily on her cane, with
Gwyn following only a few steps behind.

Char gave them a big wave. "Over here, girls," she
hollered.

Gwyn patted her straight shoulder-length hair as she
walked, putting it neatly back into place. "Sorry we're
late, I couldn't get Mom out of the bathroom this morning," said Gwyn, giving Char and Phyllis each a
small hug.

Hazel stopped walking and leaned back stiffly to scan
the faces of the onlookers. "Hell, Gwynnie. Do you have to
tell the whole damn restaurant that I was having problems
with my morning constitutional?" she snapped. "I can't rush
the process at my age, or I'll give myself a hernia trying."

Char grinned. Something about Hazel seemed to
make her smile. Then she looked over at the table full of
men. It occurred to her that since Gwyn and Hazel were
moving into the community, she should provide some
introductions.

"Gwyn and Hazel, this is Sergeant Bradshaw," said
Char, gesturing towards the white-haired man at the end
of the table. She pointed to the next man over, a blond
wearing a navy suit and tie, by far the youngest of the

small group of men. "That's Mayor Adams, obviously the mayor of Aspen Falls."

Gwyn nodded at the men in turn as Char continued her introductions. Sitting across the table from Mayor Adams was a tall stretch of a man with gangly arms and a long, narrow face etched with deep lines around his mouth. "This is Marcus Wheedlan. He runs the hardware store."

She pointed to the man next to Marcus. "This is Sam Jeffries. Mr. Jeffries is retired now, but he used to be a city councilman." Sam was an elderly man, perhaps the oldest at the table. At one time he'd had coal-black hair, but now it was dusted with time. He barely looked up after being introduced.

Char pointed at the last man at the table. "And that is Benny Hamilton. He writes for the *Aspen Falls Observer*. He wrote poor Kat's obituary," she tacked on at the end for Gwyn's benefit. Then Char gestured towards Gwyn and Hazel. "Gentlemen, this is Gwyndolin and Hazel Prescott, Aspen Falls' newest residents."

From the end of the booth, Mayor Adams offered his hand, as did Marcus Wheedlan. Neither Sam nor Benny offered the same nicety and instead only stared back at Gwyn and Hazel, making Gwyn shift uncomfortably in her brown Skechers.

Sergeant Bradshaw, however, made a point of standing to shake Gwyn's hand. "It's a pleasure to meet you," he said with a deep bow. "I take it you're friends of Phyllis and Char's?"

Gwyn nodded. "I went to college with them years ago."

"Oh, very nice," he said, lifting his white eyebrows. "What brings you back to Aspen Falls?"

"I just accepted the activities director position at the Aspen Falls Retirement Village," she explained as Hazel ignored the men and took a seat next to Phyllis at their table.

"Oh, they've been trying to fill that position for quite a while. You must be something special," he said with a wide smile, revealing his perfectly white teeth.

Gwyn lifted a shoulder shyly. "Oh, I wouldn't say I'm anything special..."

"They couldn't fill the position because they couldn't find anyone with experience who also had experience with *the paranormals*," said Benny. He said *the paranormals* as if it were a dirty word.

"Yes, well, I'm a witch," said Gwyn with a nervous little titter. "So, I had the experience they were looking for."

Benny rolled his eyes. "Great, more witches. Just what this town needs."

Sergeant Bradshaw's eyes darkened with embarrassment as he looked down at Gwyn. "Don't mind him," he whispered loud enough that everyone could still hear. "He's a little salty. He got beat out for a promotion recently *and* he hasn't had all of his coffee yet this morning. That's a bad combination for a journalist."

Gwyn smiled and batted her eyelashes at Sergeant

Bradshaw. "Oh, it's fine. I'm used to people being a little skittish about my *abilities*. I appreciate it, though."

"Well, I'll let you get to your friends. It was a pleasure to meet you, Gwyndolin," he said, patting the top of her hand as he shook it.

"My friends just call me Gwyn," she said pleasantly. "You're sure welcome to call me Gwyn as well."

Sergeant Bradshaw smiled broadly. "In that case, I'm thrilled to be extended that honor. It was a pleasure to meet you, Gwyn. I hope we bump into each other again sometime."

"Likewise," she agreed before sashaying around a chair and sliding into her seat at the round table with the girls.

Char leaned over and whispered into Gwyn's ear. "What was all that eye batting about?"

"Eye batting?" Gwyn asked, feigning horror.

"Yes, eye batting," agreed Phyllis. "Oh, Sergeant Bradshaw," she added in a mockingly high voice.

Gwyn threw the napkin in front of her across the table at Phyllis. "Oh, quit it. You girls are ridiculous. I wasn't making eyes at that man. I was just being polite," she hissed.

"It's about time you flirted with a man. I think you should go home with him and see if he needs his broomstick polished. Maybe that'll help you take the edge off," said Hazel with a chuckle.

"Mother!" gasped Gwyn. Her wide eyes contained a mixture of shock and embarrassment.

Phyllis slapped her thigh, threw back her head, and let

a howl of laughter escape her mouth. "Haze! There's a child present," she finally said when her convulsions had finally settled.

Hazel lifted her eyebrows, which in turn hefted the heavy bags beneath her eyes. "I'm just sayin', her basement's gotten a little dusty. Maybe she should let the man come over and help her clear away the cobwebs."

Char laughed. "Hazel, you're terrible!"

Gwyn's face flushed bright red. "Mom, you are so embarrassing," she hissed, looking down at the table and shielding her forehead with her hand. "Please tell me he didn't hear all that."

Char looked over Gwyn's shoulder to see Sergeant Bradshaw back in heavy conversation with the men at his table. "Nah, he's moved on, he's not listening."

Gwyn straightened in her seat and then smoothed the invisible wrinkles on her sweater in an attempt to shake off her mother's words. "Good!" she sighed. "Now, we don't have much time to visit. Have you ordered us coffee yet?"

Phyllis shook her head. "No, we just got here too." She looked back at the bar and caught sight of a tall, slender young man with thick wavy black hair and olive skin. "Excuse me, young man. Over here," she called to him, lifting a curled finger into the air.

The waiter approached the ladies with a tray of coffee mugs and a coffee carafe. "Good morning, ladies," he said with a smile.

"Good morning," chirped Phyllis. She turned to her friends. "Girls, this is my grandson, Reign Alexander," said Phyllis. "He's my daughter Linda's oldest child. Reign, this is Gwyn Prescott. She was an old college friend of mine, and this is her mother, Hazel."

"It's nice to meet you both. Hazel, that's a terrific color for you," said Reign, referring to the blue shirt Hazel wore that made her eyes pop.

"Eh?" asked Hazel, cupping her hand around her ear.

"He said you look great, Mom," said Gwyn, leaning closer to her good ear.

Reign smiled and plucked a piece of material at the breast of his shirt. "That's a great color for you, brings out your eyes," he said more loudly this time.

Hazel wagged a crooked finger at him. "Uh-uh, Sonny. I'm off-limits. I don't date my friend's children or grandchildren. You're quite the looker, though."

Reign held back the smile that threatened his easy-going composure and pretended to crumple next to the table. "Aww, just my luck." Then he straightened himself. "Well, can I at the very least get you a cup of coffee?" He put a cup in front of Hazel.

"Yes, and you can get me some French fries," said Hazel.

He set coffee cups around the table in front of each of the women. "French fries?" asked Reign with a lift of his brows as he poured the coffee.

"You got wax in your ears, Sonny?" she snapped. "Yes, French fries."

"Fries are on our lunch and dinner menus, but I could probably do you a special favor because you're a friend of my grandmother's," said Reign with a little wink at Hazel.

"See, there he goes, flirting with me again." She turned to Char. "The men. They can't resist my charms."

"Mother, he's just trying to be polite," whispered Gwyn, exasperated. She shook her head and reached out to touch Reign's elbow. "No fries, please, just bring her a Danish or a roll or something. I'll have the same." She looked at her mother and shouted, "Mom, you can have French fries at lunchtime. Don't make this poor man go to the extra trouble."

Hazel scowled at her daughter. "See what I'm saying? She's wound so tight. She needs to have the edge taken off," she said, elbowing Char in the ribs.

Reign smiled. "Okay, so two rolls. Char, Phyllis, can I get you anything?" he asked.

Gwyn eyed Phyllis curiously but remained mum.

"Oatmeal with a side of wheat toast," said Char decidedly. "And I'll take my senior discount, please."

"I'll have the special," said Phyllis. "Extra bacon, please. Not too crisp."

Char shook her head. She was going to have to work on Phyllis's diet, so she didn't have a heart attack on her. She couldn't bear the thought of losing *another* friend.

Char touched Reign's arm before he ran off. "What's going on today? Why's the place so busy?"

Reign looked around. "I think we've got a lot of tourists in today for the festival. And then, of course, there's Sergeant Bradshaw's coffee club over there," he said, gesturing towards the group of men. Then he tipped his head in the other direction. "And that group meets twice a month for breakfast. It's the Aspen Falls Master

Gardener Club. Okay, ladies, I'll have that out for you in a jiffy." He snapped his notepad closed, tucked it in his apron pocket, and took off.

"Your grandson calls you Phyllis?" Gwyn asked Phyllis after Reign had gotten out of earshot.

"Oh, well, yeah. We're sort of working on our relationship," explained Phyllis uncomfortably. She waved a hand at Gwyn. "It's a long story."

"And unfortunately we don't have a lot of time today. You'll have to tell me about it another time. We need to figure out what to do about finding that spell book," said Gwyn.

Char grinned and leaned into the table conspiringly. "I agree. I've been thinking about that. I think we start with the first person that discovered Kat dead. We start with the paperman."

"It's the only thing that makes sense," agreed Gwyn. "So maybe at lunch, the three of us go pay him a visit?"

"The three of us? You, me, and Phil?" asked Char, counting them each off in turn. "What about Hazel?"

Hazel furrowed her brow and pointed at herself. "Yeah, what about Hazel?"

Gwyn shook her head. "Oh no. You're staying at The Village. I'll have someone keep an eye on you while I'm gone."

"What? No way. Things are just starting to get interesting!" she whined.

"I'm sorry, Mom. But you tend to blurt things out, and we can't have you messing things up for us."

"What are you geniuses gonna do? Just go knock on

the man's door?" asked Hazel. "You think he's just gonna tell you he stole the book?"

Phyllis made a face. "The woman has a point."

Gwyn's jaw dropped. "Yeah, at the tip of her devil's horns," she sighed.

"Okay, so what do we do about it? How do we figure out if he really took the book?" asked Phyllis.

Hazel rolled her eyes. "Obviously you take me. I read minds. Hello? Anyone home in the bat cave?" she asked, knocking gently on the side of Phyllis's temple with her knuckle.

Phyllis swatted Hazel's hand away. "Okay, okay. I get it." She looked at Gwyn. "Sorry, Gwyn. Your mother's right. We need her to go with us. I vote to bring the old witch." She raised her hand.

Hazel raised her hand next. "I vote to bring the old witch too," she said with a devious smile.

Char raised her hand too. "I vote to bring her too."

Hazel let out a little cackle. "Three to one. Motion carried. Sorry, Gwynnie. Oh, look. Breakfast's here."

Gwyn sighed as Reign began to serve the table.

Char smiled. She had a feeling Gwyn was going to be outvoted a lot from now on where Hazel was concerned. "It's alright, Gwyn. We'll take good care of her!"

14

"*I*t's too bad we couldn't convince Loni to go with us to look for the book," said Char as she put on her turn signal and scanned the road for pedestrians.

"That old biddy's plumb crazy if you ask me," said Phyllis. "She thinks the FBI is after her."

Gwyn leaned forward into the front seat. "What makes her think that anyway?"

"Who knows?" said Char. "I think her warped imagination makes her think that."

"We need to keep an eye on her," sighed Gwyn. "It's not healthy for her to be all cooped up in that house day after day with no human interaction."

"We'll put that on our to-do list. Right after finding out who stole our spell book and figuring out what to do with Kat's house," said Char as she pulled up to a small bungalow on the other side of town. "This is his house," she said, her voice dropping into a lower register as she came to a stop.

"What are we going to do?" asked Gwyn.

"We don't need to do anything. We've got Hazel. We just need to ask him if he has the book," said Phyllis bluntly.

Hazel turned her head and stared out the window. "I feel like the class slut on prom night."

Phyllis chuckled. "I'm sorry, Hazel. We don't want you here just because you put out. We all enjoy your company as well. It's those snappy little retorts we enjoy so much."

"Like I said the other day, she doesn't need any more encouragement on those snappy little retorts. In fact, I think she could tone them down a bit. Don't you think so, Mother?"

Hazel snorted air out her nose. "Well, I think you could tone down that fake strawberry-blond hair of yours, but what do I know? I'm just an old lady."

"Can we go in now?" asked Char, changing the subject. "I have a roast to get in the oven."

"Yes," agreed Gwyn. "I think sitting out here talking is fruitless and a waste of my time. Let's go."

The four women got out of the car and followed Char up the sidewalk to a simple little tan house with brown shutters. Char knocked on the door. They didn't have to wait long before a woman in a tight pink sundress, big poofy brown hair, and cleavage to spare opened the door. The sound of a blaring TV poured through the open doorway.

"May I help you?" she asked.

"We're looking for Ruben," said Char.

The woman looked surprised, but turned and looked into the house. "Ruby, there are some women here to see you."

A man with a head of thick, dark hair popped up from the sofa as if he'd just been poked with a needle. "Women?" he asked.

Char could hear the nervousness in his voice. Ruben came to the door and seemed to visibly relax when he saw the four old ladies standing in front of him. His head turned slightly as his eyebrows furrowed. "May I help you?"

"Hi, Ruben," began Char, extending her hand. "I'm Char Bailey. You deliver the *Aspen Falls Observer*, right?"

He nodded curiously as he shook her hand. "Yes?"

"You delivered the paper to one of our friends. Katherine Lynde."

Ruben's eyes shifted around uncomfortably as he fidgeted with the chain lock on the door. "Oh, yeah, uh, Kat." He looked into the house and hollered at the woman who'd answered the door. "Sweetheart, I'm just going to be outside for a moment." He stepped over the threshold as Char and the rest of the women took a step backwards. When he was all the way out, he shut the door behind him. He looked at Char. "You were at her funeral, weren't you?"

Char nodded. "Phyllis and I were," she said, pointing at Phyllis. "Why were you there?"

Ruben ran a hand across the back of his neck. "I was kind of *friends* with Kat," he admitted.

Phyllis's eyes narrowed. "You and Kat were friends?"

"Sort of," he said uncomfortably.

Phyllis eyed Hazel. The old woman blinked but didn't say anything.

"And you were the one to find her dead, is that right?" asked Gwyn.

"Yeah. It took me a while to realize that she wasn't picking up her papers. I guess I was preoccupied and not really paying attention. It's a monotonous job. That happens sometimes, you know? I'd get home and wonder if I even delivered to certain streets because I didn't remember doing it."

"So what made you realize it the day you finally found her?" asked Char.

He shrugged and suddenly seemed suddenly not to know what to do with his arms, crossing them and uncrossing them. Finally, he jammed his hands into his pockets and looked down at his white socks. "I needed to, uh, talk to her. That's when I realized that her papers had been piling up and a light was on inside her house. I tried knocking, but she wouldn't come to the door. So I went around to the backyard, and that was when I found her."

Phyllis peered at him curiously. "What did you need to talk to her about?"

Ruben put a fist to his lips and cleared his throat. "You know, I can't remember anymore." His voice seemed to rise an octave.

Char glanced at Hazel, wondering if she was getting a

reading on the guy. It seemed to Char that he wasn't being forthcoming with what he knew.

Hazel acted nonchalant, as if she weren't even paying attention to the conversation.

"Okay, so you went around to the back. And where did you find her body?" asked Gwyn.

"She was just lying by the entrance to her garden. It was obvious she'd been there for quite a while. I'm surprised an animal didn't get to her or something. She smelled horrible, and her body was all bloated and grotesque." His tone got lighter then. "I've had some nightmares about it, to be honest."

Gwyn rubbed his arm. "Oh, you poor man. I'm sure that was extremely difficult. It's difficult for us as her friends just thinking about it."

He nodded and then whispered, "Thank you."

"Ruben, did Kat have anything with her when you found her? Like maybe lying on the ground next to her or something?" asked Gwyn.

"Like what?" He peered out through his long, dark eyelashes at the women.

"I don't know. Anything. A book, perhaps," suggested Gwyn.

He made a face as he tried to recall exactly what he had seen. "Not that I remember. I didn't see anything. Of course, I wasn't really in the mind-set of looking around. I'd just found a dead body on my route. I'd found a *friend* dead. I knew I needed to get the police called immediately. So that was really my only concern."

Char patted him on the back. "You did the right thing, Ruben."

"Yeah," he said, getting a little choked up. "I felt really horrible finding my friend like that. Kat was a nice woman. She kept to herself mostly, but she always had time for me."

"She really was a nice woman," agreed Char. "We'll all miss her."

Phyllis peered at him curiously. "So did you happen to take anything of hers after she died?"

His demeanor shifted when he looked at Phyllis. "Take anything? No. I didn't take anything. I'm not a thief." Ruben looked at all of the women's faces then. "Is that why you're here? You think I took something of Kat's?"

"Don't go getting your dander up," snapped Phyllis. "We just wanted to find out what happened to our friend. You were the first person who discovered her body, so we're starting with you."

Ruben lifted both hands in a shrug. "I don't know what you want to know, but I've told you everything I know. I'm sorry about your friend." He opened the door behind him. "I need to go."

"Okay, well, thank you for visiting with us," said Gwyn before turning to walk away first.

The rest of the women said a simple goodbye and followed her down the sidewalk and back to the car. Once inside, they all turned to Hazel in the backseat.

"Well? What did you make of him?" asked Char.

"Yeah, what did you think?" asked Phyllis.

Hazel crossed her arms across her chest. "Well, look who's the popular girl now," she said with a crooked smile.

"Mother. Please. Just tell us what you know," begged Gwyn.

Hazel lifted her brows. "You're going to have to do better than that, Gwynnie."

"Better than that?"

"I want French fries for breakfast all week," said Hazel staunchly.

"All week? Mother, that's so unhealthy!"

She closed her eyes and shrugged. "It's what I want."

Gwyn sighed, slumping forward in her seat. She glanced up at the girls who nodded their heads encouragingly. "You can have them tomorrow."

"Four days," Hazel countered.

"Three days."

"Deal!" she said, holding out her hand out for her daughter to shake.

Gwyn shook her mother's hand. "Now tell us what you figured out."

Hazel smiled at them. "He does *not* have the book."

"I thought he was telling the truth about that, too," said Phyllis knowingly.

"What else did you figure out?" asked Char.

Hazel looked at her curiously. "What am I? A mathematician? You said you just wanted to know if he had the book! You didn't tell me I was supposed to listen to the rest of that gobbledygook."

Char swiveled back around in her seat to face the

windshield again. "You seriously weren't paying attention to *any* of that conversation? The man was obviously withholding *something*."

Phyllis nodded. "That whole thing about being *friends* with Kat. What was that about?"

"I don't know, but he didn't seem to want his wife to know that he was *friends* with Kat," she said, air-quoting the words *friends*. "The only reason I know of that a man would want to hide a friendship from his wife is if there's some hanky-panky going on," said Char with a little chuckle.

Gwyn sucked in her breath. "You don't think *Kat* and *Ruben* ... ?!"

"Say it, Gwynnie. It's not a dirty word," said Hazel.

"Oh, Mother," she gasped.

"Say it!"

"Mother, please!" Gwyn's cheeks reddened.

"Say it, and I'll tell you what else I know!"

"Oh, for goodness sake, you don't think that *Kat and Ruben had sex*, do you?"

Hazel threw her hands up to the ceiling. "Hallelujah, my daughter knows how to say the S-word!" She leaned over and whispered to her, "Now see if you can do it next time without blushing."

"I'll try, Mother," Gwyn said, rolling her eyes. "Now what do you know?"

"Well. I really wasn't paying much attention to that entire conversation, but I did hear him thinking that he hoped we wouldn't find out."

"Find out what?" asked Char, swiveling around in her seat again.

"If I knew that, don't you think I would have included it?" asked Hazel.

Gwyn leaned back in her seat and cupped her chin. "Now I'm really curious what he doesn't want us to find out. If he doesn't have the book, then what else is he hiding?"

"This is turning into a bigger mystery than we originally thought," said Phyllis. "Maybe we need to talk to the Aspen Falls Police Department and see if there was anything suspicious about Ruben Moreno finding Kat's body."

Gwyn looked at her watch. "I still have a half an hour left of my lunch break. Let's go."

---

*C*har drove the women to the Aspen Falls Police Station, where they all unpiled from the car. Inside, a small waiting room fronted a plexiglass window with a speaker embedded in it.

"May I help you?" asked the man in blue behind the window. He had big bushy black eyebrows, a solemn expression on his face, and a name tag that read *Officer Vargas*.

Gwyn approached the window first. "We'd like to talk to someone about our friend's death."

"Name, please?" he asked.

"Katherine Lynde," she said.

"Not the deceased's name, your name, ma'am," said the police officer.

Gwyn giggled and glanced back at her friends. "Oh. I'm Gwyndolin Prescott."

"Just a moment," he said and switched off the microphone. He dialed a number and spoke into the phone. Seconds later he flipped the microphone and speaker back on. "You can come on back. I'll have you talk to the detective." He pushed a buzzer, and the door to the right unlocked.

Gwyn opened the door and let Hazel, Char, and Phyllis go first. Officer Vargas led the women through the station to a door on the right. He poked his head in. "Gwyndolin Prescott and friends to see you about their friend's death."

The man behind the desk nodded and the women filed in.

Detective Mark Whitman sat behind his desk eating a burger and fries. He was a broad-shouldered man with dark wavy hair and a thick mustache and bore a striking resemblance to Tom Selleck. He wore a khaki-colored blazer over a white button-down shirt and no tie. His top two buttons were undone, and a thick mound of dark, curly chest hair spewed out.

"Good afternoon, Detective Whitman," said Char as she breezed in first.

His mouth was full when he stood up to greet the women. "Char, Phyllis, what are you two doing here?" he asked through his food.

"Detective Whitman, this is Gwyndolin and Hazel Prescott," introduced Phyllis. "We went to college with Gwyn. Hazel is her mother."

Detective Whitman's eyes smiled warmly at the two women. "It's a pleasure," he said. "What brings you in to see me today?"

"We've come to inquire about the death of our friend, Katherine Lynde," said Gwyn, leaning on the seat back of her mother's chair.

He nodded. "Yes, Ms. Lynde. That wasn't that long ago. I remember the case well. What can I help you with?"

Char looked at her friends. She wasn't really sure what kind of information they were looking for, besides wanting to find the spell book. Char felt kind of silly now saying they'd confronted Ruben Moreno at his house.

Phyllis piped up first. "Ruben Moreno found her body, correct?"

Detective Whitman wiped a smudge of mayonnaise from the side of his mouth. "That's correct."

"Was there anything suspicious about him finding her body?"

"Suspicious?" He furrowed his eyebrows and looked at the four women curiously. "What do you mean?"

Phyllis shrugged and leaned back in her seat. "I don't know. Does he seem like an honest guy to you?"

Detective Whitman made a face. "Ruben Moreno has been in the community for a number of years. There's nothing suspicious about him. It's unfortunate he had to discover Ms. Lynde's body like that, but I didn't suspect foul play or anything if that's what you're asking. Her head was on a rock when she was discovered, and the damage to her skull was consistent with that kind of head trauma."

"Was Ruben questioned at all?" asked Gwyn.

"My officers spoke to him regarding his usual route. There really wasn't much else we needed to know from him. Is there a problem?"

Char looked at the girls. "I trust Detective Whitman. I think we can tell him what's going on."

Gwyn nodded, silently giving her the go-ahead.

Char turned back to Detective Whitman. "Kat left us her house and all its contents," began Char. "Years ago, we were given a spell book by our old headmistress. It's been a source of tension between our little group all these years, and now that Kat's gone and she's left us the house, we'd like to find the book."

"But it's missing," said Phyllis, cutting to the chase.

"Missing," he began. "And you're sure that Ms. Lynde had the book before she passed?"

Gwyn leaned her head to the side. "We're fairly sure. Honestly, we can't prove she had the book. We kind of think that perhaps she died after doing a spell in her garden."

A small smile played around Detective Whitman's mouth. "Yes, my officers told me about the cauldron in the center of her garden. I wondered if a spell wasn't involved."

"It's possible she had the book outside with her, and someone took it after her death," explained Char.

He leaned back in his seat and steepled his fingers. "Ahh, now I understand. You're looking for your spell book."

"Obviously we want to know if there's anything else suspicious going on," said Phyllis.

"You think something else suspicious is going on?"

"We went to see Ruben," admitted Char.

"And he seemed shady as an oak tree if you ask us," clucked Phyllis, leaning back in her seat.

Detective Whitman's fingers went to his temples. "You ladies went to see Mr. Moreno?" he asked. It was clear by his expression that that admission surprised him. "To see if he had the book?"

Gwyn nodded.

"And did he have it?"

"No," said Char as she cast a glance towards Hazel, who was sitting quietly with her hands folded in her lap like a proper old woman. "And we have strong reason to believe that he was telling the truth."

"I see. So the problem is…?"

Phyllis put her elbows on Detective Whitman's desk and leaned towards him. "The problem is, he said he had a *relationship* with Kat. He told us!"

"What kind of relationship?"

Phyllis shrugged. "He didn't say. But it seemed strange. Like he didn't want his wife to know."

"But it could have just been a friendly relationship," suggested the detective.

"Well, yes, but it *seemed* like there was more to it," said Phyllis.

"Let me ask you this. Do you think Mr. Moreno had something to do with your friend's death? Is that what this is really about?"

Gwyn sucked in her breath. "Oh no. I don't think we're accusing Ruben of anything like that. He just seemed, I don't know...*off*."

Detective Whitman nodded and sat forward in his seat. "Well. You don't think he took your book. You don't think he killed Ms. Lynde. I'm not really sure how I can help you. It's not illegal to be *off*."

Char sighed. Hearing all their suspicions out loud now, they really did sound silly. She cleared her throat. "Did the police find the book? Maybe they took it into evidence or something?"

He shook his head. "Not that I'm aware of. I'm sorry, ladies. I wish I could help you more."

Char exhaled the breath she'd been holding. "So do we, Detective. So do we."

15

"*Y*ou should put on a sweater, Mom," suggested Gwyn as she combed her hair in their small shared bathroom later that evening. "It's supposed to be cool tonight."

Hazel scowled as she hobbled over to the faded floral armchair under the window in the living room. The chair had become her new favorite, and after only a day or two in the retirement village, she'd quickly laid claim to it.

"I don't understand why you're making me go with you."

Gwyn put down her brush and peered out the doorway at her mother. "You're the one who always wants to have fun. I plan something fun, and now you don't want to go?"

"You act like watching water falling is fun. If I wanted to look at water falling, I'd turn on the faucet," complained Hazel as she tried to lower herself into the chair.

"Oh, Mom. The fresh air and the exercise will do you some good." Gwyn touched a bit of lipstick to her lips as she peered into the mirror. It was the first time she'd caught her reflection in anything all day, and she was horrified by what she saw. When she tilted her head down, the horrible fluorescent lighting in the bathroom magnified the dark rings beneath her eyes. She pulled back the skin just above her eyes, and it lifted the lower half of her face. She silently wished it would just stay like that all day. *Someone should invent clips for your face*, she thought to herself. *Hmm, I'll have to Google that later*. With her thumbs, Gwyn prodded at the flesh at the base of her jaw and pushed it back towards her earlobes. The wrinkles below her mouth and at her chin vanished. Holding her face, she moved it in all directions in the mirror and then sighed. *If only I had the money for a face-lift I could get rid of these darn frown lines. I'd feel so much better about myself.*

She let go of her face and straightened her spine. Who was she fooling? There was no extra money in their budget for her to get a face-lift. Plus, she was an old woman now. She didn't need to look young. She smoothed her hair one last time, then dipped it to assess her roots. The strawberry-blond hair color was enough of a grasp at youthfulness, and the only thing she could afford on their tight budget. Letting her hands fall to her sides, she spun around to face her mother.

"Besides, Mom. I'm not leaving you alone. If you don't think you can walk that far, then I'll push you in a wheelchair. It's only a few blocks."

From her armchair, Hazel pointed her cane at Gwyn and chortled. "Oh no. You're not pushing me in one of those rolling contraptions. Not when I've got two good feet."

She knew her mother would say that. Gwyn had threatened to push her in a wheelchair before. "Good. Then you'll walk." She grabbed her compact and hairbrush off the counter, tossed them in her purse, and flipped off the bathroom light. "Should we go?"

Hazel groaned. "Only because you're making me."

Gwyn tossed her purse onto the kitchen counter and went to the closet. She considered wearing her blue sweater, but then Loni's extreme dislike for blue popped into her consciousness. Even though Loni wasn't going to be attending the festival, she opted for her emerald-green sweater instead. She pulled it out of the closet and tugged it on. "I don't understand why you're being like this, Mom. What would you do if I left you here?"

Hazel looked around uncomfortably. "I don't know. I'd find something."

Gwyn pulled her hair out of the back of her sweater, gave it a little spring, and then pulled another sweater out of the closet for Hazel. "I know exactly what you'd do," she answered for her. She reached a hand down and pulled her mother out of the chair. "You'd start a poker game with some unsuspecting resident."

Hazel poked a finger into her chest. "Who, me?!"

Gwyn wrapped the sweater around her mother's shoulders. "Yes, you. We both know the minute I leave, you'll get into trouble. I can't have you getting into trouble here. I finally got my old friends back. I don't want to have to leave Aspen Falls because you got the two of us into trouble. Isn't it kind of fun to have friends to go do things with now?"

Hazel shrugged. "They're your friends, not mine."

"They're *trying* to be your friends," said Gwyn quietly.

"Are we gonna go or not?" asked Hazel after Gwyn stared at her for several long seconds.

Gwyn walked to the counter, grabbed her purse, and threw it on her shoulder. "Yes. Come on. Let's go."

After Gwyn pulled the door shut behind them and double-checked the lock, the two women took off down the hallway. Just as they rounded the long corridor towards the meeting hall, they ran into a man in an all-black outfit with a white collar. He was tucking a Bible into a black messenger bag slung across his chest. Gwyn had met him the day before, when he'd stopped in to visit the facilities director.

"Oh, Father Donovan. It's nice to see you. What are you doing here this late at night?" asked Gwyn as she stuck her keys in her purse.

He stopped when he heard her voice. "Gwyndolin, Hazel, hello," he said with a pleasant smile. As the two women continued walking, Father Donovan walked with them. "One of the residents is sick. Her family asked that I stop in and pray over her. I just came from her room. The poor thing has pneumonia."

"Oh," said Gwyn, the single word coming out as a

heavy sigh of disappointment. "I hadn't heard we had a sick resident. I'll make it a point to stop in there tomorrow."

"How are the two of you adjusting to life in Aspen Falls?"

Gwyn smiled broadly at him. "We're adjusting well. Everyone's been very friendly."

Hazel wrinkled her nose. "There's not much action," she complained.

He chuckled. "It does seem to be a pretty sleepy town. Not that I would know well enough to say. I'm actually from another parish. Father Bernie is on a retreat. I'm just covering for him for a few more weeks. Where are you two headed this evening?" he asked, looking at his watch.

Gwyn smiled at him. "I'm taking a group of the residents to the Falls Festival for a night walk. Would you like to join us?"

He patted her gently on the shoulder. "Oh, I'd love to, but I've been invited to have supper with one of my parishioners, and I'm already running a little behind."

Gwyn smiled at him pleasantly. "Well, we won't keep you. It was very nice seeing you again."

"You as well," he said before starting down the corridor towards the parking lot. Then he stopped and looked back at them. "Oh, and ladies—be careful out there tonight. I don't know if you know much about the history of Aspen Falls, but it"—his eyes glanced off in both directions—"it's a *paranormal* community—lots of *witches and wizards*. Satanic rituals and cults and things. Very, very dangerous. I hope you'll be extra cautious," he whispered sternly. Then he took in a deep breath and let it out slowly. "This town should really do something about that, but it is what it is."

Gwyn's head reared back, as did Hazel's. She could feel the anger welling up inside of her. She didn't practice satanic rituals! And she most certainly wasn't *dangerous*! What a horrific thing to say about witches! Her mind, though, drew a blank as she tried to think of how to respond to such a hateful thing to say.

He gave both of the women a little wave and began to walk away without realizing how insulting his comments had just been. Hazel held up a finger before hobbling after him at full speed, which was almost as fast as the line at the DMV.

Gwyn had to reel her in. "Hold on, Mother. There's nothing you can do about people like that. They don't know how spiritual witches really are. They don't understand that we commune with nature and our inner spirits. They can't comprehend that good witches don't do black magic and satanic rituals. It's sad, really. But it's attitudes like that that get witches killed."

"You don't have to tell me. Tell that guy!" sputtered Hazel. "How they can call themselves men of the cloth and be that narrow-minded, I'll never understand."

"Me either," said Gwyn sadly. She'd run into far too many narrow-minded people like him over the years, and every time, without fail, she'd faltered on how to react. A bit flustered, she reached into her purse and pulled out her cell phone. "I'm going to call Char and Phyllis and let them know we're ready."

"Are they walking from here with us?"

"Yes, they said they wanted to, and quite honestly I could use the extra help," said Gwyn as they rounded the corner to the meeting hall. No sooner had Gwyn dialed Char's number than they saw Char and Phyllis standing in the lobby with a strange-looking short man and a Chihuahua wearing sneakers. "Oh, they're already here!"

"Who's the short guy?" Hazel muttered out of the side of her mouth.

"I have no idea," Gwyn whispered back. With a broad smile on her face, Gwyn greeted the group energetically. "Hello, girls! Are we all ready?"

"Sure are," said Char. "I hope you don't mind I brought along my hu—my dog." She looked around at the rest of the senior citizens quietly mulling around the meeting hall, waiting for the rest of the group to gather.

Gwyn took in a breath and squatted down in front of the dog. She loved dogs and was excited to meet Char's. She scratched his chin. "I don't mind a bit! What a cute puppy. What's his name?"

"Oh, uh, his name is Vic," stammered Char.

Gwyn stood up and cocked her head to the side. "Isn't that your husband's name?"

Char swallowed hard and nodded her head uncomfortably. "We named the dog after my husband."

Gwyn looked at her curiously but didn't say anything.

Some people named their children after their husbands; perhaps it wasn't entirely weird to name your dog after him, too? "I see. Well, it's nice to meet you, Vic," she said, smiling down at the little dog, who almost seemed to smile back at her. Gwyn pushed the thought aside. *Dogs don't smile.* "Speaking of your husband..." She turned her attention to the short man standing next to the women. He was a peculiar-looking man with an oddly tanned face that shone in the light, giving his skin an almost rubbery appearance. He wore black round glasses, a top hat, dark baggy denim trousers, and a black trenchcoat that swept the ground as he moved. She cleared her throat. "Is this him?"

"Your husband is a George Hamilton impersonator?" asked Hazel, bringing light to the elephant in the room.

Char's eyes widened. "Vic? Oh, heaven's no, this isn't my husband!" She couldn't help but laugh. Her eyes glanced down at the dog and then back up at Gwyn and Hazel. "I decided to leave my husband at home. He wasn't quite feeling up to a walk."

Gwyn lifted her eyebrows. "Oh! Well, then, who do we have here?" she asked, turning her face towards the unusual man.

"Oh," snickered Phyllis. "You don't recognize our old friend, Loni?"

Gwyn's jaw dropped, and her eyes widened as she stared at the small person. "Loni! Is that really you?" she whisper-hissed.

Loni's head bobbed up and down, but she didn't say

anything, lest someone hear her voice and realize she wasn't really a pint-sized weird-looking man.

Hazel threw an arm up in the air. "Well, now I've seen it all!" She looked at her daughter. "These are the people I sent you to college to meet? You couldn't have picked a few *normal witches*?"

Gwyn swatted the air. "Oh, Mother," she breathed with a small chuckle. Then she looked at Char and Phyllis curiously. "How'd you get Loni to come?"

"We got to thinking about it this morning and decided you were right. It's not healthy for Loni to stay all cooped up in her house. So we went over there after you left to go back to work this afternoon," explained Char.

"We promised her we'd make her an amazing costume," added Phyllis.

Char rolled her eyes. "And we had to pick her up in the alley and zigzag through back roads to make sure we weren't being followed."

Gwyn nodded, still stunned. "It is pretty amazing. Is this a plastic mask?" She looked around, and when it seemed no one was looking, she touched Loni's face.

"It's silicone," said Char. "My ex-husband bought it for a Halloween party we hosted years and years ago. Back when George Hamilton was the 'it' guy."

"It's actually really good," said Gwyn with a chuckle. "You look like a man, Lon."

"A strange man," snapped Hazel. "No one's going to buy it."

Phyllis pooh-poohed Hazel's negativity. "No one's

going to notice anything. It's dark outside. She'll just blend into all the activity."

"Don't you mean, *he* will just blend into all the activity?" asked Gwyn with a little giggle.

Phyllis pointed at her. "Exactly. Are we ready?"

"Let me get my group rounded up. Why don't you girls just wait for us outside?"

16

*I*t felt so good to breathe in the fresh, cool evening air and to be surrounded by friends and family that Gwyn practically skipped her senior citizen group all the way to the Falls Festival. She'd hated the fact that her mother had gotten them kicked out of Scottsdale Manor, but it was almost as if fate had done that for a reason now. She felt like she was where she was supposed to be.

Gwyn glanced over her shoulder at Loni and Hazel, who walked side by side, visiting like old friends. To her right, Char chatted with Eliza Emerson, a Village resident, and several steps behind her Phyllis kept Frank Dodson company. Just to see them all together and so happy, a feeling of contentment settled over her. This felt good! She wanted to squeal and tell the girls and her mother how much she loved them all, but she didn't want to lose her composure in front of her residents. She'd tell them later, when they were alone. They all needed to know how much they meant to her. Kat's untimely death and the fact that Gwyn had never gotten a chance to say goodbye hadn't been lost on her. Gwyn was going to make it a point to tell those she loved how important they were to her on a more frequent basis.

Gwyn had felt the low rumble of bass in her body before she'd even stepped foot outside of The Village. Now that they were getting closer, she could make out the distinct sounds of the instruments. The piano and the sax had her wanting to dance. The drums had her snapping her fingers in time with the music. The creamy smooth voice that poured out of the speakers and reverberated off the buildings was simply another instrument, one that blended with the music, but Gwyn couldn't understand the words. As they walked towards the Falls, people from all over parked their cars down side streets, and little by little The Village group was joined by people from everywhere, like a slow-moving flood headed towards the festival.

As they moved closer to the central part of downtown Aspen Falls, Gwyn could hear the Falls, a waterfall in the center of town. The town had been built around the magnificent natural feature, and tonight they'd lit it up with colorful lights and set the band up on the wide bridge that spanned the river that ran through town.

"Oh, it's beautiful!" gushed Gwyn as the group wound their way through the crowd to the waterfall. "It's been so long since I've seen it at night!"

And then like sleigh bells in the sky, giggling could be heard from above. Gwyn looked up to see four broomsticks flying in from the north. Her face lit up. *Oh, to ride a broomstick again!* It had been years since she'd ridden a broomstick. Yes, she was a witch, and Hazel was a witch, but they didn't use their abilities like they had when they were younger. It was almost as if they'd both grown too old for witchcraft and their abilities had weakened with age just like their bodies had.

"Oh, girls, come here, I'd like you to meet some people." Phyllis tugged on Gwyn's arm.

Gwyn swung her eyes back to look at the two handfuls of senior citizens she'd brought to the festival. "Oh, Phil, I really shouldn't leave my group. I don't want us all to get separated."

Phyllis nodded. "Don't move, I'll bring them to you, then," she announced before disappearing into the crowd.

Gwyn turned around to face her residents and discovered several of them had gotten into the groove and started dancing. Even Char was dancing with her dog! The energy in the air was lively and felt contagious, and with Loni keeping Hazel occupied, she felt free and younger than she had in years. A smile crept across her face, and her shoulders relaxed slightly. What a great feeling!

Suddenly, she felt a tap on the shoulder. "Good evening, Gwyn," said a man's voice from behind.

Gwyn spun around to see Sergeant Bradshaw standing behind her. He looked quite dapper in a tweed sports coat over a plaid button-down shirt and a newsboy cap. He flashed her a brilliant smile. "It's so lovely to see you out enjoying the festivities this evening."

Gwyn smiled at him and suddenly felt self-conscious. She'd felt so old when she'd looked in the mirror earlier, and now this incredibly attractive man was smiling ear to ear at her. She tugged at the ends of her hair, wishing she'd had time for a trim.

"Hello, Sergeant Bradshaw. It's so nice to see you. Are you here alone?" she asked, working fiercely to keep it together.

He moved the beverage he carried from one hand to the other hand and pulled up his sleeve, revealing a tattoo on his forearm that Gwyn guessed had come from his days in the military.

"Sort of," he admitted with a smile. "I was persuaded to come by my daughter, Elena." He looked around. "But now she's nowhere to be found. We ran across some old classmates of hers, and she ditched me, I'm afraid. How about you?"

Gwyn tipped her head backwards towards the girls and her residents. "I brought a group of my senior residents on a night walk," she said. "Of course I brought my mother along, and Char and Phyllis decided to join us, too."

He looked back towards the group of people who chatted together in a big group just behind Gwyn. "That was a great idea to bring your group down here. It's such a perfect evening. Isn't the band terrific?"

Gwyn's head bounced on her shoulders in an emphatic nod. "They are *wonderful*. They make me want to dance."

His eyes lit up then. He held a hand out to her. "I love to dance. Would you like to join me?"

A little flutter of excitement bubbled up in Gwyn's chest. It had been *years* since she'd danced with a man. Her girls' father hadn't been one for dancing, and after they'd split up, she'd been too busy mothering them on her own to find a new dance partner. Then she'd moved in with her mother, and there had hardly been a single day when she'd had time for herself, let alone the time to find a man.

Gwyn worked hard not to look overly eager, blinking hard to keep her smile at bay. "Umm, you don't think your wife would mind?" she asked coyly.

His jovial smile broadened even further, if that were possible, and Gwyn thought she caught a bit of a twinkle in his eye. "Gwyn, I wouldn't have asked you to dance if there were a Mrs. Bradshaw in the picture. I'm a one-woman kind of man."

Her heart nearly shot out of her chest after that, and she found herself almost unable to form a complete sentence.

His face sobered a bit. "Though, perhaps there's a Mr. Prescott in the picture I should be concerned about? I just assumed that since you had the same last name as your mother, perhaps—"

"No, no. You were right. There's no Mr. Prescott," said Gwyn, cutting him off. "I'd love to dance with you. Just let me make sure the girls will keep an eye on my mother."

He squeezed her hand. "Hurry back, now. I don't want to miss the rest of this song."

Gwyn turned her back to Sergeant Bradshaw and rejoined her group. Char and her dog, she discovered, had been watching them with keen interest.

"Oh, Gwynnie, you're leaving the sergeant already?" asked Char with a frown. "I thought maybe you were going to dance with him!"

Gwyn smiled shyly as she nodded. "I am going to dance with him," she admitted. "I just wanted to make sure you'll keep an eye on all of my residents for me."

With her dog in her arms, Char smiled from ear to ear. "Absolutely! Now get out there and shake your stuff!"

"You'll keep a close eye on Mom?" Gwyn clarified.

The three of them looked at Hazel, who stood only a few feet away with Loni. Neither of them could hear a single thing that was going on over the music, but together they swayed in time with the beat. Gwyn smiled at the sight of her mother dancing with a mini George Hamilton. It made her want to squeal happily. They were *both* having a fun night.

Char waved a hand at Gwyn. "Haze isn't going anywhere, you go have some fun," she hollered.

Gwyn beamed at her. "Thanks, Char, I owe you one!"

She returned to Sergeant Bradshaw, who took her hand almost immediately. "Shall we?"

Gwyn wanted to giggle out an excited and emphatic *YES!* Instead, she merely nodded her head and let him lead her away from the crowd standing around and into the area where couples were spinning each other around to the old Fats Domino song, "I'm Walking."

On the dance floor, Gwyn and Sergeant Bradshaw barely stopped moving once during the entire song, and she discovered the two of them laughing through most of it. His movements were intuitive and rhythmic. She couldn't believe she was able to keep up with him. When the song ended, Gwyn found herself nearly out of breath. Perhaps he was winded too, but if he was, he kept that to himself.

Gwyn didn't even notice until they were back near the rest of the crowd that Sergeant Bradshaw still kept a tight hold of her hand. He stopped several feet short of their little senior group and turned to face her. The crowd, which seemed to ebb and flow in time to the follow-up song, smashed the two of them together immediately.

With their chests pressed against each other and his mouth just above her ear, he couldn't help but chuckle. "That was fun," he said. The scratchy stubble on his cheek touched her temple when he spoke, and the warmth of his words trickled down Gwyn's exposed neck. Goose bumps crawled across her arms.

She looked up at him and gave him a shy smile. "It *was* fun. I haven't danced in years," she admitted.

"Neither have I." He looked down at her.

With his silvery-blue eyes interlocked on her own blue eyes for several long seconds, Gwyn half-wondered if he felt the same sudden urge to taste her lips as she felt to taste his.

She'd never know, because a second later, Phyllis approached, dragging a young woman along by the arm.

The girl had a thick red braid down one shoulder and wore thick black-rimmed glasses, skinny jeans, and a pair of black Converse sneakers. Several other girls in their early twenties followed closely behind her.

"Gwynnie, I want to introduce you to my grand-daughter!" shouted Phyllis above the music.

17

*P*hyllis shoved the young woman in front of Gwyn and Sergeant Bradshaw. "Gwyn, this is Mercy, Linda's girl. She and her friends go to the Institute."

Gwyn's eyes widened, and as heat tinged her face a crimson red, she once again felt self-conscious. Though Sergeant Bradshaw hadn't kissed her, she still felt awkward, like she'd just been caught with her hand in the cookie jar. Trying to shake it off, she turned from him, hoping the cover of the night hid her flushed cheeks. She smiled at Phyllis's granddaughter. She held her hand out to shake the young woman's hand. "Oh, how lovely! It's nice to meet you, Mercy. I'm Gwyn Prescott. I went to college with your grandmother."

Mercy gave her a tight smile and shook her hand. "It's nice to meet you, Gwyn. Gran hasn't told me much about her days in college." She cast her grandmother a sideways glance.

"Oh, the stories I could tell you about your grand-mother," said Gwyn with a smile. She looked up at Sergeant Bradshaw, who stood less than a half an inch behind her. She could feel the warmth emanating off his body, and it sent a thrill zipping through to every cell in her body. He had a wide smile on his face.

Gwyn cleared her throat. "Oh, I'm sorry. Mercy, this is Sergeant Bradshaw."

Mercy smiled from ear to ear. "Sergeant Bradshaw! How are you? Funny to see you here, too. We just ran into Elena a little while ago."

"Good to see you, too, Mercy. Girls," he said and nodded towards the rest of the girls who stood unintro-duced behind Phyllis. "Yes, Elena ditched me to go hang out with some old friends." Then he looked down at Gwyn and gave her an almost unnoticeable wink. "But I don't mind. I bumped into some friends of my own."

Gwyn felt the air leave her lungs. Was that just a *flirt*? Had Sergeant Bradshaw just *flirted* with her in front of Phyllis and all these young women? She lifted her eyebrows and turned to face Phyllis, who cocked her head sideways. Gwyn could see the lightbulb turning on in her friend's brain. Phyllis had just realized what she'd interrupted.

"I see that," said Mercy with a knowing grin. "How do you two know each other?" She moved her finger in the air, pointing at both Gwyn and Sergeant Bradshaw.

Sergeant Bradshaw looked down at Gwyn again. "We met at coffee a few days ago. She was with your grandmother."

"I see," said Mercy. "My Gran the matchmaker!"

Gwyn wanted to crawl into a hole and die. "You know, Mercy, I could tell you some stories about your grandmother," said Gwyn in an attempt at changing the subject. "She was quite the wild child in those days."

Mercy lifted her eyebrows as she pushed her glasses further up on her nose. "Oh, were you, Gran?" She looked at Gwyn. "Please, do tell!"

Phyllis waved a hand in front of her face, the flesh below her arms wobbling. "Oh, this isn't the time nor the place for that. Mercy, don't be rude. Introduce the girls to Gwyn."

Mercy stepped aside and pulled a small girl with a big black witch's hat, striped purple leggings, and exposed, tightly defined abs in front of her. The girl looked younger than the rest and quite innocent. "This is my roommate, Jax."

The tiny little thing curtseyed in front of Gwyn. Gwyn couldn't recall a time anyone had actually curtseyed at her. She suddenly felt like the Queen of England or something. She put a hand to her mouth to cover up her delight.

"Hello," chirped Jax. "It's so nice to meet one of Gran's friends!"

Mercy's friends called Phyllis Gran also? Gwyn looked at Phyllis curiously but bit her tongue.

"And this is Holly," said Mercy, gesturing towards a voluptuous blonde with a low-cut shirt and a pair of short shorts that barely covered the underside of her bottom.

"Hello," said Holly with a little wave as she flipped a curled wave of hair off of her shoulder.

Gwyn nodded back at her. "It's nice to meet you both."

Mercy pointed at the next girl. She was the tallest of the group. She had short brown hair and a dark, flawless complexion. "This is Alba."

"Hey," she said barely lifting her chin towards Gwyn.

"Hello, Alba."

"And this is Sweets," finished Mercy, pointing to a girl with chubby cheeks and a dimpled smile. "She just took over the bakery."

"The bakery?" asked Gwyn.

"Yeah, Bailey's Bakery & Sweets. She works for Char and Vic," she explained, tilting her head towards the Char and her dog, who were still with the senior group.

"Oh! I see. It's nice to meet you, Sweets, and the rest of you. I'm Gwyn Prescott, and that's my mother over there, sitting on that bench talking to that, uh-hum, *man*," she stuttered. "Her name is Hazel Prescott. We just moved back to Aspen Falls."

"Where did you move here from?" asked Jax.

"Arizona. Scottsdale. It's quite nice moving back to Aspen Falls. I just realized how much I've missed it."

"My grandmother recently moved back too," said Jax.

"Oh, how lovely," said Gwyn, wondering if she'd ever met Jax's grandmother. "What's her—" she began but was cut off by the sound of the band starting up a new song, her voice drowned out by the heavy beat of the bass.

"Jax, we should go," Mercy hollered over the music. "I told Mom we'd stop in and see her. It was nice to meet you, Gwyn. Bye, Gran. Are you coming to the B&B for dinner on Sunday?"

"Yes, I think I will," said Phyllis, giving her granddaughter a prize-winning smile.

Mercy gave her grandmother a quick hug and then dashed off with her girlfriends.

"They're so young and spry," Gwyn hollered to Phyllis over the sound of the music.

"Oh, don't I know it. They're always off doing this spell or that magic and getting themselves twisted up into one mystery or crazy caper or another."

A wistful smile spread across Gwyn's face. "I really miss doing magic. I've let it go over the years."

Phyllis puffed air out her nose. "Ha. I don't miss it at all. I think I'm getting too old for that."

Sergeant Bradshaw chuckled behind them and startled Gwyn. She'd almost forgotten that he was still standing there. "You aren't too old, Phyllis. Hardly."

Gwyn looked uncomfortably back at her group. She'd had a lovely time with the man, but it was time she got back to work. She looked up at him, but before she could speak, he put a finger to her lips.

"I know. You have to get back to work," he said with a brilliant smile. "Thank you for the dance."

Gwyn's heart lightened. "It was exactly what I needed tonight. Thank *you*."

"Phyllis, it was good to see you as always," he said, tipping his head to her.

"You too, Henry," she said with a little chuckle. When he'd gone, Phyllis leaned into Gwyn. "What was that all about?"

Gwyn let out a deep breath. She was too giddy to want to talk about it just yet. Instead of sharing, she just offered her friend a tight smile. "Nothing!" she sang.

"Nothing my fat ass," she said. "That was a whole lotta *something*. I felt the sparks. They were there."

Gwyn wanted to giggle and act like a schoolgirl who'd just gotten her first kiss, but she didn't. She put a straight face on and lifted a brow. "It was nothing, Phyllis. Come on. It looks like Char and her dog made a new friend." Gwyn tilted her head towards the senior group.

The music changed, and the band began to play a softer song, making it a little easier to hear. Gwyn and Phyllis returned to the group to find Char chatting with a man in his mid- to late fifties with exceedingly dark hair and matching eyes.

"Girls, meet Boomer Wallace. I recognized him from the meeting they were having this morning at Habernackle's. It was the Aspen Falls Master Gardeners' Club. Boomer is the president and a friend of Kat's."

Phyllis narrowed her eyes. "He was a friend of Kat's? Funny, I didn't see him at the funeral," she said pointedly.

Gwyn elbowed Phyllis and whispered at her. "I wasn't at the funeral either, but I was a friend of Kat's."

Phyllis ignored Gwyn and stared at Boomer. It was clear she wanted answers.

His mouth smiled, but his eyes did not. "We weren't very close, actually."

"After all those years of putting on gardening shows, and you weren't that close?" asked Char.

"She was a member of a club I belonged to, but we didn't socialize outside of the club. Kat preferred to keep to herself after meetings."

Char grimaced. "Well, you may like to know that Kat spoke very highly of you. She always told me how hard she had to work to keep up with you."

He lifted one dark brow and showed the slightest sign of a smile. "Indeed. I had to work hard in order to keep up with *her*."

"Friendly competition?" asked Gwyn. Something about the man wasn't sitting right with her. Something about his aura was dark and gave her the creeps.

"Something like that," he purred. "Now, if you'll excuse me, I've got to get back to my wife. Have a nice evening."

Phyllis gave him a little fake wave. "Friendly fellow," she said when he'd disappeared.

"Yeah. Something about him rubs me the wrong way," Gwyn retorted, crossing her arms across her chest.

"Ooh, did I miss something good? Who's been rubbing my Gwynnie?" asked Hazel from behind her.

The women turned to see both Hazel and Loni standing behind them.

"We just met an acquaintance of Kat's. He had a bit of a personality disorder if you ask me," explained Phyllis.

Gwyn sighed and looked at Loni. It was nice knowing that Loni had finally gotten out of the house. Gwyn only wished that the woman would feel like taking off the costume. "Having fun, Loni?"

Loni looked around, wide-eyed. "It feels weird being out of the house. I feel like everyone's staring at me."

"That's because you're wearing a George Hamilton mask. You look a little ridiculous," said Phyllis.

Gwyn blanched. "Loni, why don't you just dress normally?"

"And have them find me? No way, Jose!"

"No one's looking for you, Lon. It's all in your imagination," sighed Char.

"That's what you think."

"Loni, Kat wouldn't have liked you having to hide like this. Take off the mask, for Kat," begged Gwyn.

Loni harrumphed. "Kat got me." She poked herself in the chest. "She'd understand."

Char ran a hand over her bare shoulders. "Girls, speaking of Kat, I've meant to talk to you all. I've got her ashes at the house, and we need to do something with them."

Gwyn looked at Char with surprise. "You've got Kat's ashes? She was cremated? I didn't know that."

"It was what she wanted," shrugged Char.

Gwyn felt a lump form in her throat. Hearing that Kat had been cremated was yet another reminder that her dear friend Kat was gone. They'd never see her again. Despite the fact that she'd kept Gwyn and the rest of the girls apart for all of those years, the anger in her heart didn't compare to the love she had for her friend. A cool gust of wind zipped through the crowd and made the skin on Gwyn's arms pebble. "We should do it tonight," she said. Something told her it was the right time.

"Tonight?" whined Hazel. "Gwynnie, it's already getting late."

"It won't take long," said Gwyn firmly. She didn't know why, but something had spoken to her. Something told her that they had to do it after the festival.

They all looked at Loni. Loni shrugged. "I'm already out of the house, might as well."

Phyllis nodded. "Hell, I have nothing else to do. I'm in."

Char glanced down at her dog. It almost looked like he opened his mouth to say something, but then thought better of it and just nodded his head instead. Char looked up at the group. "I'll just drop Vic off at home, and then I'll be over."

Gwyn turned her head slightly. "Did your dog just nod at you?"

Char gave a nervous laugh and then cleared her throat. "He's got a nervous tic."

Gwyn smiled as unshed tears shone in her eyes. "Alright, then, tonight's the night we say our goodbyes to our friend."

18

*C*rickets sang against an inky-black backdrop by the time Gwyn got the residents settled back into The Village. It had been a such a lovely evening, and Gwyn felt good that she'd gotten out and had a little fun in her new town, but she felt strangely ambivalent about the rest of the evening ahead as they pulled into Kat's driveway and parked behind Char's car.

"Why do we have to do this tonight, Gwynnie?" asked Hazel, hefting the car door open with a mighty shove. "I'm pooped."

Gwyn sat in the driver's seat for a long moment as she slowly shook her head. She didn't know how to describe it. It was just a feeling she had. Something was telling her that they needed to put Kat's ashes to rest immediately. She shrugged her shoulders and looked over at her mother, unsure of how to explain it. "I don't know, Mom. I just have this feeling. It has to be tonight."

Hazel stopped moving and looked back at her daughter.

"What?" asked Gwyn even though she knew full well what her mother was doing. She was trying to weasel her way inside Gwyn's mind.

Hazel shook her head and then reached across the car and patted her daughter's hand. "Nothing," she said quietly. "Come on. Let's go."

Gwyn walked around to the other side of the car and helped her mother out. Together they walked up the sidewalk.

The lights in Kat's house were on, and the front door was swung wide open, casting a dull glow across the porch and down the stairs. Gwyn held her mother's elbow as they walked up the white-painted wood steps. She pulled open the screen door and let her mother go in first. The wood door made a sharp smack as it slammed against the wood frame behind them. Gwyn's nose picked up the fresh scent of mango almost immediately. "We're here," she called out as she shut the heavier door behind them.

"Come in. I'm in the kitchen," hollered Phyllis from another room.

The gentle sound of a radio playing a familiar song filled the empty spaces around her. Gwyn wiped her shoes on the mat and followed her nose. "It smells so good in here! What's that smell?"

"Char's daughter-in-law sells those Scentsy bars. She brought in a few warmers the other day and got them going. That rotten chicken smell was just too much for her," explained Phyllis.

Gwyn grabbed the wax container from the counter. "Ooh, Cranberry Mango." She looked at her mother. "Mom, remind me to have Char order us some for our apartment. We could use a good candle. It smells like someone died in there."

"They probably did. I told you it was like a funeral home," snapped Hazel as she pulled a chair out from the kitchen table with the base of her cane.

While she got comfortable at the table, Gwyn looked around the room. "Oh, goodness, is that what I think it is?" she asked, pointing to a brass urn on a doily in the center of the table.

"Yup, that's Kat," said Phyllis matter-of-factly.

Gwyn's face fell as she felt her heart lurch in her chest. It was all that was left of her old friend. She bit her lip to keep from crying. "Poor Kat," she murmured. "You have no idea how much I'll miss you."

"We'll all miss her," agreed Phyllis. "It'll be nice to put her to rest tonight and settle her spirit."

"Where are Char and Loni?"

"They're outside. Char's keeping Loni company."

"Why's Loni outside?"

"She's having a cigar," said Phyllis as she padded around the kitchen. "Did you know she smoked cigars?"

Gwyn pulled a chair out next to her mother. "Yeah, she tried to smoke one the other day when we were over at her house. I didn't think it was such a good idea to have her smoking around Mom."

Hazel pursed her lips. "Don't blame it on me again. You just didn't want to smell the smoke."

"I knew you knew that," said Gwyn with a knowing smile. "You just *let* me blame it on you because you didn't want to smell it either."

Hazel rolled her eyes and pressed her lips between her teeth, but remained silent.

Phyllis opened a cupboard and peered inside. "Char told her she had to take it outside but said she'd keep her company out there."

"Well, why aren't you out there with them?" asked Gwyn, sitting down next to her mother.

"I wanted to make something to eat. That walk worked up an appetite. I'm starving."

Gwyn stood up and rubbed her stomach. "Ooh, does Kat have anything in her fridge? I could eat something too."

"I was just starting to look when you walked in the door," she said.

Together, the two women rummaged through Kat's cupboards in search of snack foods. Phyllis pulled a box of crackers from one cupboard. "She's got Ritz crackers."

"Oh, hand me a roll of those," said Hazel, holding out a hand to Phyllis. "Those French fries at dinner didn't fill me up."

Gwyn looked back at her mother with one eye cocked up. "Well, if you'd eat more than French fries, you might get filled up. Miss Georgia made an amazing Swiss steak for supper. I don't know why you wouldn't just eat it."

Phyllis opened the box and handed Hazel a sleeve of the round crackers.

"That steak smelled funny." Hazel's hands shook as she worked to unwrap the plastic wrapper.

"It didn't smell funny, Mom."

"I think those tomatoes she used had botulism in them."

Gwyn glanced up at Phyllis who shot her a crooked smile. "If they had botulism, I'd be almost dead right now."

Hazel stuffed a Ritz cracker in her mouth. "Would you like real flowers or fake flowers on your grave?" she asked through a mouthful of crackers. Crumbs trickled down the front of her shirt and settled into the creases.

"Mom, there was no botulism poisoning. I'm not going to die. You can't live on French fries and Ritz crackers. And you're making a mess."

Hazel wiped the front of her shirt. "Do you see how she talks to me?"

Phyllis laughed and held up both hands as she squatted to the ground to look in the cupboard under the sink. "I'm staying out of this mother-daughter discord."

Gwyn rummaged through the refrigerator. "She's got some cheese in here. We could do cheese and crackers."

"Oh, man, look what I found," said Phyllis excitedly, holding up a clear glass bottle.

Gwyn squinted her eyes. "I don't have my reading glasses with me. What is that?" She walked closer to Phyllis, who smiled devilishly. "Is that *tequila*?"

Phyllis rushed to the sliding door to the backyard.

"Ladies, hurry up and get in here. I found something you're gonna wanna see."

Char barreled in first. "Did you find the book?" Her tone was anxious and hopeful.

A brief frown flitted across Phyllis's face. "No, but almost as good."

"Where's the fire?" asked Loni as she came inside next. Her arms were spread out wide as she held the door frame. A fat brown cigar dangled from the mouth of her mask.

"You can take that mask off now, Loni," said Gwyn. "No one can see you in here."

Loni shook her head staunchly. She pointed at the sliding glass doors. "Uh-uh. Someone could be spying on us through those," she said gruffly with the cigar still hanging from her lips.

Gwyn plucked the cigar from her mouth, walked over to the doors, put the cigar out in the planter next to the door, and pulled the vertical blinds shut. "There. Now you're safe. Take off the mask. I feel like I'm talking to George Hamilton. It's creepy." She shuddered.

Loni pulled her glasses and top hat off and set them on the counter. Then with both hands, she pulled the mask off. "Oh," she sighed, fanning her face with one hand and searching blindly on the counter for her glasses with the other hand.

"Here, Lon," said Phyllis, handing them to her.

Loni slipped them onto her face and looked up to smile at the women. "That's so much better. It was hot in there. I was starting to wilt away. Do I look all shriveled up now?" she asked, smiling at her friends.

"You looked all shriveled up before you put the mask on," quipped Hazel. "What do you expect? We all look like prunes these days."

Char patted her curly white hair. "Speak for yourself. I eat well, I hydrate often, and I keep up with my fitness. You girls might look like prunes, but I don't."

"I don't either," agreed Gwyn, running a hand through her own shoulder-length hair. She might have some wrinkles, but she certainly didn't look as weathered as Loni and Phyllis.

"Give yourself time," said Hazel, holding up a crooked finger. "Wrinkles are like underwear. They creep up on you when you least expect it. You'll all look like prunes someday. Even you, Gwynnie. A bottle of hair dye isn't going to keep you young forever."

Phyllis held up the bottle of tequila in her hand. "No, but a bottle of this might keep us young for the night. What do you say, girls?"

Char sucked in her breath as she looked at the bottle. "What is that? Is that tequila? Phyllis Habernackle! Where did you get that?"

"In Kat's cupboard. She wanted us to have it," Phyllis said with an ornery smile, hugging the bottle to her chest. "It was a gift from beyond."

19

*L*oni shoved Phyllis aside and walked into the kitchen. "Make mine a double," she croaked while opening Kat's other cupboards. "I wonder if she has any limes. I can't drink tequila without a lime."

"I'll find the salt!" Phyllis excitedly put the bottle on the counter and began to look for the salt.

"We're not drinking tequila," said Gwyn firmly. "Tonight is supposed to be about putting our friend to rest. Not getting wasted like a bunch of college girls."

Phyllis pulled several glasses from the cupboard she was searching and let it slam shut before staring at Gwyn. "Tonight is about celebrating Kat's *life*. On the way here, we stopped by Char's place to drop off her hu—" She glanced up at Char and then cleared her throat. "*Her dog*. We grabbed an old photo album Char hung onto for all these years. It's over there." She pointed towards the parlor. "Why don't you grab that, and I'll make us some drinks?"

"I found some lemon juice in the fridge. I'm good with lemon juice. How about you girls?" asked Loni, popping her head out from around the fridge door.

Phyllis gave her a broad smile. "Perfect."

"I'll have mine on the rocks," said Hazel from the table. "Bring that cheese over here too. I'll cut it up. We shouldn't drink on empty stomachs."

"Here, give this to Haze," said Phyllis, passing Char the cheese. Then she pointed to a drawer at the end of the counter. "Knives are in that drawer."

Char shook her head. "I can't believe we're seriously doing this."

"Mother, you are *not* drinking tequila. Girls, are you off your rockers? We're too old to drink straight-up tequila. We'll die of alcohol poisoning!"

"You're already going to die of botulism poisoning. Wouldn't you rather be drunk when you kicked the bucket?" asked Hazel with a little chuckle.

"Oh my gosh, Mom. Those tomatoes did not have botulism. You can't *smell* botulism. Would you stop?" She pointed a finger at Phyllis. "I'm going to go get the photo album. *Do not* give my mother any tequila," she added, shooting Phyllis a stern look.

Phyllis held up two hands as if to say, "Say no more," but the minute Gwyn turned her back, Phyllis ran a tumbler with ice and two fingers of alcohol over to Hazel.

Hazel waved a hand in the air at Phyllis before she walked away. "I can't drink this without salt."

Loni held the salt shaker up. "Here. I found it."

Gwyn came back in the room to find her mother licking the soft, fleshy part of her fist. "Mother! Don't you dare!"

"Over the lips, over the gums," said Hazel, grabbing the tumbler and rushing it to her lips. She made a little squeal as it went down the hatch.

"Mother!"

Loni handed her a shot of lemon juice she'd poured. "Here, chase it with a little of this."

Hazel nodded and swallowed a bit of the juice. "Whew!" she bellowed, stomping her cane down on the ground several times as the alcohol settled inside her belly.

"I can't believe you girls. You're trying to get my mother drunk! What is wrong with you?"

"What is wrong with you, Gwyn? Your mother is old; she's not fragile. There's nothing wrong with her having a few drinks," bellowed Phyllis.

Loni squinted her eyes at Gwyn. "Yeah, what happened to my old roommate? She was a reckless, wild child. A free spirit. A blazing saddle. You aren't any of those things! Makes me wonder if you're really Gwyn Prescott." She stared at Gwyn for a moment, leaning her head sideways. "Are you wearing a wire?" she asked, reaching out to pat down the front of Gwyn's shirt.

Gwyn hugged her arms to her chest to keep Loni's hands off of her breasts. "Do you mind, Loni?!"

Loni pointed a finger at her as she stood her ground. "Don't make me rip that shirt open!"

"Ooh, old witches gone wild," cracked Hazel. "Someone record this. We'll make a mint on the interweb."

"I'm not wearing a wire!" cried Gwyn, holding her blouse together with her hands. She lowered her eyebrows at Loni. "And if you touch my shirt, I'll scream."

Hazel threw her arms up. "Houston, we have a screamer! Phil, pour me another one. Make it three fingers this time. I'm not driving."

With her shirt still bunched up around her neck, Gwyn frowned at her mother. "You are not having another one. Phyllis, do not make my mother any more drinks."

"You *are* wearing a wire!" insisted Loni. "The Gwyn I knew wasn't this uptight!"

"The Gwyn you knew wasn't taking care of her elderly and extremely insolent mother!" she spat back.

Loni's mouth crooked up on one side. "How do I know you're the real Gwyn and not some imposter sent here to infiltrate my defenses?"

Gwyn spun around, out of Loni's reach. She grabbed the photo album she'd just set down and paged it open to a picture of her and Loni. "This is you and I. See?" She pointed at her face and then at the picture. "That's me."

Loni stared at Gwyn's face and around her ears and neck. "It could be a mask."

"Oh, lay off, Loni. It's Gwyn," said Char, rolling her eyes.

"How do I know you're actually Charlotte Adams?

You could've all been sent here for me," said Loni, slowly backing towards the sliding glass doors.

"Because you know me?" asked Char.

"I haven't seen Char Adams in years. You don't even look like Char anymore." Inch by inch, Loni's arms wrapped around towards her back.

"Oh, for Pete's sake, Loni. I got old. We all got old. You don't look like you used to look either."

"That's what the FBI would say, too." And then in a flash, Loni produced a small black handgun. With trembling hands, she aimed it at the women. "Don't move! I'm on to you!"

With wide, astonished eyes, Char, Phyllis, and Gwyn all held their hands up.

"Oh hell, Loni. Are you off your meds? It's the real Gwyn," said Hazel from the table. "Put the gun away. You'll kill someone with that thing."

Loni shook her head as her other hand rose to connect with the handle of the gun too. "Like I should believe you? You were the one that told me the other day that she kidnapped you."

Hazel rolled her eyes and slammed her hands down on the table. "Oh, for the love of Walter Matthau. When they were handing out brains, did you think they said trains and miss yours? You're crazier than the crazies in the mental ward, you crazy loon."

"Mother, you're not helping any," hissed Gwyn with her hands still up. "Loni, what my mother is trying to say is that she was *joking* when she said that the other day."

"I don't believe you!" hollered Loni.

Phyllis moved a filled shot glass to the other counter and slid it towards Loni. "Take a drink, Lon. Just to take the edge off. You're wound up tighter than Kim Kardashian's underwear."

Loni eyed the drink suspiciously but lifted it to her lips and slammed it, closing her eyes for a split second as she did so. "Oooh!" she yelped as it burned her throat.

The three women staring at her used that tiny moment to unleash a torrent of electrical energy from their palms in her direction. It snaked around her like a glowing neon straitjacket, binding her arms to her body. The handgun clattered to the floor.

"See! I knew you were the bad guys!" hissed Loni, struggling to get her arms out of the stronghold.

"We're not the bad guys, Loni Hodges!" barked Phyllis. Then she held a hand up to the side of her mouth and whispered to the other women, "Does her elevator not go to the top floor anymore?"

"I don't know, but if it does, the doors certainly aren't opening," Char whispered back. She walked towards Loni and bent down to pick up the gun from the floor. "We bound you for your own good, Loni. Why are you so paranoid?"

Loni stopped struggling and lifted her head. "She wasn't acting like the real Gwyn!"

"I *am* the real Gwyn!"

"Prove it!"

"I proved it the first day I saw you again, Loni. Don't you remember?"

Loni was quiet for a moment. She pursed her lips and narrowed her eyes. "Remind me."

"I reminded you that I stayed over at your house during college and we snuck out your bedroom window. We climbed down that tree in the backyard."

Loni's shoulders visibly relaxed. "That tree came down in a storm twenty years ago."

Hazel and Gwyn exchanged a look. Hazel swirled a finger in a circle next to her temple and widened her eyes as her mouth formed a little circle.

"I know," said Gwyn. "You told me. Don't you remember?"

"Of course I remember," snapped Loni. She tried to move her arms, but they were still bound to her sides. "Now take this damned spell off of me."

Gwyn's eyes widened. "You just tried to kill us, Loni."

"I wasn't going to *kill you*."

"How can we believe that?" asked Phyllis.

Loni shrugged and refused to make eye contact with the women.

"Do you believe it's really Gwyn now?"

Loni hung her head. "Yes," she grumbled.

"Loni?" pressed Char.

"I believe it's Gwyn," she mumbled.

Char held up the gun. "I'm not giving this back to you."

"Where'd you get a gun from anyway?" asked Phyllis suspiciously.

"I'd tell you, but then I'd have to kill you," said Loni

with a half-smile. "It's better if some things are left unsaid. Now take this off me."

Gwyn, Char, and Phyllis exchanged a look. Char gave a little nod, and Phyllis sighed. "Fine. But if you so much as point a finger in my direction, I'm gonna make you wish you never left your house."

Loni nodded reluctantly. "I'll be good," she said in a solemn voice with lowered brows.

"Ready, girls?"

The three women held their palms, arms outstretched, towards Loni once again. This time, they slowly pulled their hands backwards. Their magic reversed, unwinding Loni and spinning her in a circle as it did. When the magic was completely released and Loni was done spinning, she shook her head wildly.

"What a trip!" she exclaimed, stumbling around. "A tequila shot and a magic spin. Heavy!"

"Sit down before you fall off the floor," said Phyllis dryly. Then she looked up at the girls in the room. "Well! I think that calls for another round. On the house." She held up the tequila bottle. "Char, you, me and Gwyn are behind by one, so we get doubles." Phyllis filled two shot glasses and slid them towards Char.

"Oh, fine. But I'm only having one." Char took the glass, salted and licked her hand, and downed the small amount of liquid, chasing it quickly with a bit of juice. "Yow!" She wiped her mouth and shook her head. "It's been years since I've had one of those!"

"You're only having one," repeated Phyllis with a chuckle. "Saying you're only having one tequila shot is like saying you're only going to eat one M&M. It's highly unlikely, and really what's the point of that?"

Char shoved the second drink towards Gwyn. "Your turn, blondie."

Gwyn looked at the drink with hesitation and then up at her friends.

"Gwyn, Gwyn, Gwyn," chanted Hazel, pounding her small fists on the table.

Loni joined in next. "Gwyn, Gwyn, Gwyn!"

Phyllis and Char added their voices to the chant next as their tempo increased. "Gwyn! Gwyn! Gwyn!"

Gwyn closed her eyes, wrapped her hand around the cool glass, and brought it to her lips. She blew out a breath and then whispered, "Lord help me."

20

*B*y eleven o' clock that evening, the noise level in Katherine Lynde's house had ratcheted up several decibels. Not only had the music gotten turned up, but the ladies had gotten turned up as well.

Phyllis spun the empty bottle of tequila, which lay sideways on the kitchen table next to the open photo album. Cracker crumbs and bits of cheese littered the floor. Hazel was passed out at the table, facedown with her head cradled in her outstretched arms.

"Too bad we didn't have any good-looking men here to play spin the bottle with," hollered Phyllis over the blaring music.

Loni tipped her head back as she poured her last shot down her throat. She slammed the glass down on the table. "Yee-haw!" she bellowed. "That one went down *smooth*," she slurred.

"Pass me those crackers!" Phyllis's eyes were thin slits of green as she looked at Char across the table. Strands of her grey hair had freed themselves from her bun, and they tufted out wildly around her face. "My belly don' feel so good."

Char slid the last few crackers in the sleeve across the dining room table. "That's all we got left. I'm gonna hafta go to the store t'morrow an' buy Kat some more crackers."

"Kat's dead," shouted Loni. "She don' care if we ate alla her crackers."

"Oh no, I can't steal crackers from my dearly departed friend," cried Char over a new loud song that blared from the speaker in the kitchen. "What is this song?" she bellowed, plugging a finger in one ear. "It sounds like she's bangin' a hammer inside a my head."

"It's the *new music*," shouted Phyllis. "It's what my granddaughter listens to. You don't like it?"

"That girl sounds angry," said Gwyn through narrowed eyes while holding her head. "She's giving me a migraine. Maybe we should listen to something else."

Phyllis leaned back and pointed her finger at the AM/FM radio on the counter. Slowly the dial turned on its own until it hit another station. A slow country ballad drizzled out of the speaker.

Loni closed her eyes and swayed to the steady rhythm with her hands waving in the air. "This sounds like a love song," she said dreamily. "Who wants to slow dance with me?"

"Keep going," said Char spinning a finger in the air. "I'm not dancing with her. And that song'll put me to sleep in two shakes."

Phyllis magically turned the dial until it hit a golden oldies station and the sound of the Del-Vikings' "Come Go with Me" poured out of the speaker.

Gwyn hopped up and started swaying her hips and snapping her fingers in time with the music. "Oh, girls! Do you remember this song! It was playing the night we had that mixer with the boys from the wizards school! Dom-dom-dom-dom-dom dom-de-doo-be ..." she sang excitedly. "I can picture it like it was yesterday!"

Loni hopped up next to her and began clapping her knees together and fist pumping the air. "I remember! I was dancing with Avner Kleinfelder when this song came on!" Suddenly she stopped moving and put a hand to her chin. "Gosh, I haven't thought about Avner Kleinfelder in years. I had a huge crush on that boy. I wonder whatever happened to him."

Char leaned back in her chair. "Dead."

"No, he is not," said Loni, lifting her heavily sketched on brows.

Char nodded. "No, he is. A gal I go to bingo with told me. Her ex-sister-in-law or ex-brother-in-law or some in-law or another married him." She thought about it, but her head was too scrambled from the alcohol to make much sense of her memory. She waved a hand in the air. "Anyway, it was her third marriage. His second. He died about eight years ago."

Loni put a hand to her heart. "Well, hell's bells. I can't believe it."

Char crossed her arms. "The man died of diarrhea, if you can believe that."

"Oh, now you're fooling," said Loni with a snort.

"No, that's what she told me. He got ahold of some kind of parasite. They think through the water. He got so dehydrated that he ended up biting the big one."

"What a way to go," clucked Phyllis as she stood up to go into the kitchen. "I hope they didn't put that in his obituary. Died of diarrhea. Can you imagine? You'd be glad you were dead."

"Come on and dance with me!" sang Gwyn, who had danced her way to the other side of the room. "Whoa oh-oh-ohhh…"

In a jerk, Hazel lifted her head off the table. A line of drool stretched from her chin down to the puddle she'd left on the Formica table. She looked around dazedly. "Who lit her candle?" she asked, thumbing the air.

"Haze! You're awake. Welcome back to the land of the living," said Char, rubbing her arm.

Hazel felt her chin with the tips of her fingers. She took a tissue from the table and wiped off the slobber. "What happened?"

"You passed out cold after the second shot. You're a lightweight," said Loni as she joined Gwyn on the dance floor.

"What the hell happened to Gwynnie while I was out? Did hell freeze over? Have pigs learned to fly?" she asked, pretending to look out the drawn shades.

"No, Hazel. Gwyn had five shots of tequila, that's what happened. She's feeling no pain right now," said Phyllis. "You missed it. She let Loni check her top for wires."

"Did you get it on tape?" asked Hazel. "I can't believe you didn't wake me."

"They're kidding, Mom," said Gwyn with a giggle. "I've been a perfect angel. You'd be proud of me."

"Hell, Gwynnie, I'd be more proud of you if you'd have let Loni strip-search you."

"Come dance, Mom," said Gwyn, ignoring her remark.

Hazel turned her head away from Gwyn. "And throw my hip out again? I'll pass."

"You threw it out doing the limbo. You won't throw it out shaking your moneymaker," she argued. "Come on. I love this song! Come on, Char, let's go, Phil!"

"I'm not too old to cut a rug." Char got up and lifted her arms as she spun around Gwyn and Loni. "Let's see if you two can keep up."

Phyllis joined next. Hazel sat quietly, watching the four younger women dance around like teenagers in the kitchen.

"Come on, Haze," shouted Char. "It's good for your heart!"

"I'm not worried about my heart. I'm worried about my hip. I can't throw it out now. I just met a new man at The Village. I gotta keep my business in working order in case he gets frisky."

"Mom!" breathed Gwyn. "Who did you meet?"

"You just mind your own business, and I'll mind mine," snapped Hazel. "I don't have to tell you every-thing. You don't know my life."

"I do know your life, but I feel too happy right

now to let your bad attitude bring me down, Mom."
Gwyn danced with her friends until a different song
came on the radio. When it did, the four women
laughed the way that old college friends should.
Gwyn felt light and free and more than a little
buzzed.

"Oh, that was fun," she remarked as she fell into the
chair next to her mother. She took a napkin off the table
and blotted the perspiration around her forehead. "I miss
those old days, don't you, girls?"

Char sat down next to her. "I do sometimes. When I
see Phil's granddaughter Mercy and all of her friends
running around town, sometimes I wish I was that young
again and got to use my magic more."

"I don't use mine enough either," agreed Phyllis. "It's
almost like I'm rusty. Can our magic get rusty?"

"Absolutely. Anything can get rusty from lack of use,"
said Char.

"Hear that, Gwynnie? You better get that Army
fellow to grease your hoo-ha before it gets rusty and stops
working altogether!"

"Mother! Why do you have to be so perverted?"

Hazel shrugged. "It's fun."

"Well, we're talking about magic! You don't use your
magic anymore, and neither do I."

"I use it," said Hazel, lifting her chin.

"When?"

"I read minds all the time," snapped Hazel
indignantly.

"I'm not talking about reading minds. When is the

last time you conjured anything or made a potion?" asked Gwyn.

"The last time I conjured anything, Jimmy Carter was president. What a mistake that was. Just because a man is a good actor and looks good on the television screen does not mean he should be president."

"Hazel! Are you trying to say you're responsible for putting Ronald Reagan in office?" breathed Char.

Hazel's eyes widened, and she turned her head towards the wall. "I got nothing else to say about that."

Gwyn's eyes widened. "Alright, well, that's exactly what we're talking about! You haven't conjured anything since the eighties. Why not?"

That made Hazel stop and think. "I guess I haven't had a need."

"Me either," agreed Loni. "I haven't had a need for a very long time."

"Char, when's the last time you healed someone with your powers?" asked Gwyn.

"I volunteer at the hospital. I help people all the time!" she retorted.

"You *heal* them?" asked Gwyn.

Char hesitated. "Well, I don't exactly heal them. Vic's a baking potion maker, or at least he was. We make things to bring to the patients. It eases their symptoms."

"You used to heal people when they were sick and injured. Why don't you do it anymore?" asked Phyllis.

"People at the hospital think that witches healing their patients is bunk," explained Char. "I'd be banned for life if they thought that's what I was trying to do. I guess I've gotten used to not pressing the issue. It's exhausting, to be honest."

"How about you, Gwyn?" asked Char.

"Me?" Gwyn pointed at herself. "I'm too busy to think about magic. Between work and taking care of Mom, I barely have time to use the restroom during the day."

"Taking care of me?!" screeched Hazel. "I'm a grown woman. I can take care of myself."

Gwyn's eyes were droopy as she patted Hazel's hand. "Of course you can, Mom."

Hazel widened her eyes. "Don't patronize me, Gwyndolin Prescott. I might be old, but I'm not feeble. I'm perfectly capable of looking after myself. I just let you think you're taking care of me because I want you to feel important."

Gwyn gave her mother a drunken smile. "Alright, whatever you say, Mom."

Hazel pointed at her daughter. "See how she patronizes me? You'd think I was an invalid or something."

"We know you're not," Char assured her with a gentle smile. "So does Gwyn. She just worries about you is all."

"I wish we had Kat's spell book. Wouldn't it be fun to do a big spell together? I haven't done a spell with another witch since we graduated!" said Loni.

"I wish we had the book, too," agreed Char.

"Maybe we could do a spell to find the book?" suggested Gwyn.

The women all looked around the room. No one seemed to know a spell that could produce those results.

Finally, Hazel tipped her head forward. "If Kat were here, we could do a spell on her and force her to tell us what she did with the book."

"Well, obviously we can't do that, she's dead," said Loni.

"Right, she's dead. But she's *here*," said Hazel, nodding towards the urn.

Gwyn sucked in her breath. "Her ashes! Mother! You're a genius!"

Hazel lifted a shoulder. "Not really, I slept my way to the top."

"Girls. What if we used Kat's ashes to do a spell in the garden? We could do a memory spell and figure out what happened to the book!" suggested Gwyn.

"Hot damn, I like it," said Phyllis, swiping her hands together briskly.

"Me too," agreed Loni. "We need to get that book back."

"I'll go gather the ingredients from Kat's casting room upstairs," said Char, standing up.

"I'll go with Char," said Gwyn.

"I'll find candles. I saw some the other day when we were looking for the book," said Phyllis.

Loni hobbled over to the kitchen counter. "I'll put my mask back on."

Everyone looked at Hazel as she stood up next. "I'll warm up the recliner in the living room. Call me when you're ready."

21

*A*s they tiptoed out to Katherine Lynde's garden in the middle of the night, Char held up the urn she carried, leaned over, and whispered, "Don't you think Kat would be upset that we're not scattering her ashes around her roses?"

"We're only doing this because she stole our spell book and then lost it. It's her own damn fault for stealing it from us in the first place! She owes us," Phyllis hissed back, carrying an armload of supplies. "Besides, if she were here, she'd tell us to do this very thing."

Walking in front of them, Gwyn swiveled her torso around. "Don't worry, when we're done with the spell, we'll pour the potion out onto her roses. Maybe it'll make good fertilizer."

"All I know is that when I'm dead, you better not make me into fertilizer," snapped Hazel. "I want to be buried facedown and naked, so anyone who didn't like me can kiss my ass."

"Oh, Hazel, you're terrible," hissed Char as she maneuvered through the flower garden to the very center, where an empty cauldron waited to be used.

"Point that flashlight over here, Loni," hollered Phyllis.

"Are you crazy, Phyllis Habernackle?! Take my name outta your mouth! Someone might hear you!"

"It's midnight, Loni. Who's outside at this hour?"

"You can never be too sure," Loni hissed back. "Call me George."

"I'm not going to call you George," said Phyllis.

"Okay, fine. Just don't say my name, then!"

"Oh my gosh, Loni, you're being ridiculous," said Char.

"You can't say my name either!" railed Loni into the darkness. "What is it with you people? Can't you respect my right to privacy?"

"We're skulking around Kat's fenced-in backyard, in the dark, at midnight. What's more private than this?" asked Phyllis.

Gwyn sighed. "Girls, can we please do this spell? I need to get Mom home. I have to work in the morning. I'm going to be exhausted."

"And hungover," quipped Loni.

"Okay, well, we need water," said Gwyn, pouring the two ice cream buckets she carried into the cauldron.

Loni held up the two buckets she carried and then poured each one into the cauldron too.

"Sprinkle those frog warts in there," Gwyn instructed Char. "Phyllis, did you find the candles?"

"Yes, I have them," said Phyllis, looking around the area for a place to put them. "I'll get them set up while you four get the water boiling."

Without a word, Gwyn spun a bright ball of glowing orange electrical energy in her hands. She worked it up into a frenzy by rolling her hands as if she were rolling a ball of dough between her palms.

"Wait, Gwyn, let me put down some kindling first. That grass is too wet," said Char, rushing to a small pile of firewood that Kat must have brought out for her own spell. She put several split logs beneath the hanging cauldron and then stepped back.

Gwyn sucked in a deep breath and threw the fireball at the base of the cauldron, and the pile of wood burst into flames.

"You've still got it!" cheered Loni.

Gwyn blew on her fingertips and rubbed them on her shoulder. "Nice to know!" she said with a smile. "Go ahead, girls, finish adding the ingredients."

"Two cloves of amethyst root," said Char as she dropped the woody tendrils into the water. "A pinch of spiderweb silk. Two shakes of nightshade pollen, a scoop of elephant memory dust, and four dried blueberries for color."

"And most importantly," added Phyllis as she lifted the lid off of Kat's urn, "Katherine's ashes."

Gwyn looked down into the pot. "Goodbye, Kat."

"I'll say my goodbyes when her memories show us what happened to the book. Are we ready?" asked Phyllis. "The water is boiling, and my bunions are burning."

"I think we are," said Char. "Okay, everyone. Stand back. Circle the pot."

The five women moved slowly around the cauldron. Gwyn took hold of her mother's hand and then turned to take Phyllis's. Phyllis took Gwyn's and Char's hands. Char took Loni's hand, and Loni took Hazel's hand.

"I sure hope this works," said Gwyn. The flesh on her arms pebbled as they began to chant in unison.

> *We call to the North that time be reversed.*
> *We call to the South that history be repeated.*
> *We call to the East that memories be unearthed.*
> *We call to the West that truths be revealed.*

An electric blue steam bubbled up from the cauldron and surrounded the women, clouding their vision and camouflaging their bodies. In turn, they each looked up to the sky and slowly released each other's hands. In a gentle scooping motion, they pulled the steam to their faces, inhaled the mist and let it cover them completely.

> *In this misty haze of truth*
> *Clear away the cobwebs from our third eye*
> *Show the memories of Katherine Lynde*
> *On the night she died.*
> *Show us what she saw and heard*
> *Give us the truth that we deserve.*

"It's working!" cheered Gwyn as the fog began to lift. "Again, girls, again!"

In this misty haze of truth
Clear away the cobwebs from our third eye,
Show the memories of Katherine Lynde
On the night she died.
Show us what she saw and heard,
Give us the truth that we deserve.

The mist lifted higher into the air and slowly swirled into a cloud. And just as clouds begin to form shapes in the sky, so did the mist begin to form a scene.

"Oh my gosh," whispered Gwyn with a hand to her mouth. "It's Kat!"

"Kat!" breathed Char.

Lines and shadows formed in the scene, making Kat's face more clearly defined, and showed her standing in front of the very cauldron they stood in front of now. With her arms held out wide to either side, she stood with her eyes closed as she chanted to the heavens. A spell book was in front of her.

"The book!" exclaimed Phyllis as wind picked up around her, blowing tendrils of her hair up around her shoulders. "She had the book that night! I knew it!"

The cloudy outline of Kat slowly lowered her arms. Thunder and lightning bellowed in the sky above them. Kat closed up the book, tucked it under her arm and headed towards the house.

"She's leaving!" shouted Phyllis. "She's got the book."

"Wait. Did you just see something move over there?" asked Gwyn, pointing to a dark, shadowy cloud in the lower corner that seemed to be moving towards Kat.

"I didn't see anything," said Loni, squinting her eyes.

"Me either," agreed Char.

"There!" Gwyn pointed at the dark shadow as Kat turned around.

"Oh my God," breathed Char, staring as the cloaked figure reared back with a shovel.

"He's going to hit her!" screamed Gwyn, her heart racing in her chest.

"Zap him, Kat, zap him!" hollered Char with hands on either side of her cheeks.

"She dropped the book!" breathed Phyllis. "She's gonna get him!"

"Oh my God," they all breathed in unison as they watched their friend take a hit to the head with a shovel and immediately crumple to the ground.

"Kat!" screamed Char. "No!"

Tears sprung up into Gwyn's eyes, and she felt the immediate urge to vomit. "Kat!" she whispered, reaching a hand out to touch her friend's face in the cloud.

Phyllis pointed at the cloudy mist. "Look, he bent over to pick up the book!" And then, as if someone had flicked off the television set, the cloud went black. "No! Keep showing us! We need to see his face!"

"It's too late. She's gone. It only shows us her memories," whispered Loni. "I can't believe this. Kat was murdered!"

"We have to do something," said Char. "We have to tell the police."

"It's after midnight. We can't go now. We'll go in the morning," said Phyllis.

"What are the police going to do?" asked Hazel. "You saw her killed in a magical cloud and the body's been cremated. You have no proof."

"We can tell them what we saw!" breathed Gwyn.

Hazel let out a puff of air. "You can tell them, but what evidence do you have?"

"We don't," said Char sadly.

"Exactly," said Hazel. "You need to go to them with some hard evidence. Maybe then they'll take you seriously."

The girls looked around. "Where are we supposed to find any evidence? The man came out of nowhere!" said Gwyn in shock. Her heart was still pounding in her ears, and her hands shook after seeing one of her dearest friends murdered in front of them.

"Well, we know one thing. He took our book. Find the book, find the murderer," said Phyllis. "And when I find that man, he's not going to know what hit him!"

"We're going to find him and turn him over to the police," said Gwyn. "He deserves to spend the rest of his days rotting in a jail cell for what he did. Death is too good for him!"

"I agree with Gwyn," said Char.

"Not me," said Loni, rubbing her hands together. "I think we should teach him a lesson. You don't mess with a witch in our coven!"

"Settle down, Loni. First, we have to find him," said Phyllis. "I only wish I knew where to start looking."

"We'll figure it out in the morning," Char assured her. "Come on, girls. We need to get home and get some rest, so we have our wits about us tomorrow. We're going to need all the sleep we can get."

"I'm not sure I'll be able to sleep tonight," whispered Gwyn. "Not after seeing that!"

Loni rubbed her head. "Me either."

"And what are we going to do about this?" asked Gwyn, pointing to the cauldron. "Kat's ashes are in there! We haven't spread them around her garden like we said we were going to."

Char frowned. "Can we truly put her to rest now?"

Phyllis looked down into the pot. "We let the water evaporate out. Once we've figured out who did this to her, then we'll put her to rest."

The girls all exchanged glances before Gwyn finally nodded after swallowing back the lump in her throat. "We have to get him, girls. For Kat."

22

The next morning after Char pulled on her favorite pink visor, she slipped on the darkest pair of sunglasses she owned and headed for the front door. Her head throbbed as it hadn't in years. If things had been different, she'd have called Phyllis and Gwyn and canceled coffee that morning, but things weren't different, and they now had a murder to solve.

Char glanced down at Vic, who had just hopped down off the sofa. "I can't believe you want to go to Linda's for coffee with me. You never want to go with me to have coffee with the girls." She held the door open for him, and he trotted outside, his spry little tail curled high in the air.

"There's usually not a murderer running around Aspen Falls," he said, following Char down the front steps. "I have to keep my little love muffin out of harm's way!"

Char stopped walking and shot her husband a wry smile. "What are you going to do if a murderer comes after me, Vic? Growl at him?"

"Trust me, sugar buns. In our wedding vows, I promised to love and care for you, and I'm not going to let the little fact that I've been turned into a dog stop me from holding up my end of my vows."

"Suit yourself, but I promise I can take care of myself. Besides, I'll be with the girls."

"No, *we'll* be with the girls," said Vic, panting happily as he bounced next to his wife.

Minutes later they were outside Habernackle's with Phyllis in tow.

"Oh, my head is pounding," said Phyllis behind her own dark glasses. She reached a hand out to steady herself on a lamppost and rubbed her temples. "I feel like I got scraped off the bottom of a shoe."

"I know what you mean," agreed Char. "The sun hurts my head just by being in the sky. Uh, that's the last time I'm drinking cheap tequila with you four."

"You're absolutely right. Next time we'll drink vodka. Much easier on the stomach. Or we'll all pitch in and spring for the good tequila. Kat always was a cheapskate."

"My poor little apple bottom, how about you take me over to the bakery, and I'll have Sweets whip you both up a special loaf of my Cure What Ails Ya Bread."

Char leaned down and scratched beneath Vic's chin. "That's so sweet of you, darling, but we'll survive. I just need to get some black coffee in me. That should start to fix the problem."

Just before they went inside, Gwyn's silver Buick pulled into a parking spot across the street.

"Oh, Gwyn and Hazel are here," said Char. "Should we wait for them?"

Phyllis looked down at Vic and cocked an eyebrow up. "You haven't told them about Vic yet. Why not?" she asked.

Char shrugged and then let out a heavy sigh. Her head hurt much too badly to get into it now. "I just haven't had the time, to be honest."

"No time like the present. I've almost slipped up more than once during the last few days. I'm tired of having to mind my p's and q's around them."

"Yes, I know. There have been a few awkward moments," agreed Char. She looked down at Vic. "Mind if I tell them, sweetheart?"

Vic sat down on his bottom. "No. I think your friends deserve to know the truth."

"Alright, if you two think so," she said, looking at the women crossing the street.

"Well, look at what the cat dragged in," shouted Phyllis.

Gwyn held her head with one hand and her mother's arm with the other hand. "Do you have to yell, Phyllis Habernackle? My head is throbbing so bad I can feel it in my toes."

"How are you feeling this morning, Hazel?" asked Char, grabbing her other elbow.

"Huh?" the older woman hollered back.

"Her head hurts so bad she put cotton in her ears," explained Gwyn. "She was complaining that I was breathing too loud, so I handed her the bag of cotton balls and told her there was nothing I could do about breathing."

"Oh, I know the feeling," said Phyllis. "We're all hurting. We decided next time we're drinking vodka."

"Oh, there's not going to be a next time. That was so irresponsible of us," clucked Gwyn. She headed towards the front door to Habernackle's and nearly tripped over Vic, who was sitting quietly on the sidewalk. "Oh! Char, you brought your dog to coffee? Are you going to tie him to the lamppost? I would assume that they don't allow dogs inside?"

Char held a hand against the door, blocking Gwyn's entrance. "Yes, I brought Vic along. I've brought him many times, as a matter of fact. Linda has her own dog, and she's never minded that I brought mine. Listen, uh, Gwyn. I need to tell you something about Vic."

Gwyn straightened her sunglasses and looked at Char curiously with one hand over her eyes as if it were a visor. "I wasn't going to say anything," said Gwyn in a bit of a hushed whisper, "but since you've brought it up, don't you think it's a little *odd* that you named your dog after your husband? What does your husband think about that? Surely he doesn't care for that?"

Char nodded as a small smile flitted across her face. "Well, that's sort of the thing I wanted to tell you."

With her hand still on the door hand, Gwyn slumped forward. "Can't you tell me inside? This sun is doing nothing for the throbbing in my skull."

"It'll just take a moment, and I don't exactly want everyone inside Habernackle's to hear this. It's sort of my little secret."

That interested Gwyn. She lowered her other hand from the door handle. "What is it?"

Char looked down at Vic with a soft smile. "My dog," she began slowly, "is...well, my dog is... oh, goodness. There's really no good way to say this, but my dog is my husband," she finally said. The words made her feel foolish to say out loud, but it was the truth.

"Your dog is your husband?" Gwyn looked at Phyllis. "Is this a joke? Why are you joking like this right now? Kat was murdered. We're all hungover. I can barely keep my eyes open I'm so exhausted, and you want to joke?" Gwyn put her hand on the door handle again.

Phyllis touched her arm. "She's being serious, Gwyn. That's Vic Bailey."

Gwyn looked down at the dog on the sidewalk. "You married your dog? I'm sure there's got to be a law against that ... cruelty to animals or something..."

Char put a hand on her hip. "I'm not cruel to him, for crying out loud, and he wasn't a dog when I married him."

"He wasn't a dog when you married him? What was he? A cat?! A hamster?! Oh, for heaven's sake, please don't tell me you married your hamster," asked Gwyn, horrified. "Here I thought Loni was the crazy one of the group!"

"No, he wasn't a hamster," shot back Char.

Phyllis chuckled. "A hamster, good one, Gwyn. That's funny. A hamster…"

"I'm being serious. What was he when you married him?"

"He was a man," barked Char. "Goodness' sakes. He was a man, and he was the victim of a spell gone bad. A couple spells, actually. It's a long story, really."

"You mean this *dog* is *actually* your husband?" asked Gwyn, wide-eyed behind her dark shades.

Char nodded. "*Yes*. It's *actually Vic*."

"Does he talk?" she asked, touching the dog with the tip of her toe.

Char swatted at Gwyn's shoulder. "Well, don't kick him for crying out loud. He's my husband!"

"To answer your question, my dear, yes, I do talk," said Vic quite clearly.

"Ahh," shouted Gwyn, throwing her arms up to cover her mouth and heart. "He talks!" She held her head. "Ow, and that hurt."

Hazel flinched at Gwyn's scream. She looked up and backwards at her daughter curiously.

"Shhhh," hissed Phyllis.

"Keep your voice down. We haven't told many people about Vic's—er—condition," hissed Char.

"You call this a condition? It isn't a rash, Char!" said Gwyn.

Char lifted a shoulder as if to say, "Eh." "You could

look at it like it's a rash. But instead of his body being covered with red, scaly patches, it's covered with fur."

"Ha-ha, very funny," said Gwyn. "I can't believe this. Have you tried to reverse the spell?"

"Well, if I reverse the spell, he becomes a ghost. And we decided we'd rather have him be a dog than a ghost. At least I can see and hear him this way."

Hazel pulled the cotton out of one of her ears. "What are we doing sitting out here looking at that scrawny dog? I need a cup of joe. And get that poor fella some bacon, he's nothing but skin and bones," she said, nodding towards Vic. Without another word, she shuffled towards the restaurant door and opened it. "What are you waiting for?"

A split second later, the door burst open and Benny Hamilton lurched out. He nearly bowled Hazel over as he ran out of the restaurant.

Hazel shook her cane at the man as Gwyn rushed to her side to catch her before she fell backwards. "Watch it, Buster!" Hazel hollered.

Gwyn's brow furrowed as she looked up at Benny. She wrinkled her nose at him. "Hey, watch it. That's my mother!"

"You watch it, witches," hollered Benny as he ran up the street towards downtown Aspen Falls.

"Where's the fire?" Char shouted after him, but he was already around the corner.

"People have no manners these days," snapped Gwyn as she dusted Hazel's dress off with her hands. "Are you alright, Mom?"

Hazel swatted her hands away. "Get your hands off me," she snapped. "That fella better watch his step. Next time he knocks me over like that I'm gonna get my step stool and punch him in the chin."

Phyllis rubbed her shoulder. "You won't have to go to the trouble. Next time that man lays a hand on you, I'm gonna sock him where it counts!"

The women went inside and found Sergeant Bradshaw and his buddies having coffee at their usual booth.

Phyllis stopped at the table. "Where was Benny off to in such an almighty hurry?"

Gwyn pushed her sunglasses up on top of her head and into her hair. "He almost knocked my mother over," she added with her eyebrows knitted together.

"He got a big scoop on a developing story down by the Falls," said Marcus Wheedlan.

Sergeant Bradshaw stood up. "Benny pushed your mother?" he asked with a concern-filled voice. He bent over to peer down at Hazel. "Mrs. Prescott, are you alright?"

Hazel's face was red. "What?" she asked, looking up at him.

"Are you alright?" he repeated.

Hazel blinked up at him blankly, causing Gwyn to pull the cotton from her ears. "He asked if you're alright?"

"No, I'm not alright. I'm fired up! I want to punch some manners into that man!" snapped Hazel.

Sergeant Bradshaw nodded. "I imagine you do. That was terrible of Benny to be in such a hurry that he'd push you over! I'll have a talk with him."

"Mom, you're shaking," said Gwyn.

Hazel's hands curled into small fists, and she swung them at the air ineffectually. "I just wanna get my hands on that feller."

Sergeant Bradshaw watched her with a kind expression on his face. "She just wants to let her anger out. It's not good to hold all that aggression inside. I tell you what, Mrs. Prescott, why don't you hit me in the stomach? It'll make you feel better." He stood up straight and flexed his abdominal muscles.

"Oh no, Sergeant, please don't ask her to do that. My mother would actually take you up on that offer," said Gwyn as her face began to flush with embarrassment.

Sergeant Bradshaw smiled. "Please, Gwyn, call me Henry," he said, tipping his head towards her.

Char sucked her in her breath. "Sergeant Bradshaw, I've known you for almost thirty-five years and you've never asked *me* to call you Henry. I don't even know that I knew that was your first name!"

He smiled at her. "Oh, didn't you? I'm sorry. I assumed everyone in town knew my first name, though almost everyone just calls me Sergeant. You can all refer to me by my first name if you like. I only mention it because your friend here allowed me to call her by a shortened name the other day, as she said her friends do. I was only extending the same courtesy."

"You call me Char. That's a shortened name," said Char with a hand on her meaty hip.

"Oh, is it?" he mused with a finger to his chin. "Indeed. Please, feel free to call me Henry. Although to be completely honest, I'll share a little-known fact. My first name is actually Harrison. My mother nicknamed me Henry when I was a small child because my brothers were starting to call me Harry and she thought that sounded offensive." He smiled at Hazel. "Now, back to my offer. Mrs. Prescott, if you'd like to take that aggression out on me, I'd sure allow it. It'll make you feel better."

Hazel fisted her hands. "I might hurt you," she warned, looking at her fists. "These are powerful weapons."

He chuckled. "Oh dear, you couldn't hurt me. I've got abs as solid as a brick house." He flexed his stomach muscles again, widened his stance, and put his arms behind his back as he watched Hazel gearing up to inflict her best damage.

She licked her lips, then reared her fist back. Then at the last moment, she closed her eyes and let loose. Her hand headed south, and before anyone could stop her, she landed a punch squarely between Sergeant Bradshaw's legs.

"Oooof!" he breathed. His knees buckled together, and his hands dropped to cover his sensitive area.

Gwyn's eyes opened wider. "Mother!" she screamed. "You hit him in the…"

"I think you just ruined any chance he had of becoming a father again," said Phyllis with a little laugh.

"Harrison, are you alright?" asked Gwyn, her arm around his shoulder as he crumpled lower. "I'm so, so sorry!"

Sergeant Bradshaw tried to wave to her as he couldn't

yet form words. "It's okay," he breathed between clenched teeth.

"Mother!"

"What? I closed my eyes. He told me to hit him," she said matter-of-factly, patting the man on the shoulder. "You were right. I do feel better."

23

*G*wyn's heart thumped erratically in her chest as she stared down at Sergeant Harrison Bradshaw's nearly purple face. She felt horrible that her mother had punched the poor man at all, let alone in his nether regions.

"Phyllis, take Mom to get some food. Her blood sugar's got to be low after that adrenaline spike with Benny."

Phyllis nodded and took Hazel by the elbow. "Sure thing. Want me to order you something?"

"Coffee and a roll, please," said Gwyn curtly. "And don't forget, Mom gets French fries today." She turned back to Sergeant Bradshaw as Char, Phyllis, Hazel, and Vic left to find a table.

"Oh, Harrison, I'm so sorry!" she cooed, rubbing his back.

He tried to get to his feet but struggled. The men at his table had all howled as they'd watched the scene unfold. Now that the shock had worn off, they all wiped away the tears that had formed due to their fits of laughter.

"Don't worry," said Marcus, holding his stomach. "He's a tough old coot. He'll shake it off."

Harrison nodded his head. "I'll be okay," he puffed out.

"At least let me buy you coffee and a roll," begged Gwyn, pulling her purse up to her hip. How embarrassing! And after the lovely dance they'd shared the night before, too. She was going to have to have a stern talk with her mother.

He touched her hand gently. "No need," he whispered.

Marcus laughed. "The sarge gets free meals and all the coffee he can drink here."

Gwyn's eyes widened as she looked down at the man. "He does? Whatever for?"

"Long story," said Harrison as he got to his feet and began to slowly recover. "I'll be fine. I'm sorry Benny knocked your mother over."

"I'm so sorry my mother punched you!" said Gwyn.

Sergeant Bradshaw turned back towards his friends. "I better let you get back to your mother and your girlfriends," he said, limping back to his seat.

Gwyn's heart sank. He didn't want anything to do with her anymore. *Ugh! Mother!* "Okay," she whispered, her heart in the pit of her stomach. "I'm really sorry."

Gwyn left the table just as Char was approaching them with Vic in her arms. "Hey, fellas," she said, getting all of their attention again. "What was the big scoop that had Benny's britches on fire, anyway?"

Sam Jeffries, the older gentleman who hadn't wanted to make eye contact with Gwyn the day she'd met him, made a face. "A body was found down by the Falls."

"A body?" breathed Gwyn.

Sergeant Bradshaw leaned backwards when he heard Gwyn's voice. "A woman's body," he said more precisely.

"She was dead?" asked Gwyn.

He nodded. "Be careful out there. There could be a killer on the loose. I wouldn't want anyone to hurt you." He looked over at Hazel, who had taken a seat at the bar across the room. "Of course, with your mother's mean uppercut, I don't think anyone is going to hurt any of you."

The women all piled into Gwyn's Buick and took off up the street. Gwyn's tires screeched, and her back end skidded out sideways as she made the turn towards Hemlock Road.

Vic danced across Char's lap and onto Phyllis's. "Can you please take it easy? I don't have the best center of gravity anymore," said Vic.

Gwyn glanced in her rearview mirror. "You should be wearing a seat belt, Vic."

"And just how exactly is he supposed to do that, Gwyn?" asked Char, lifting Vic back onto her lap.

"I don't know, put the lap belt across his legs."

"That's not going to work," said Char, trying to fashion something around her husband's waist.

"I can't believe we couldn't even wait for my French fries to finish cooking," grumped Hazel from the front passenger seat.

Gwyn glanced at her sideways. "I don't want to hear another word about those French fries of yours," she snapped. "Don't you have anything to say for what you did?"

Hazel turned towards her daughter stiffly. "For what I did? What the hell are you talking about, Gwynnie? I didn't get my French fries, that's what I did."

"You punched Sergeant Bradshaw in the…" She gripped the steering wheel tighter. She was so steaming mad, she couldn't even say it.

"In the giblets?" asked Hazel, lifting her brows and widening her eyes.

"Yes, Mother!"

With her eyes still wide, Hazel let an *uh* escape the back of her throat. "He told me to!"

"He told you to punch him in the stomach, Mother, not his… *sensitive region!*"

"Really, Gwyn? His *sensitive region?* They're called balls," said Phyllis plainly. "It's not hard to say. *Balls.*"

"I've always called them meatballs myself," said Char, looking down at Vic as he put a paw to his forehead. "Or marbles."

"Ladies," he sighed, thoroughly embarrassed. "Just call them testicles."

"Testicles?!" screeched Phyllis. "I can't call them testicles. That sounds so… so… *clinical*."

"Sweetheart," said Char, looking down at her husband, "*you* don't even call them testicles."

"Well, what do *you* call them, Vic?" asked Phyllis.

Vic buried his face beneath his paws on the seat.

Char smiled. "I think I've only ever heard Vic refer to them as the family jewels, although there was that one time I'm pretty sure you called them the Gruesome Twosome."

"Love muffin!" cried Vic. "There are *ladies* present!"

"No ladies here," cracked Phyllis. "The Gruesome Twosome, that's cute, Vic. Nice."

"We were on our honeymoon," explained Char as an aside.

"*Girls!*" shouted Gwyn in exasperation. "Why are we even discussing this? The point is, Mom, you shouldn't have punched him at all. That was so embarrassing!"

"I was just testing his fortitude." Hazel shrugged.

"You were testing the fortitude of his balls, that's for sure," agreed Phyllis with a chuckle.

Gwyn turned the steering wheel. "Well, I hate to break it to you, but that little stunt just cost you your three days of breakfast fries."

Hazel sucked in her breath. "Gwynnie! You scoundrel! You wouldn't?"

Gwyn touched a hand to her chest and turned to stare at her mother. "Oh, *I'm* the scoundrel?! Mother! You punched Sergeant Bradshaw in the nuggets!!" she bellowed into the car.

The car went silent for several seconds after that, until finally, Phyllis nodded from the backseat. "Nuggets. I like that one. Good call, Gwynnie."

"Ugh," groaned Gwyn. "Why are we even going up here? The dead woman is back that way!"

Phyllis nodded, crossed her arms across her chest, and leaned back against her seat. "I don't know. She's not going to want to go with us anyway."

"Well, she'll be madder than a wet hen if we don't invite her," chided Char. "And we don't want her pulling a gun on us again anytime soon."

Phyllis threw a flattened palm towards the girls. "Oh no, I put that woman's gun on ice."

"What'd you do with it?" asked Gwyn.

Phyllis smiled. "I just told you. I put it on ice. I hid it in Kat's deep freezer in the garage. She'll never find it out there."

"What are we doing, girls? Kat was murdered. We were supposed to spend our breakfast talking about how to figure out who killed her, and now we're off chasing another murder and talking about man parts," said Gwyn. "I didn't even have time to finish my coffee. I can't think straight."

"Nothing new there," grumbled Hazel without moving her head.

Gwyn looked at her mother sideways. The woman was riding her last nerve. She pulled two cotton balls from the pockets of her cardigan and handed them to Hazel.

"Put these back in your ears, Mother." She steered the car around the corner and pulled to a stop at the curb.

"Who's running in?" asked Phyllis.

"Not me," said Char.

"I'm not going back into that loon's house," snapped Hazel.

"Ugh, looks like it's you and me, Phyllis," said Gwyn.

"If I have to," sighed Phyllis. "We should have just gone over to the Falls without her."

"She'd want to know what happened," said Gwyn as she got out of the car. "Come on. I'm not going alone."

The two women marched up the front steps and were promptly greeted by a swarm of cats on the porch, enjoying a leisurely breakfast of dry cat food and saucers of milk. The cats all looked up at Gwyn and Phyllis as they navigated through the crowd and to the front door.

Gwyn knocked. She could hear Loni moving around inside, but no one opened the door. "Open up, George. It's Gwyn and Phyllis."

No one answered, but the noise inside stopped.

Phyllis pounded on the door. "Open this door right now, Loni Hodges!"

The door opened a crack. "Why are you yelling my name? Someone is bound to hear you," she hissed.

"As if whoever you *think* is watching your house doesn't know who lives here?" asked Gwyn, looking around. "Besides, there's no one out here but your army of cats."

Loni looked down at the cats. "Clifford, Emma, did you two see anything?"

Two cats looked back at the door and meowed. Loni nodded her head. "Okay," she said. She nodded towards the rest of the herd. "Are all of you ready to come back in yet?"

Several cats meowed in response and Loni opened the door wider. "They aren't ready to come back in, but you two are cleared for entrance."

Gwyn sighed and took a step forward. She was greeted by Loni's palm in her face. "You're not wearing a wire or anything, are you?"

"Not that again, Loni. Of course I'm not wearing a wire. What am I going to have to do to prove to you that you can trust me?" asked Gwyn.

Loni shrugged. "I don't know. I'm sure that time will present itself at some point, but it hasn't just yet. Just know I'm keeping my eye on you." She put two fingers to her thick glasses and then pointed them at Gwyn and Phyllis. Loni let Gwyn pass but then held her palm up in Phyllis's face.

"I'm going to need you to remove your shirt," said Loni. Her face was stone cold Steve Austin serious.

Phyllis frowned. "Like hell."

"It's blue," said Loni, her lips barely moving.

Phyllis threw her arms out on either side of herself. "And?"

Gwyn sighed and tugged off her green sweater. "Loni has a thing about the color blue. Here, put this on so we can get on with our day."

"Are you serious right now?" asked Phyllis.

Loni blinked without changing her expression. "Serious as a dead man."

Phyllis took the sweater from Gwyn and in a big huff pulled it on and buttoned the middle button.

Loni pointed at her shirt. "I can still see a little of it right—"

Phyllis smacked her hand away. "Don't touch me," she grumped as she buttoned the sweater up to her neck. "You're weird, Loni." She pushed her way inside Loni's house. "We don't have time for this nonsense. We stopped by because they found a dead body over by the Falls."

Loni sucked in her breath, and her hand went to her mouth. "Was she murdered?"

Gwyn shrugged. "We don't have any details yet. All we know is that the police found a body, and I guess there's a big scene over by the Falls. We were going to head over there, but we thought maybe you'd like to ride along with us."

"Out in public?!" she demanded. "In broad daylight? Someone would be sure to spot me then!"

Phyllis waved her hand dismissively towards Loni. "Then put on one of those dumb disguises you have."

"Those only work if I'm hidden. Or it's dark. Those don't work during the *daytime* out in *public*!"

"I hate to break it to you, but they don't work at night-time either," huffed Phyllis. "You look like an idiot in them."

Gwyn sighed. "I hate to say it, Loni, but Phyllis is right. All you're doing is calling *more* attention to yourself, not less. You've got to figure out more of an incognito disguise. Something that's not so flashy!"

"Like what?" asked Loni.

Gwyn looked around the room at the myriad articles of clothing strewn on chairs, hanging from light fixtures, and draped across the backs of sofas. She saw a black scarf dangling from the corner of a curtain rod. It was covered in dust and cat hair. She shook it off and wrapped it around Loni's head. "I think we can make something work!"

24

"*A*re you sure you can't tell who I am?" asked Loni.

Char and Phyllis looked at her, sitting between them, and smiled. "You are completely unrecognizable," said Char as Gwyn pulled the car away from the gate in the backyard.

Gwyn and Phyllis had found a blond wig that they'd pulled over Loni's hair. They'd added the black scarf, wrapping it around the majority of her lower face, and had put on a pair of sunglasses that fit over her pop-bottle glasses. She wore a long black dress with heeled pumps to give her some height. She simply looked like a woman in mourning and not like the crazy old cat lady who lived on Hemlock Road.

"You look great, Loni," Gwyn assured her from the front seat.

Hazel threw a snort over her shoulder. "You look like the grim reaper's wife."

"Can we get out of here, before someone sees us?" asked Loni, slinking down in her seat.

Gwyn pulled out of the alley and wound her way through side streets until they found a parking spot downtown near the Falls. Carloads of people pulled in from all directions as they got out and began to walk towards the main attraction.

Police tape cordoned off a small white bungalow with a fenced-in backyard just across the street from the Falls. Next-door neighbors on both sides of the house stood in their yards, watching the events unfold as passersby stopped to ask them what had happened.

"Pick up the pace, girls," hissed Char as she sped past them towards the police cordon, carrying Vic in her arms.

"Coming through," Vic shouted into the crowd.

Phyllis and Loni shoved their way to the front of the crowd to stand next to Char. Gwyn followed behind closely, holding her mother's elbow so she wouldn't get shoved over by one of the many people on the street. Hazel whacked at ankles with the end of her cane, causing many unhappy stares down at her.

When they were all the way up to the front of the crowd and up against the police's yellow tape, Phyllis looked around. Police officers searched every part of the property and could be seen coming in and out of the small house.

"Whose body did they find?" asked Phyllis.

Char shook her head. "I haven't heard, but this is Margaret Sutton's house."

"Who's Margaret Sutton?" asked Phyllis.

"I don't know her very well. She plays bingo at the senior center. I only know she lives here because I brought her dinner once when the word at bingo was that she had slipped on some ice and thrown her hip out."

"Have I ever met her?" asked Phyllis.

Char frowned. "I haven't seen her at bingo since you've been to town." Then a thought occurred to her and she held up a finger. "But, she was at Linda's the other day when we had coffee."

"Oh, really? You didn't point her out."

Char nodded. "Yeah, she was at that gardening meeting. The one that Boomer Wallace was presiding over."

"The one that Kat was a member of?" asked Gwyn.

Char nodded. "Yeah. I remember seeing Margaret there and thinking I didn't realize that she was in that club."

"Well, that's peculiar." Gwyn scratched her jaw. "Two women from the same gardening club dead within a few weeks of each other?"

"You don't think the two deaths are connected, do you?" asked Loni.

Gwyn shrugged and looked around. "I think we have to consider it. Doesn't it seem suspicious to you?"

Loni nodded, the ends of her blond wig dusting the tops of her shoulders. "Maybe, but we need to find out more. Maybe it wasn't even the woman who lives here that was killed."

Suddenly a familiar face walked by. "Detective Whitman," hissed Char from behind the tape.

"Hello, Char, Phyllis," he said, nodding at them both and then at their friends.

"What happened here?" asked Phyllis.

He looked back at the house and rubbed the back of his neck. At least sixty sets of eyes were on him when he turned back around. "I can't talk about it, I'm sorry."

"Just tell us who was found," hissed Char. "We won't tell anyone."

Detective Whitman glanced up at the crowd. He lowered his head and whispered back at them. "I'm not worried about you telling anyone. I'm worried about *them* telling everyone."

"Is it Margaret Sutton?" asked Char.

"We aren't releasing the victim's name at this time. The family hasn't been notified."

"But there definitely *is* a victim?" asked Gwyn.

"Again, I can't say any more. Listen, I need to get back to my investigation," he said uncomfortably.

"Just tell us how you found out something happened and we'll leave you to your work," suggested Char.

He looked around once again and then lowered his head towards the women. In a hushed tone, he said, "One of the neighbors saw something and called 911."

"Which neighbor?" asked Char, looking at the other small houses on either side of Margaret's house.

"I'm sorry, ladies, that's all I can say. Now, you'll have to excuse me," he said before returning to the inside of the house.

The women stood looking at each other curiously. "Now what?" asked Loni.

"Look," hissed Gwyn, pointing across the yard. "Isn't that the man that pushed Mom this morning?"

Hazel perked up. "Where?"

Gwyn stuck her finger out further, towards the house on the north side of Margaret's. "Right there. See?"

All the women's heads turned to see Benny Hamilton with a camera hanging around his neck, slinking off into the backyard of the next-door neighbor's house.

Phyllis narrowed her eyes. "He's a reporter. He's got a lead. We've got to get over there. I bet that was the neighbor who called 911."

"I bet you're right," agreed Gwyn. "We've got some investigating to do."

"Don't you have to get to work?" asked Char, looking up at her.

"The Falls event last night gave me a little flexibility on what time I come to work. Mom and I have some time before we have to be back. But we need to hurry."

After pushing their way through the crowd, the five women and Vic slipped off unnoticed around the north side of the police tape to the nearly identical house next door to Margaret Sutton's. They looked down the narrow grass walkway between Margaret's privacy fence and the small detached garage on the neighbor's property. From where they stood, they saw Benny Hamilton standing on top of a pile of wood, snapping pictures over the fence.

With Vic slung over one shoulder, Char eyed Benny. "Girls, can you believe what you're seeing right now?"

Hazel elbowed her daughter in the ribs. "I told you you shouldn't have worn that hideous blouse."

Gwyn frowned at her mother and then pointed down the alleyway. "Mom! She's talking about Benny Hamilton taking photographs over the fence."

Hazel looked around her daughter. "Oh. You still shouldn't have worn that hideous blouse."

"Ugh," groaned Gwyn.

"He sees something. We need to find out what it is," whispered Phyllis. "Come on, shh," she hissed, holding a finger up to her lips.

Slowly, she tiptoed down the alleyway with Char and Vic close by her side. Gwyn followed just slightly behind them but held on to Char's arm. Loni and Hazel clung to each other as they brought up the rear.

"Don't spook him," whispered Loni from the back.

"Shhh," hissed Char.

They hid behind a large hemlock tree in the neighbor's backyard and watched as Benny snapped his camera at different angles. And then, seconds later, they heard a low, deep voice on the other side of the fence.

"Hey, you. No photography. Get out of here," growled a police officer.

Gwyn peered around the tree to see Benny hightailing it off the stack of wood and into the alley at the back of the house. "He's gone, girls."

"Do we dare look over the fence?" asked Char.

"Just a little peek," said Loni. "We need to know what happened."

Phyllis nodded in agreement. "We have to try. We'll boost you up, Lon. No one will recognize you in that disguise. Alright?"

Loni saluted Phyllis. "Aye-aye, captain! You can count on me!"

"Let's go," whispered Char, waving them forward. Wordlessly the group clung to one another, and when they got to the fence, Char put Vic down on the grass, and they boosted Loni up on top of the wood pile.

"What do you see?" asked Phyllis.

Loni readjusted her wig and scarf. "Lots of police officers," she whispered down to them. "I don't see a body yet. Too many people in the way. I'm not tall enough. Can you girls get me a little higher up?"

Phyllis and Gwyn each took one of Loni's legs and tried to boost her up higher.

"Just a little bit more," said Loni, adjusting the black scarf again as the wind continued to blow it in her face. "I can almost see."

Gwyn tried to get Loni higher, but Loni began to move as she tried to arch her back so she could see better. And then just like that, Gwyn felt Loni rock backwards. "Quit it, Loni, you're going to fall," she hissed up at the smaller woman.

"No, I'm just trying to pull myself up higher," Loni hissed back.

"I'm losing my grip," whispered Phyllis, trying to readjust her hands on Loni's butt. "Char, grab her backside before she—"

But before anyone knew it, the whole pile toppled over backwards. Char managed to catch hold of Loni's dress before she hit the ground, but it was a near disaster. "Ooh!" hollered Loni.

"I told you not to move!" cried Gwyn, dusting herself off.

"I couldn't see! My scarf got in my eyes," she barked back.

"Well, you shouldn't have moved while we were trying to readjust your weight," argued Phyllis. "Come on. We'll boost you up again."

The women lifted Loni up off the ground, and this time, Gwyn put her on her shoulders and boosted her up.

"Can you see now?" asked Char as Gwyn got into position, staring at the fence.

"I'm going to have to ask you to get down, ma'am," said the same deep voice they'd heard earlier from the other side of the fence.

"Oh, I, uh, was looking for my dog. Is he over there?" asked Loni uncomfortably.

"There are no dogs over here, ma'am. Please get down, or I'll be forced to come over there and take you down myself," said the police officer.

Gwyn felt her heart tumble into the pit of her stomach.

"Oh, no problem. If you see my dog, I'll just be over here," said Loni awkwardly. "Toodeloo," she said, giving him a little flutter of her fingers as Gwyn slowly lowered her to the ground on the other side.

The minute they were all back on solid ground, Phyllis wrinkled her nose. "Darn it! We have to figure out what is going on over there!"

"I'll tell you what's going on," said a voice from

behind them. The girls all spun around to see a woman in her midfifties with curlers in her hair, wearing a bathrobe. "Margaret Sutton is dead!"

25

"So it *was* Margaret," breathed Char, making the sign of the cross. "That poor woman! What happened to her?"

The woman shrugged. "I have no idea. I woke up this morning to the sound of a dog barking like mad. I came out here to see what was going on and discovered the dog on the other side of Margaret's fence going crazy! So I climbed up on the woodpile and looked over the fence to see if I could see what his problem was, and there she was. Dead in her flower garden."

Gwyn covered her open mouth with a trembling hand. "Was she murdered?"

"I have no idea. I didn't see how she died. I couldn't see anything. She was just lying there on her back in her garden. I went back in the house and called 911 and waited for them to show up. I was too scared to go back outside."

"What time was that?" asked Char.

"Well, my alarm goes off at seven, but I probably listened to that dog bark for about forty-five minutes before I actually went out to see what his problem was. That was at about a quarter to eight. He could have been barking longer, though. I sleep with the fan on and the windows closed. My house is pretty well insulated. I never hear him bark. It wasn't until I woke up and opened the windows this morning that I started hearing him."

"Do the police think she was murdered?" asked Gwyn.

The woman shrugged. "Beats me. They knocked on my door, and I told them where the body was. A detective was over here for about a half an hour asking me questions, but I wasn't much help because I didn't see anything. Poor Margaret," sighed the woman.

"Do you know Margaret well?" asked Char.

"Not real well. I mean, we visited once in a while. She was a nice old lady. She liked to be outside. She was a bit of a night owl. I don't think she slept very well. I'd see her out walking late at night all the time. I always figured she'd be hit by a car or something because she never wore reflective clothing, and sometimes if I came home late at night, I'd almost hit her pulling into my garage because she was so hard to see. I suggested to her on numerous occasions that she should wear bright clothing when she went out to walk late at night, but she seemed to feel safe."

"Is Margaret from Aspen Falls originally?" asked Gwyn.

The woman shook her head. "I don't really know. She

lived here when I moved in almost fifteen years ago. I'm embarrassed to admit that I never asked her anything about her past. This is just so sad. I'm really going to miss seeing her around."

"It is sad. I'm very sorry for the loss of your neighbor." Gwyn hugged the woman. "Are you going to be alright?"

She nodded. "Yes, I'll be fine, thank you. I called my daughter and told her what happened. She just lives over in Bakersdale. She's on her way right now to spend the day with me because I was pretty shaken when I called her."

"I don't blame you," said Char. "Finding anyone dead would be horrific."

The woman dotted at her eyes with her tissue. "It was," she agreed.

"Thank you for all the information," said Gwyn. "The police aren't saying anything out there."

"Oh, I'm sure everything will be in the paper soon enough. There was just a news reporter in my backyard a few minutes ago."

"We saw him," said Loni.

"Well, if you ask me, it *should* be in the paper. If there's a murderer running around Aspen Falls, I think the citizens have a right to know, don't you?"

The women all nodded agreeably. "Yes, absolutely," said Phyllis.

"That's why I didn't chase the reporter off my property," she said. Then she waved a hand at the women.

"Well, I better get inside and get these curlers out. Janie will be here shortly."

"Thank you," called the women as the neighbor retreated into her house.

"Girls, I think we need to talk to the neighbor on the other side of Margaret's house," said Char. "Maybe they saw something."

"Absolutely," agreed Phyllis. "But instead of going back through that crowd, I think we should go around the back, through the alley."

Char bent over and scooped up Vic, who had been silent during the conversation with the woman. "Let's go, girls."

The house on the other side of Margaret Sutton's property had a chain-link fence surrounding the back-yard, and inside the fence, a full-grown German shepherd paced the length of Margaret's privacy fence. The dog didn't even have to see the group of women before he began barking like mad. "Roof roof roof roof roof!"

The dog's deep, lumbering voice made the hair on Gwyn's arms stand straight on end. She was afraid that all the action had the dog on edge and maybe he'd jump the fence and attack them.

"Hey, buddy," said Loni, shoving her arm over the chain-link fence.

"Loni, are you crazy? Don't stick your arm in there! He'll bite you!" hollered Char, holding Vic as far away from the fence as she could.

The dog barked again. This time there was an inflection in his tone. "Roof roof *roof!*"

Loni smiled at him calmly. "I'm Loni. These are my friends, Gwyn and her mother, Hazel. This is Char and Phyllis. And the little guy is Vic. We just wanted to know what happened to Margaret."

"Ra-ra-roof!" he bellowed.

"Yeah, I know she died, but did you see what happened?" she asked as if the dog were answering her.

Gwyn stared at the two of them, wide-eyed. She knew her friend could talk to animals, but she hadn't even considered asking an animal for help.

"Can you understand him?" asked Phyllis incredulously.

Loni nodded excitedly. "He said he saw everything!" She looked at the big, scary-looking dog again. "Gimme a minute, will ya?"

Phyllis held her arms out to silence the rest of the group while Loni continued communing with the animal.

"What exactly did you see?"

The dog began to bark wildly, relaying as much information as he could to Loni. "That had to be horrible. I suppose you wanted to tear him to pieces!"

The German shepherd paced back and forth along the fence then.

"He's very upset," whispered Loni. "He liked Margaret. She snuck him doggie snacks."

"Well, what happened to her?" demanded Phyllis.

"Someone attacked her," whispered Loni. "Last night after the festival at the Falls. It was late, though. Everyone else was long gone."

"Ask him if he knows what time it was,"

suggested Char.

Loni nodded and looked at the dog. "Darwin, what time was she killed?"

The dog stopped pacing and gave her a little yip.

She waggled her head back at him. "Well, excuse me!" She turned to the girls. "He says he's a dog. Dogs can't tell time," she said matter-of-factly. Then she put her hand beside her mouth and whispered to the women. "He was kind of snotty about it, too."

"Did he see who it was that attacked her?" asked Gwyn. "We need a description."

Loni nodded and said to the dog. "What did the attacker look like?"

The dog barked, yipped, and cajoled.

"It was a man. He was tall. He had on a black hooded gown, just like the one we saw in our vision of how Kat died!" said Loni anxiously, repeating what the dog had just told her. "And he carried a book. A big brown book."

Gwyn sucked in her breath. "It's the same person. It has to be!"

"Girls, we have a serial murderer on our hands. This is bad, very, very bad," said Phyllis, her skin going pale as the blood drained from her face.

"We need to find out what time she was killed. It might help us track down who was at the Falls that time of night. Can you ask Darwin if we can talk to his owner?"

Loni nodded and looked at the dog, who stared up at her, wagging his tail excitedly. "Darwin, my friends want to know exactly what time Margaret was attacked. We need to talk to one of your owners and find out what time you were outside last night. Can you get them for us?"

Without another sound, Darwin turned tail and ran towards the house. He slipped inside his doggy door, and from the alley, the women could hear Darwin howling like crazy. Soon, the back screen door opened and Darwin came running out dragging a man behind him. "What is it, Dar?" asked the man.

Darwin lunged ahead and nearly dragged the man to the back of the yard where the women stood waiting. When he got to the fence line, he sat in front of Loni, pleased with himself, and wagging his tail.

The man looked down at Darwin in shock. "Who are you?" asked the man incredulously. "And what did you to do Darwin? He never sits like this when he sees strangers."

Loni smiled at him. "I have the magic touch when it comes to dogs."

"Apparently. What's with the scarf?" he asked, giving her a little nod as he held on to Darwin's collar.

Loni touched the black veil covering her face.

"She's in mourning," said Hazel, piping up for the first time.

Loni nodded solemnly. "My, uh, dog died," she said with a pronounced fake accent.

The man made a face. "I've never heard of being in mourning after your dog dies."

Loni lowered her head reverently. "It's what they do in my country," she added.

"Oh. What country are you from?"

She cleared her throat. "Romania," she said curtly. "It's a tradition to be in mourning after our pets die. When my horse died, I was in mourning for two years."

"Two years?" he asked. "Wow. That's a long time to have to wear a scarf over your head."

Loni nodded. "I take great pleasure in speaking to your dog," she said.

"He's been a bit worked up today," said the man. "You know, with Mrs. Sutton's passing and all."

"Yes, we heard about that," said Char. "Such a shame."

"It is a shame. She was a nice gal. Lived alone. She really liked Darwin."

"I am getting a vibe from the dog," said Loni, playing up her fake accent. "Did Darwin act strangely at all last night?" She glanced down at the alert, pointy-eared dog.

The man nodded. "He did. I'd let him out in the front yard during the festival. He likes to people-watch. But I went to bed around eleven and brought him inside. Around midnight he must have heard people back out at the Falls, and he begged to be let back out. Usually, I don't let him out in the front yard at night because once in a while he'll see something and jump the fence. I didn't want to take the chance, so I leashed him to the front porch and went back to bed.

"Then about twelve thirty or one o'clock in the morning, he began to go nuts—barking like crazy. I went outside and looked around, but I didn't see anything. So I brought him in the house. He was real antsy after that, but eventually, he settled down."

"The neighbor on the other side of Mrs. Sutton was the one that called the police," said Char. "She just told us that she called 911 because Darwin was barking early this morning, and when she looked over the fence to see what he was barking about, she saw Mrs. Sutton dead in her backyard."

"Yeah, he's been a mess since last night," agreed the man.

"What time did you let Darwin into the backyard this morning?" asked Phyllis.

"It was early. Probably about six. He woke me up earlier than usual, begging to go out back. I guess he must have sensed something happened to Mrs. Sutton."

The women all looked down at Darwin, who seemed to be nodding. "I think you're right," said Loni.

"We appreciate your help, Mister…" began Phyllis.

"Oh, Martinez," he said, reaching a hand out to shake Phyllis's hand. "Ernesto."

"Thank you, Ernesto," repeated Phyllis. "We really appreciate the information."

"No problem." He started to tug Darwin's collar back towards the house.

"Oh, Ernesto," said Char. "Do us a favor and tell the police what time Darwin went nuts last night. We have a sneaking suspicion that Mrs. Sutton didn't die from natural causes. I bet Darwin saw something last night."

Ernesto looked down at his dog. "You think?"

"One hundred percent," said Gwyn.

Now they just had to figure out who it was that Darwin had seen.

*a*fter leaving Darwin, Ernesto, and Margaret Sutton's backyard, the group drove back to Kat's house on the edge of town.

With all her friends crashed on the furniture around her, Char rubbed her temples. "I can't believe Margaret's dead now too."

Vic snuggled up in the warm crook of his wife's arm. "That poor, poor woman! I used to see her walk past the bakery every day. This is horrible news!"

From her seat in the recliner, Hazel leaned forward and stared at Vic. "Gwynnie," she whispered. "I think you forgot to give me my pills this morning. I'm hearing the dog talk!"

Gwyn reached across the armrest and patted her mother's hand. "You didn't forget to take your pills, Mom. The dog can talk."

"I'm not surprised that the dog can talk. I'm surprised

that I can *hear* the dog talk," said Hazel, wide-eyed and frozen in her seat.

"Hazel, this is my husband," said Char, speaking louder than usual so Hazel could hear her across the room. "This is Vic. You didn't hear the man's voice talking in the car ride earlier?"

Hazel blinked. "I thought that was Phyllis."

"You thought I sounded like a man?" asked Phyllis from the other side of the sofa.

Hazel's head reared back as she shrugged. "You always sound like a man." Then she pointed at the dog. "So you're married to your dog?"

Char nodded with an uncomfortable grimace. "Yes, Hazel."

"That's legal?"

"I guess."

Hazel's eyes widened as she shook her head. "The things people will do to get their pets covered under their Medicare."

Char laughed. "Hazel, I didn't marry him so he could get covered under my Medicare. He was a man when I married him. Some witches did a spell on him, and he turned into a dog."

"Well," drawled Hazel, lifting her heavy brows, "I bet that puts a damper on things in the bedroom."

"Mother!" snapped Gwyn. "That's none of your business! Stop being rude."

"What?" Hazel threw her hands out on either side of her and looked around the room. "It's not what everyone is wondering?" Then she pulled the lever on the side of the recliner, leaned back in her seat, and closed her eyes. "Fine, wake me when it's time to go."

Loni stood up and walked towards the bathroom. "I'm going to look and see if Kat has any ibuprofen in her bathroom. This damn headache won't go away."

"Bring me some too," hollered Phyllis.

Gwyn nodded. "Me three."

"Bring us all some," Char hollered after Loni. She leaned back in her seat. "Well, this has been quite the exhausting morning."

Vic patted his wife's arm. "My poor, poor sugarplum."

"Girls, we have to figure out what happened to Kat and Margaret. There is someone going around killing people in Aspen Falls. No one is safe until we find out who it is and bring him to justice!" said Gwyn.

"We need to make sense of it all," agreed Phyllis. "But I don't even know where to start!"

"Well, what do we know?" asked Gwyn. "I think that's where we start. We put together the pieces of the puzzle that we have."

Char nodded and leaned forward. "Gwyn's right. Okay. We know that the person in question is a man, and he wore a black hooded robe in both murders."

"And we know that he has our spell book," Loni chimed in as she came back with a bottle of ibuprofen and a glass of water. She handed both to Gwyn.

"Right," agreed Phyllis. "He's got our book. So we find our book, and we find our murderer."

"We also know that Margaret was killed after the festival, sometime between twelve thirty and one o'clock," said Gwyn.

"That's going to be an important clue," said Phyllis nodding. "If we can come up with a list of suspects who had a motive to hurt both women, then we'll be able to narrow down that list if they have alibis."

Vic hopped up on Char's lap. "Not so much. That's a bad time of day for an alibi. What would all of our alibis be?"

"We were partying together last night at that time," said Char with a groan.

"Yes, but the rest of Aspen Falls was probably at home sleeping," he said.

"Vic's right. That doesn't make for a very strong alibi for anyone. If we go nosing around, how are we supposed to believe anyone is telling us the truth?" asked Phyllis.

"Well, we've got the world's best lie detector test sleeping on the chair right there," said Gwyn, looking at her mother.

"This is true," agreed Char with a nod. "Now we just need a suspects list. Who would want both of those women dead?"

"I don't know, but Margaret was found dead in her flower bed, and so was Kat. Is that coincidence, or is it the killer's calling card?" asked Gwyn.

"You think it's his calling card?" asked Char, hugging Vic to her chest. The thought of there being a killer who left a *calling card* in Aspen Falls made her pulse go faster.

"Don't you think it would be too coincidental not to be?"

Char and Vic exchanged a knowing look. She knew he was worried for her safety. After hearing that Margaret had been killed, she had to admit that she was now worried about all of their safety. "I suppose if you look at it like that. Both women belonged to the same gardening club."

"Maybe we need to look at the members of the club, then," suggested Phyllis, taking the water and ibuprofen Gwyn handed her.

"I think we start with the most obvious member, Boomer Wallace," said Char.

"I hate to say it, but he didn't seem very upset about Kat's death," said Vic.

"Agreed. We definitely need to pay him a visit. Anyone know where he works?" asked Gwyn.

Char nodded. "He owns Wallace Garden Supply, on the east edge of town."

Phyllis pulled herself to her feet. "Well, what are we waiting for? I think that's where we start our investigation!"

"Mom, wake up," said Gwyn, patting Hazel's leg. "We need a mind reader!"

Hazel jerked awake. "What?"

"We need a mind reader!" she repeated.

"I was dreaming that Walter Cronkite invited out for a nightcap. You woke me up for that?" she snapped.

"You told us to wake you up when it was time to leave!"

"I also told you never to interrupt your mother when

she's having a good time! I think I was just about to get lucky!"

---

*W*allace Gardening Supply didn't just sell rakes, hoes, and garden hoses. It also had an enormous greenhouse in back full of interesting hybrid flowering shrubs, antique perennials, and ornamental trees. The young man working the counter had pointed the women to the greenhouse, and they found Boomer with his hands buried in the soil of an obscure species of an azalea plant that he was transplanting.

"Boomer, hello," said Char from behind him.

On his hands and knees, Boomer casually looked back at the women. "Hello. Rodney at the counter will assist you with all your gardening supply needs."

"Oh, we didn't come to shop, we came to see you!" said Phyllis pointedly.

Boomer's shoulders slumped. He rocked back on his toes and wiped the black soil from his big hands into the azalea pot. Without standing, he peered up at the women.

"How may I help you?" he asked, more than a little perturbed to have been interrupted.

"Do you remember us?" asked Gwyn. "We met at the festival last night."

Boomer narrowed his eyes and then grudgingly nodded his head. "Yes," he said gruffly. "I remember. You're friends of Katherine Lynde's."

Gwyn smiled at him pleasantly. "Yes."

Char put Vic down on the gravel floor and took hold of his leash. "Unfortunately we've come bearing bad news."

Boomer looked at them blankly but didn't say anything.

"Do you know Margaret Sutton?" asked Phyllis.

Boomer nodded. "Of course I do. She's in my gardening club."

"Are you aware that she died in the wee hours of the morning?" asked Phyllis.

That made him lumber to his feet. "No, I hadn't heard." He pulled a shop rag from his back pocket and wiped his hands with it. "So Maggie's dead? How'd she die?"

"We aren't sure," admitted Char. "The police are investigating. The downtown area is full of cops right now."

"I've been in my greenhouse all morning. I hadn't heard a peep about it. Well, that's unfortunate. First Kat, now Maggie."

"Yes," agreed Char with a frown. "It *is* unfortunate. Such a kind woman taken, far too early."

Boomer stuck the rag in his back pocket. "And next month is time to re-up their dues. Now the club will be short those funds."

The women all exchanged shocked looks. How dare he be so flip over the death of both women!

"Mr. Wallace!" breathed Gwyn. "Another woman in Aspen Falls has died, and all you're concerned about are the club fees that you'll be missing out on?"

His squinty brown eyes widened. "The dues are one hundred dollars apiece! That shorts my club two hundred dollars! Now we'll have to recruit new members or do some fundraisers to replace those funds. I already had plans for that money!"

"Well, it's unfortunate that your mother never taught you not to count your chickens before they hatched!" snapped Gwyn.

"It's also unfortunate his mother didn't teach him empathy!" added Hazel, with her brows lowered.

Boomer crossed his arms across his chest. "I have a lot to do today, ladies. I'm sure you didn't drive all the way out here just to tell me that Maggie Sutton met her maker. What do you want?"

"We want to know where you went last night after the festival," said Hazel bluntly.

Boomer's face twisted into a snarl. "I'm pretty sure it's none of your business where I went after the festival. What's it to you?"

"We're just trying to understand why two women from *your garden club* were both found dead in their gardens in the last month," said Phyllis. "It's a bit coincidental, don't you think?"

"I have no idea about that. Now, if you'll excuse me. I have to get back to my Rhododendron vaseyi." He turned his back to the women and squatted down.

With his back turned, the women stared down at Hazel. Had she been able to read anything from him? She shrugged.

Suddenly, Gwyn had an idea. She looked around her

feet, searching for something that would work. Spotting a rock, she squatted down and scooped it up. When she was back on her feet, she handed Loni the rock and gave her a wink. Loni seemed to know what to do. She held the rock in the palm of both hands out in front of herself. Gwyn closed her eyes, took a deep breath to center her energy, and then wiggled her fingers towards the rock. It bounced like a jumping bean in Loni's hands, and then suddenly it began to turn. As it did, it transformed into the shape of a pot, and from the pot shot forth a crop of beautifully cupped rosettes on hardy green stems. The rose bush, with its oversized pale peach buds, made the women gasp. It was the most elegant flower any of them had ever seen.

"Mr. Wallace, perhaps I could persuade you to share with us where you were last night after the festival," said Gwyn sweetly, plucking the pot from Loni's hands.

Boomer stopped messing around in the dirt and let out a deep breath as he turned around. "I told you, it's none of your business. I'm going to have to ask you ladies to…" He stopped when he caught sight of the plant in Gwyn's hands. With a slack jaw, he rose to his feet, unable to take his eyes off of the plant. "Where did you get that?"

Gwyn gave him a little shrug and a casual tip of her head. "I thought you might like it." When he didn't answer immediately, she began to turn around. "But I guess not."

Boomer caught her elbow gently with his hand. "Wait! That's a Juliet rose! It's exquisite!" he breathed.

Gwyn looked down at the flower in her hands. "Yes,

isn't it?" she replied wistfully. "I thought you might be interested in having it, but I guess not. Come on, girls. We should go. We don't want to take any more of Mr. Wallace's precious time."

The women began to head towards the entrance of the greenhouse. Boomer chased after them. "Wait, wait, wait! I might have a few minutes to visit. What exactly is that you want to know?"

Gwyn feigned surprise as she stopped walking and turned around to face him. "We were just curious where you went after the festival."

"My wife and I went to visit my mother," he said. "We'd planned to take her to the festival with us, but she's been sick, and we couldn't bring her along."

Gwyn looked back at the girls. She wasn't sure what to say to that. The girls stared back at her blankly. They didn't know how to respond either. Gwyn lifted a brow. "Your mother lives in town?"

He nodded but kept his eyes trained on the potted flower. "Yes, at The Village. My wife and I stayed for quite a while."

Gwyn looked at Boomer with surprise. "Your mother lives at The Village?" she asked.

"Yes. Ellison Wallace."

Surprise washed over Gwyn. She knew that name! "Ellie Wallace is your mother? I hadn't put the names together. Of course. I wasn't thinking. Ellie had wanted to go on the walk with us, but had to back out at the last minute."

"You know Mom?" he asked, pulling his head back in surprise.

Gwyn nodded. "I just took the activities director position at The Village. My mother and I live there."

"I see," he said absentmindedly. He nodded towards the rose bush. "Where did you get this plant?"

Gwyn smiled at him coyly. "I have my sources."

He reached his hands out slowly to take it from her hands. "I answered your question, now may I have the plant?"

Gwyn pulled the plant just out of his grasp. "One more question. Do you have any idea how Margaret Sutton died?"

He lowered his brows, casting shadows across his dark brown eyes. "I can honestly say that I have no idea." He plucked the plant from her hands. "Thank you. With this plant, and with Katherine out of the running, I think I have a pretty good chance of winning the Aspen Falls Master Gardener award this year. No one around here has ever entered a Juliet rose into the event."

Gwyn rolled her eyes and groaned. "Ugh, you're welcome."

"It was a pleasure, ladies. Now if you'll excuse me, I have an entire nursery to tend to."

"Thank you, Mr. Wallace," said Phyllis as they marched away.

Back in the car, Gwyn turned the key in the ignition and then all eyes turned to Hazel.

"Did he do it?" demanded Phyllis.

Hazel shrugged. "You asked if he had any idea how

she died and he said he had no idea. I think that was the truth."

"So he didn't do it?" asked Gwyn.

Vic hopped up on Char's lap. "I didn't like how he phrased his answer."

Char smiled at her husband. "You read my mind. Your question to him was vague, Gwynnie. You asked him if he knew how Margaret died. If he hit Margaret over the head with a shovel like Kat was killed, perhaps he doesn't know what actually ended her. That doesn't mean he wasn't the one who whacked her."

Gwyn frowned. She hadn't thought about it like that. "So now what?"

After strapping Vic in over her lap, Char looked up at the women. "Well, considering the fact that I didn't like how flip he was about both women's deaths, I think we need to pay a little visit to Ellie Wallace."

Gwyn put the car in reverse and backed out of her parking spot. "Say no more, I'm on my way!"

27

"Good morning, Gwyn," chirped Arabella Struthers, the front desk clerk at The Village. "Hello, Hazel, I see you brought some friends with you this morning."

Hazel tapped the floor with her cane. "I see you took your annoying pills again this morning."

"Oh, Arabella," said Gwyn with a pleading smile. "Please forgive Mother. That's just her way of saying good morning."

Arabella's bright smile faded only slightly as she nodded. "No problem, Gwyn. Have a nice day, Hazel."

"We're off to visit Ellie Wallace," said Gwyn as she breezed past.

Arabella's eyes widened. "Oh, wait, Gwyn. Mrs. Wallace is sick. I'm afraid she caught a case of the sniffles."

"Is she not allowed visitors?" asked Char.

"No, visitors are fine. I just wanted to warn you all, so

you don't catch it as well. We would hate for this little bug to get passed around The Village."

Gwyn smiled at her. "No problem at all. Thank you for the heads-up, Arabella."

"Glad to help," she said. Then she looked down at Vic and plumped out her bottom lip. "And unfortunately that little fellow isn't allowed past the lobby."

Gwyn snapped her fingers. "Darn it! I should have known that. I'm so sorry, Char. I'm not up on all of the rules here at The Village just yet."

Char nodded. "I understand. I think Vic and I will just wait outside, then."

"I'm really sorry," said Arabella.

Char smiled back at her. "Not a problem. It's a beautiful day. We'll just wait by the car, girls."

"We'll make it fast," promised Phyllis as she walked towards the residents' living quarters.

"Have a nice day, ladies," said Arabella, her voice resuming its usual chirpy tone.

Char waved goodbye to the women as Phyllis and the rest of the crew followed Gwyn out of the lobby and towards Ellie's room.

"You as well," called Gwyn with a little wave.

"She's sure perky," Phyllis whispered to the girls as they walked down the long corridor.

Gwyn nodded. "I just love Arabella."

"I don't," snapped Hazel. "When a woman's personality is as perky as her breasts, something about her just rubs me the wrong way."

"If that's the case, you shouldn't rub anyone the

wrong way," quipped Loni, overtly eyeing Hazel's sagging chest.

Phyllis giggled.

"Oh, no, she rubs everyone the wrong way," sighed Gwyn with a nod. "I only wish her breasts were perkier."

Hazel laughed. "He-he. I haven't heard any complaints from the old perverts around here."

Gwyn swatted gently at her mother as they continued down the hallway and rounded a corner. A man in black was just coming out of Ellie's apartment.

"Father Donovan!" said Phyllis in surprise. "What are you doing here?"

"Oh, hello, ladies. I was just visiting a sick resident," he said.

Hazel eyed the man with venom-laced daggers in her eyes. After his unkind words about witches the day before, she didn't have much interest in speaking to the man.

"That's Ellie Wallace's room," said Gwyn. "Was Ellie the one you were visiting last night when we saw you before the festival?"

Father Donovan turned to look back at the door he'd just exited. "Indeed she was," he said. "The poor thing has a terrible bout of pneumonia and is feeling just miserable."

Gwyn grimaced. The thought of Ellie feeling miserable made her feel bad. She also worried about her own mother and wondered if perhaps she shouldn't go in the room lest she catch a virus. "She isn't any better today?"

He shook his head, "No, I'm afraid not." He gave a tight smile to the small group and headed towards the exit. "Well, I better be going. I have a lot of people to visit today. You ladies have a nice day."

"Oh, Father Donovan. How was your dinner last night?" asked Gwyn.

He stopped walking midway down the hall and turned back around, separating their group in half. "Oh, it was quite lovely, thank you for asking," he said. "I got an opportunity to see the lights at the Falls. The weather was just perfect for the event."

"Oh, I guess I assumed you'd miss the festival since you were going to supper with that family."

He nodded. "They just lived a few blocks away from the event, so after dinner, we walked over."

Loni scratched her face beneath her veil. "What did you do after that?"

He looked curiously at the short, heavily disguised woman. "Oh, I went home after that."

"Were you alone?" she asked bluntly.

He cleared his throat uncomfortably. "Well, yes, of course. I live alone. Why?"

"Ignore our friend," said Gwyn with a fake smile as she elbowed Loni in the ribs. "She's not from this country and isn't familiar with the concept of manners."

"Oh, I understand," said Father Donovan with a stilted bow. "Welcome to America. Now, if you'll excuse me—"

"Oh, Father Donovan," said Gwyn, catching him once again before he rushed off. "Has anyone told you that a woman who lived across the street from the Falls was found dead this morning?"

His eyes narrowed. "Hmm. What was her name?"

"Margaret Sutton," said Phyllis.

He turned to look at Phyllis and Hazel, who stood behind him. His cheeks fell slightly. "Yes. I did hear about that," he said calmly. Then he put a hand aside his mouth and whispered. "I heard she was a *witch*."

Hazel's head reared back, as did Phyllis's.

"Father Donovan!" chided Phyllis. "So what if she *was* a witch? Is it any less of a tragedy if she was?"

His head bobbled from side to side on his shoulders as he mulled that notion over. "Any culture that challenges God's role in the universe is gravely contrary to the tenets virtue of my religion, I'm afraid."

"I don't see how a group of people that values nature and utilizes the gifts that God has given the world should be seen as any different than anyone else!" argued Phyllis.

Gwyn's face was red as she threw in her two cents. "And aren't all of God's creatures inherently valuable?"

He puffed air out of his nose and gave them a tiny smirk. "I'm afraid you ladies have been around this culture for much too long. They've gotten to your heads," he said, tapping the temple of his nearly black hair. "I just don't understand how Father Bernie has ministered to this community for so long."

From the corner of her eye, Gwyn saw her mother lift the end of her cane and aim it at Father Donovan's back. When Hazel closed her eyes, Gwyn knew what was to come next. She'd been on the receiving end of those little electrically charged zaps her entire life.

"Mother, no!" shouted Gwyn, holding her hand out in front of her.

But it was too late. The blunt end of Hazel's wooden cane glowed with a fiery green ember, like the tobacco end of a cigarette as it puffed to life. Gwyn watched it discharge, emitting a slow, gurgling sound. She did a double take, looking curiously at the cane. Usually, Hazel's cane emitted a sharp zapping sound when it discharged, not a slow gurgling sound.

The charge it chugged out slow-danced its way towards Father Donovan. The green ball hung in the air as it moved excruciatingly slowly and then stopped almost six inches before hitting him and dropped limply to the floor. The electrical discharge sizzled and then evaporated harmlessly into the air.

Hazel looked down the length of her cane with one lip curled, disappointment covering her face. "Well, that was a bust," she said.

Father Donovan sucked in his breath and then cast his long condemning finger at Hazel. "*Witch!*" he sneered.

"Was it the wart on my nose that gave me away?" snickered Hazel.

"Was it your intent to use your magic against a man of God?" His face was crimson as he fired off his righteous indignation at the small woman.

"I don't know how you can call yourself a man of God and not love all of God's creatures," she snapped back.

"Pagan!" he fired back, still holding his pointed finger in her direction.

"Hypocrite!" shouted Hazel. "And you better remove that finger from my face before I remove it from your body!"

"Mother!" breathed Gwyn.

He reeled around to look at Gwyn. The whites of his glowed as his eyes widened into round balls. "And she's your *mother?!* That means *you're a witch too?!* I hope you know that I intend on telling the directors of this institution about your...*condition.*"

Gwyn smiled at him, keeping her composure despite the fact that inwardly, a storm raged. "You go right on ahead. That was the reason they hired me in the first place. They wanted someone who wasn't narrow-minded and intolerant of others. I only wish Aspen Falls had selected a temporary minister that possessed the same attributes." She lifted her chin to give her an air of authority. "Good day, Father Donovan."

She turned her back to him, knocked on Ellison Wallace's door, and upon hearing an immediate 'come in,' breezed inside.

Phyllis stared icily at him as she walked past him, as did Loni.

Hazel stopped on her way past him and wrinkled her nose. "You're lucky my stick jammed, Buster. Next time, don't plan on being so lucky."

Father Donovan let out an indignant, "Uh," before storming down the hall towards the front doors.

Inside, Ellie Wallace lay back in her bed. Surrounded by fluffed pillows and covered up to her neck with a soft peach afghan, she looked like a tiny little thing.

"Good morning, Ellie," chirped Gwyn as she walked over to the woman's bedside. "How are you feeling?"

"I'm afraid I've got a touch of pneumonia." Her small voice was frail as she spoke.

"I heard," said Gwyn with a drooping bottom lip. "I'm so sorry you aren't feeling well. I brought some friends to cheer you up." Even though Gwyn trembled with anger inside, she tried to keep it together and put on a positive attitude for Ellie. She didn't need to know about the little squabble they'd had with Father Donovan in the hallway. "You know Mom, of course, but this is Phyllis Habernackle, and this is… umm…" She stopped and thought about it for a minute. "Olga Patterson, from Romania," she said, pointing at Loni in the black scarf.

"From Romania!" said Ellie. Excitement lit up her pale face, and she tried to sit up a little higher in her bed. "That's so far away!"

Loni nodded and held up her hand with her fingers parted down the middle in a Vulcan salute. "I come in peace," said Loni with a fake accent and a slight nod.

Ellie smiled at Loni. "It's so nice to meet you, Olga."

Gwyn took a seat on the chair next to Ellie's bed. "Oh, Ellie. It's such a shame you were sick last night! You missed the walk to the Falls, and it was such a lovely evening."

"Oh, I know dear. I heard all about the festival from my son and my daughter-in-law," she said, her watery grey eyes brightening slightly. "Walter said he and May had a lovely time dancing the night away."

"Walter?" asked Phyllis.

"Yes, dear. Oh, I'm sorry. Most of the people in Aspen Falls know him as Boomer. I still call him Walter, though."

"Walter Wallace is your son's real name?" asked Hazel with lifted brows.

She nodded. "Walter was my father's name," said Ellie. "I know Walter Wallace is a bit of a mouthful, but my father had just passed before Walter was born, and it meant so much to me to honor him in that way," she said with a light smile. "Of course everyone wanted to nickname him Wally. Can you imagine a little boy in school called Wally Wallace? My husband was just sure that little Walter would get laughed out of the first grade with that name!" She snickered behind her hand at the memory. "So my husband started trying out nicknames, and somehow he started calling Walter Boomer, and that one stuck. He's been Boomer to everyone but me since he was six months old."

Gwyn laughed politely. "Oh, Ellie, what a fun story."

Ellie's broad smile brought some much-needed color to her pale cheeks. She sat up a little higher in bed. "Yes, it really is. I haven't told anyone all of that in quite a few years."

"Can we get you anything, Ellie?" asked Phyllis, sitting down at the foot of her bed? "Are you hungry?"

Ellie pointed across the room to her water bottle on a table. "You could pass me my water bottle, dear. I was going to ask Father Donovan to pass it to me, but we got to talking, and I plumb forgot."

Phyllis patted her leg and then got up to get the bottle. "Sure thing."

Hazel took a seat on the other side of Ellie's bed. "Are you going to feel up to playing poker later tonight, Ellie? I hear someone's putting together a game in the dining room after dinner."

Ellie smiled at her. "I'm afraid I'm really not much of a poker player, Hazel."

Hazel scooted further back in her seat. "Oh, that's alright. You really don't have to know how to play. It's all in good fun," she said with a half-smirk.

Gwyn stared down her mother. "Mother, I think I heard that that poker game was going to be canceled, unfortunately."

Hazel puffed air out her nose. "They're always canceling the fun stuff, aren't they, Ellie?"

Ellie smiled at her. "Yes, it does seem like it, doesn't it?"

"Would you like me to come to your room tonight? We could play a game of poker just the two of us. You have any money on you?"

Gwyn sighed. Her mother wasn't going to let up on her own. She glanced over at Phyllis with pleading eyes. "You know, Phyllis, if Ellie has pneumonia, maybe Mother shouldn't be in here." She looked at Ellie then. "I just don't want to pass it around The Village, you know?"

Ellie nodded her head as Hazel rolled her eyes and crossed her arms across her chest.

"Phyllis, maybe you could take Mom out to see how

Char and Vic are doing? Olga and I will stay and visit Ellie."

Phyllis stood up. "I think that's a great idea. Come on, Haze. Let's go see what Char's up to."

"I already know what she's doing," snapped Hazel. "She's watching the talking dog outside. I don't need to go check on her."

"Mother, maybe you could go visit Miss Georgia and see if she's gotten your French fries cooked already. I bet you're starving since we didn't have time for breakfast this morning. You could have an early lunch."

Hazel pushed herself out of her chair and made a beeline for the door. "Bye, Ellie. If you're feeling better later, I'll bring my cards over."

"Goodbye, Hazel, thank you for visiting me," said Ellie as she waved goodbye.

When Hazel and Phyllis had gone, Gwyn leaned back in her seat. "Speaking of visits, that was really nice of Boomer to visit you after the festival."

Ellie smiled agreeably. "Walter is such a good boy. And his wife, May, of course."

"Did they stay long last night?" Gwyn scratched the base of her scalp as she spoke, trying to convey mild disinterest so as not to arouse any suspicion about her reason for asking.

"Oh, yes, they stayed quite awhile," she said, crossing her hands politely in her lap. "There was a *Matlock* marathon on the television last night. I think Walter and May stayed for several episodes. I fell asleep a time or two, and when I woke up the two of them had fallen asleep on my sofa. I'm afraid I dozed off again, and when I woke up, they were gone."

"You don't have any idea what time that might have been?" asked Gwyn.

"That I woke up?" she asked.

Gwyn nodded.

"Oh dear, I'm afraid I don't. It was probably two or three in the morning."

Gwyn couldn't help but sigh in disappointment. "Okay."

"Is there a reason why, dear?" asked Ellie.

Gwyn shook her head. "No. I was just curious."

Ellie nodded and leaned back in bed again. "Alright, because I was going to say that if you really needed to know, Arabella at the front counter should have the checkout sheet. I'm sure Walter and May checked out before leaving."

Gwyn's eyes widened as she shot Loni a repressed look of excitement. "Oh, sure. It's not a big deal at all. You know, Ellie, talking about those French fries has really gotten me hungry. I think I might grab a bite to eat with Mom and Phyllis. Can I bring you anything?"

"Thank you, but Miss Georgia has already been in to visit me this morning, and she's going to send lunch over in another half an hour. If you're going to go, I think I might try and squeeze in a nap before she comes."

"Perfect," said Gwyn. She spent a moment helping Ellie pull the blanket up around her shoulders. "Would you like us to turn the lights off on our way out?"

Ellie nodded. "Please do. It's been lovely talking to

you. Maybe you could stop back with Hazel later and we'll all play cards together. I'm afraid I might need someone to help me out a little."

Gwyn stopped in the doorway before flipping off the lights. "I have a better idea. How about Mom and I come later and play Scrabble with you?"

Ellie smiled as the lights turned off. "Oh yes. I'm much better at Scrabble, and then I won't lose my shirt either."

28

*I*t was well past lunchtime when Gwyn drove the women back to Kat's house. They had all had lunch together at The Village, but it had been so busy and there had been so many sets of hearing aids turned up high that Gwyn and Char hadn't felt comfortable discussing the case there.

"What's taking Gwyn and Hazel so long?" asked Char the second she got into the car and had Vic belted in.

"Ellie didn't know what time Boomer left The Village last night," said Loni, straightening her scarf across her blond hair. "So she's checking the sign-out sheet at the counter."

"But did he actually go to see her after the festival?" asked Vic.

"Yep. He and his wife were really here," sighed Loni. "She said they all fell asleep watching *Matlock* reruns."

"*Matlock!*" said Char. "Oh my word, I haven't seen an episode of *Matlock* in years!"

Phyllis looked at Char with a smile. "Don't you just love Andy Griffith?"

"Oh, most definitely!" said Char.

The car doors opened and Gwyn slid into the driver's seat.

"Okay, spill," said Loni. "You checked the visitors' log?"

Gwyn nodded as she plugged her key into the ignition. "I did. I'm sorry to report that everything Boomer said checked out. The Wallaces were both with Ellie until one forty-five in the morning. There's no way Boomer could be our murderer!"

Hazel opened the passenger side and slowly climbed in.

"Hazel, what happened with your cane earlier?" asked Phyllis.

Hazel pulled her legs into the car and slowly shut the door. "I think it needs cleaning. It jammed. That never happens!"

"Or maybe you're losing your magic touch," suggested Gwyn with a half-smile. "I guess if you don't use it, you lose it!"

"Gwyndolin Prescott, bite your tongue," chastised Hazel. "I'm not losing anything!"

"When's the last time you used your cane to zap anybody, Mom?"

Hazel's mouth opened to shout back a snappy reply,

but it suddenly became apparent that she couldn't remember when the last time she'd used her cane to zap somebody had been! She stuttered, "I-I'm sure it was just the other day."

"Mom," Gwyn said, gently touching her mother's leg, "I haven't seen you zap anyone with your cane in probably five years. You can't do it anymore, can you?"

"Of course I can!" shouted Hazel. "I just need to clean it is all. It jammed. I'll have it up and running again in no time. And you'll be the first to find out! Just to prove it to you! He-he," laughed Hazel before turning to look out the window as Gwyn pulled away from the curb.

"Did you girls fill Char and Vic in on what Father Donovan said to us about Margaret Sutton?" asked Gwyn.

Char leaned forward. "They did!" she breathed. "I just can't believe that a man of the cloth would say such horrid things!"

"I can," snapped Hazel. "Just because they're wearing a white collar doesn't mean anything."

"But to be so crass about a dead woman, just because she happens to be a witch, is infuriating!" said Phyllis.

Gwyn peered back at Char in her rearview mirror. "That's the first time anyone told me that Margaret Sutton was a witch. Is it true?"

Char shrugged. "There are tons of witches in Aspen Falls. I don't know them *all*. Not everyone went to school at the Institute."

"If it *is* true, that's just one more thing that Kat had in common with Margaret," said Phyllis. "They were both in the gardening club, and they were both witches."

"And now we know that Boomer Wallace couldn't have killed her. Maybe one of the other members of the gardening club hated the fact that Kat always won that dumb award every year with her magical roses," suggested Gwyn.

Gwyn turned the car down Blue Spruce Lane and parked in Kat's driveway. "I think we need to check Kat's garden for clues. The police thought she fell and hit her head, so they probably weren't looking around much."

"Yes!" agreed Phyllis. "Come on."

Gwyn turned off the ignition, and together, the group walked up the front steps. But no sooner had Char unlocked the front door than a familiar face happened by, carrying a messenger bag of newspapers.

"Good afternoon, Ruben," said Phyllis, taking the newspaper he handed her.

"Good afternoon, ladies," he replied, tipping his baseball cap to the women.

Char heard Ruben's name and turned around. She still felt like there were unanswered questions when it came to him. He'd seemed as suspicious as a cat with a mouse tail hanging out of his mouth. "Say, Ruben. Before you run off, do you have time for a glass of lemonade?" called out Char.

Ruben wiped the beads of sweat off his brow and looked down at his watch. "I actually I do have time for a little break. It sure has turned into a mighty warm day," he said. "I'd love a glass of lemonade."

Gwyn looked at Char curiously, and when Char winked at her, Gwyn smiled sweetly. "Oh, wonderful! I'll just run inside and make us all a glass, and we'll sit out here on Kat's covered porch and enjoy the breeze. I wish we had some cookies to offer you, but unfortunately, we need to do a little grocery shopping this afternoon."

Ruben smiled politely. "Oh, thank you, but the lemonade is just fine anyway."

"Alright, I'll be back in a jiffy!"

"I'll help you," said Loni and followed Gwyn inside.

Phyllis waved Ruben up to the porch, where he took a seat on the little green settee in front of the parlor window. Phyllis sat down next to him. "How's your morning going, Ruben?" asked Phyllis.

He took off his ball cap and combed his fingers through his damp curly hair. "It's going well. I'm actually a little ahead of schedule today." He flashed a set of perfectly straight teeth at the women.

"Oh, how nice," sighed Char, lifting Vic up off the ground and settling him on her lap. "Sit, sit," she said, offering him a place to sit across from her.

Vic sat squared up to Ruben, with his ears on high alert and one eye open wide.

Ruben regarded Vic with a hesitant smile. "Your dog is sure...cute," he said with a nervous laugh as he scratched the fur on Vic's head.

Vic growled at him, causing Ruben to pull his hand back.

"He's not fond of new people," Char assured him, giving Vic a little squeeze. "But *he'll be nice.*" It was a warning to Vic to relax until they had a little bit more information. They had to treat him as if he were innocent until proven guilty.

Ruben smiled uncomfortably and then settled back into his chair. "How are you ladies today?"

"Oh, we're alright," said Char with a bit of a sigh.

"That didn't sound very encouraging," said Ruben.

Char looked down at Vic and then lifted her brows. "Well, another friend of ours passed away today," she said and then peered at him out of the corner of her eye. The news didn't seem to shock him.

"Are you talking about Maggie Sutton?" he asked as his head nodded knowingly.

Char put a hand to her heart and looked at him. "Why yes, we are," she said. "You knew her too?"

"Of course I did. She was on my route," he explained.

Phyllis lifted her head slightly. "They say she was killed in the wee hours of the morning. I suppose they'll be asking everyone in town for their alibis if they suspect murder."

Ruben shrugged with a blank look on his face. "Oh, maybe. I don't know."

Phyllis looked at him pointedly. "Anyone who had contact with her might be on that list."

He nodded. He didn't seem to get where she was going with it, but Char picked up the cards she was putting down. "Yes!" she said brightly. "Like, for example, I knew Margaret through my bingo group. So the investigators might want to know where I was between midnight and one. Of course, I can tell them I was with my friends all night."

"Ahh," said Ruben, shifting in his seat uncomfortably.

Phyllis sighed. The man was offering *nothing* up. "Will *you* have something to tell the police if they ask?"

Smooth, Phil, real smooth, thought Char, laughing to herself.

Ruben nodded and leaned back in his seat, extending one leg and crossing his arms across his chest. "Oh, yeah. I mean, I was at work last night."

"Delivering papers at midnight?" scoffed Phyllis.

He shook his head. "Oh, no. Sometimes I fill in for a guy at Rawley's Pub downtown. I'm supposed to work tonight too. Eight to close."

Char frowned and wondered if he was telling the truth. She glanced up at Hazel, who closed her eyes and shook her head. *The little scoundrel was lying!* The table went quiet for several long, awkward moments while Char debated what to say next.

Eventually, Ruben tried to fill in the empty spaces. "Yeah, Maggie was such a sweet woman. It's hard to believe both her *and* Kat are gone," he said.

Phyllis nodded but kept a close eye on Ruben. "Will you be attending Maggie's funeral as well?" she asked a bit snarkily.

Ruben let out a puff of air. "Likely not," he said. "I didn't know Maggie *that* well."

"And yet you knew Kat that well," asked Phyllis, drumming her fingers across her chin.

Ruben's jovial nature seemed to come to a screeching halt then as he visibly sobered up. "Yes, I did."

"Funny, Kat never mentioned that the two of you were friends," said Char.

Ruben shrugged. "It was kind of a secret," he admitted. "My request."

"Really," purred Phyllis, leaning towards him. "How interesting."

He looked up at Phyllis and smiled. "Not *that* interesting," he chuckled.

From behind them, Hazel stood idly by, watching their conversation. When she'd had enough of listening to them beating around the bush, she finally chimed in. "If it wasn't *that* type of relationship, then what kind of relationship were you having with her?"

Ruben looked over his shoulder. Hazel flashed him her best intimidating scowl, but it didn't seem to faze him. "Okay. You're curious. I get it." He shrugged. "I can't explain it. Kat was just an easy person to talk to. We visited a lot, and we became friends. Is that so hard to believe?"

"Yes," snapped Hazel before going inside.

She passed Gwyn in the doorway, carrying a serving tray with a pitcher of lemonade and glasses. "Mom? What's wrong?" she asked, but Hazel didn't stop to respond. Gwyn peered outside curiously. "Where's Mom going?"

"I'm sorry if I offended her," said Ruben.

"Offended her?" asked Gwyn, looking over her shoulder. "How on earth could you have offended my mother?"

He shrugged and took the glass of lemonade that Gwyn offered him. "Your friends were just asking me why I was friends with Kat. I explained that we were just really good friends, but she didn't seem to want to believe me."

Gwyn narrowed her eyes at Ruben. "My mother is an excellent judge of character, Ruben. She almost has what you might call a sixth sense. If she doesn't believe you, I'm afraid that puts a little concern in me as well."

Ruben sucked down the lemonade in several easy swallows and then stood up. "I'm sorry that you don't believe me either. But Kat *was* my friend." His glass made a loud clink when he set it down on the table. "Thank you for the lemonade. Kat used to make me lemonade too," he said somewhat remorsefully. "Now, if you'll excuse me, I need to get back to my route." He pulled his cap back on and tipped his head towards the ladies. "Have a nice day."

Char waved at him uncomfortably. "Thank you for visiting with us, Ruben," she called after him. Then she swatted at Phyllis. "Did you girls have to make him feel so uncomfortable?!"

"*Uncomfortable?!*" barked Phyllis. "He might have been the one that killed Kat! Not only was he the one that *conveniently* found Kat's body, but he had a mysterious relationship with her that he can't explain. The man showed up at her funeral, and now he got Hazel's dander up!"

"Let's talk about this inside," whispered Char. "We don't need the neighbors fueling our speculation."

After ushering everyone inside, they found Hazel seated in her recliner chair in the corner.

"Mom, what was that all about?"

Hazel pretended to be startled. "Oh, Gwynnie. I was just about to take a nap."

"No time for naps now," said Gwyn. "I have to get to work shortly. But first, we need to know why you don't believe Ruben was friends with Kat."

Hazel crossed her arms across her stomach as she closed her eyes and settled her head back into the plushness of the recliner. "I believe they were friends."

"Then what don't you believe?" asked Phyllis.

All the women stared at Hazel, wondering if she'd already dozed off. Finally, the old woman let out a puff of air. "Well, for starters, he wasn't working last night."

Char sucked in her breath. "He wasn't?!"

Hazel didn't open her eyes. "And he's not working tonight."

Phyllis tossed a hand in the air. "I *knew it!*"

"Sure ya did," snapped Hazel. "He's also keeping a secret."

"A secret?" asked Gwyn.

"Yeah, you know, like the fact that I know that you still stuff your bra."

Gwyn's face soured. "Mother! I don't stuff my bra!"

"Eh, push-up, padded—I know the truth. Those puppies aren't your own," said Hazel, finally opening her eyes and pointing at Gwyn's breasts.

"Mom!"

"He had a secret and Kat knew," she said. "Kat was keeping his secret for him."

"What was the secret?" asked Char.

"What am I? God? I don't know everything! He didn't think of the secret!" snapped Hazel.

"So Kat was keeping a secret of Ruben's?" mused Phyllis.

Vic hopped up on the arm of the sofa and curled his tail around him as he sat. "Maybe he killed her to keep the secret safe."

Loni appeared out of the kitchen and leaned against the door frame. "People have gotten popped for much smaller things," she said.

"Popped? What do you know about people getting popped, Loni?" asked Phyllis.

Loni sucked her lips between her teeth and mashed them together as if to say, "You'll never get it out of me."

"Listen, the point is, we might just have figured out why Kat was killed," said Gwyn.

"You really think *Ruben* could have done it?" asked Char with a hand on her hip. "He seems like such a nice man."

"Good people do very bad things when their backs are up against a wall," said Gwyn. "We need to find out exactly what secret Kat was keeping for Ruben."

"Gwyn's right. I think we need to turn up the heat on Ruben Moreno," said Phyllis.

Gwyn sighed as she looked at her watch. "Unfortunately, I can't right now. I've got to get to work. Let's meet back up after I get off. How about at seven?"

The girls all nodded. "Fine. At seven we're going to figure out the truth about Ruben Moreno," said Phyllis.

29

*P*hyllis stood in Katherine Lynde's kitchen doorway later that evening. "So now what?"

"Well…" began Char. "I've given it a lot of thought today. What do the police do when they put someone on their suspects list?"

"High-five each other and then go have donuts?" asked Hazel.

"Very funny, Mother," said Gwyn. "No, I agree with Char. We need to think like detectives."

Char nodded as she wagged a finger at the women. "They do stakeouts."

Phyllis laughed. "You think we're up to doing a stakeout?"

Hazel shook her head. "Not me. My bladder's the size of a pecan. Unless we're parked outside of a port-a-potty, I'm not going."

"Oh, come on, Hazel. We might not have to be out that long," said Phyllis.

"Yeah, I'm out too," said Loni. "Someone might trail us. I can't have that."

"You'd be in disguise!" said Char with a harrumph. She looked around at the women. "Oh, come on, girls! Do you want to solve Kat's murder or don't you? The killer isn't just going to fall into our laps!"

Phyllis nodded. "Char's right. Two dead women by the same killer has got me rattled. My daughter and my granddaughter live in Aspen Falls. They could be next!"

"Any one of us could be next," agreed Char. "We have to get this dirtbag off the streets!"

Phyllis put a hand in. "Who's with us?"

Char put her hand on top of Phyllis's. "Let's go, girls. For Kat!"

Gwyn smiled and put her hand on top of Char's. "For Kat!"

"For Kat," sighed Loni, adding her hand to the pile. Then she aimed a fist at the sky. "You owe us one, Katherine Lynde!"

All eyes turned towards Hazel. She widened them exaggeratedly. "I didn't even *know* the woman!"

"Well, for heaven's sake, are you part of this coven or aren't you?" asked Phyllis, pointing to their hands.

Hazel thought about it for a second. "We're taking Char's car. That way if I pee, it'll be on her seat, not Gwyn's."

Char smiled at her. "Actually, I had a better idea. Are you in, or are you out?"

Hazel put a hand on her the pile. "Fine. For Kat."

"You really think all this is necessary?" asked Gwyn as she smudged the last bit of her fair skin with black shoe polish. Only the whites of her eyes showed through the makeup. With the rest of her lithe body dressed all in black, she looked like a cat burglar.

"For what I've got in mind? Definitely!" said Char followed by a wicked laugh.

"Oh man," said Phyllis rolling her eyes. "I know that laugh. That's the Charlotte-Adams-is-going-to-get-us-in-trouble laugh."

Char's upper lip smashed against her teeth as she smiled devilishly. "You know me so well, dear."

"It would be really nice if we all could be in on your little plan," said Gwyn as she finished smudging Hazel's face with black.

"Trust me. You're gonna love it. It's going to be just like old times!"

"Are we going to Ruben's house to steal all of his bras?" asked Loni with a chuckle.

"Hey!" shouted Phyllis. "That's not a bad idea."

Gwyn's hands went to either side of her face. "Oh man, that brings back memories," she said with a smile.

"Focus, ladies, focus. We have a very important job to do!" said Char, clapping her hands in the air to bring them back to the present.

Loni wrapped her makeup-covered face with the

black scarf again and topped it off with a big black witch's hat. "We know, we know."

"You're not wearing that thing, are you?" asked Phyllis.

Loni's eyes swiveled up to look at the brim sticking out above her eyes. She pointed at the hat. "This thing?"

"Well, obviously that thing. Did you think we were still talking about bras? Because I certainly wouldn't tell you to take yours off, although the floors could use a good dusting," snapped Phyllis.

Loni furrowed her eyebrows as she turned to the group. "Has anyone fed her today? That one's getting a mite cranky."

"She's eaten, I assure you," said Char. "She was referring to your hat, Loni. You're not seriously going to wear it, are you?"

Loni looked down at her outfit. "Why wouldn't I wear the hat? It's black. Isn't that the theme of the night?"

"The theme is black. Not idiot," snapped Hazel. "Take that thing off. You give witches a bad name."

Loni's mouth fell open. "Uh! I never get to wear my witch's hat. Where else am I supposed to wear it but on a secret night mission?!"

Char pointed at her. "I'll put it on your head when you're buried. How's that?"

Loni stomped a foot on the ground. "Not good enough. I want to wear it while I'm alive."

Phyllis palmed her forehead. "Look. A witch's hat is about the most clichéd thing a witch can wear. Do you want to be a cliché?"

"If it means I get to wear the hat, then yes."

Phyllis threw her hands out in a huff and strutted off towards the kitchen. "Talk some sense into her," she said to Gwyn.

Gwyn walked over to the strange-looking black-clad woman. "Look, Loni. I think what the girls are trying to say is that the hat calls *more* attention to you. The goal tonight is to have *less* attention."

"That girl at the festival was wearing a black witch's hat," said Loni, stoutly crossing her arms across her chest. "No one crawled up her ass."

"We're not crawling up your, uh-hum, *bum*, Loni," said Gwyn.

"Besides, if you're talking about that little thing with my granddaughter, she's a peculiar thing," said Phyllis. "You really can't compare yourself to Jax. I mean, she's a few fries short of a Happy Meal."

"Uh-hum," coughed Char. She covered her mouth and pointed a finger at Loni. Yolanda Hodges was *nothing* if not a few fries short of a Happy Meal. In fact, Char wondered if they'd even remembered to put fries *in* her Happy Meal.

Phyllis's eyes widened as she got what Char was hinting at. "Oh. Yeah. I get it. Fine, Loni. Forget it. Wear whatever floats your boat."

"Thank you," she said with a smile and a curtsey.

"Alright, well, Mrs. Bailey," said Phyllis, surveying the girls, "it looks like we're all ready. Hazel, have you used the little witches' room?"

Hazel nodded and then just as suddenly frowned. "Maybe I better go use it one more time, just to be sure I don't flood the car."

"Well, that's sort of the thing, Haze. We're not taking the car," said Char, rubbing her hands together evilly.

Phyllis scratched the back of her head. "Umm, Char. I'm not quite sure you get how this stakeout thing works. Do you want us to walk to Ruben's and then chase his car down the street when he goes somewhere?" Phyllis smiled at her. "Might be a tad obvious that he's being followed when he sees a bunch of old ladies in black costumes running after him."

Char smacked Phyllis across the arm. "Don't be ridiculous! I have a better idea! Follow me, girls!" Char led the women through the hallway to Kat's dining room, where a blanket lay on the floor, covering something up.

"What the hell is this?" asked Loni. "We going on a magic carpet ride or something?"

"Better." Char grinned. She leaned over and grabbed one side of the blanket and gave it a tug. "Voilà!"

On the ground beneath the blanket lay five broomsticks in a neat row.

"Shut up!" shouted Loni with a broad smile across her face as she bent over to pick up the handle of one of the broomsticks.

"Oh, hell no," said Phyllis, shaking her head. "There's no way I'm getting on that. Have you seen my ass? I'm pretty sure I'll have to start paying property tax on it because it lives in another zip code these days. There's no way it's gonna be able to fit on that."

"I'm with Phyllis. Char, what were you thinking?" sighed Gwyn as she eyed the broomsticks disdainfully.

"I was thinking we could have a little fun while doing the stakeout!" said Char. "Oh, come on, girls, where's your sense of adventure?"

"Mine's on the TV set," said Phyllis. "Take me all over the place, but I don't have to fall off a broomstick to do it."

"Char, you can't be serious!" Gwyn looked at Hazel. "You really expect this geriatric, arthritic, feebleminded—"

"Hey! Who you callin' geriatric?" asked Hazel in a huff. "I resemble that remark!"

"Hazel, I think you meant *you resent that remark*," said Phyllis.

Hazel shook her head with a caustic smile. "No, I actually do resemble that. I'm pretty old. When you've been through as many presidents as I have, you earn the badge of being called geriatric."

"We're getting off topic again," sighed Char, shaking her head.

"Right. The topic is Char's crazy. Nuff said," said Phyllis with a flourish. "Gwyn, you're driving."

Char held her palms up in the doorway to stop the stampede. "Girls, you aren't thinking about this. What better way to stay undercover than to fly overhead? He'd never see us. It's the perfect cover!"

"I'm telling you, this is not safe," objected Gwyn. "My mother is old. She could fall and break her hip."

"Or worse, I could break my lady parts," said Hazel.

"Then how am I supposed to satisfy the boys at The Village?"

"Oh my God, Hazel. Focus?" asked Char. "You do remember how to ride a broomstick, don't you?"

Hazel shrugged. "It's been a few years. But I'm sure I can still do it. I mean, what do they say? It's just like riding a broomstick. Oh, wait…"

"My mom is not getting on a broomstick by herself, and that's that!"

"She can ride with me," volunteered Loni. "You wanna ride with me, Haze?"

"If Mom is going to ride with anyone, she's going to ride with me," said Gwyn.

"Or you can ride with me, Hazel. I'm probably the safest choice," said Char.

Hazel looked at Phyllis. "You want to throw your name into the hat too?"

Phyllis frowned. "And have you pee on me mid-stakeout? Pass."

"Fine. I've got plenty of other takers. No need to fight, ladies. There's plenty of ole Hazel to go around."

"I'm pretty sure I saw that written on the back of a bathroom door somewhere," said Phyllis.

"He-he," laughed Hazel, raising her brows. "That was from my younger days."

"So who's it gonna be, Haze?" asked Loni. "I'm not getting any younger over here."

Hazel took a deep breath and eyed Gwyn, Char, and Loni carefully. Finally, she shrugged. "I pick Loni. She's going to be the most fun."

"Ha! I win!" cheered Loni. "Put that in your broom-stick and smoke it!"

Gwyn rolled her eyes and then looked down at her mother. "Mom. I don't think it's a good idea. What if you fall?"

"Then I fall. Maybe I'll kick the bucket, and you can have your own apartment," said Hazel flippantly.

"I don't want you to kick the bucket," said Gwyn. "Although, I wouldn't mind having my own apartment. Loni, you want Mom to move in with you?"

Loni smiled. "She wouldn't get along with my cats. They're a tad insecure, and they don't like it when I hang out with other people."

"Well, Gwynnie, I guess you're stuck with me. Your only chance now is to let me ride the broomstick and fall off."

"Do you have to be so melodramatic, Mom?"

"Yes, I do. I enjoy it. I find it gives me purpose in an otherwise boring world."

"So Hazel and Loni are in. I'm in, of course," said Char. "Now we're just waiting on Party Pooper and Sour-puss. What do you say, ladies?"

Phyllis groaned. "There's no way my butt is fitting on one of those things."

"Hey. You had quite the badonkadonk back in college if I remember correctly," said Char with a grin. "It didn't stop you from riding a broomstick then."

Phyllis made a face. "What are you talking about? I didn't have a big ass in college."

Loni grimaced. "I hate to break it to you Phil, but your jeans used to cringe when they saw you coming."

"Oh, stop it. You girls are terrible," snapped Phyllis. "Tell them I didn't have a big butt in college, Gwynnie."

Gwyn put a hand to her mouth. "Oh, well, I—uh…"

"Her mother taught her it was naughty to lie," said Hazel. "You want the truth, or you want her to keep her lips zipped?"

"Ugh," groaned Phyllis. "Fine. I'll fly on the damn broomstick, but if I fall off and Medicaid doesn't cover my hospital bills, you girls are taking up a collection."

They all looked at Gwyn.

"Well. You're all that's left, Gwyndolin. You ready for the night of your life?" asked Char.

30

Gwyn's heart raced as she looked down at the broomsticks lying in a row on the ground. It had been years since the last time she'd ridden a broomstick, and while the idea excited a tiny piece of her deep inside her heart, the rest of her—the calm, cool, and *rational* side of her—wasn't as excited. Gwyn realized that that tiny piece of her was a remnant of a wild childhood. She'd been raised by a free-spirited, fun-loving mother who was no stranger to impromptu broomstick rides in the middle of the night. Gwyn remembered those days fondly. Riding with her mother, the wind in their hair... the bugs in their teeth...

"Well? What's it going to be, Gwynnie?" asked Hazel.

Gwyn smiled. She knew it wasn't the responsible thing to do, but how could she let her million-year-old dinosaur of a mother go up in the air *alone*? Yes, she'd be with

Loni, but that was *practically* alone. "Oh, fine. I'll go," she sighed.

Char clapped her small hands together. "Fabulous! Oh, girls, you won't regret this. It's going to be such a fun night! Now, I've already saved us some time and enchanted the broomsticks, so let's all pick one and then go out back and have a little practice ride before we take off for Ruben's house."

The rest of the women surged forward. Phyllis took the fattest stick she could find. Not that it mattered; even with a fat stick, it was still going to be difficult for her to maintain balance on it. None of them were the size they used to be in college, Gwyn included. While she had maintained some semblance of a trim body, she'd also packed on a few extra pounds after each of her girls were born. Then, when she'd gone to live with her mother she'd lost a few. But eventually all of the pounds had come back, and they'd brought friends.

Loni grabbed the longest stick because she and Hazel were riding tandem. Char already had her favorite selected too, so there were two sticks left when it was Gwyn's turn to choose. Gwyn looked down at them uncomfortably. One was a short, squat stick painted red with nylon bristles. The other was a long bare wooden stick with the more traditional straw bristles. Gwyn leaned over and scooped the second one up.

"Ahh, going for tradition," said Char with a smile. "Good pick. Good pick."

"Like anyone was going to go with the modern broom?" asked Gwyn.

Char shrugged. "I figured Hazel wasn't going to ride alone. That one was just a gag."

"Ha-ha," said Gwyn, rolling her eyes.

"Follow me, girls!" said Char, leading the way through Kat's dining room and back to the kitchen. She threw open the sliding doors to the backyard and tromped outside. "Perfect weather, isn't it?"

Gwyn looked up at the inky night sky. Char was right. There was no humidity. The temperature was a perfect seventy-five degrees, the stars were out, the moon was bright, and it cast an illuminating glow across Kat's rose garden. Crickets and a bullfrog in the distance provided the night soundtrack, and the smell of Kat's early blooms scented the air.

"It *is* perfect," said Gwyn lightly. She looked across the yard at Hazel and Loni. They were talking animatedly about how they were going to mount the stick together. It warmed Gwyn's heart to see Hazel so excited about an activity for once. She loved seeing her mother happy. Gwyn didn't like having to be the one who said no. But she also liked having her mother in her life. She only said no to protect her.

Phyllis zipped past Gwyn on her broomstick. "Wheeeee!" she called. Phyllis pulled the nose of her broomstick up in the air and gained elevation. "Check this out, girls," she hollered down and then rode by with her hands over her head. "No hands!"

"Phyllis Habernackle!" shouted Gwyn as her heart lurched into her throat. "Two hands on the stick!"

"Yes, Mother," Phyllis hollered over her shoulder into the wind.

Gwyn sighed. She wished she could be as carefree again as Phyllis and the rest of the girls. Soon Char was in the air. Char was more cautious than Phyllis, but she was still a little speed demon. She leaned into the stick and zoomed past Phyllis.

"Eat my dust, Phil!" she yelled.

Hazel and Loni had finally figured out how to mount their stick tandem and were readying for takeoff. Loni pushed her glasses further up her nose and looked back at Hazel. "You're not going to let go of me, right?" she asked.

"I'll cling to you like ones on a sweaty stripper," said Hazel with a bit of a cackle.

"Alright, then, let's go!" said Loni. The duo didn't get a running start like Phyllis and Char had, but took off at a less-than-brisk walk, with Hazel's arms wrapped around Loni's waist.

"Up, up and away!" shouted Hazel, giving the stick a little bounce in back, but they failed to take off.

"Magic broomstick uppo," said Loni, lifting it higher between her legs as she walked. She looked back at Hazel. "Maybe we need to jump-start it."

Hazel nodded. "On three. One…two…go!" The two women bounced on their feet.

Gwyn couldn't help but laugh. In their minds, they'd probably gotten some serious air under their feet, but in reality, they'd barely gotten a blade of grass under their feet.

"Let's try again," suggested Loni. "One, two, three!" They bounced again. This time, Gwyn could see the broomstick shaking to life a bit.

"It moved! I saw it!" said Gwyn. "Try jumping again."

"One, two, three!" they shouted in unison as they gave the biggest bounce they had. The broomstick lifted them both into the air, but they only hovered over the ground instead of taking off.

Loni looked down at the ground. Then she looked back at Hazel. "Let's try rocking it," she said. The two old women began to grind their pelvises back and forth on the stick.

"Oh my God," cried Gwyn, shielding her eyes with her hands. "If I could have gone my whole life without seeing my mother hump Loni Hodges's back on a broomstick, I think I could have died a happy woman."

Loni laughed. "Well, then, give us a little push, will ya, Gwynnie?"

With her hand still covering her eyes, Gwyn walked over to where they hovered near a lilac bush. She turned the front of the broomstick away from the hedge and gave them a shove.

"To infinity and beyond!" hollered Hazel as they moved forward at the speed of a slow-moving pony.

"Look at us, Gwyn! We're flying! I haven't flown in years! Hell, I haven't left the house in years! This feels amazing!" cheered Loni.

Gwyn clapped for them. "You're doing great, ladies.

You just have to see if you can gain elevation and pick up some speed. Mom, you hold on tight to Loni!"

As the two women worked on their skills, Gwyn realized she was next. She bent down to pick up the broomstick she'd dropped when giving the girls a push and saw a black piece of material clinging to the lilac bush. She pulled it loose and examined it.

It was black nylon of some sort, about four inches wide and maybe three inches long. It had obviously been ripped off of something. What it was torn from, Gwyn couldn't be sure. Perhaps Kat had had a purse or something that had lost part of its strap. She tilted her head sideways as she looked at it, flipping it over in her hand, feeling the bumpy texture against her fingers. She was getting a strong feeling about the piece of material. So strong that she waved the girls back in.

"Girls! I found something. My witchy instincts are zeroing in on it," hollered Gwyn.

Char landed first, followed by Phyllis. "Whatcha got?" asked Char.

Gwyn shrugged and handed her the small piece of material. "I don't know what it is."

"Looks like a strap off of something," said Phyllis, grabbing it out of Char's hand.

Char gave Phyllis a dirty look. "Watch it, Habernackle," said Char with a half-grin.

"You watch it, Bailey," Phyllis said with a chuckle. "Who has better intuition about objects? You or me?"

Char rolled her eyes and put a hand on her hip.

"Well, then, hurry up and get a reading on it. Where did you find it, Gwyn?"

Gwyn pointed to the lilac bush near the corner of the rose garden. "It was caught in the branches. At first, I thought maybe it had been Kat's, but I got a really strange reading on it when I touched it."

Phyllis nodded. "I'm getting a really bad vibe from it too. This wasn't Kat's."

Char rubbed her arms. "That just gave me goose bumps," she said. "Do you think it was the killer's?"

Gwyn and Phyllis exchanged a look. Then Gwyn nodded. "That's kind of what I feel like."

"Me too," said Phyllis. "I bet it tore off of something the killer was wearing the night of the murder. He was standing over here when he hit her." She handed it to Char. "Here, put it in your pocket."

"Why don't you put it in your pocket?" asked Char, who looked down at the item disdainfully. "I don't want to touch it."

"You just bellyached at me for taking it from you because you *wanted* to touch it."

"That was before we established that it's probably the killer's!"

"What do you think it's going to do? Kill you next?" asked Phyllis.

Loni and Hazel landed next to them with a flourish. "What a trip!" bellowed Loni exuberantly.

Hazel had a broad smile on her face. She wiped her eyes with the sleeve of her sweater. "The air is making my eyes water," she said. "But man, does it feel good to fly again!"

Loni looked at all the straight faces. "What's with the saggier-than-usual faces? Did we miss something?"

Phyllis held out the small piece of black nylon. "Gwyn found this in the lilac bush."

Loni took it from Phyllis, but the minute her fingers touched it, she let it drop to the grass as if it were a hot potato. "Oh, man. That's got majorly bad vibes," she said. "There's no way that was Kat's."

"We think it was the killer's," said Gwyn, staring at the small piece of fabric on the ground.

All the women looked at it.

"Why are we staring at it? If it's evidence, don't you think we should keep it or something? I mean, if it was the killer's, it's got to be a clue," said Hazel.

"No one wants to touch it, Mom," said Gwyn.

Loni nodded agreeably. "That thing's got bad juju. I'm not touching it again."

Hazel hiked up her skirt and then bent over to pick it up. "Oh, you Fruit Loops," she said, grabbing the material from the ground. "It's just a piece of a strap off of something."

"Something evil," agreed Char.

Hazel held it up in front of her as if she held a hex in her hand. "Oooh," she jeered spookily. "I'm cursed. Look at me..."

"Mom! Don't say things like that!" snapped Gwyn. "You'll jinx yourself."

"I'm not going to jinx anything. This is a clue.

Evidence. Some kind of sleuths you losers are. Can we go now?" asked Hazel as she stuffed the strap in her pocket.

"Yes, let's fire up the canons," agreed Char.

Hazel made a face. "Oh, wait. I gotta go see a man about a horse."

"Again?" asked Loni.

"Hey, you don't want to come home with a wet skirt, do you?"

"Take your time!"

31

*G*wyn tugged her sweater tighter around her shoulders as she flew. It might be a pleasant seventy-four degrees on the ground in Aspen Falls, but in the sky and traveling at such a brisk pace, it was nowhere near that warm. Her arms and legs pebbled from the chill in the air. She glanced down at the ground, something her flying instructor had cautioned her against when she'd first learned to fly a million and a half years ago, but today, she needed to be reassured that there was a ground below her. Gwyn preferred keeping treetops between her and the ground too, just to break the fall in case there was a mishap. And while they were infrequent, mishaps *did* happen to witches.

From her vantage point, all the cars on the dimly illuminated streets were like Matchbox cars, and the people like the little Polly Pocket dolls that her granddaughters had loved years ago. She wondered if anyone could see them flying, although she knew it was highly unlikely. The sky was dark, they were all wearing dark clothes and face paint to cover their skin, but she wondered nonetheless. She was sure a little girl peering out her bedroom window would find it exciting to see a witch's coven fly by in the darkness.

Char and Phyllis led the pack, Gwyn hung just behind them towards the middle, and Loni and Hazel brought up the rear. Gwyn glanced back at her mother, who was still clinging to Loni's waist. It was quite the sight to see Loni and Hazel stuck together like Legos. Her heart felt like a buoy bouncing happily in the ocean, and she couldn't help but smile at them. Gwyn was glad that they'd decided to go on such an exciting outing. She knew full well that her mother would talk about it for days to come.

"This way," shouted Char to the group behind her. Her arm waved over her head so the witches could see her in the darkness.

Gwyn followed the slow curve Char and Phyllis made to hover over a familiar row of houses. Gwyn pulled up next to the girls. "Is this his house?"

"Yes, that one right there," said Char, pointing down to the small bungalow they'd visited earlier in the week.

Gwyn sat up on her broomstick, and with one hand still firmly wrapped around her handle, she pulled back the sleeve of the black gown she wore to squint at her watch. In the darkness, she had to hold it up to the moon to see the time. "It's almost eight o'clock," said Gwyn. "What if he already left for work?"

Phyllis snorted out her nose as Loni and Hazel pulled

up next to them. "I'll bet you dollars to donuts that that man is not working at a bar."

"You don't think he's working tonight?" asked Gwyn.

"Not tonight. I'm talking *ever*. I bet you he doesn't even have a job at a bar."

Hazel nodded. "I agree. That man lies like a basset hound on a front porch."

"So if he doesn't have to work, then why are we even here?" asked Loni as she straightened her back, holding the broomstick with one hand. She put a finger to the bridge of her glasses and pushed them up her nose.

"We're here because he *told* us he has to work tonight. That means he probably *told* his girlfriend he has to work tonight too. I think we need to find out where he's really going," said Char.

"What if he's going to kill someone else?" asked Phyllis.

Loni threw both of her hands up in the air. "Damnit, girls! This is why I need my gun back!"

Gwyn's heart jumped up in her chest. "Two hands on the stick, Loni. You're carrying my mother, you know."

Loni looked over her shoulder at Hazel. "Don't I know it. She's been wiping her nose on the back of my dress the whole time."

Hazel's saggy eyes widened. "I can't help it! The wind whipping in my face is making my eyes water up and my nose run. I feel like a damn faucet!"

"We happen to be witches, Lon," said Char. "We don't need guns. We have magic. Hello?"

Phyllis rolled her eyes. "The woman is like a glow

stick. I want to snap her and then shake the hell out of her until the light comes on."

"Phyllis!" breathed Gwyn. "Don't be rude!"

"What? The old lady gets to say whatever she wants. I'm an old lady too. Granted, she's got more wrinkles than I do, but why don't I get to say whatever's on *my* mind?"

Gwyn sucked in a breath. "You know that little voice deep inside your head that keeps you from saying things you shouldn't?"

Phyllis nodded.

"Yeah, my mother doesn't have that. You do. Be nice."

"It's alright, Gwyn, I can take it from her. You know why? Because I know I can kick her ass whenever I want to," said Loni with a nod.

Phyllis puffed air out her nose. "I'd like to see that, Hodges."

"Keep talking and maybe you'll get your chance!"

Phyllis flicked a finger in Loni's direction, and a little green burst of electricity zapped out and knocked Loni's black witch's hat off her head.

"Oh, nice, Habernackle. You lost my hat!"

"You shouldn't have worn that stupid hat anyway," said Phyllis. "We all told you not to."

"Can you girls please shut up? We aren't invisible, you know," said Char with a sigh.

Gwyn kneaded one temple with her fingertips. "I really don't like the word *shut up*, Char."

Char's mouth dropped open. "Phyllis, Loni, and

334

Hazel all have mouths like sailors and you don't want me to say shut up? Are you kidding me right now?"

"It's really cold up here," said Phyllis, rubbing her shoulders.

"Then maybe you should go down there and get my hat," said Loni.

"I'm not gonna go get your hat, Hodges."

Loni crossed her arms across her chest and looked away. "Fine. Then you owe me a new hat."

"I'm not getting you a new hat either," said Phyllis. "The hat was dumb."

"You really do have a bad attitude tonight, Phyllis," said Gwyn.

Char nodded in agreement. "Yeah, what crawled up your shorts?"

"Nothing!" insisted Phyllis. "She just gets on my nerves sometimes. And it's cold out here, and I really don't want to be on a broomstick with my fat ass right now. Why couldn't we just have staked his place out in the car? Cars have heaters, you know."

"I thought this would be more fun," said Char. "Besides, I knew for sure he wouldn't see us this way."

"So are we just gonna sit here all night and stare at his house?" asked Gwyn. "Because Phyllis is right about the fact that it's cold up here. I didn't wear a thick enough sweater." She looked at Hazel. "Mom, are you too cold? I don't want you to catch a chill. You know Ellie Wallace has pneumonia. It could be going around. I wouldn't want you to get it."

Hazel waved a hand at her daughter. "You worry too

much, Gwynnie. Tonight's about cutting loose and having a little fun. Don't worry about me. I'm fine." Hazel tapped Loni on the arm. "This is boring. Let's fly down there and get your hat."

Loni sighed. "Alright. If Habernackle's not going to get it for me, I guess we'll have to."

"Well, be careful. Two hands on the stick," Gwyn reminded her.

Loni steered their stick around to face the other direction and pointed it towards the ground. "Toodeloo!" she shouted into the wind as they flew away.

Gwyn looked at Char and then down at the ground. Her mother was right about one thing. This stakeout thing *was* boring. Gwyn should have brought a book and a glass of wine to keep her company while they waited. "Maybe Ruben just lied to us about going out at all. Maybe he was actually home last night."

"Or maybe he was out killing Maggie Sutton," suggested Phyllis. She leaned forward on her stick and put her palm under her chin. "Haze was right. This *is* boring. Maybe we should just go."

Suddenly, Char smacked both Phyllis and Gwyn on the arms. "Girls. Girls! Look, he's coming out of his house!"

Gwyn stared down at the tiny little house. She couldn't see the door opening, but she could see Ruben Moreno heading down the front steps. "He's going to his car!"

"This is getting good," said Phyllis.

"I thought you said it was boring," said Char with a smile.

Phyllis smiled back. "Well, now I said it's getting good. I can't change my mind?"

"Oh, look, he's heading south. Come on," said Char, forgetting about her conversation with Phyllis.

"Well, we can't leave until Mom and Loni come back," said Gwyn, looking behind her and down at the ground.

"If we lose him, we'll have to do this whole thing again tomorrow," sighed Char.

"And it's not like they won't know where to go afterwards," said Phyllis. "We know we have to meet back at Kat's because our cars are there."

Gwyn sighed. She didn't like the idea of leaving her mother in Loni's care any longer than necessary. "Maybe I should just wait here for them," she suggested.

Char rolled her eyes. "Then *you'll* be lost. What difference does it make, Gwyn? They'll find us. Come on. He's leaving. I don't want to lose him."

Char and Phyllis took off, leaving Gwyn hanging alone in the night sky. Suddenly she realized that if Char and Phyllis got too far ahead of her, she'd never find them again, and it occurred to her that perhaps Loni and her mother wouldn't be able to find her in the dark anyway. "Ugh, wait for me, girls, I'm coming!"

They followed Ruben's dark grey sports car down the block. He took a right, making all the women glance at each other knowingly. All the bars were downtown and would have required a left-hand turn. Taking a right-hand turn only wound him further into residential developments. Ruben's car zigzagged through neighborhoods as if he were indeed trying to assess whether or not he was being followed.

"Look at that," Char pointed out. "He's weaving through town."

Phyllis nodded. "That's not suspicious or anything."

"He's trying not to be followed is what he's doing," said Char.

"Girls, I'm nervous. What if he really is going to go kill another woman?" asked Gwyn.

Phyllis's eyebrows dipped down into a V and her mouth straightened into a straight line. "Then we pounce."

"Before he can kill them. Right?" asked Gwyn worriedly.

Phyllis rolled her eyes. "Of course before he can kill them. Do you really think we'd let him kill another woman on our watch?"

"Okay," said Gwyn with a small, timid voice. Her well-manicured fingers went to her lips. She wasn't much of a nail-biter, but now all she wanted to do was rip off each and every nail off her fingers. What if Ruben tried to attack some poor woman. How would they handle it? What if he tried to hurt one of *them*? How would she handle it? Gwyn's stomach churned anxiously. Suddenly the fun evening had taken a much more sinister tone, and she wished she hadn't signed up for the night broomstick flying group activity.

Sensing her ambivalence as they slowly trailed Ruben,

Char reached over and put a hand on Gwyn's arm. "It'll be alright, Gwynnie. Nothing bad is going to happen. Okay?"

Gwyn nodded. "Okay," she said with a nod. She could only hope that Char was right.

Phyllis, who had taken the lead as Gwyn and Char had slowed down, pointed up ahead at a pair of red tail-lights glowing in the dark. "Girls, he's stopping up ahead," she said. "Hurry up!"

Char zoomed past Phyllis and then past Gwyn. "We need to get lower. We can't see faces from this high up." She lowered the tip of her stick and slowly began to descend towards the ground. Phyllis and Gwyn followed closely behind until finally the three of them hovered behind a tree in front of a light grey house with quaint pink shutters.

"Whose house is this?" Gwyn whispered to Char.

Char shrugged. "It used to be Rick Voorman's place, but he moved to Dallas last spring. I think it's a rental now."

"Shhh," hissed Phyllis. "He got out of the car!"

Indeed he had. Ruben went around to his trunk, messing around inside it for a while. Finally, he grabbed a dark duffle bag and slung it over his shoulder.

Gwyn's heart went wild. What if there was a gun in the bag? Or a knife? Or any number of other things that were intended to harm whoever lived in the house?

Char touched both women's shoulders. "Girls! What if that piece of material we found came from the strap on that bag? We have to get closer."

"If we get any closer, we'll be flying up his ass," said Phyllis. "I think at that point he'll realize he's being followed. Don't you?"

"Oh my gosh, he's knocking on the door. What do we do?" asked Gwyn as she ripped the polished fingernail off her index finger.

"Shh, the door's opening, the door's opening," said Char, patting Phyllis and Gwyn's arms excitedly.

"Who is it?" asked Phyllis as the door slowly creaked open.

Char sucked in her breath as a face became visible. "Oh my God, I know her!"

32

*P*hyllis and Gwyn peered around the tree to get a look at the woman opening the door. She was extremely petite, standing no more than five feet tall. Her straight golden-blond hair fell to the middle of her back, and she wore a black silk robe that hung to her knees.

"You know her?" asked Phyllis incredulously.

Char nodded. "That's Ida Washington's granddaughter."

"Who's Ida Washington?" asked Phyllis, making a face.

"She goes to our church. You know, that super tiny woman who sits in the front row and sings really loud and off-key?" asked Char.

Phyllis nodded.

"Well, that girl"—she pointed at the young woman who had answered the door—"is Elizabeth, Ida's granddaughter. She moved to Aspen Falls about a year ago. She works part-time for the gift shop downtown and part-time at the gas station."

"Does Ida live with Elizabeth?" asked Gwyn.

"Ida lives across the street from the church. So if this is Elizabeth's house, then no, they don't live together."

"Maybe Ida's visiting Elizabeth," suggested Gwyn nervously. What if Ruben was plotting to kill Ida at her granddaughter's house?

They watched as the young woman stepped out on her doorstep while talking animatedly with Ruben.

"It kinda seems like she knows him," said Phyllis, peering out the tree.

And then, out of nowhere, the woman stepped up on her tiptoes and threw her arms around Ruben's neck to plant the kiss to end all kisses on him. All jaws dropped. When the kiss was over, she took him by the hand and led him inside her house.

"Oh my gosh! She's his *girlfriend*!" breathed Gwyn.

Phyllis lifted her brows. "Well, I gotta say, I didn't see that one coming."

"Me either," said Char, shaking her head.

"What if he's really going to go in there and murder her?" asked Gwyn. "We don't know."

Phyllis chuckled. "I don't think *murder* is what he has in mind," said Phyllis. "But, just because he's got a woman on the side doesn't mean he didn't murder Kat and Maggie. In fact, I think it makes him even *more* of a suspect. It proves he's as shady as we thought he was. We need to find out where he *really* was last night."

"And just exactly how do we do that?" asked Gwyn.

Char lowered herself until her feet touched the grass. She dismounted her broomstick, leaned it against the trunk of the tree in the woman's yard and then looked up at the women. "There's only one way to find out. Ask!"

"Charlotte Bailey," said Gwyn, sucking her breath and scrambling to get her feet on the ground. "You can't just go up to the house and *ask* the woman."

But all that was left was Charlotte's broad backside as she strutted towards the house.

"Char!" hissed Phyllis.

Gwyn switched fingernails in her mouth. "Should we go with her?"

"Ugh," groaned Phyllis. "Why does she have to be in such an almighty hurry! This could jeopardize the entire operation."

"We can't let her go alone," said Gwyn. "What if Ruben pulls out a gun on her or something?"

Phyllis rolled her eyes, grabbed Gwyn by the arm, and dragged her towards Char, who had already knocked on the front door. By the time it opened, Phyllis and Gwyn stood right behind Char. Gwyn's heart pounded in her chest anxiously.

The small blonde woman answered the door, with Ruben nowhere to be seen. "Hello, may I help you?" She looked at the three awkwardly dressed women curiously, the black makeup smeared on their faces likely doing nothing to assure her of their sanity.

Char smiled sweetly at her. "Good evening, sweet-

343

heart. We're friends of your grandmother, Ida Washington."

The woman's smile faded immediately, and a hand went to her heart. "Oh my God, is Gamgam alright?"

Char's smile faded too as she reached a hand out to touch the woman's arm. "Oh, Elizabeth, yes, your grandmother is fine. I'm so sorry to scare you!"

Elizabeth let out a heavy sigh and covered her mouth with her hand. "Oh, wow. That freaked me out! With that other woman being found murdered in her garden, I was concerned that maybe there was a serial killer on the loose or something, and maybe something happened to Gamgam. I'm so sorry to freak out on you!"

"Oh, not at all," sighed Gwyn. "It was our fault for not being clear from the beginning."

The woman cleared her throat and worked to regain her composure. "I'm sorry. Now what is this about?"

Char looked at her curiously. "You heard about Maggie Sutton's death?"

Elizabeth nodded her head. "Of course! Everyone in town has heard. It was all over the front page of the newspaper this morning!"

"Wow, word travels fast," said Char.

Elizabeth nodded. "I've been worried about it all day, to be honest."

"They haven't found who killed her, then, I assume?" asked Phyllis, eying the woman curiously.

The tiny blonde woman shrugged. "I haven't heard. But I did warn Gamgam to keep her doors locked at all times until this gets resolved."

"You should keep your doors locked as well," said Gwyn.

Elizabeth smiled brightly. "Aren't you sweet? Don't worry, I am!"

"We couldn't help but notice a man going into your house a few minutes ago," said Phyllis carefully. "That's actually the reason why we're knocking. We were on a little, umm, walk, and we saw a strange man pull up and go into your house."

Char nodded. "We just wanted to make sure that you're alright."

She looked uncomfortable then. "Oh, you saw him pull up?"

All the women nodded as the woman continued to look uncomfortable. Gwyn had to assume it was because their relationship was supposed to be kept private.

Elizabeth cleared her throat again. "Ruben's just a friend of mine. No need to worry."

"*Ruben Moreno?*" asked Phyllis, feigning surprise. "That was Ruben Moreno? It was so far away we couldn't see who it was."

"Oh," she said, shifting on her feet. "Yes. It was Ruben Moreno."

"Funny, we ran into Ruben today on his route," said Char.

"Oh, did you?" Elizabeth glanced back towards the house.

"Yeah, he mentioned he had to work tonight, though," said Char.

Elizabeth peered back into the house again and then

345

stepped out onto her porch and closed the door behind her. "You ladies look sweet. Can I possibly ask you to keep a secret?"

"Oh, of course, dear! We're the best secret keepers in all of Aspen Falls," said Char, camouflaging her lie behind a brilliant white smile.

The woman seemed to relax visibly. "Well, here's the thing. He doesn't actually have a job at a bar. It's just what he's been telling his wife." She sighed heavily as if she were preparing to let out a burdensome secret. "Ruben and I are actually seeing each other. Maybe you already figured that part out. I don't know. I know it's wrong."

Char nodded. "You know he has a wife?"

Elizabeth ran a hand through her blond hair. "Yes. I know. He wasn't married when we met, though. You have to understand. They were only dating when he first started coming into the gas station where I work."

"Ahh," said Phyllis with a knowing nod.

"We became friends over time. Before he got married, they weren't together for a time, and that's when we started dating. But then he got back together with her, and she pushed him into eloping. He rushed into it, and now he regrets it, but he doesn't know how to end things with her."

"So when he said he was working last night…" began Gwyn.

The woman finished her sentence as she nodded, pointing at herself. "He was here, with me. He's been pretending to have that bar job for a while now."

Gwyn's eyes widened as a lightbulb went off in her head. "Do you know if he told anyone else that?"

"That he was thinking about leaving Gloria?" asked Elizabeth. She nodded. "Yes, I know he'd confided in a woman on his route. She found out somehow, and they'd been trying to figure out how he could tell her without hurting her. Ruben doesn't want to hurt her. It's his main concern."

"Was the woman he told Katherine Lynde?" asked Gwyn.

Elizabeth nodded. "Yes! Lynde, that was her last name. But I think he called her Kat. Do you know her?"

Char sighed. "Yes, we knew her. She passed away several weeks ago."

Elizabeth frowned. "Yes, I'd heard that. Ruben and Kat were very close. He was pretty shaken over her death. Not only did he lose her friendship, but he was the one that found her, you know."

"Yes, dear, we know," said Phyllis. "Well, we better get back to our, umm, *walk*. We just wanted to make sure that you were alright."

Elizabeth smiled at them. "You ladies sure are sweet to check on me." She pointed at Char's face. "Next time you go for a night walk, though, it's probably not a very good idea to dress so...umm, darkly. I think you're supposed to wear flashy colors so cars can see you."

Phyllis shrugged as she took the concrete step to the sidewalk. "We just didn't want the murderer to see us."

Elizabeth gave them a soft smile. "Good idea. If you have some time, maybe you could check on Gamgam?"

"I'll stop in tomorrow," promised Char.

"Please don't tell her about Ruben and me. She'd be horrified to find out that I had a relationship with a married man," begged Elizabeth.

Gwyn swallowed hard. "It's probably best you convince Ruben to come clean to his wife, sweetheart. Secrets don't make friends in small towns."

Elizabeth's eyes widened. "Oh, don't I know it! I'll work on him. Thanks for the tip."

"Good evening, dear," said Char with a little wave as she headed back towards the tree where they'd stashed their broomsticks.

"Good night!" Elizabeth called out before going back inside.

Phyllis sighed as the three of them met under the tree. "Well, there goes that suspect. Ruben Moreno isn't a killer. He's a cad!"

"Now what, girls?" asked Char.

"Your guess is as good as mine. We're out of leads," said Phyllis.

"I know what's next," said Gwyn. "We go back to Kat's and hope that Loni and Mom are there waiting for us!"

---

*L*oni felt Hazel's face grind into her back as the duo zipped through the night sky towards the ground. The wind whipped the scarf she wore so that it beat at her cheeks and covered her glasses, impaling her vision.

"Stop wiping your nose on my back," she hollered over her shoulder.

"I can't help it! I feel like a five-year-old with a cold!"

Loni took one hand off her stick and tried to move the scarf so she could see, but the brisk air moved it right back into her line of sight. In the darkness, it was difficult to see anyway. They'd cruised past the same area twice, looking for the hat Phyllis had knocked off her head. By now she was sure the girls had already left without them in their quest to follow Ruben to his job.

"We're never going to find that stupid hat," said Hazel, ducking behind Loni's back. "We should just go home. I'm cold."

"I'm cold too," agreed Loni. "We'll head home in a few minutes. That hat has to be down here somewhere. It couldn't have just disappeared."

"It fell from a few hundred yards, the wind probably carried it halfway across Aspen Falls by now," said Hazel. "Come on."

"I want my hat back!" said Loni adamantly. "It's an heirloom. My great-great-great-great-great-grandmother gave me that hat."

"It's only an heirloom if that great-grandmother of yours had a Walmart back in her day. I saw the tag on it. *I'm* more of an heirloom than that hat!"

Loni frowned. She didn't care that it wasn't an heirloom. It was still her hat, and she wanted it back. How dare Phyllis Habernackle! She was going to make her buy her a new hat if she couldn't find her old one. Skimming the tops of the trees, Loni looked down at the ground.

"I think we're too far away, that's the problem. It's dark, and we're too far off the ground. I'm going to fly closer to get a better look."

"Drop me off at The Village, then. You can spend the rest of the night looking for your stupid hat for all I care. It's past my bedtime."

Loni descended and did her best to weave through a grove of trees, while looking over the edge of her broomstick towards the ground. "Ugh, just let me look down in that little valley, I thought I saw something, there's... AHHHHHH!"

She felt branches clawing at her face, scratching her skin, and stealing her glasses from her as they became entangled in the branches of a tree, slowly bringing them to a halt. The broomstick attempted to surge forward but was firmly held in place.

"I can't see!" The back of the broomstick tilted down towards the ground, unable to hold both of their weight.

"Ahhh!" screamed Hazel. "Abort mission, abort mission, abort!"

Loni tried to pull up on the front of her broomstick, but it was stuck in the branches, and she felt the powers of the stick being disabled. Without her glasses, the world around her was completely black and now completely fuzzy. Loni could see nothing.

"I'm trying! But I can't see!"

And then, she felt Hazel's grasp on her waist loosening. Gravity began to tug at the old woman and then

Loni heard her scream in her ear. "Ahhhh! Heeeeeeelp!!"

Where Hazel had once been warm on her back, Loni now felt a cool breeze in its place, and Hazel's voice had faded away in the distance.

"Hazel? You back there?" she asked, suspended blindly in the tree branches.

No one answered.

"Hazel?!"

But the world was silent around her.

"Haze!" she hollered even louder. What was she going to do? Gwyn was going to kill her if she lost Hazel. "Damnit, I gotta get out of this stupid tree!" She kicked her feet and felt the branches clawing at her limbs.

Time to break out the magic, Yolanda, she thought to herself. She rubbed her hands together, then blew in them to warm them and loosen her cold joints. Then she held them out in front of her as the tree suspended her above the ground. She closed her eyes and summoned as much energy from the tree as she could. She felt it gathering between her hands. She felt her body becoming a receptacle for nature's graces. Slowly, she opened her eyes and saw the glowing orange ball of the force of nature in her hands.

With one giant flourish, she cast the ball down towards the ground. When it hit the grass, it fired back up at her in a stream of light. Slowly, she maneuvered her body onto the stream until she could feel herself being levitated by the current. By moving her palms parallel to the ground, she could feel herself being carried out of the tree. "It's working!" she cheered. It had been years since she'd had to levitate herself in such an awkward way.

When she could no longer feel the branches touching her arms and legs, she slowly lessened the amount of energy she fired at the ground, and inch by inch it lowered her closer to the grass until finally, she could feel her feet on the ground. She'd done it!

"Hazel, I did it!" she cheered excitedly. "Hazel?"

But she couldn't hear Hazel, and she certainly couldn't *see* Hazel. Not without her glasses. Without her glasses she was blind. Without her glasses *and* in the dark, she was completely helpless. She got down on her hands and knees and began to feel around the grass, searching for her glasses. Her gown kept catching between her knees and the ground, tripping her up. She put a hand to her head, and that was when it hit her that her scarf was gone! She had no scarf and no glasses. Her face was more exposed to the world than it had been in decades! She'd not left her house without a costume since…well, since *then*.

Her heart lurched into her throat. What if someone saw her? She couldn't be seen out in public without a scarf. But she couldn't go anywhere because she didn't have her glasses and she couldn't see where she was going. Panic began to overwhelm her. She pictured FBI agents surrounding her. She was sure there was a sniper on a house over her head. Did she have one of those little red glowing dots on her forehead?

"Hazel?" she asked weakly, her voice trembling along

with her hands. "Hazel, I don't know where you are, but we have to get out of here. It isn't safe."

She continued to feel around on the grass. Then she stopped what she was doing and took a deep breath, trying to center herself. She rocked backwards until she was sitting pretzel-style. With her eyes closed, she put her hands out on either side of her, her palms facing upwards towards the heavens.

> *Mother Nature heed my call*
> *You took my glasses in the fall*
> *Give them back and let me see*
> *The way back home will comfort me.*

Loni felt the air shift around her.
She chanted again...

> *Mother Nature heed my call*
> *You took my glasses in the fall*
> *Give them back and let me see*
> *The way back home will comfort me.*

Her hair began to whip around her head. And then suddenly, she felt something touch her hand. She felt around the grass and immediately felt the familiar touch of her thick glasses. She let out a breath of relief.

"Thank you!" she shouted into the night sky.

With her glasses on, Loni could still see nothing around her. It was much too dark for that, but she did stand up.

"Hazel?" she asked trepidatiously, scared to yell too loudly. What if *they* heard her? She wasn't safe here. "Hazel, we really need to go."

No answer. She knew in her heart that Hazel knew the way home. She was a tough old bird. And she had magic. She'd figure out her way home. Loni looked around her and then slipped back behind a tree. She'd find her way home without Hazel.

33

*G*wyn paced the length of Kat's covered porch, waiting for Loni and her mother to return home after their late-night fly. The hour they'd been waiting seemed to drag on, making Gwyn progressively uneasy. They'd already taken the black gowns off and removed the shoe polish from their faces. Now all they had to do was wait for the other two to return, but Gwyn could sense in her bones that something had gone terribly wrong.

"We should be out there looking for them," said Gwyn as she rubbed her arms to stifle the goose bumps threatening to pebble them.

Char shook her head and leaned back in the small iron chair. "It would be a waste of our time. Those girls could be anywhere."

"Like in the hospital," said Gwyn. She stopped pacing, then swiveled on her heel and started for the house.

"Where are you going?" asked Phyllis.

"To get my car keys from the house. I'm going to go check the hospital."

"Someone would have called you by now if they were in the hospital. Knowing Loni, she probably took your mom out for a late-night joy ride over the mountains or something."

Gwyn's eyes widened as she felt a lump form in the back of her throat. "Oh, great, now I'll picture them being stranded in the wilderness with a pack of wild boars breathing down their necks!"

Char smiled at her. "You're being ridiculous, Gwyn. There are no wild boars in the Appalachian Mountains."

Gwyn crossed her arms across her chest. "Shows what you know. I heard a story on National Public Radio on the drive here from Arizona. There are indeed wild boars on the Appalachian Trail."

"Well, that passes through the eastern side of the state. We're not even close to the Appalachian Trail. Besides, don't wild boars eat like nuts and wild berries? What would boars want with a couple of bony old women? There isn't even enough meat between the two of them for a boar's midnight snack."

"I didn't say the boars wanted to *eat them*! Oh my goodness, Char, are you *trying* to freak me out?!"

"I'm just saying, I'm sure your mother and Loni are just fine. Quit worrying!"

Gwyn felt her lungs constrict, making her unable to inhale a deep breath. Something was seriously wrong. She could feel it. "Maybe we should call the police," said

Gwyn, rubbing her wrists. "They've been missing for over an hour."

Phyllis stood up and walked across the porch to put both of her hands on Gwyn's shoulders. "Take a deep breath, Gwyn. Listen to yourself. They've been missing for an *hour*. Not a couple of hours. Not a day. Not a week. They've been missing for an *hour*."

Char nodded. "Phil's right. The police wouldn't even take you seriously if you called them. I don't even think you can call someone missing if they've been gone for an hour. Knowing your mother, she probably conned Lon into stopping off at the all-night diner for French fries or something."

Phyllis tried to smile. "Or maybe she had to use the restroom again. That's probably what happened."

Gwyn forced herself to nod. Maybe her friends were right. Maybe everything was just fine. She shook out her hands and rolled her shoulders. "Okay," she said, more to herself than the girls. "I'll try to let it go. Loni's an adult. She can watch out for my mother, right?"

Phyllis hugged her. "Exactly. Plus Hazel isn't a child, Gwyn. She can take care of herself. They'll both be fine. Come on. Sit down with us and enjoy the beautiful evening." Phyllis took a seat next to Char at the little settee.

Gwyn walked around the two of them and scooted herself up onto the white porch swing on the far corner of the porch. "It *is* a nice evening," she said, trying to convince herself everything was alright.

"And we got some new information," said Char. "We know Ruben isn't the killer."

"Yeah, we know that, but now that puts us back to square one!" complained Phyllis.

"We've got that piece of vinyl," said Gwyn.

Phyllis harrumphed. "Some clue. We have no idea what it came from. How are we supposed to use it to find the killer?"

Suddenly, they heard a rustling on the side of the house. "Girls, did you hear that?" asked Char, getting to her feet.

Phyllis stood up next and held her hands out, palms flat in front of her to zap whatever came her way. "Yes, I did. Who's there?" she hollered into the night.

Gwyn hopped up next, praying it was her mother and Loni. Perhaps they'd flown in and landed in the backyard. "Mom?" she called out, rushing to the edge of the porch steps.

"It's me," said Loni, hobbling towards them. Her dress was torn in several places, her glasses were crooked, she walked with a limp, and not only did she not have her hat, but she also didn't have Hazel with her.

"Loni!" said Phyllis. "It's about time! Where have you been?"

"Where's Mom?" asked Gwyn as she ran down the stairs and started around the side of the house towards the backyard. "Did she go in through the back?"

"Gwyn, wait!" Loni hollered at her. "She's not in the house."

Gwyn walked back around to look at Loni curiously. "Why do you look like that? Where's Mom?"

Loni's eyes darted around the neighborhood. "We'll talk about it inside. Not out here. Come on," she said and pulled Gwyn's elbow towards the house.

Gwyn felt her dander starting to spring up. Something was indeed wrong. "No, we'll talk about it out here! Where's my mother?"

Loni shook her head and ignored Gwyn. She hobbled up the stairs with a very pronounced limp.

"What's with the limp?" asked Char as she followed Loni inside the house.

"We had broomstick problems," she said to the group once she'd pulled the drapes in the parlor and shut the front door.

"Broomstick problems? What kind of problems?" asked Char. "Mechanical difficulties?"

"Ha-ha, very funny," said Loni.

"More like user error, I'm sure," snapped Phyllis.

Loni frowned at the group. "We ran into a tree crossing, I'll have you know."

"A tree crossing?" asked Phyllis. "What's a tree crossing?"

"A tree crossed in front of us," said Loni indignantly. "It wasn't my fault. It just popped up out of nowhere."

"Trees don't just pop up out of nowhere, Loni," snapped Gwyn. She was starting to get the picture. Loni hadn't been paying attention to where she was going, and she'd crashed the broomstick. "Where is my mother? Is she hurt? Is she alright? Did you leave her somewhere safe for us to go pick her up?"

Loni took off her glasses and held them up to the light so she could bend them back into the correct shape. Once she'd put them back on her face, she looked at Gwyn. Her big eyes blinked matter-of-factly. "Well. Here's the thing. Once we got tangled up in the tree, Hazel sort of disappeared."

"Disappeared? How?!"

Loni threw her hands out on either side. "I don't know. One minute she was there, one minute she was falling out of the tree."

Gwyn's jaw dropped, and she felt her limbs go numb. "My mother *fell* out of a tree?"

Loni shrugged as she took a seat on the nearest chair. "I guess. I couldn't see anything. I lost my glasses in the fall. That damn veil was in my eyes. It was dark. I was blind. One minute Hazel was behind me, and the next minute she was gone."

Blood began to rush to Gwyn's cheeks. "Loni. Where is my mother?"

"I don't know," she sighed. "I looked for her…"

"But you just left her?"

"I couldn't find her!" argued Loni.

Gwyn ran for her purse. "She could be hurt. You need to take us to where you last saw her."

Loni's magnified eyes blinked behind her lenses. "I have no idea where that was…"

"You don't know where you came from?" demanded Gwyn.

Loni's mouth opened, but for once the woman seemed speechless, "I—uh…"

Phyllis and Char, who had remained mum thus far, let out sighs. Char spoke first. "Loni. Take a deep breath. You're shaken up. One thing at a time. Are you hurt?"

Loni looked down at her ankle. She leaned down and felt it with her hand. "I turned my ankle in a hole on the way here," she admitted quietly.

"You walked all the way back here? Why didn't you fly?" asked Phyllis.

"My broomstick—I think it's still stuck in the tree."

"This is ridiculous. Why are we sitting around talking to her? She's clueless. Completely clueless," snapped Gwyn. She was at her breaking point. There was a serial killer on the loose in Aspen Falls, killing old witches, and now her mother was out there. *Alone!* She needed to find her mother before she lost it completely.

Char turned to Gwyn. "Gwyn. You need to take a deep breath too. We're going to need Loni to help us find where she crashed. Okay? Relax for a minute. We're going to find Hazel. But first I need to help Loni. Just give me a minute or two. Alright? Then we'll all go out looking for your mom."

Gwyn closed her eyes and inhaled a deep breath. Her shoulders were tense and as she slowly exhaled she tried to release the tension the best she could. With her eyes closed, she could hear Char tending to Loni.

"Where's it hurt exactly, Loni?" she asked.

Gwyn parted her lashes and stared down at Loni hatefully as she showed Char where her pain was.

She could scream at the nutjob of a woman. What had Gwyn been thinking to have let her precious mother ride on the back of a broomstick with the craziest woman in Aspen Falls? She hadn't been thinking! She'd been too consumed with learning to "loosen up" and having more fun. Well, no more! Safety was going to resume its number-one spot in her life!

"Are we ready yet?" demanded Gwyn.

Char looked up from the ground. "Give me just a minute. Her ankle's pretty badly swollen." Then she looked at Phyllis. "Phil, hand me my purse. I think I have some amethyst in there."

Phyllis handed Char the purse she'd brought with her, and Char dug through it to find an amethyst crystal. She held it between her hands with her eyes closed and then held the crystal over Loni's ankle.

> *Ancient moon and starlit night,*
> *Heal this witch's limb just right.*
> *Soothe her pain with nature's powers,*
> *By the magic witching hour.*

Gwyn could see an energy swirling around Loni's ankle. Char's powers of healing were working. She could see it in Loni's face.

Relief washed over Loni's face like a wave across the sand, smoothing the lines of pain. "It's already feeling better."

"It doesn't take long," said Char. "Let me help you to

your feet, and we'll see if putting weight on it changes things."

With a boost from Char, Loni got to her feet. She took a few crooked steps as she looked down at her leg. "The pain is still there a little bit, but it's definitely improved."

Char smiled at her and patted her on the back. "It takes a few minutes for the pain to go away completely, but it'll be healed before midnight, I guarantee it."

"Good. Can we go now?" demanded Gwyn.

Loni looked down at her hands as she approached Gwyn. "I'm sorry, Gwynnie, I really am…"

Gwyn held a palm up to Loni's face. "Don't. I don't want to hear it, Hodges. You can explain once we've found her. Come on, let's go."

Loni's feet seemed to be bolted to the floor. "Gwyn, I —I can't…"

Phyllis's eyes widened as she stared at Loni. "What do you mean you can't? You *lost* the woman's mother! Of course you can!"

Loni looked fretfully at the door. "They're out there," she whispered. "I can't leave."

"Who's out there?" asked Char, looking at the door curiously.

Loni looked almost uncomfortable enough not to say what she was thinking. "The FBI. They found me when I fell off my broomstick. I—I lost my hat, and I lost my veil, and I didn't have my glasses on. It was a really close call."

Gwyn's eyes narrowed as she peered at Loni. "Are. You. SERIOUS?!" Gwyn hollered. "There was no one following you, Loni. You're nuts. Flat-out nuts. And if you won't come help me find my mother, so help me, Loni, I'm never speaking to you again," she hollered down at the small woman while poking a finger into her chest.

Char got between them. "Okay, okay. That's enough. Let's not say things we can't walk back once Hazel is found safe and sound."

"We don't *know* Mom's going to be found safe and sound, do we?"

Char sighed and then tugged on Gwyn's arm. "Come on, Phil. Help me get Gwyn to the car. We'll go hunting for Hazel without Loni. Loni, you stay here. If Hazel comes back, call us."

Gwyn fought to leave. "We're not leaving with her? She's the only one that knows where to look for her!"

"We'll find her, Gwyn. There are places we can look without Loni's help."

Gwyn looked over Char's puffy white head as she and Phyllis dragged her to the car. "I'm coming after you, Hodges. You can hide all you want, but I know where you live!"

34

"*I* can't believe you just let Loni stay back at the house," complained Gwyn as Char backed the car out of the parking lot of the Aspen Falls Medical Center. "We've checked the hospital. Mom's not there. We've checked The Village, no Mom. I think it's time to go get Yolanda Hodges and *force her* to help us figure out where she last saw Mom. She could be lying somewhere bleeding to death right now!"

Phyllis stuck her head forward between the two seats. "Haze is a tough old bird. She's not bleeding to death."

"You don't know that!" snapped Gwyn. "Or the serial killer could have her by now!"

"Unlikely," said Phyllis. "Haze would put up too much of a fuss."

Gwyn's eyebrows set into a straight line. "Turn the car around, Char. We need to get Loni. She's the only one of us who knows where to look."

"She doesn't remember, Gwyn. The woman was

flustered. It was dark. She twisted her ankle. She lost her glasses. And she thought the FBI was coming down on her. There's no way she'll have any clue which tree in Aspen Falls she crashed into," said Char. "Cut her a break. I think she's got a bolt loose in the attic."

"I don't care if all the bolts in her attic are loose. She holds the key to finding Mom." Gwyn crossed her arms across her chest staunchly. They'd been driving around the city streets for the last half hour in the general vicinity of where they'd been flying earlier, and there was no sign of her mother.

Phyllis sighed. "I hate to say this, girls, but I think maybe it's time to go to the police station. Maybe they can get a couple of cruisers out looking for her."

Gwyn nodded and looked at Char. "I agree. I don't care if it hasn't been twenty-four hours. An elderly citizen of Aspen Falls is in danger. Shouldn't they do *something* to help?"

Char turned at the next block and laid on the gas. "Fine by me."

Minutes later, they'd parked the car and were standing in front of Officer Peterman, the police station's night shift desk clerk. He was a young, gangly fellow with long arms and a mop of blond hair.

"Officer Peterman." Gwyn read his name tag as she approached him. "We're looking for a missing woman. My mother. She—she took a tumble and now she's missing. Is there any way we can get a police officer to help us find her?"

Officer Peterman spoke into the microphone on the plexiglass. "What's your mother's name?"

"Hazel. Hazel Mae Prescott," said Gwyn. "Do I need to fill out a missing person's report first? Or can you just have a cruiser go out looking for her?"

"I'll have you talk to one of our officers." He reached over and pressed a button, sounding a buzzer. "Come on back." He stood up and led the women through the maze of offices, finally stopping in front of a conference room, where he gestured for them to enter. "You can wait here. I'll have someone brought in to talk to you," he said before shutting the door and disappearing.

Gwyn paced the floor while Phyllis and Char took seats at the table. "I literally cannot believe this is happening right now." Her stomach felt scrambled and nauseous, and her mind raced.

"Calm down, Gwyn, we'll find her," said Char, dropping her face into her cupped hands.

"You don't know that! You really don't," said Gwyn. She was tired of people telling her to calm down. It wasn't their mother that was missing! How dare they tell her to calm down!

The door opened a second later, and a short bulldog of a man wearing a police uniform and carrying a clipboard stepped in. He had a short buzz cut of brown hair, and shoulders that settled next to his earlobes. "Good evening, ladies. I'm Officer Gerard. I hear you're looking for your mother?" His eyes scanned the room as he tried to assess which person he should be speaking to.

"Yes, Officer." Gwyn stepped forward, nodding as she

walked towards him. "I'm looking for my mother. Her name is Hazel Mae Prescott. She's about this tall," said Gwyn, holding a hand up to her chin. "Well, maybe more like this tall." She lowered her hand to the top of her shoulders.

Officer Gerard lifted one overgrown brow as he looked up from his clipboard. "Hazel, you say?"

Char nodded. "Yes, Officer. Little old lady with a cane."

Officer Gerard stopped writing and looked at the women curiously. "What was she wearing?"

"Well, she was wearing a white cardigan over a floral shirt and a greenish skirt. But we put a black robe on her when we went out," said Phyllis. Then she sighed uncomfortably. "And her face was smeared with shoe polish."

He peered at Gwyn curiously. "You took your mother out late at night and dressed her in black and smeared her face with shoe polish?"

With one hand covering the unease in her stomach, Gwyn lifted her other hand to her forehead. *How stupid do I sound right now? What was I thinking?* she berated herself.

Phyllis pushed Gwyn out of the way. "It's a long story, Officer. Mostly we were concerned about Margaret Sutton's killer being on the loose. How's that investigation going, anyway?" Phyllis didn't wait for an answer. "So can you help us find Hazel or can't you?"

He gave the women a half-smile and then peered around Phyllis to speak to Gwyn. "Well, I'll be honest with you. I do have a woman in custody fitting that description."

Gwyn's heart leapt in her chest. "You found my mother?"

Phyllis pulled back her head. "You have her in custody? As in arrested?" she asked incredulously.

He held a hand up in front of the ladies. "Well now, one thing at a time. I said I have a woman in custody *fitting that description*. Unfortunately, she didn't have any ID on her, and the name she gave us was not Hazel Prescott."

"Well, what did she say her name was?" asked Char.

"Gwyndolin Prescott," said Officer Gerard with a half-smile.

Gwyn sucked in her breath. "I'm Gwyndolin Prescott," she said with a hand to her chest. "My mother got arrested, and she used my name?!"

He nodded. "Apparently."

At that moment, Gwyn didn't even care. "Is she alright? Physically, I mean?"

He smiled and put a hand on Gwyn's shoulder. "Yes, your mother seems to be fine. She's got a bit of a mouth on her, but physically she's okay."

Gwyn let out an audible sigh and relaxed her shoulders. "Oh, thank God."

Char cocked one eyebrow up. "So what did she get arrested for?"

Officer Gerard rearranged the papers on his clipboard almost as if he were stalling. Finally, he sighed. "Grand theft auto."

"What?!" demanded Gwyn. "My mother is being

charged with grand theft auto? You've got to be kidding me! She's an old woman!"

"An old woman who was trying to steal a car," he pointed out. "Now, she hasn't been *officially* charged, yet. We were trying to find out a little more about her and see if we couldn't establish who she belonged to."

Gwyn lifted her brows and pointed at herself emphatically. "Me! She belongs to me!"

He nodded. "I see that now."

"What happened?" asked Phyllis.

He leaned his round bottom against the door frame and crossed his right foot over his ankle. "My partner and I were cruising tonight near the intersection of Donovan and Pine street when we heard a car alarm going off. We responded to the alarm and discovered your mother trying to hot-wire the car. Apparently, she crossed some wires and set the car alarm off instead."

All three women looked at each other with slack jaws. Gwyn's mouth went dry.

Char cast a curious glance towards Gwyn. "Hazel can hot-wire a car?"

Phyllis shook her head. "Apparently she can't! That was her first mistake!"

Gwyn couldn't wrap her head around what the officer was telling her. "My mother was trying to hot-wire a car? I—I didn't even know she knew how to do that! This can't seriously be happening right now."

"Can we see her?" asked Char.

He nodded. "Absolutely. Right this way."

He led them through a series of hallways until they

came to a windowed holding cell. "We were trying to get information out of her when you showed up, but that woman is tighter than a clamshell with lockjaw."

Gwyn rushed to the window. Behind it, Hazel lay faceup on a hard wooden bench with the black gown she'd worn tucked behind her head for a pillow.

Gwyn knocked on the glass. "Mom!" she hollered. "Mom, it's Gwynnie. Can you hear me? Are you alright?"

Hazel's limbs flinched before she opened her eyes. Her head lifted as she looked at the window with narrowed eyes. "Gwynnie?" She lifted her glasses from her chest and put them on. That was when she saw Officer Gerard staring at her through the window too. She glanced back at her daughter. "I mean, Hazel. Hazel! My sweet daughter Hazel! You've found me, your dear old mother, Gwyndolin."

Gwyn rolled her eyes. "Mom, he knows you're Hazel, and I'm Gwyn. Why did you give them my name?"

Hazel lifted her brows as her mouth formed the outline of an O. "I panicked. They asked for my name and your name just sort of popped out of my mouth."

"Mom, they arrested you for grand theft auto. What in the world? Why were you trying to steal a car?"

"I was tired," she complained. "I'd just fallen out of a tree. I wanted to go home and go to bed. I was just going to borrow it and have you return it first thing in the morning! I didn't think anyone would miss it for the evening."

"You don't even have a license, Mom. You're not supposed to be driving. You can't see at night."

"Which is exactly why I needed the car. Was I supposed to walk all the way home half-blind?" Hazel grabbed her cane and pulled herself to her feet. She ambled towards the glass. "There aren't exactly cabs on every street corner in Aspen Falls, you know."

"Oh, Mom," said Gwyn. She was so happy to see her mother in one piece that she didn't care about the theft charges, or the hot-wired car, or about the fact that her mother had used Gwyn's name instead of her own.

Hazel touched the palm of one wrinkled hand to the glass. "Gwynnie, can you take me home? I can hardly keep myself upright; I'm so tired."

Gwyn turned to look at the officer. "Officer Gerard, isn't there something we can do about this? My mother didn't know what she was doing. She's off her medication. It was late at night. She was injured. Can't we just make this all disappear?"

The officer leaned back and ran a hand across the back of his tree stump of a neck. "She's off her medication?"

Gwyn nodded. "Yes, and we've had a really long day too. There's no way she's in her right mind. Couldn't we just let this go? I can pay for any damages done to the car."

He looked down at the papers on his clipboard, lost in thought. It took him a while, but finally, he nodded. "Alright. I think maybe we can let this incident go. Of course, if it happens again…"

"Oh, it won't!" promised Gwyn with an ear-to-ear

smile as she took his hand from him and pumped it excitedly. "I promise. I'll keep an extra-close eye on her from this moment forward. I won't let her out of my sight again!"

"Oh, great," said Hazel with a flip of her hand. "I think I'm probably better off taking my chances with Officer Fun Squasher here."

Gwyn let out a nervous giggle as Officer Gerard removed his keys from his belt. "I'll get her released. You go back out to the front desk. Officer Peterman will have the paperwork to sign her out."

Gwyn nodded. "I'll be right back, Mom," she hollered through the glass. "Girls, will you please stay with her and Officer Gerard while I go get her checked out?"

Char nodded. "Absolutely. You just take care of things, Gwyn. We've got this."

Officer Gerard took Gwyn out to the hallway and pointed her back in the right direction just as Detective Whitman rounded the corner from another hallway.

"Whitman, would you take Ms. Prescott back out to Peterman? I've got to finish up something in here."

Detective Whitman looked down at Gwyn. "Ms. Prescott! What are you doing here at the station this late at night?"

"Oh, Detective Whitman, it's nice to see you again. Oh, umm…" Gwyn looked back at the door that Officer Gerard closed behind her. "My mother sort of got into some trouble."

He looked at the closed door, and then his eyes

widened as the pieces clicked in his brain. "Gerard's elderly woman is *your* elderly woman?"

Gwyn shifted uncomfortably and nodded. "I'm afraid so."

He chuckled and held a hand out in front of him as if to say *after you*. "I'm sorry. He mentioned the name to me, but it didn't click until just now. Maybe if I'd seen your mother, I would have recognized her, but I've been holed up in my office all night working the Maggie Sutton case. But it looks like we got it all worked out. Gerard knew she had to belong to *someone*."

Gwyn held a hand to her wildly pounding heart as she walked. "I'm just thankful we found her before the serial killer did!"

Detective Whitman stopped walking and looked back at her. "What did you just say?"

Gwyn felt the blood drain from her face. Had she seriously just said that out loud? She tried to laugh it off by waving a hand in front of her face. "Oh, nothing."

Detective Whitman didn't move but instead narrowed his eyes as he stared closely at Gwyn. "You said serial killer? What are you talking about?"

Gwyn cleared her throat. "Oh, you know. Maggie Sutton's death and everything. The whole town's just a little on edge."

"Maggie Sutton was only one person. One dead woman doesn't imply that there's a serial killer out there."

Gwyn smiled and nodded at him politely. "Oh, yes. Of course. My brain is just all muddled up right now. Silly old woman." She clunked her palm gently against her skull as a nervous laugh escaped her throat. "Sometimes the funniest things come out of my mouth."

"Is there something you know that you're not telling me?" asked Detective Whitman.

Gwyn giggled and headed towards the front desk. "Not at all. What would I know? I just moved to town. I'm sure Maggie's death was just a coincidence."

"A coincidence?" He rubbed a thick-fingered hand across the scruffy five-o'clock shadow that covered his chin. "A coincidence would also imply a second death. As far as I'm aware there's been only one suspicious death in Aspen Falls that we're dealing with. You know something, don't you?"

She shook her head dismissively. "I don't know anything."

"You would make a poor poker player, Ms. Prescott."

Gwyn nodded. "You're right about that. My mother got all the poker playing genes, I'm afraid." She looked at her watch and frowned. "Oh my, it *is* late! I need to get Mother home, Detective."

"Listen, I can't protect the citizens of Aspen Falls without all the facts," he said softly.

Gwyn sighed. Should she just tell him what they knew about Kat? Why did they need to keep it a secret anyway? "Fine," she sighed. "As you know, our friend Katherine Lynde died a few weeks ago."

Detective Whitman nodded. "I remember you came in to see me about some questions you had. Did you ever find your missing book?"

Gwyn shook her head. "No, but we're pretty sure we know who has it."

He lifted one brow. "Oh?"

"Yes, we think the person who killed Maggie Sutton has the book."

This seemed to intrigue Detective Whitman. "Is that so? And why do you think that?"

Gwyn looked around. She was oddly worried that the girls would be mad at her for telling Detective Whitman what they knew, but at the same time, she just wanted this all to be over and everyone to be safe. And she wanted justice for Kat. "Because the man who killed Maggie Sutton also killed Katherine Lynde before taking our book."

35

*D*etective Whitman's eyes widened to the size of half-dollars. "Why in the world would you think that? Katherine Lynde's death was ruled accidental."

Gwyn smiled at him calmly. "We're witches, remember? We have our ways."

He was silent for a moment as he mulled over her theory. "So then tell me who the killer is!"

Gwyn shook her head sadly. "I wish I could! Our magic got us as far as seeing Katherine's murder happen, but the man wore a hooded black robe during both murders, so his face was obscured."

"But you're sure that he *killed* Katherine?"

Gwyn nodded. "Sure as I am that my mother's going to fall asleep on the car ride home."

"How did he do it?"

"He hit her across the head with a shovel."

Detective Whitman's jaw hung open. Then he inhaled a deep breath, and as he exhaled, he said in a low voice, "Maggie Sutton had injuries that would be consistent with that."

Gwyn nodded. "See? I told you. The deaths are connected. Therefore we have a serial killer on our hands."

"I really wish you had some evidence to substantiate your claim," he said. It was almost a question. Like he was hoping she'd come forward with more to help his case.

"Evidence we do not have, unless you count a talking dog and a few magic spells. But we're working on it. If we find anything, we'll let you know."

He nodded. "Please do. I am, however, concerned about you ladies snooping around on a killer. That's not something to be taken lightly, and I'm concerned about your well-being. It's dangerous to get involved in a murder investigation."

"Oh, Detective Whitman," said Gwyn with a chuckle as they approached Officer Peterman's desk. "I assure you, *nothing* is more dangerous than taking care of your elderly mother."

"All I'm saying is, Mom, you shouldn't have left Loni like that," said Gwyn as they pulled away from the curb to head back to Kat's house.

Char nodded from the backseat. "I agree, Hazel. If

you and Loni would have stayed together, none of this would have happened."

Hazel readjusted the cane that had settled between her knees. "It's not my fault the loon crashed into the tree. When I landed in a bush, she wasn't around, so I took off. Was I supposed to stand there and *wait* for her to crash too?"

Gwyn gripped the steering wheel tighter. "Don't you understand, Mom? Running off is the problem. It's not like this is the first time you've run off and gotten arrested."

"The other times weren't my fault either," snapped Hazel before looking out into the darkened town. "How was I supposed to know that there were male prostitutes in Scottsdale? I just thought I was looking especially hot that night."

Gwyn groaned as she turned the steering wheel.

Phyllis piped up from the backseat. "Next time you run off, Haze, Gwyn's putting your picture on a prune juice bottle." Phyllis and Char laughed.

"Don't give her any ideas," said Hazel over her shoulder.

Char leaned forward, poking her head between the seats as Gwyn drove. "Now that we have Hazel back and everything's somewhat back to normal, I want to know exactly what you said to Detective Whitman and what he said to you!"

"Yeah, I'm shocked you told him about Kat," agreed Phyllis.

Gwyn leaned her head back against the headrest.

"I'm so sorry, girls. It was an accident, really. I said something to him about a serial killer and a coincidence, and he just needled me until he got it all out of me."

"Well, what did *you* say? What did *he* say?" asked Char.

"Basically I just told him that magic showed us that Kat was killed with a shovel and that whoever did it has our spell book. And he said that Maggie was killed similarly, so I think he believes me, but he can't do anything about it without evidence. And a killer, of course."

"Girls, we've got to solve this. Now that we know Ruben didn't do it and Boomer Wallace didn't do it, we've got to explore some other options," said Phyllis.

Gwyn took both hands off the wheel for a moment and shook her open hands at the windshield. "What other options? We *have* no other options."

"We have a swatch of vinyl belonging to the killer," said Char. "You still have it, right, Hazel?"

Hazel lifted her chin but didn't look back at the car full of women. "Of course I do."

"Okay, then there has to be a spell we can do that would use the swatch to figure out the killer. Everyone, put on your thinking caps and think about spells you know that might work," instructed Char.

The car went silent for the next few blocks before Gwyn piped up. "It's too bad we didn't have our book back. I bet it would have had some appropriate spells in it."

"You know, I do know of one thing we could try, but there are no guarantees," said Phyllis.

"What is it?" asked Char.

"My grandmother passed down her premonition blanket to me. It's really old. It was one of my ancestors'."

"A premonition blanket?" asked Gwyn skeptically. "How's that supposed to work?"

"Well, you wrap yourself in the blanket at night, and any dreams you have while wrapped in the blanket are actually premonitions."

"So how does that help us?" asked Char.

Phyllis held up a finger. "Bear with me. So, what if we sewed that swatch of material to my blanket, and I slept with it? Maybe I'd get a premonition about the killer."

"What good would that do?" asked Gwyn.

Phyllis shrugged. "You never know. I might see where he lives. I might see where he works. I might even see his face. If we could just get another clue, it might lead us to find him."

"There's no harm in it, I suppose," said Char. "We've got no other leads, and it's late. Are you sure you want to sew that thing your grandmother's blanket? It could give you nightmares!"

Phyllis scratched the side of her face. "I don't *want to*. But we're running out of options. I'm willing to take one for the team."

"Kat would thank you, I'm sure," said Char. "Alright. So then we'll meet back up again for coffee tomorrow morning and see if the blanket worked?"

A noise from Hazel's side of the car caused all the women to turn their eyes towards her. Her eyes were closed, her glasses had fallen off of her face, and her head lolled partially against the door frame. "Nughhh," she snored, a guttural inhale escaping her throat.

Gwyn smiled at her mother and let out a heavy sigh. "Alright, girls. Consider it a date."

36

*C*har was the first one to coffee the next morning, and by the time she entered Habernackle's, she'd already gone for her morning walk with Vic, baked a loaf of pumpernickel bread to bring to an ailing neighbor, and read the morning paper.

"Good morning, Linda," she chirped sunnily as she breezed into the restaurant.

"Don't you look spry this morning, Char," said Linda as she wiped a hand on her apron.

Char fluffed the puffy white hair that foamed out beneath her visor and tipped her head back. "Why, thank you. It's all the herbal breads and such," she said. "Vic wants to keep me looking young for him."

Linda laughed. "Are you meeting the girls?"

Char nodded. "Indeed I am. I'll just seat mys…"

"Yeah, I was just going to break the bad news. Your usual table is taken."

Char furrowed her eyebrows as she stared at the

men's group who'd invaded her turf. "I see that. What's up with that?"

"Oh, a group of tourists were the first ones in this morning. When I came out of the kitchen, they had already seated themselves. Then the men's coffee club came in and just sort of spread out all over the tables back there."

A door chimed behind Char. She turned around to see Phyllis wearing black shades and looking more hungover than she had the day after their little tequila party. Phyllis held her head.

"Coffee, Linda. Your mother needs coffee. Black."

"Wow, Mom. You look terrible."

Char looked her up and down. "For heaven's sake, Phyllis. You look like you went to hell and the devil didn't want you, so he spat you back up."

"I feel like it too," said Phyllis, rubbing her head. "The night I had...we need to sit so I can tell you about it." She started walking towards their usual table when she pulled up short. "Why are those *men* in our seats?"

"They got here first," sighed Char as she led them back towards the men, Linda following them both with menus. She immediately noticed that Sergeant Bradshaw was absent from the group.

"Where's your fearless leader?" Phyllis asked, her tone sharper than the point of a pin.

Only Marcus Wheedlan looked up from the conversation at the table. "If you're talking about Sarge, he's late. His truck wouldn't start."

"So y'all just decided to steal *our* table?" asked Phyllis, slamming her purse down on one of the two tables they'd shoved together.

"Sarge is usually the first one here, but since he was late, we weren't able to get our usual table," said Marcus, nodding towards the tourists in their seats.

"Well, do you need *both* of these tables?" asked Phyllis, looking down at a ratty old camera bag on the table they usually sat at. "There *are* only four of you."

"Well, Benny's in the bathroom. Sarge will be here any minute, and Mayor Adams thought he might join us for coffee today." He smiled at the two women kindly. "I'm really sorry. Everyone was here before I was, or I would have picked a different spot."

Phyllis held a hand to her temple. "Ugh," she groaned. "Fine. Come on, Char, let's go sit at the bar today."

"I'm right behind ya."

The two women pulled up to the bar and seated themselves.

Phyllis looked around. "Where's my coffee?" she grumbled. "Linda!"

"Gosh, I haven't seen you this grumpy since...well, since last night. What has gotten into you?"

Phyllis crossed her arms on the bar and laid her head down in the cradle it formed. "Ugh," she groaned. "I slept with that premonition blanket last night and had nightmares all night long."

"So it worked?" asked Char, brightening up.

With her cheek smashed against her arms, Phyllis tried to nod. "Yes, it worked."

"So what did we find out?"

"Aren't we going to wait for Gwyn and Hazel?"

Char looked behind her. They still weren't there, and she didn't want to wait. She wanted to know what Phyllis knew now. "You can just tell me. I'll tell them when they get here."

Linda split the swinging doors open, two empty coffee mugs in hand. She put them in front of Char and Phyllis and poured them each a cup of coffee. "You need some ibuprofen, Mom?"

Phyllis shook her head as she stirred a packet of sugar into her coffee. "No, thank you, dear."

"You want your usual breakfast?"

"Yes, but I need carbs. Throw down an extra slice of toast for me this morning."

Linda nodded. "You got it. Do you want that extra bacon too?"

"Yes!" said Phyllis emphatically.

"Okay. You, Char? Oatmeal?"

"Yes, dear. Same as always."

When Linda disappeared back into the kitchen, Char turned to her old friend. "Come on, now. I'm dying to know. What did you see?"

"It's going to happen again," said Phyllis in a hush.

Tingles raced down Char's arms. "What's going to happen again?" she breathed.

"The killer is going to strike again." She took a sip of her coffee. "I could sense it."

Char's lungs felt dammed in her chest, and she couldn't catch a deep breath. "You sensed it? Like how?"

"You know when you have a dream, and you're vaguely familiar with what's going on, but you don't really see it? You just know you're late for something, because you have that feeling, but you don't actually see it in the dream."

Char shrugged. "I guess."

"Well, that's what happened. I had this horrible sense of dread through the whole dream. You and I and the girls were all looking for someone, but we couldn't find her. But throughout the whole dream, I knew he was going to kill her if we didn't find her in time."

Char's eyes widened. "Who were we looking for?"

With her cup to her lips, Phyllis shrugged. "That's the thing. I really don't know. It was just that we were looking and he had her."

"But did you see *him*?"

"I saw his house."

Char's face brightened. "The outside?"

"I wish. But I did see the inside. And you're never going to believe what I saw!"

Char put a hand to her mouth. "What?" she breathed.

"I saw something hanging on his wall."

Char made a face. "And that's supposed to help us figure out who this guy is? By some decor hanging on the wall of his house?"

Phyllis put her cup down and turned to Char. "It was a cross, Char."

"A cross? As in Jesus died on the…" Char's words trailed off as she made the sign of the cross.

Phyllis nodded. "Yup. As in that."

"Oh my gosh," breathed Char, her mouth dropping open as Gwyn and Hazel pulled up barstools next to them.

"Good morning, ladies," sang Gwyn.

The two women looked up at Gwyn with slack jaws and wide eyes.

"What?" asked Gwyn.

When no one spoke, Gwyn looked at Hazel, but Hazel was busying herself with her barstool. Gwyn turned to face the girls again. "What?!" asked Gwyn again.

"We think we know who the killer is!" said Phyllis.

Gwyn's eyes widened. "The premonition blanket worked?"

Phyllis nodded. "Sort of. There was a cross on one of the walls inside his house."

"I don't get it. A cross? That tells us who it is?"

Phyllis shrugged. "It doesn't tell us *with certainty*, but I feel like it points us in the right direction."

"It does?" asked Gwyn, shaking her head in mild confusion.

"Gwyn, you need to have some caffeine, and maybe your brain will kick into gear," said Phyllis.

Char rolled her eyes. "Don't mind Mrs. Grumpy Pants. She didn't sleep very well last night. She also had a premonition that the killer is going to strike again. And then, of course, she saw the cross on the wall."

"Well, we assumed he was going to strike again," said

Gwyn. "That's not a shocker to anyone. I mean, don't serial killers usually keep killing until they're caught?"

"Well, yes, but we didn't know for *sure* that he was a serial killer. He could have been a two-time killer, and that was it."

Gwyn nodded as Linda slid a cup of coffee in front of both her and Hazel. "Thank you," she said with a kind smile to Phyllis's daughter.

"Would you like some breakfast?" asked Linda.

"Mom, you want another one of their rolls this morning?" asked Gwyn, leaning towards her mother. "Weren't they good the other day?"

Hazel frowned. "I want French fries."

Gwyn scowled at her mother. "They don't serve French fries in the mornings, remember? And besides, after that little stunt you pulled with Harrison the other day, you lost out on that deal we made."

"Deal, schmeal. I'm sure *someone* else in this town serves French fries in the morning," said Hazel gruffly.

"Perhaps," agreed Gwyn with a nod. "But we're here. And this place doesn't cook French fries until lunchtime, *and* you're grounded. So you'll have to pick something else."

"I don't want something else."

Gwyn sighed. "Really, Mom? After everything you put me through last night, you're going to be stubborn about French fries again?"

Hazel shrugged.

Linda looked at her with a kind smile. "I'm sorry,

Hazel. We have hash browns, would you like some of those? They're potatoes too."

"Do you have any hash browns in the shape of French fries?" asked Hazel petulantly.

Linda laughed. "I'm sorry, we don't. Just the regular old shredded kind."

"Then I don't want anything," said Hazel, sticking her nose up into the air in the opposite direction.

"Mom, you're going to starve," begged Gwyn. "Girls, tell my mother to eat something other than French fries?"

From the opposite end of the bar, Phyllis craned her neck around Char and Gwyn to see Hazel gazing off in the other direction. "Meh, she'll live if she goes without a meal."

Char patted Gwyn on the back. "Hazel, you really should eat something besides French fries, dear. Didn't your mother ever tell you that you are what you eat?"

"Of course she told me that. Why do you think I eat French fries? I wouldn't mind being tall, thin, and French," said Hazel with a dentured smile.

Char and Linda chuckled. Char sighed. "Oh, Gwyn, I think Hazel will be fine. If she's hungry enough, she'll eat. Maybe you shouldn't be so hard on her."

"Seriously?" asked Gwyn. "I shouldn't be so hard on her? Do you *not* recall her running off yesterday and hot-wiring a car?"

Linda looked across the bar at Hazel in astonishment. "Hazel, you hot-wired a car?!"

"*Tried*," said Phyllis.

Gwyn looked down the bar at Phyllis. "What?"

"She *tried* to hot-wire a car. She failed. If she hadn't failed, she wouldn't have been caught. I think the problem here isn't that she got arrested, it's that she *failed to properly hot-wire the car.* Maybe this is simply a lack of education, and we should have someone teach her," said Phyllis with a wicked smile.

Gwyn lowered her eyebrows. "Phyllis Habernackle, that is not funny. You're encouraging her!"

"The woman's a million years old, Gwyn. If she wants to eat French fries for breakfast, let her! We're too old not to get what we want in life. How would you like someone telling you that you couldn't have ... I don't know. Wine?"

Gwyn buried her head in her hands, then let her fingers comb over her scalp before slamming her palms down onto the counter. "Fine, Mom. Don't eat. You can eat at The Village at lunchtime. Linda, just one roll this morning, please."

"You got it." Linda smiled at her before disappearing back into the kitchen.

Gwyn swiveled her chair so her back was to Hazel and looked at Char and Phyllis. "Okay, now can we please talk about this premonition dream you had?"

Phyllis leaned her forehead on her hand. "I can't talk about it anymore. It shot my nerves to hell."

"It was that bad?" Gwyn asked Char.

Char nodded as the smile on her face vanished. "Someone else is gonna bite the bullet soon if we don't find this psycho."

Gwyn sucked in her breath. "She *saw* that?"

"I had this feeling of dread through the entire dream. He's going to strike again soon. I know it," groaned Phyllis.

"But you didn't see a face?" asked Gwyn.

Char shook her head. "Nope. She didn't see any faces. But she saw the cross."

"So what does the cross signify? He's religious?" asked Gwyn.

Char pointed a finger heavenward. "I think it means more than just 'he's religious.' I think we need to go pay a little visit to our loaner priest."

"Father Donovan?" breathed Gwyn with shock. "You think a *priest* killed two women?"

Char held up a finger. "Two witches. I think he killed *two witches*!"

Phyllis leaned down to look past Char at Gwyn. "Are you kidding me, Gwyn? Are you that naive? Priests are human too. They do all sorts of wicked things. You don't think there's a priest out there that's killed anyone before?"

"Well, I mean, I suppose it's *possible*, but you really think he could have killed Kat and Maggie?"

"Let's look at the facts," said Char, opening one hand on the bar so she could count on her fingers. "We've got the fact that he's completely opposed to witchcraft and thinks witches are pagan spirits. So we know *why* he might have done it. That's motive." She checked off one finger.

"We know he was down at the Falls the night of

Margaret's murder. And we know he came to Aspen Falls right before Kat was murdered. That's opportunity times two," she said and ticked off two more fingers.

"Both women were hit with a blunt object. Like that's hard to find? Kat had a shovel in her garden. Maggie could have been hit with a rock for all we know. There are our means," she said, checking off two more fingers. "Not to mention the fact that he's a priest and owns a black robe. Case closed."

Phyllis nodded her head knowingly. "*And* I've seen him carrying around a messenger's bag with a black strap on it. That could be where that piece of black nylon came from!"

Gwyn's head reared back. "Listen, I know Father Donovan was a bit harsh on witches, but do you really think he hates us enough to want to *kill* us all?"

Phyllis shrugged as Linda appeared from the kitchen again to refill the women's coffee. "I don't think we can put it past him. Overlooking him as a suspect might just be the opening he needs to put another witch into the ground."

Linda topped off Gwyn's coffee. Then she leaned forward to speak in a hush. "You know, I don't mind putting a few French fries into the fryer for your mother. I didn't want to offer it in front of her before because I know you're opposed to it, but it's really no big deal, and I hate for her to go hungry."

Gwyn gave Linda a funny look. Then she turned her head to look over her shoulder at Hazel. When she realized that Hazel wasn't sitting next to her anymore, she spun completely around to inspect her chair more closely, as if Hazel was actually sitting in it, but she just wasn't able to see her for some reason.

"Mom?" Gwyn said aloud.

"Where'd Haze go?" asked Char.

Gwyn threw a hand out on either side of her as her mouth hung open. "I don't know. She was just here."

"She probably went to use the little girls' room," said Char. "Don't worry. Sit back down. Cut her a break. You don't have to follow her *everywhere* she goes. She's a grown woman."

Gwyn's head shook as she boosted herself off her seat. "You don't understand. Yes, I do have to follow her everywhere she goes." She ran around the bar towards the bathroom.

Seconds later, Gwyn was back with an ashen face. "She's not in there. The bathrooms are empty."

Char sat up a little higher. Surely Hazel hadn't just *run off*. Not after last night's fiasco. She looked at Gwyn in confusion. "Well, surely she's around here *somewhere*."

Char and Phyllis both spun their seats around so the three of them could face the breakfast crowd in the restaurant.

"I don't see her," said Phyllis.

"Me either," agreed Char.

Gwyn headed for the front door without a word to the girls.

"Where you going, Gwyn?" asked Char.

"To look for my mother!"

37

"*H*ow do you know where to look?" Char asked Gwyn as the women blasted out of Habernackle's front door.

Gwyn looked both ways down the street. "I don't see her."

"How'd she get away so fast?" asked Phyllis, straightening the dark shades she'd just pulled back on.

"I have no idea how she can move that fast when I'm not looking, but it takes her an hour to walk from the bathroom to the chair," said Gwyn. "Ugh, this woman frustrates me. Come on," she said and began heading towards the main street.

"Where are we going?" asked Char.

"We're going to try the cafe down the street. What's it called?"

"Aspen Falls Eclectic Eatery," said Char. "Julius Marcel owns it."

"Julius Marcel from the Paranormal Institute for Wizards?" asked Gwyn with surprise.

Char nodded. "Yes. Julius moved back to town about fifteen years ago."

"Alright, let's go check it out. Maybe they serve French fries in the morning. I know my mother, and if she took off, she went to find fries."

The three women went on a mad dash towards the small eatery. Beneath the striped awning out front was an outside eating area that consisted of a waist-high black wrought-iron fence and matching wrought-iron tables and chairs. The women walked around the fence to the opening and hurried inside the small eatery. Only a handful of customers sat in the booths lining both walls, and the tables in the center of the dining area were empty.

"It doesn't look like she's here," said Phyllis.

Gwyn rushed to the hostess standing near a podium.

"Table for three?" asked the woman as she grabbed a stack of menus from a shelf inside the podium.

"No, we're looking for my mother. She's about this tall, white hair, cane," said Gwyn, holding her hand up to her shoulder. "She would have ordered French fries."

The woman shook her head. "I'm sorry," she said with a bit of a French accent. "I have not seen anyone here like that today."

"You're sure?" asked Gwyn in a bit of a panic.

"Yes, I am sure," said the woman kindly.

Gwyn nodded. "Thank you." She turned around and headed back for the door. "Let's go girls."

Outside Char squeezed Gwyn's hand as the panic Gwyn felt in her heart began to bubble up to her face. "It's okay, Gwynnie. We'll find her. We found her last night, didn't we?"

"The police station!" said Gwyn. "We should try there again."

"She's only been gone a few minutes, Gwyn," said Phyllis. "There's no way she got arrested *already*."

"Let's go back to Habernackle's," suggested Char. "Someone else in there had to have seen which direction she went."

"Good idea," said Phyllis.

The three women went back to the restaurant and found Reign behind the counter. "Reign," said Phyllis, curling her finger towards her grandson. "Reign, you didn't happen to see Gwyn's mother, Hazel, anywhere did you? Perhaps she wandered into the kitchen in search of French fries?"

Reign smiled. "Mom just mentioned that Hazel wandered off. I haven't seen her, sorry. But you're welcome to check the bedrooms upstairs."

Gwyn sighed. "I'll check with the men's coffee table. Char, can you check the rooms? And Phyllis, can you please check with the rest of the customers?" suggested Gwyn.

Char and Phyllis took off as instructed while Gwyn walked over to the men.

"Gwyn, what a pleasure," said Sergeant Harrison Bradshaw, getting to his feet. "Would you like to join us for coffee this morning?"

397

Gwyn shook her face, lips pursed. "No, thank you, Harrison. I'm actually looking for my mother."

"Hazel's missing?" he asked in surprise. "I could have sworn I saw her at the counter when I came in just a bit ago."

Gwyn nodded. "Yes, I know. She was there a moment ago. I'm afraid I took my eyes off of her for just a second, and she wandered off. It's fairly typical of her to do so, but now I can't find her."

He shook his head. "I've been buried in a political debate with the mayor here for the last few minutes, so I'm afraid I didn't notice anything." He looked at the men at the table. "I'll see what I can find out for you, though."

"That would be very helpful."

"Excuse me, gentlemen," he said, clearing his throat. "Gwyn here is looking for her mother, Hazel. She's the tiny thing with a cane and the mean right cross."

Several of the men's eyebrows lifted as they tried to control their laughter. Sergeant Bradshaw looked at them sternly, and they promptly fought to swallow back their jokes.

"She was just sitting up at the counter, and now I'm afraid she's wandered off. Did anyone here see which way she went?" asked Gwyn.

Mayor Adams looked up from his Danish. "I saw her heading towards the bathroom only a few minutes ago."

Benny Hamilton nodded his head. "I saw her heading that way too, just as I was coming back from the bathroom."

Sam Jeffries, Marcus Wheedlan, and two other men

Gwyn had never seen before shook their heads as if to say they hadn't seen any of it.

"I'm sorry," said Marcus. "I wasn't paying attention."

"Me either," agreed Sam.

"Would you like some help looking for her?" asked Harrison, straightening the collar on his polo.

Gwyn smiled politely. She barely knew the man. She could hardly ask for his help in finding her mother. "I appreciate the offer, Harrison, I really do, but unfortunately I wouldn't even know where to ask you to look."

"Gwyn, no one saw anything," said Phyllis, as she came up behind her. "Sergeant, did you fellas see anything?"

He shook his head. "A few people saw her going towards the restroom, but that was it."

"But I checked both the women's and then men's rooms. They were both empty," said Gwyn with a sigh. "I just don't understand where else she would go!"

Char came bounding down the stairs. "Rooms upstairs are all empty. Let's go check The Village. Maybe she caught a ride from someone back there," suggested Phyllis.

"Good idea." Gwyn smiled at Harrison. "Thank you for the offer, Harrison, but I think we'll do a little snooping around town before we call in the Army."

"Well, if you can't find her, I'd sure be happy to help!" he said.

Gwyn looked at him coyly. "Even after my mother punched you in the *Gruesome Twosome?*" she asked, lowering her voice when she said the silly moniker.

Sergeant Bradshaw's eyebrows lifted up into his forehead. "The Gruesome Twosome?" He couldn't help but chuckle. "Oh, Gwyn. You are just something else, aren't you?"

Gwyn felt color flooding her cheeks. *Something good or something bad?* she silently wondered.

"But *yes*, even after that. Hazel didn't mean anything by that little nudge, and I'm quite alright now, so I hope you haven't been too hard on her. It was my own fault, for trying to show off."

"Trying to show off?" mused Gwyn.

"I hate to keep you. I know you need to find Hazel. It was good to see you again. Perhaps we'll bump into one another for coffee tomorrow?"

Gwyn smiled at him. The worry over her mother's disappearance had vanished in those few moments, and all she felt was a little spin of excitement that welled up in her chest. It was something she hadn't felt in quite a long time.

"Perhaps," she answered with a little wave as she followed Char and Phyllis towards the front door.

"I think that man's sweet on you," said Char as they crossed the street to Gwyn's car.

"Oh, stop," said Gwyn.

"No, I'm serious. I've never seen *Harrison* talk to anyone the way he talks to you, and I've known that man for years."

"Well," breathed Gwyn, "there's no time to think

about that now. I have far too many things on my plate at the moment. Like finding my mother, for starters."

The three women got in the car. "Should we go pick up Loni?" asked Char. "She might want to help us look."

"Ha!" sputtered Gwyn as she backed the car out of her parking spot. "She was the one who *lost* Mother last night and couldn't be bothered to help look for her! Why would she want to help now?"

"Oh, cut her a break. Something's loose in the attic and the woman's blind as a bat. She had a rough night too, crashing into that tree and then having to walk home," said Char.

Gwyn slunk back in her seat. "Oh, fine, we'll pick up Loni to help us look, but then our one and only priority is finding Mom."

*M*inutes later, the women were outside Loni Hodges's house, honking their horn.

"You really think Loni's coming outside to us honking?" asked Char.

"I'm not going in there," said Gwyn adamantly. "You wanted her to come. You go get her."

Char rolled her eyes and ambled out the passenger door. "Fine. I'll go."

Phyllis leaned her head back against the seat back. "Ugh, I feel like hell, Gwynnie," she groaned, her raspy voice filling the car.

"I'm sorry, Phyllis. We'll get back to your premonitions as soon as we find Mom."

"You know, I've had premonitions before, but none like this. It was so dark and so ominous. It just really shot my nerves to hell."

Despite her own anxiety, Gwyn reached back to rub Phyllis's knee. "I'm so sorry, Phyllis."

The minute Gwyn's hand touched her leg, Phyllis's body went rigid against the seat. "Phyllis?" Concern colored Gwyn's voice. "Are you alright?"

Phyllis didn't say anything. She was in some type of paralysis. Her face appeared frozen and her limbs stiff.

"Phyllis!" shouted Gwyn in a panic. She reached around the seat to shake her, but Phyllis's absent expression didn't change.

Gwyn let go of her, opened the driver's-side door, and climbed out so she could go in through the back door. She opened the door and looked down at Phyllis, who was now completely cognizant.

"Don't touch me!" she squealed, nearly jumping out of her skin to back away from Gwyn's hand.

Gwyn looked down at her fingertips. "Don't—don't touch you? Did *I* do that?"

Phyllis nodded without taking her eyes off Gwyn's hands. "Yes, you did that. Oh my God, I had another premonition!"

Gwyn scooted into the backseat next to Phyllis, careful not to touch her friend. "What did you see?"

"He's got her," she breathed as her chest pumped up and down anxiously.

"The killer has someone?" asked Gwyn, her mind swirling with confusion. "Is it his next victim? Who is it? Can you see her face?"

Phyllis rubbed a hand across her face as if to wipe away any traces of the memory. "I—I can't—I don't want to…" She looked up at Gwyn and then turned her face to look out the window at Loni's house. Both Char and a heavily costumed Loni were coming down the steps.

Gwyn got out of the car and slammed the back door. "Girls, get in. Phyllis had another premonition. But she can't bring herself to tell me what she saw!"

Char and Loni hurried into the car. "What did you see, Phil?" asked Char as she twisted her torso around to look into the backseat.

With all eyes on her, Phyllis bit her bottom lip. "I don't know if I can tell you," she said quietly.

"Why can't you tell us?" asked Char.

"Because he's got her, and I don't want it to be true," said Phyllis quietly.

"Who has who?" asked Loni, her eyes bouncing from face to face around the car, out of the loop of the conversation.

"She saw the killer's house last night in her dreams," explained Char. "She thinks he's going to strike again."

Phyllis covered her forehead with her hand. "I don't think, I know. He's got her."

"Who does he have!" demanded Char. "Another witch? Do we know her? Can you see her face?"

Phyllis pressed the button on her door handle to roll down her window. She sucked in several large lungfuls of air. "Yes, it's another witch. I didn't see her face, but I recognized her voice."

"You only heard her voice?" asked Gwyn. "Then how do you know it's a witch?"

"Because…it's Hazel," breathed Phyllis. "He's got Hazel!"

38

*G*wyn didn't remember running off the road after that, but as she sat parked with one wheel up on the curb, she struggled to regain her breath.

"Gwyn? Breathe, Gwyn," shouted Char while rubbing her back as she wheezed through an anxiety attack.

"Someone get her some water," said Phyllis.

"We don't have any in the car," said Char, looking around.

"Well, someone conjure her up some, for goodness' sake!" barked Phyllis.

"I don't know how to conjure water," said Loni.

"Me either," agreed Char. "Gwynnie, breathe. You're having a panic attack. It's going to be alright."

Suddenly, tears burst loose from Gwyn's eyes, and she yelled through choked sobs, "Mom! We have to find her."

"There, there. I know we have to find her. And we

will. Don't you worry!" Char glanced back at Phyllis as she consoled Gwyn. "Where is she, Phyllis?"

"I don't know. Wherever she is, it's completely dark. I heard her calling for help."

"Then how are we supposed to find her?" asked Loni.

With her fingers spread open wide, Phyllis grabbed her face between her palms. "Ugh," she groaned. "I don't know! I'm so sorry, Gwyn. I couldn't see anything else."

"We can't waste any more time, girls," said Char. "Father Donovan's our only lead. We have to investigate him. Hazel could be at his house right now! Phil, help me get Gwyn into the back. She can't drive like this."

Char and Phyllis got out of the car and rushed around to the driver's side. Together they managed to pull Gwyn out of the front seat and get her into the back next to Loni. Char slid into the driver's seat while Phil rushed around to the front passenger's side, and the women peeled away from the curb, practically taking two wheels around the corner.

"Ahhh," screamed Gwyn as Loni tumbled on top of her in the backseat. "Char!"

"Sorry about that, girls! Gwyn, your gas pedal takes a light touch, doesn't it?" Char looked in her rearview mirror and smiled at Gwyn apologetically.

Driving at that speed, it took them only a few minutes to get to the church rectory. Char came to a screeching halt in the driveway, and the four women exploded out of the car. Gwyn pounded on the front door and Char tried the garage door, while Phyllis and Loni peered through the windows.

"Father Donovan!" hollered Gwyn while she pounded.

"Father Donovan!" Phyllis yelled into an open window on his porch. "We need to talk to you immediately!"

When there was no answer, Gwyn wrapped her hand around the doorknob and turned. The door opened with a pop. "Girls, his front door is unlocked!"

"Because who in their right mind would break into a priest's house?!" asked Char as she hobbled up the porch steps.

They all stared at the open door. "Can we just *go* into a priest's house without being invited?" she asked.

Gwyn made the final decision, pushing the door open wide and barging ahead. "If he's got my mother, we surely can!" She took one look around and hollered into the empty living room, her voice filling the dead air around her. "Mom!"

"Hazel!" shouted Phyllis heading towards the kitchen.

Loni took a left and went down a hallway. "Hazel! It's us! Where are you?" she hissed into the quiet hall.

Phyllis came back to the living room. "She's not in the kitchen."

"I've been in the rectory before. There's a basement," said Char. "It's this way."

The sound of the word basement left a bad taste in Gwyn's mouth. The *basement*. A dank cellar of eerily cold darkness. Gwyn's heart leapt into her throat as she felt the air leaving her lungs. She could picture her mother now, bound at the hands and wrists with zip ties, her mouth gagged with a dirty bandana. *Mom!*

Char was the first to get to the door just off of the garage, but Gwyn was the first down the stairs. "Mom!" she hollered, her voice sucked into the darkness.

The other three women hobbled down the stairs behind Gwyn, each of them calling Hazel's name in turn. At the bottom of the stairs, Gwyn flicked on the light. She had expected to see her mother sitting on the dirt floor in the darkness. She'd blink back the sudden burst of light and look up at her daughter with fear-stricken eyes. She'd rescue her, and her mother would be so thankful that they'd saved her from the serial killer. Instead, a perfectly normal, though barren, tan-carpeted basement greeted her, with a pile of cardboard boxes on one side of the room and a vacuum cleaner with an unwound cord on the other side.

"There's nothing down here," said Gwyn in surprise. "I thought for sure Mom would be down here."

"I thought she might be too," sighed Loni. "But we haven't checked all the rooms."

The women wasted no time in opening the last three doors in the house. They discovered a utility closet, a stark laundry room, and a partially finished bathroom, but no Hazel.

Back upstairs, they decided to go through the priest's bedroom a little more carefully to search for clues. "I'll check his closet for the black robe," volunteered Loni.

Gwyn headed for his nightstand while Char rifled through the pockets of a pair of pants slung across a chair. Suddenly, Gwyn heard Char's breath catch in her throat.

"Girls!" she said.

"What?!" they all asked in unison, craning their necks to stare at Char.

"This is the messenger bag he carries everywhere he goes!" she said, holding up a black bag with a nylon strap. "Look!" She showed off the handle. "It's not torn!"

"And there's no black gown in here," said Loni, shutting the closet door.

"Dammit," cursed Phyllis under her breath. "I was sure we'd find something to tie him to the murders!"

"Let's go over to the church. Maybe the robe is over there, and we'll find a clue," suggested Gwyn.

The women put everything back as they'd found it and slid out the back door. They trudged across the church's lush green carpet of grass to the side door of the church. A handful of cars parked out front had gone unnoticed when the women had pulled into the rectory driveway.

"There sure are a lot of cars here for this time of day. Mass was earlier this morning. I wonder if something is going on," said Phyllis, looking around.

"I don't know," said Char with a shrug. "I guess we'll find out!"

The women opened the side door and were immediately greeted by the sound of organ music pouring out of the main room. The melodic sound of a woman's voice floated in next. The women peered through the doorway and into the room filled with pews and a smattering of people gathered around the altar. Father Donovan stood at his pulpit, holding a hymnal and singing in a baritone voice.

"It looks like they're having choir practice," hissed Char.

"I wonder what time they started," said Gwyn.

Phyllis nodded. "There's only one way to find out!" she said before entering the religious sanctuary.

Gwyn, Loni, and Char watched as Phyllis slid into a pew with a husband and wife who were singing along with the organ. When the music stopped, they could see her whispering to the wife. Seconds later, she returned to report back to the girls.

"Practice started an hour ago, but they were at mass before that. Father Donovan has been here since the beginning of the service and hasn't left once."

Gwyn and Char's mouths dropped open.

"He isn't the one that took Mom?" she asked breathlessly. Thoughts swirled in her mind like a tornado refusing to touch down.

"We're barking up the wrong tree?" asked Char in shock. "I thought for sure it was going to be him."

"I did too," said Phyllis with a nod. She put a hand on Gwyn's shoulder. "I'm so sorry, Gwynnie. I thought we had…" Her voice trailed off as her body went rigid once again.

"What's happening?" asked Char, grabbing hold of her before she toppled forward.

Gwyn and Loni each caught ahold of Phyllis as well. "She's having another premonition!" Once they'd gotten

Phyllis steady, Gwyn withdrew Phyllis's arm from around her shoulder. "Touching me is what did it last time."

And as if her trance had been lifted, Phyllis awakened from the momentary spell. She held a hand to her head as if she were dizzy. "Oh, my head!" she whined.

"Are you alright, Phyllis? I'm sorry I keep having this effect on you," said Gwyn.

Phyllis shook her head as if she were trying to remove the cobwebs from the inner recesses of her mind. "It's okay. It's not your fault."

"Did you see anything?" asked Gwyn. "Did you see Mom?"

Phyllis pulled the women towards the door of the church in a panic. "Not in here. Let's talk about it in the car. We have to go."

"Gwyn, I'll drive," shouted Char as they ran. Phyllis refused to say another word until they were all seated back inside Gwyn's car.

"Well?" demanded Char. "What did you see?"

Out of breath from having sprinted back to the car, Phyllis leaned forward between the two seats. "I saw Hazel. She's in a cage."

"Oh my God," whispered Gwyn with a hand to her mouth. Tears flooded her blue eyes. "Mom's in a cage?"

Phyllis nodded. "It's a small cage. Like a dog kennel or something."

"Is that all you see?" asked Loni.

Phyllis shook her head. "I saw his back. He was chanting. He had our spellbook."

Loni's eyes widened. "The person who stole Hazel has powers?!"

Phyllis shrugged. "I don't know. I guess. He was trying to use the spell book, anyway. But I saw the room. It was dark and unusual. There was something familiar about it."

"How was it familiar?" asked Char.

Phyllis leaned back in her chair and thought about it for a moment. "I'm not sure. It's not like I've been there before, but it felt like something I've seen before."

"Like what do you mean?" asked Gwyn.

Phyllis looked out the window. "You know what it felt like? It felt like a darkroom. There was this weird glow."

"A darkroom? As in for developing photographs?" asked Gwyn.

Phyllis nodded. "Yeah, like that."

"Aspen Falls used to have a developing center downtown, but that closed a few years ago," said Char. "Once digital pictures became the new big thing."

"So where would we find a developing center?" asked Loni.

Phyllis's eyes widened. "Newspapers probably still have developing studios!"

"You think Mom's over at the newspaper office? That seems unlikely."

Phyllis shrugged. "I have no idea. But we have nowhere else to check."

Char nodded. "Phil's right. We have nothing else to go on right now. Let's go."

Minutes later, Char pulled Gwyn's car up to the curb

in front of the *Aspen Falls Observer*. The women rushed inside and were promptly greeted by a plump man with a collared shirt and a necktie that had already been loosened to his sternum.

"Good morning, may I help you?" he asked, pulling a pen from a pen cup in the corner.

"Do you have a darkroom?" asked Phyllis.

The man nodded. "We do. In our basement."

"Is there anyone down there?"

He made a face. "I couldn't tell you. There are only a few of us in the office. I wouldn't think so."

"Is there any way that we can go down there and check?" asked Char, pushing her way to the counter.

"Check our basement? You want to go in our basement?"

The women all nodded.

He cleared his throat and wiggled the tie that hung between his oversized breasts. "That's somewhat of a strange request."

Char nodded. "Yes, we know. My friend's mother is missing," she said, pointing to Gwyn. "We have reason to believe she might be hiding in your basement."

"Huh," he said in almost a grunt.

They heard a noise coming from an office just off the reception area. "Dennis? Is there anything I can help you with?" called a woman's voice.

Dennis leaned his head back. "There are some women out here who have somewhat of a strange request. Maybe you could speak with them?"

They heard a chair squeak back on the floor and then the clack of high heels walking towards them.

"Hello," said a tall, slim woman wearing heels, a pencil skirt, blouse, and a small strand of pearls. "I'm Minnie Cooper, is there something I can help you with?"

Gwyn nodded. "My mother is missing, and we have reason to believe that she may be in your darkroom."

One of Minnie's perfectly plucked eyebrows lifted. "In the *Observer*'s darkroom? What would make you think that?"

Gwyn sighed. How could she possibly tell this woman the truth? She glanced over at Dennis, who looked at them curiously. "Uh-hum," she cleared her throat. "Can you give us a moment?"

Minnie smiled at Dennis. "Those documents on my desk are ready to be faxed, Dennis."

Gwyn and the rest of the women smiled awkwardly at him as he left the room without a word. When he was gone, Gwyn leaned forward. "Can you keep a secret, Minnie?"

Minnie leaned forward stiffly. "Secrets aren't really my forte. I *am* the editor-in-chief of a small-town newspaper."

Gwyn sighed. *Of course.*

Phyllis pushed Gwyn aside. "Listen, Min. It shouldn't be a surprise to you that there are witches in Aspen Falls. This is a paranormal community, is it not?"

Minnie gave a light smile. "I suppose."

"Okay. Well, the truth of the matter is, we're witches. And our supreme, fearless leader is missing. We thought she ran off to find French fries, but we've come to discover that she's being held by the same person that killed Margaret Sutton and Katherine Lynde."

Minnie's eyes widened as she sucked in a breath. "Katherine Lynde was murdered? I thought she died of an accidental fall."

"Of course. That's what the killer wanted us to think," explained Char. "But we know the truth."

"And now you think your mother is with the same man that killed those women?" she asked.

Gwyn could see both the shock and excitement of getting such a big scoop register on her face.

Phyllis nodded. "Yes. We think so. I had a premonition, and I think he's holding her in a darkroom. This is the only darkroom in town that we could think of."

"Riiight," she drawled, pulling on one of her earlobes.

"So we're just wondering if we could *please* check your darkroom for my mother. It will just take a moment, I swear. And then we'll be out of your hair."

Minnie smiled at the women and then tipped her head back toward her office. "Dennis, watch the counter, please. I'm going to take these ladies to the darkroom."

$\mathcal{M}$innie's heels clicked on the wooden stairs all the way down to the basement of the *Observer.* "I really don't think we'll have anyone down here. I mean, Dennis and I are the only ones in the office right now, and I haven't heard anything suspicious."

"It'll just make us feel better to check," Char assured her.

"Of course, I understand."

At the bottom of the stairs, she flipped on the light. It was a cobbled-up old basement with stone walls and a dirt floor. "Not very pretty," she said with a gentle laugh. "The darkroom is over here."

Across the room, she put her hand on the door handle, took a deep breath, and opened it. Gwyn's pulse raced, and she prayed that her mother would be inside. The door screeched open to darkness. Minnie flipped on the light, and the women all flocked inside.

"There's no one in here!" exclaimed Char with disappointment.

"Well, that was a bust!" said Loni.

Gwyn's heart fell. She had put all of her hopes into finding her here. "Do you have another darkroom?" asked Gwyn in a meek voice.

Minnie shook her head. "I'm afraid not. I'm sorry."

Gwyn let out a heavy sigh. She didn't know what to do now. Her mother was in a cage somewhere in some madman's lair. Her hands trembled at the thought of her mother helpless, scared, and alone.

"Okay. Well, she's not here," said Char. "Let's not waste any more time dwelling on it. Let's get back out there and figure this out."

"Char's right. We need to go. Thank you for at least letting us look," said Phyllis.

Minnie smiled as she shut off the darkroom light and closed the door. "Not a problem at all."

She led the women back up the stairs. When they were all safely above ground, she shut the door behind them.

Gwyn looked back at the young woman with a heavy heart and tear-filled eyes. "Thank you for believing us, Minnie. I know we probably sound crazy. I'm sure it's probably not every day that you get witches making wild claims in your office."

Minnie's hazel eyes smiled warmly. She put a hand on Gwyn's arm. "It's okay. It wasn't a wild claim. And you certainly don't sound crazy. I'll let you girls in on a little secret," she said and leaned towards them, lowering her voice. "I'm a witch too."

All eyes widened. Phyllis smiled at her. "I knew I sensed something witchy the minute I walked into the building."

Minnie nodded. "I don't tell many people in the business world. Only because many people, especially men, think you're trying to get ahead by bewitching them instead of earning your stripes."

Gwyn knew all too well what Minnie was talking about.

Phyllis patted the woman's arm. "Oh, Minnie. You poor thing. We've been around a lot longer than you, and I hate to tell you, it doesn't get any better."

Minnie blanched as she began ushering the women out of the offices and towards the front of the building. "I just recently got promoted to editor-in-chief. One of the people I was up against for the job found out I'm a witch, and let's just say...he didn't take it very well. He was *sure* I'd bewitched my way into the position."

Suddenly, Phyllis, who had been leading the pack back towards the front door, came to a screeching halt in front of a desk. "Whose desk is this?!" she demanded.

The woman looked down at the desk. "Oh. Uh, this is Benny Hamilton's."

"What's up, Phil? You got some type of ESP going on right now?" asked Char.

Phyllis shook her head. She reached down and grabbed hold of a ratty old camera bag on top of the desk. She held up the strap. A big chunk of the handle had been torn off. "Girls. Look at this."

Gwyn sucked in her breath and grabbed part of the handle to inspect it closer. It was the same color and had the same bumpy texture as the piece they'd found in Kat's garden. "Oh my gosh!"

Char looked at Minnie curiously. "You said that Benny had problems with you getting the promotion because you're a witch?"

She nodded. "Yeah. He's ranted about it ever since I got the job. He's barely in the office anymore. He just stops in in the morning to get his mail and check his computer and then he's out beating the streets trying to come up with things to show he can out-scoop me."

"He tries to out-scoop you?" asked Phyllis. "Has he done it?"

Minnie nodded with wide eyes. "Yes! Several times, in fact. He reported on Margaret Sutton's death almost immediately. So much so that we were able to print it in the paper the morning that her body was found."

"How did he know about it so early?" asked Char with narrowed eyes.

Minnie shrugged. "I assumed he'd been listening to the police scanner, but I guess I didn't ask him. He wouldn't have told me anyway. He's not my biggest fan."

"Have there been any other stories he seemed to know about before they happened?" asked Phyllis.

Minnie's eyes swiveled up towards the sky. "Hmm. Well. Now that you say it, he had some *amazing* pictures of that big storm we had about a month ago, and he was able to get a write-up about it before the paper went to press. That was a little surprising."

Gwyn's jaw dropped. That was the night that Kat had died. Benny was there! And they had the torn strap on his camera bag to prove it!

The women exchanged anxious glances. "Alright. We have to go now, Minnie. Thank you for all of your help."

Minnie looked at them curiously. "I wasn't much help."

"You were more help than you know!" said Phyllis.

"Toodeloo," said Loni, waving her fingers at Minnie and Dennis as they exited the office.

In the car, Gwyn had trouble breathing.

Char rubbed her back. "Breathe, Gwynnie, breathe!"

"I can't," she said forcibly while holding her chest.

"You're having an anxiety attack," said Char. "I'm going to chant over you to help calm you down. Just be still."

Gwyn's head bobbed up and down.

> *Through fear and pain, she cannot breathe,*
> *Bring her peace, calm, and tranquility.*
> *Wrap her in your calm embrace,*
> *So her fears will displace.*

Char repeated her calming mantra several times over Gwyn until finally, Gwyn could breathe. Her heart stopped beating so fast, and her hands stopped trembling.

"I'm feeling better," she assured the girls.

"Good," said Char. "Because we need to find Benny

now, and we all need to be at our best if we're going to get Hazel back."

"What if she's already gone?" asked Gwyn, panic filling her voice.

"You'd know if she were gone," Phyllis assured her. "She's your mother."

"I agree," said Loni. "Where do we start looking for Benny?"

Char pulled Gwyn's car away from the curb. "I bet that man has a developing studio in his house. That's got to be where he's got Hazel."

"Do you know where he lives?" asked Gwyn.

Char shook her puffy white head. "Nope. But I know someone who does!"

40

"*L*et me get this straight. You think Benny did *what?!*" asked Sergeant Bradshaw from his chair.

"We think he's the one that took Hazel and killed Margaret Sutton. We even think he killed Katherine Lynde," said Char, leaning against the booth at Habernackle's.

Sergeant Bradshaw's eyebrows furrowed into a deep V. "I'm afraid you girls have overactive imaginations. Benny Hamilton couldn't have killed anyone. He's a good guy."

Phyllis grimaced. "Good guys can do bad things, you know. Are you going to tell us where he lives or not?"

Sergeant Bradshaw stood up. The rest of the men in his coffee club had all gone on to start their day, leaving him to debate if he'd rather go golfing or maybe take the boat out and throw a line in the water at the lake. But now the ragtag group of women stood in front of him, sure as thunder that Benny Hamilton had *kidnapped* the ornery little lady that had punched him in the cojones the other day.

"Well, I mean, I'm sure it's public record. The man lives in his mother's old house on Eighth and Eucalyptus." He glanced over at Gwyn. She nibbled at her fingernails with a pensive look on her face. *Poor woman*, he thought. "But I'm sure you'll find that he doesn't have your mother, Gwyn. I wish that you'd let me help you look for her."

Gwyn gave him a strained, tight smile, but it didn't reach her eyes the way the rest of her smiles usually did. He could tell that her heart wasn't in it.

"Thank you, Sergeant, I appreciate it, but we'll sort it out ourselves. We need to go now." Her voice was clipped.

He gave her a stiff tilt of his head. *No Harrison today*, his inner voice mused. *She must really be worried.*

"Who's Benny's mother?" asked Char, lifting a brow.

"Doris Hamilton. She passed a number of years ago. I believe she was a teacher at the elementary school for many years."

Char nodded. "Oh, sure, I remember Mrs. Hamilton. She taught my grandson. I vaguely remember taking him trick-or-treating at her house on Eucalyptus. I think we can find it." Char turned on her heel.

He nodded. "Alright, well, when you're ready to let me help you look, please holler."

The women were out the restaurant door before he

could even give Gwyn a proper goodbye. He slumped back in his seat. *Should I have offered to go with them to Benny's?* The feeling he'd gotten from Gwyn was that he'd angered her by not believing their wild accusations. Should he have at least pretended to be a little bit more concerned about Benny?

He crooked his head to the side and rubbed the opposite side of his neck. *Women!*

"*W*hat is it with men?" huffed Gwyn as they rode in the car towards Benny's house. "Why don't they ever believe women?"

"Men are more logical thinkers," explained Phyllis. "Whereas women are more intuitive thinkers."

Gwyn frowned and spun in her seat to look at Phyllis. "I'm a logical thinker."

"Well, of course you are," said Phyllis. "But our brains process information differently. We didn't give Sergeant Bradshaw any reason to believe our claims, so I don't think you can hold it against him."

Gwyn crossed her arms and looked out the window. The fact that he hadn't believed her frustrated her. "Can you drive any faster? It feels like we're walking."

Char gave her a sideways glance. "I'm going as fast as I can. The speed limit is thirty-five!"

Gwyn leaned over and pressed on Char's knee. "I'll

pay for the speeding ticket! My mother's life is in jeopardy!"

"Hazel's still got some magic left in her. She'll handle business," Loni assured her.

"You saw her trying to fire her cane at Father Donovan. It jammed on her. She's too rusty for magic." Gwyn groaned. She gave an angry glance over her shoulder. "I don't even want to hear anything else out of you, Hodges."

Loni put a hand to her chest and widened her eyes. "Out of me? What did I do?"

"Are you kidding? You abandoned my mother last night!"

"You're still mad at me about *that*?!"

"Of course I'm still mad at you about that! Did you think I was going to forget?"

Loni frowned at Gwyn. "Well, no, but you found her! I wasn't the one that lost her today, you know."

Gwyn swiveled around in her seat. "Oh, so you're saying this is *my fault*?!"

Loni shrugged. "If the tights fit."

"Loni!" breathed Char. She looked over at Gwyn. "You *both* need to settle down. I know you're worried about Hazel, Gwyn, but picking fights will not find her any quicker."

Gwyn stared at Char in shock. "Uh! She basically said that it's *my fault* that Mom's gone. I watch that woman 24/7. Some nights I get up in the middle of the night three or four times just to make sure she's still in her bed. Mom fights with me every step of the way about what she eats, what she does, sometimes even what she wears or who I let her hang out with. It's literally like I'm parenting a teenager again!" cried Gwyn, her fingers combing through her fake strawberry-blond hair. "I'm stressed. I work full-time, and I have to keep watch over Mom at the same time, and to have *Loni Hodges* insinuate that *I don't watch my mother* is frustrating!"

The women in the car went silent.

Finally, Loni reached a hand into the front seat and put it on Gwyn's shoulder. "I'm sorry, Gwyn. I didn't mean to insinuate that. I don't know what it's like taking care of Hazel. I'm sure she's a handful. I wasn't a very good friend yesterday." Loni looked down at her purple galoshes. "I know I have some *issues*. I'm going to work on them."

Phyllis nodded and put a hand on Gwyn's other shoulder. "I'm going to help you out with Hazel, Gwynnie. You shouldn't have to do it alone. I'm here for you."

Char squeezed Gwyn's knee. "We're all here for you, Gwynnie. You're back with your family where you belong. We'll all support each other. Through the good and the bad."

Gwyn wiped away the tears that fell down her cheeks and squeezed Char's hand. "Thanks, girls," she whispered. "I'm just so scared that something bad has happened to Mom. I don't know what I'd do if I lost her."

"We know, sweetie. We know. But don't worry. We're

427

going to get her back, and then we're all going to help you keep an eye on her. We get it now. Hazel likes her freedom," said Char. She looked up and pointed to a simple ranch-style house. "We're here. That's the one, the beige one. Where should I park?"

Gwyn eyed the property and then pointed to the back. "It looks like there's an alley. I don't think we should come in through the front. We've gotta sneak up on him."

Phyllis nodded. "But he'll see a car parked in his alley. Why don't you park at the neighbor's, and we'll walk to the back?"

"Maybe we should call the police," Gwyn suggested nervously. Suddenly the idea of confronting a murderer scared the ever-loving shit out of her.

Loni shook her head. "No way. You don't want the cops messed up in this," she said, her coarse voice completely serious. "Trust me. They'll come in here guns blazing, sirens wailing, and ole Haze will be gone faster than a toupee in a hurricane."

"You think he'd kill her?" asked Gwyn, nibbling on the tips of her nails.

"Absolutely." Loni nodded. "We're here. We're witches. We got this."

Phyllis squeezed Gwyn's shoulder. "Loni's right. We can handle that little weasel Benny Hamilton."

Char pulled the car to a stop in the alleyway of the house next door to Benny's. "Well. Now what?"

"We'll start by casing the perimeter," said Loni, lifting an eyebrow her head swiveled on her neck like a deer in the woods.

"Casing the perimeter? Did you work for CSI in another life, Lon?" asked Phyllis.

"I might not get out much, but I do have a television," said Loni with a smile. "Let's go."

The women got out of the car and approached Benny's house. It was quiet, with the exception of a dog barking in the distance. Gwyn peered down at the egress basement windows. "The windows are covered with something from the inside," she hissed to the girls.

"That's probably where he's got his darkroom," whispered Phyllis. "We need to get down there. It's gotta be where he's keeping Haze."

When they'd walked around the entire house and seen no signs of movement, Loni climbed the two concrete steps to the back door. "Try the door," whispered Char to Loni.

Loni turned the handle. "It's locked."

"Shoot," sighed Char.

Gwyn looked around and without a pause scooped up a small stick off the ground. She handed it to Loni. "Hold this."

Loni smiled excitedly and held it in her hands out in front of her. She knew what was coming. Gwyn wiggled her fingers at the stick and concentrated on the object she had in her mind. The stick bounced off Loni's hands and quickly evolved into a wooden key.

"Nice one, Prescott," said Phyllis.

Loni put the key into the door handle, and it clicked in the lock. "It worked!" she hissed excitedly. "Come on."

Slowly she pushed the door open, squatting low as she entered the house.

They found themselves in the kitchen. Char pointed towards a door, which they all assumed to be the door to the basement. The girls ducked walked past the kitchen table and were almost to the basement door when the doorbell rang.

"What the?!" hissed Char.

"Of all times!" Phyllis whispered back.

Suddenly, footsteps ascended the basement stairs. They scurried to hide behind the kitchen table and all held their breath, hoping they wouldn't be seen.

Gwyn pinched her eyes shut as the basement door popped open. When she didn't hear anything for a second, she opened one eye to see Benny Hamilton wearing a black robe and rubber gloves. Working quickly to shed the robe and gloves, he didn't even seem to notice the four witches hiding behind his kitchen table. Benny grumbled as he went to the door.

"Now's our chance," whispered Char. "Get to the basement before he comes back!"

Phyllis led the pack down the stairs. At the bottom, she opened the first closed door and found it to be completely dark. She flipped on the light. It was a dark-room! Just like in Phyllis's vision! A long table sat in the middle of the room. On top of the table was the spellbook!

"Our book!" breathed Phyllis.

Char looked around. "But where's Haze?"

Gwyn's heart pounded out a quick staccato in her chest. "Where's Mom?"

Her eyes surveyed the room. Photography equipment and boxes covered the small room, but something in a corner caught her eye. It looked like a bedsheet covering a box. Gwyn rushed towards it and yanked off the sheet. A frail body lay limp inside of a cage.

"Mom!" she said with a gasp.

41

*G*wyn squatted down in front of the small mesh dog cage to see Hazel curled up in a ball on her side inside of it. "Mom!" she hissed. "Wake up!" But Hazel didn't move.

Gwyn lifted her arm and shook it. Yet Hazel didn't move. Gwyn let go of her hand, and it fell limply to the ground. "Girls, she's not moving! What if she's…"

Loni squatted next to Gwyn and felt Hazel's wrist. The room went silent for a moment as Loni fought to find a pulse. Finally, her face lit up. "She's not dead. She's either passed out or sleeping."

Gwyn's pulse boomed loudly in her ears. "We've got to get her out of here before Benny comes back!"

Loni unhooked the cage door and pulled it open wide. "How are we supposed to get her out of there? Pull her legs out?"

Phyllis lifted one corner of the cage. "It's light. I think we each take a corner and carry her out in the cage."

Loni shook her head and pushed her arms out wide on either side of her to stretch. Then she folded them in front of her and cracked her knuckles, rolling her head on her neck at the same time. "Girls, I've got this. Just stand back."

"Wait!" Phyllis rushed back and grabbed the spell book off the table. Quickly she put it inside the cage next to Hazel's legs and shut the cage door. "Okay. Go."

Loni took a deep breath, furrowed her eyebrows and then shoved her palms towards the cage. A steady flow of electrical energy surrounded the cage, gradually lifting it off the floor.

"Good job, Loni!" said Char. She darted ahead of Loni and opened the door, peering out into the basement. "The coast is clear."

The women watched with hearts pounding anxiously as Loni hefted Hazel telekinetically up the stairs to the kitchen. Gwyn held her breath the whole way, praying that Benny wouldn't return.

At the top of the stairs, she finally let out the breath she'd been holding, thankful that at least they'd gotten Hazel as far as the upstairs. Maybe now if Benny returned, they'd have a better chance of fending him off.

Loni gently set the cage down at the top of the stairs and exhaled. "She's heavier than she looks," she whispered, leaning on the railing as she gathered her breath.

Please, Loni, just a little bit further, Gwyn begged silently, too scared to speak her plea out loud. But Loni still had to maneuver the cage around the table and the chairs, all the while knowing that Benny could show up at any minute.

Finally, Loni gathered her strength and levitated the cage once again. But instead of going around the table, she just lifted her over it. Phyllis quietly cracked the back door open and held it open wide enough for Loni to transport the cage outside. Char followed next. Just as Gwyn got to the threshold, she thought she heard a familiar voice carry into the kitchen from the living room. She paused for a brief moment.

Char waved her on from the outside. "Come on, Gwynnie!" she hissed. "Hurry!"

But Gwyn was sure she recognized the voice, though it was on the other side of the house, and she couldn't quite make out what was being said. "I wonder who rang the doorbell," she whispered back.

Char frowned at her. "Are you kidding? We don't have time for that! We have to get out of here before Benny comes back!"

Gwyn nodded. Char was right. Her main priority was getting her mother to safety. She closed the kitchen door behind her and never looked back.

---

*S*ergeant Bradshaw pulled his truck into the driveway of the beige ranch house on the corner of Eighth and Eucalyptus and shut off the engine. While it seemed completely farfetched to him that Benny Hamilton had had anything to do with the deaths of

Margaret Sutton and Katherine Lynde or the disappearance of Hazel Prescott, he did know one thing. It concerned him that Gwyn and her friends were all running around town playing detective when there was an actual murderer on the loose. Someone could get hurt, and he felt it was his duty to make sure that that didn't happen.

He looked out his window. The trees shading the driveway were all greened up, and the tulips in front of Benny's house had just gotten some color on them. A pair of squirrels darted across the top of the privacy fence next door, and birds chirped overhead. The cozy residential neighborhood seemed quiet, and there appeared to be no action going on at Benny's house. He was glad that he'd beaten the women there. Then he'd have a chance to chat with Benny before they came and prepare him for the accusations that were to come.

He got out of his truck, walked up the front steps, and rang the bell. While he waited, he looked around. Surely the women would arrive any minute, and he'd get his chance to apologize to Gwyn if he'd offended her in any way and insist on helping in the search for her mother.

The front door opened.

Sergeant Bradshaw turned around to face Benny. "Hey, Benny, how ya doin'?" asked Sergeant Bradshaw, extending a hand.

Benny Hamilton looked at the sergeant curiously and then awkwardly accepted the handshake. "Hey, Sarge. What are you doing here?" he asked, looking outside the door in both directions.

"Oh, listen. I wanted to talk to you about something," said Sergeant Bradshaw. When he saw his old coffee club pal standing in front of him, he almost felt silly for driving all the way over to see him. This was *Benny*. Not some murderer. But he was sure that Benny would get a good chuckle out of the whole thing.

The muscles in Benny's face tightened slightly. "Oh? You've got my number, Sarge. You could have called."

Sergeant Bradshaw rubbed a hand across the back of his neck. Yeah, he probably could have called, but then he wouldn't have been able to bump into Gwyn Prescott and apologize. "Oh, sure. But I had the time. It's just…listen, do you have a second to talk? Am I interrupting anything?"

Benny looked backwards into the house. He cleared his throat. "Uh. I only have a minute. I'm actually developing some photographs in the basement right now. I— uh, can only let them sit in the solution for a few minutes before they'll go bad. What's up?"

Sergeant Bradshaw nodded. "Right, right. Well, I won't keep you." He didn't quite know how to tell him that four women were on their way over to accuse him of two homicides and an abduction. He cleared his throat. He'd make a joke out of it, lighten the situation.

"I just wanted to let you know that I'm on to you."

"On to me?" Benny's brows dipped.

Sergeant Bradshaw kept his straight face even longer than he thought he'd be able to. "Yeah. I know what you did."

Benny swallowed hard. "What I did? You—uh—

know what I did?" Benny rubbed his glistening brow with the heel of his hand. "I'm not followin' ya, Sarge."

Sergeant Bradshaw pointed at him then. "With the little old lady. Where's she at?"

"The little old lady?" asked Benny, reaching around to his back. "I still don't—uh…" He paused. "You wanna come in, Sarge?"

Sergeant Bradshaw nodded. Benny sure was looking awfully uncomfortable. He seemed to have a better sense of humor at coffee. But then again, he'd left before he'd finished his first cup. Maybe this was a caffeine deficiency problem. "Sure. I can stay for a minute. You sure your pictures will be alright? I'd hate for them to get ruined."

Benny nodded and shut the door behind Sergeant Bradshaw. "Oh, yeah. The pictures will be fine. No worries." He took a step back and looked at Sergeant Bradshaw curiously. "Now what's this about a little old lady?"

"You know, Hazel Prescott. One of those gals that have coffee at Linda's?"

Benny swallowed again. "Uh-huh."

One last poke and then he'd deliver the punch line. "You got her tied up in your basement, don't you?" said Sergeant Bradshaw with a half-smile.

Benny didn't look amused.

Maybe it was time to drop the humor and just come out with it. Sergeant Bradshaw backed up to lean against the door, when suddenly, Benny pulled a gun from behind his back and pointed it right at Sergeant Bradshaw.

"What do you know about it?" asked Benny.

Sergeant Bradshaw looked down the barrel of the gun, and the smile that had just begun to form as he prepared to release the punch line evaporated. "Hey—uh, Ben. What's this about?"

Benny scowled at him. "Really? It didn't occur to you that coming down here unarmed to confront me might result in a gun in your face? I think you've been out of the military a little too long, Sarge. Might be time to brush up on your interrogation skills a little. Don't you think?"

"My interrogation skills? Ben, I was joking! Gwyn and her friends came to the coffee shop with this crazy notion that you'd kidnapped Hazel." Sergeant thought about it for a second. Benny Hamilton was holding a gun to his face and sweating profusely. He let out a heavy sigh. "But I guess it wasn't a crazy notion, was it?"

Benny smiled wickedly at him and tilted the gun sideways. "Not so crazy, no."

"Oh, Benny!" sighed Sergeant Bradshaw, hanging his head. "Did you kill those women too?"

Benny's cheeks pinched into his eyes as he grimaced. "I've told you on quite a few instances. There are *way* too many witches in this town. I'm tired of it."

Sergeant Bradshaw couldn't believe what he was hearing. "So you just decided to kill them all off one by one?"

"Well, that hadn't *exactly* been the plan," admitted Benny. "Katherine was simply a piece of investigative journalism gone awry. I'd been scouting that big storm for years! I knew it had to be a witch causing it, and I'd finally narrowed it down to either Kat Lynde or Mabel

Anderson, but I got lucky. That night I got my hands on a pretty exciting piece of magic."

"Piece of magic?"

Benny wagged the business end of the gun towards Sergeant Bradshaw, encouraging him away from the door and further into the living room. "I found a spellbook. And inside was the perfect spell. With it, I can take away the powers of all the witches in Aspen Falls! Then we'll all be on a level playing field."

"Ohhkay. Benny, I hate to break it to you, but you don't have magical powers."

"Well, duh," said Benny, rolling his eyes mockingly. "I tried it by myself, just in case. The book said the spell had to be done at midnight in a central location. So after the Falls Festival, I attempted the spell there, and of course, *because I don't have magic*, it didn't work."

"That was the night you killed Margaret?"

Benny nodded. "That one was her own fault. She was out walking around and saw me chanting. If she would have just gone on about her business, she'd still be alive today. But, no. She had to stop and ask me what I was doing."

"Well, you didn't have to kill her for being nosey!"

"I didn't kill her for being nosey! I killed her because once she realized I was chanting from a spellbook, she got suspicious and asked if I was a wizard. She knew I wasn't, and she pointed out that only a paranormal could make a spell in a spellbook work. I told her she needed to do the spell for me and she refused. *That* was why I killed Margaret Sutton. Not to mention the fact that I got a big scoop out of the deal, since I was the first reporter on the scene."

"So why did you take Hazel?"

"Simple. Once Margaret pointed out the obvious, that I couldn't do the spell because I wasn't paranormal, I realized I needed my very own witch to cast the spell for me. I saw Hazel this morning heading to the ladies' room at Habernackle's. I ran her out the back door, stuffed her in my trunk, and came back inside until the coast was clear to leave. The unfortunate part is that lady's got a mouth on her! She would *not shut up!* Even with a gag in her mouth, she wouldn't shut up. I had to manually shut her up!"

Sergeant Bradshaw felt the blood drain from his face. "Oh, Benny—you didn't!"

"Kill her?" asked Benny, taking a seat on the edge of his armchair with the gun still aimed at Sergeant Bradshaw. "Oh, no. I wouldn't do *that*. She hasn't served her purpose yet! I'll get what I need out of her and *then* I'll kill her."

Sergeant Bradshaw took a step towards him menacingly. He held a hand out towards Benny. "I'm sorry, Benny. I can't let you kill Hazel."

Benny laughed manically as he put the gun in Sergeant Bradshaw's face. "Oh, and you think you're going to stop me? You think I would have confessed all of that to you if I thought you were going to be around to repeat it? Sorry, Sarge. I enjoy our talks over coffee. You're an intelligent and insightful guy, but you know my secret. I can't keep you around any longer." He grabbed him by the arm and shoved him towards the kitchen. "Now. I'd rather not get a bloodstain on the carpet. It's only two years old, and my mother would roll over in her grave if I killed someone up here. So, if you don't mind heading right this way, I think we'll do both you *and* Hazel in the basement."

Sergeant Bradshaw dropped his head. He couldn't believe he'd come all the way out here to help Gwyn and her friends and now he was the one needing help. "You don't have to do this, Benny. I can walk out of here and not say a word to anyone."

Benny laughed. "Yeah, riiight. Like I believe that one." He pressed the gun harder into Bradshaw's back. "Keep it movin', Sarge. It looks like the day's killing to-do list just got a little longer."

42

*O*utside, Loni put the cage with Hazel inside next to Gwyn's car. Hazel hadn't stirred the entire time they'd moved her. Gwyn couldn't help but worry that Benny had done something to her. Had he drugged her? Or maybe he'd hit her across the head the way that he'd hit Margaret and Kat!

"Girls, we've got to get her out of the cage so we can examine her and see what Benny did!" cried Gwyn anxiously.

Char looked at the cage's construction. "It doesn't come apart."

"We'll just have to lift her out," said Phyllis, reaching inside and grabbing Hazel's legs. "Loni, levitate Haze inside the cage, and I'll pull her out."

Loni nodded. "Good plan," she agreed and did just as Phyllis had suggested. Together the two of them maneuvered Hazel's limp body outside the cage.

"Put her in the backseat of the car," said Char, rushing to open the doors.

Loni moved Hazel to the car, where the women were finally able to examine her.

"She's got a head trauma. He hit her, alright."

"Mom!" breathed Gwyn.

Char touched Gwyn's arms. "Keep it together, Gwynnie. It's not that bad. She's still alive, and I have full confidence I can heal her. It's just going to take a little bit of time. But I don't want you to worry. We got to her in time!"

Gwyn sighed with relief. Those were just the words she needed to hear. "Oh, thank you, Char!" She looked back at the house. "Girls—just before we left, I heard a familiar voice in there. I think we need to go see who rang the doorbell before we leave."

Char nodded. "I'll stay with Haze and start working on her. You girls go check it out."

"Come on, girls," said Gwyn, leading Loni and Phyllis back towards Benny's yard. Carefully, they crept to the front of the house.

Phyllis sucked in her breath when she saw the truck parked in Benny's driveway. "It's Sergeant Bradshaw's truck!" she gasped.

Gwyn's eyes widened. That was the voice she'd heard! "Harrison's here?" she asked, putting a hand to her heart.

"It looks like it!" said Phyllis.

"Who's Harrison?" asked Loni.

"He has coffee at Habernackle's every morning. We think he's sweet on Gwyn," explained Phyllis.

Loni's eyebrows lifted, widening her already big eyes behind her glasses. "Ohhh," she sang. "Gwynnie has a boy toy?"

Gwyn swatted at Loni playfully. "He's not my boy toy," she hissed. "He's just a nice man I danced with at the Falls Festival. I'd hate for him to get hurt because we told him about our suspicions!" Then she smiled. "He believed me after all!"

Phyllis nodded. "Indeed he did. And now, he's inside with that lunatic."

"Oh, girls, what if Harrison's in trouble? We can't just leave him behind! What if Benny kills him too?"

Phyllis groaned. "Damn men. Always getting themselves into trouble."

"They are?" asked Gwyn with one lifted brow.

"Oh, is it just the men I date?" asked Phyllis with a hand pressed to her chest.

Gwyn shrugged. "Must be."

"So are we going to help the guy, or what?" asked Loni, looking around as she pulled her blond wig further down onto her head and adjusted her scarf. "This wig is itchier than my trigger finger!"

"Settle down, Lons. We'll be outta here in two shakes," snapped Phyllis. "Let's go back in through the kitchen. Hopefully Benace the Menace still has the sarge in the living room and we can sneak up on him."

The women ducked beneath the house windows and retreated to the backyard where Phyllis slowly cracked the door open and peered inside. She waved them forward. "Coast is clear," she whispered.

The three women crept inside, and just as they were about to head to the living room, they heard footsteps and voices coming their way.

"You don't have to do this, Benny. I can walk out of here and not say a word to anyone."

"Yeah, riiight. Like I believe that one," said Benny. "Keep it movin', Sarge. It looks like the day's killing to-do list just got a little longer."

The women didn't have time to hide before Sergeant Bradshaw appeared in the doorway, followed by Benny a split second later. Sergeant Bradshaw's eyes widened as he saw Gwyn, Phyllis, and Loni standing in the kitchen.

"Gwyn!" he breathed.

"What the...?" said Benny, taking the gun off Sergeant Bradshaw for a split second.

But he wasn't fast enough. Gwyn, Loni, and Phyllis all held their palms up to Benny and unleashed a stream of glowing neon energy towards him. It wrapped around him, forcing his arms to hug himself and the gun to fall to the floor. Sergeant Bradshaw acted quickly, snatching up the gun and holding it on Benny.

He smiled at the women as they held the stream of energy tightly around Benny. "Girls, what a pleasure."

"We got here in the nick of time, eh, Sarge?" asked Phyllis.

"I'd say. Benny was planning to add me to his short list. Gwyn, I'm afraid you're right. Benny does have your mother," said Sergeant Bradshaw. "I'm sorry I didn't believe you. He's got her in the basement."

Gwyn smiled at him. "Way ahead of you. Mom's in

the car with a head wound, but Char's tending to her. We came back to save you."

"To save me?" he asked, pointing at himself. "I came here to save you, but it looks like you really do have things covered."

She winked at him. They sure did have things covered. She glanced back at her friends and smiled. "We always do."

---

*D*etective Whitman finished up his conversation with his officers and then turned to the five women in the kitchen.

"You're sure we can't take Hazel to the hospital?" he asked, hunching over to look into the old woman's eyes. "She could have a concussion from that head wound."

Char put an arm around Hazel's shoulders. "I took care of Hazel. She's going to be just fine. Aren't you, Haze?"

Hazel shoved Char's arm off of her shoulder. "You think because you healed my head, you get to touch me now?" she cracked. "I'm not a cheap date. There's a two-drink minimum for touching anything above the waist. Anything below the waist, I get dinner too."

Char chuckled. "Yep. Haze is back to normal."

Gwyn giggled. "You couldn't have tweaked a few personality deficiencies while you were fixing her head?"

Loni put a hand on her hip. "Then she wouldn't be Hazel. I happen to like those personality deficiencies myself. They give her character. I like people with character."

Phyllis rolled her eyes. "Says the queen of personality deficiencies herself."

"Be nice," hissed Char.

Gwyn turned her attention back to Detective Whitman. "Yes, Mom is going to be just fine, Detective, thank you." She looked down at her mother and smiled affectionately. She was so thankful to have her mother back up and walking around again—even if she *was* back to her usual grumpy self. "We're going to take this woman home and get her some French fries."

"We are?" asked Hazel, lifting her brows. Then she lowered them and scowled. "You know, I'm really not in the mood for fries anymore. You know what sounds good?"

Finally! Something to replace her French fry addiction! Gwyn smiled expectantly, hoping her mother would say Miss Georgia's store-bought lasagna or a nice salad. "What?"

"Twinkies."

"Twinkies?" asked Char with a curled lip.

Hazel nodded and looked up at Gwyn. "Yeah. You think Miss Georgia knows how to make Twinkies?"

Gwyn threw her head back and sighed. *Here we go again.* "Oh Lord, I pray she does."

43

"Oh, girls," said Char, holding her hands out wide in the middle of Kat Lynde's living room. "What are we ever going to do with this big old house now that we've got our spellbook back?"

Phyllis looked around. "We can't sell it. Kat didn't want us to for some reason."

"Nope," agreed Loni, shaking her head. "And I'm not moving in. My cats would turn up their noses at how clean this place is."

Gwyn smiled at her. "And we certainly wouldn't want to put your cats out, Lon."

"Why don't you ladies make it into a B&B, like Linda and Reign's place?" suggested Vic from the floor in front of the fireplace.

Char laughed as she leaned over and scratched the top of Vic's head. "Oh, sweetheart, you're the only man I ever want to make breakfast for again." She lifted him up to cuddle him in her arms and kissed his cheek.

"Yeah, you don't wanna taste my cooking. I'm not saying I'm a *bad cook*, but I do use the smoke alarm as a timer," said Phyllis with a chuckle.

"And I certainly don't have the time to run a B&B between working at The Village and taking care of Mom."

Loni slapped her hand across her thigh. "Well, that settles it, then. We bulldoze it."

"Bulldoze it!" shouted Char. "This is a gorgeous house! And it's huge! Why would we bulldoze it?!"

Loni shrugged. "It was just a thought."

"I think our only option is to rent it out," said Char. "I hate to do that. I don't know that I want to be someone's landlady. I mean, what if they trash the place?"

"What other options do we have?" asked Phyllis. "Kat didn't give us much choice."

Gwyn curled her legs underneath herself. "Why do you think she did that?" She took a sip of her glass of lemonade.

"Did what?" asked Loni.

"I don't know. Gave us this house and then forbade us from selling it. It's like she's forcing us to rent it out."

"You think that's what she wanted us to do?"

Gwyn shrugged. "Well, it didn't take us long to figure out the truth about the lie she'd kept up all these years. Do you think there's another reason she wanted us to have the house?"

Char's eyes darted around the room as she shrugged. "Maybe this house holds more secrets than we thought."

Vic lifted his head from Char's shoulder. "I think you

have a point, my little snickerdoodle. I bet your old friend was hiding something else."

Char sighed. "I'm too tired to figure it out today, though. Now that Benny is behind bars where he belongs, all I want to do is sleep!"

Phyllis stretched her legs out in front of her and put her hands behind her head. "I need a nap too. We'll go through this entire house with a fine-tooth comb if you want, but first, I need a nap. This has been a very stressful week."

Gwyn closed her eyes and leaned her head back against the back of the sofa. It had been a stressful week. But at least the murderer was behind bars, they had their spellbook back, and Hazel was fast asleep on the recliner next to her. All was right in the world again.

Suddenly, the doorbell rang.

Gwyn's eyes popped open, and her head rose.

"Who in the world?" asked Char, craning her neck to catch a glimpse at the front door.

"Anyone expecting someone?" asked Phyllis.

Everyone shook their heads.

"Well, then, I guess I'll go see who it is!" said Char, still holding Vic over her shoulder.

Loni's eyes widened. "Don't get it! It could be the FBI! They found me!"

Phyllis made a face. "Sit down, Hodges. The FBI doesn't give a rat's ass about you!"

"That's what you think!" Loni walked towards the back hallway. "I'm going to go barricade myself in Kat's bedroom. If anyone asks, I was never here!"

Char rolled her eyes and went to the front door. Gwyn looked over at her mother, who was sleeping soundly, and smiled. She was just about ready for a nap herself. She drank the rest of her lemonade and set the glass down on a coaster on Kat's end table.

"Gwynnie, someone is here to see you!" sang Char excitedly.

Startled, Gwyn looked back at the doorway to the foyer. "Harrison!" she said with surprise. Her heart pattered against her chest. "What are you doing here?"

"I came to see how Hazel was feeling," he said with a perfect smile.

Gwyn glanced back at her mother who was still sound asleep. "She's fine. How did you know we'd be here?"

"Detective Whitman said he heard you say something about returning a book to Katherine's house," he explained. "I hope you don't mind me stopping by?"

Gwyn stood up. "Oh, no, not at all. Would you like to have a seat?"

He shook his head. "No, no. I won't stay long."

Phyllis looked up at him with one lifted brow and nodded towards a small box he carried. "Whatcha got there, Sarge?"

He looked down at the box and then up at Gwyn. "Oh. This is for Hazel."

Suddenly, Hazel's eyes flew open. "I'm awake. Where's my present?"

"Mom!" cried Gwyn. "Were you faking sleep?"

"I don't need to fake sleep. I'm old. At this age, there's a fine line between sleeping and being awake. What's it to you?" she asked. Then she looked up at Sergeant Bradshaw. "You bring me something?"

He couldn't help but smile as he gave her the small box. "I heard you had a craving," he said loudly.

"How'd you get the man to fit in the box?" asked Hazel with an ornery smile as she looked down at the box he'd put in her lap.

"Haze!" said Char as Vic buried his face in his wife's chest. "You're terrible!"

"That's not what the men say," said Hazel, opening the box. Her eyes lit up when she saw the dozen or more Twinkies nestled inside the box. "What's this?"

"Just a get-well present," said Sergeant Bradshaw.

"A get-well present? Or a bribe to let you date my daughter?"

"I need a bribe to date your daughter?" he asked, glancing up at Gwyn.

Gwyn wanted to crawl into a hole. How her mother managed to embarrass her in front of boys after all these years, astounded her.

"Damn straight. I prefer cash, but Twinkies will do, I guess. She's getting too old for me to be too picky."

"So do I have your permission?" he asked with a twinkle in his eye.

With her lips swished to the side, Hazel looked him up and down. "I go on all of her dates."

"Mother! You do not!" cried Gwyn.

Hazel blinked, undaunted.

Sergeant Bradshaw cleared his throat. "Uh-hum. Of course."

"No touchy-feely on the first date."

"Oh my God, *Mother*!"

"Obviously," he said with an extra-deep voice, ignoring Gwyn's admonishment.

"We like good old American food. None of that raw fish crap. I like my food cooked."

He smiled at her. "As do I."

Gwyn covered her face with her hand as Phyllis, Char, and Vic smiled at her.

"Well. Then I guess you have my permission. One date. We reassess after that."

"Of course," he said with a tip of his head. Then he looked at Gwyn. "Well? I've managed to secure your mother's permission. Now I just need yours. Gwyndolin Prescott, will you go on a date with your mother and me?"

Gwyn's heart trilled excitedly in her chest. She smiled sweetly at him. "I'd love to."

ALSO BY M.Z. ANDREWS

The main characters in this book, Phyllis Habernackle and Charlotte and Victor Bailey are characters taken from my other book series set in Aspen Falls, Pennsylvania. So if you enjoyed reading about Vic, Char, and Phyllis, there's a great chance you'll enjoy reading The Witch Squad Cozy Mystery Series.

Reading order:

Want to be emailed when new books in the series are released? Sign up for my newsletter here!

About M.Z. Andrews

I am a lifelong writer of words. I have a wonderful husband, whom I adore, and we have four daughters and two sons. Three of our children are grown and three still live at home. Our family resides in the midwest United States.

Aside from writing, I'm especially fond of gardening and canning salsa and other things from our homegrown produce. I adore Pinterest, and our family loves fall and KC Chiefs football games.

If you enjoyed the book, the best compliment is to leave a review - even if it's as simple as a few words - I tremendously value your feedback!

Also, please consider joining my newsletter. I don't send one out often - only when there's a new book coming out or a promotion of some type that I think you might enjoy.

All the best,
M.Z.

For more information:

www.mzandrews.com
mzandrews@mzandrews.com

Made in the USA
Columbia, SC
04 February 2018